Allan S. Lyons has had an eclectic career spanning the sublime to the ridiculous, from writing off-beat ad copy to sell bread to launching and managing the top-performing convertibles fund, from training raw army recruits to teaching seminars to money managers at the New York Institute of Finance, and from writing tongue-in-cheek articles twitting icons in finance to speaking at Goldman Sachs' money-manager conferences.

Sleep Not Longer is dedicated to Marjorie Beth Kahn.

Marjorie died after a long, painful battle with breast and lung cancer. A fighter, she never gave up hope, even while waiting for the final call from her doctor. *Sleep Not Longer* was written with her close help and encouragement. Sadly, she passed away the day before the news came that the book was going to be published.

I met Marjorie in September 1995, two weeks after she moved from Boston. Eight days later, we were never apart. She graduated at the top of her class in high school and ever regretted that she was not allowed to go on to college. She had a prodigious memory, read five books a week, would meet someone she knew or whose family she knew from Boston wherever we were, even at the far ends of the Earth. Like pennies that drop from heaven, the day before she passed away, Michelle, the head of the fitness center at the club where we lived, came with me to say goodbye. Getting off the elevator on the hospice floor, Michelle stopped. The woman waiting to get on the elevator, like Michelle, was from Glasgow.

Allan S. Lyons

SLEEP NOT LONGER

A Love Story

AUSTIN MACAULEY PUBLISHERS™

LONDON • CAMBRIDGE • NEW YORK • SHARJAH

Ordering Information:
Quantity sales: special discounts are available on quantity purchases by corporations, associations, and others. For details, contact the publisher at the address below.

Publisher's Cataloging-in-Publication data
Lyons, Allan S.
Sleep Not Longer: A Love Story

ISBN 9781645369912 (Paperback)
ISBN 9781645369929 (Hardback)
ISBN 9781645369943 (ePub e-book)

Library of Congress Control Number: 2019921275

www.austinmacauley.com/us

First Published (2020)
Austin Macauley Publishers LLC
40 Wall Street, 28th Floor
New York, NY 10005
USA

mail-usa@austinmacauley.com
+1 (646) 5125767

I would like to acknowledge Marjorie, together with whom I plotted *Sleep Not Longer*. She edited it page by page as I wrote it, rejecting portions she didn't feel right and suggesting changes. She was a prolific reader, reading five books a week, and remembered and discussed each in depth when called upon.

Sadly, she never got to know that a few days after she passed away in hospice, when there was no hope and after we'd finally agreed to end the long and excruciatingly painful battle with cancer, the book was finally accepted.

Author's Note

The teaching approach described in this book was used with some success by the author both as an army officer training recruits, in business training salesmen, and in seminars he taught at the NY Institute of Finance.

Chapter 1

Jaime returned to his apartment, his insides aching as if his guts had been carved out with a rusty spoon, cursing under his breath, furious with himself, furious with the Dean, fuming that the English language hadn't words adequate to describe himself that the Irish could command: maggot, donkey, git, knacker, queer, slag, fanny fart, feck hole, gobshite, falutin, knob-jockey, neddy, piss artist, scag dick. He had to forcibly clamp down on his jaw to keep from screaming invectives into the air: look no further, you knock-kneed, piss-ant spawn to see idjits and piss-ants that inhabit your planet, look no further than your campus to view the ball-less effete who dictate what is appropriate for academic syllabuses. Only the tongue of the Irish can do us justice. Can anything in Shakespeare compare to these baubles in Spike Milligan's *Puckoon*: 'With two contentious hands holding the mapping pencil, the 1924 border between the Irish Free State and this part of the UK cuts a wee village in two. It is a plus for the boozers, a minus for the stiffs. While any Catholic deceased in the North now requires a passport to be interred in the papist cemetery in the South, the boys sinking the black stuff all congregate around the cheaper end of the bisected bar. Every Anglo-Oirish stereotype known to whimsy writers staggers in and out of the story: Bible-toting priests, plummy English officers, two IRA idjits who share one cigarette and several homemade bombs... Everyone acts at the top of their voices and gives out more blarney than you'd hear in a tourist trap on a slow day in Eire.'

It was a fair day by the City's standards, overcast with fog, hardly a day to stay put and stare at the yellowish walls, but the of paying the price of consolation in expensive whiskey in a bar, or in cheap companionship on Market Street was off-putting. He pushed aside the Indian runner Chenny had laid on the breakfront celebrating the signing of the lease, opened his laptop, and began typing furiously, putting words down as they tumbled from his brain, heedless of the harping urge to edit and delete, hurling new invectives as they occurred to him, though none in his estimation were the equal of the one his buddies used back when he and them knew everything worth knowing: *'Screw the world and various inhabitants thereof.'*

As his fingers flew over the keys mindless of the backspace, deletion, and correction keys, and words tumbled onto the screen, he imagined the Dean's waspish face when the reviews came out and he realized, when his novel sat atop the Times bestseller list, that he had missed his chance as Educator of the Year.

The Bequests

There were people Conway met he knew immediately he'd want to think well of him. Ted Livermore was not one of them. Staring at the blackboard, he saw the pages of his life falling away behind him like the red and golden leaves of autumn outside. His thoughts went back to the first day he met Livermore, fresh out of grad school, entering his first classroom. He'd been dreaming of the milestones in his career, the woman who would share his life with him, how she'd beam as honors were draped over his shoulders, and the young lives he would influence with exciting, new ideas. As the bell rang, marking the end of his tenure, he turned to face his students who he once dreamed would be eager to fete him, bestow one more honor, and bid him a fond farewell. He tried to remember what it was like when he was their age. They'd not even been born when he entered his first classroom, brimming with enthusiasm, they could hardly have any idea how much of himself he had invested on their behalf, the nights he had spent in his efforts to make the great works of literature come alive for them, nor could they know how much more their appreciation meant to him than all the academic honors that had not come his way. What message could he leave that they would want to carry away with them as they set off to pursue the extravagantly naive youthful dreams, what words of wisdom could he offer that would not be shamed by those of Albert Einstein he once carved, full of youthful exuberance, into a piece of driftwood he had found that summer on a beach in Cyprus and hung above the blackboard: 'There are only two ways to live your life. One is as though nothing is a miracle. The other is as though everything is.'

There'd be no way to avoid Dean Livermore this evening, the smug knowing smile, the woman on his arm, the look that he had won. It would be the last time he could torment him, bend his will to hers.

He reread the pages, one after another, wondering if portions might have been expressed more bitingly, more tellingly. He could imagine the Dean's snarky laugh when one of the reviewers saw through the pseudonym and commented, if only Conrad had titled it, *The Taming of the Shrewd.*

"Shit, shit, shit!" he fumed, sinking into despair, almost beginning to enjoy the suffering, wrenched back into reality by the first bars of the William Tell Overture to Rossini's 'Marriage of Figaro,' the common herd knew as the theme from the 'Lone Ranger,' the ring tone on his cell phone.

He sagged, experiencing a surge of acid in his throat, sure it was the Dean calling to tell him don't bother coming in tomorrow, they'd found a replacement. "Shit, shit shit!" he exploded, wondering if he should start packing, if he'd be able to get out of his lease. When the ringing refused to quit, resigned, he reached for the phone, miserably hitting the wrong key.

"Hey," Susan quipped, eyes sparkling, "for a professor of literature, you have a rather limited command of the English language."

"Oh, God," Jaime groaned, switching onto the laptop to see her better, "I was sure it was…you don't want to know."

"You look like you're in a coal mine and the canary died," she decided.

Jaime caught sight of himself in a reflection from the screen, tried to come up with some grand response. "I had a bad day." Another failure.

"You want me to hang up so you can bitch and moan without distraction?"

"God." He smiled despite himself. She was wearing a one-piece thing revealing nothing a grandmother would call naughty. "I… I wanted to call you…but didn't think it right."

"*Right?!*" she exclaimed, color rising. "What are you talking about? *Right?*" Her eyes blazed the way they did at dinner that night when one of her friends made a snarky observation about her avoiding them.

"We agreed," Jaime offered limply, having trouble setting his face to show how overjoyed he was that she called and how miserable he was, all at the same time.

"We agreed?" Susan shook her head, the highlights in her dark hair swirling over the screen. "What did we agree?"

"Long-distance relationships…"

"You are really lame."

"I…I know," Jaime agreed, giving up trying to project delight and misery simultaneously, opting for misery, his half smile fading.

"Don't play on my sympathies. I was calling to tell you the great news. What's got you down?"

"What? What news?"

"You first."

"You don't want to hear it. I'm pathetic."

"I know," Susan sent back.

"Thanks."

"Tell me."

Jaime massaged his head, torn, wondering how much to tell, how much to admit without her thinking him an even bigger idiot. Unable to come up with something clever to soften it, he shuddered; he was his father's son: "I'm a fraud."

Susan's face fell in disbelief. "You?"

"I thought here, in San Francisco, the cutting edge of kook, they'd be eager to institute the way-out approach I promised in my application, but this morning, waiting to meet with the Dean, I discovered my track record was no secret – they needed a last-minute fill in, the Prof who was to teach the course fell ill. When I came into his office, I sat, aware he was aware. I wasn't even sure he read the course outline I placed on his desk. I can imagine entering my first class, the students sniggering at me."

Susan's face set. "I'm coming out there."

Jaime snapped up, blinked, unable to process this. His mouth opened but nothing came out.

"I never forgot the night we met when you lifted me up when we went to dinner with my friends. 'You don't know what courage it took for Susan to come here tonight,' you said, when they got down on me. Someone who would do that for a stranger, for someone who you didn't know…was…"

Christ. Jaime shook his head, felt the floor fall away beneath him. Was that only two months ago? He didn't know what to say, was afraid to say anything.

"Unless…" Susan's face fell, "unless you don't want me to…"

Jaime shook his head 'yes,' 'no,' 'yes,' 'yes.'

"I take it that's a yes. I'll text you my flight number and arrival time."

Chapter 2

The airport was the usual hive of hustle and bustle, hurrying and waiting, impatience and resignation, with an insistent background hum of energy, little different from airports the world over – with, in Susan's experience, one exception – a tiny airport in Mt. Kilimanjaro, a Quonset hut and a landing strip, at which she and Jonathan landed at two a.m. on a summer morning. The natives who met them, stowed their luggage and helped them into the canvas-covered land rover under the inky sky, Myron and Jalani, their guides that week, drove them to the base camp three long hours away over stretches of dark, often rutted roads splitting fields of dense growth. From time to time, they passed small clusters of one-room, cement-block houses, each with a single barred shuttered window facing the road, a low-watt bulb hanging high over the barred entry. In the sliver of moonlight that found its way through the overgrowth, from what they had been able to make out as they drove by, slowing mercifully at the largest of the ruts and potholes, each home was painted an identical eerie shade of watery blue. A talisman, a good-luck symbol, but didn't ask. It had been a honeymoon, once-in-a-lifetime experience they'd tell their children about one day. The base camp, no more than half a mile from a Massai encampment of stick and mud huts, was hardly the primitive jungle accommodations they expected; it had all the amenities of a Four Seasons Hotel, but not quite. Their unheated sleeping quarters – the temperature dropped forty degrees once the sun went down – was high in a treehouse, its only access, wooden stairs which Myron pulled up at night with a braided rope hung over a wooden pulley and let down in the morning, securing them from four-legged animals on their way to the adjacent water hole and two-legged visitors intent on mischief, but stranding them without means of exit in case of fire or emergency. The animals were there in abundance, but what disappointed Jonathan was how unlike it was on the Animal Channel. Instead of animals fleeing for their lives, animals of all kinds, kudus, zebras, elands, giraffes, grazed beneath the hot African sun on the Serengeti in sight of prides of lions dozing two-hundred yards away.

The San Francisco airport was so far removed from the one in Tanzania, she was surprised she thought of that and the unexpected twist of fate that brought her here today, wondering what exactly was she going to tell her mother. Had the agony of Jonathan's death driven her to act precipitously, so out of character, or was there another reason that sent her here?

"It's only speed that kills," Jonathan insisted, with that shameless quirky smile and innocent face that had her knees too weak to hold her up from the first moment she met him. "It stands to reason. The National Safety Council has it backwards. The faster you're off the road, the less the chance for an accident."

Oh, Jonathan. Why would someone who always planned so carefully now act spontaneously, almost as if not of her own accord?

As she walked off the exit ramp, pulling her carryon behind her, she was shaken from these thoughts, startled to hear her name announced over the terminal's loud speaking system: 'STAT! Dr. Susan Abramowitz: come to the Information Booth in the main lobby. STAT!' Startled, she picked up her pace, ran a few steps, slowed to a walk, ran again, dodged passengers, righted her carryon, alternately dragging and tumbling along behind her.

Coming upon the atrium, she spotted the information kiosk, alongside it a crowd milling about. High over them, a large white cardboard lettered in green suspended from three green balloons:

San Francisco Welcomes

Dr. Susan Abromowitz

Holding the strings, arm overhead, dressed like a leprechaun in a green bowler hat, green vest and green high-top sneakers, was Jaime.

"YOU ARE A NUT!" she screamed, jumping into his arms, as he tried to manage the strings and hold her at the same time, tangling them both as the balloons bobbed crazily.

"Hey," he whispered, smothering her with kisses, passengers streaming by stopping to watch in amusement, an armed security guard racing over, "You coming here for me is the best gift anyone has ever given me."

"So," Jaime asked as they pulled out of the airport onto Rte. 101 to San Francisco, "spill it. What is the news you've been bursting to tell me? You look like you're going to explode if you have to wait one second more."

Susan hunched her shoulders, "News? *Moi?*" she reported, looking like she'd stolen cookies from the cookie jar.

"Yes, *vous!*"

"Hmm. Let me think… Hey! Stop that! Keep your hands on the steering wheel."

"C'mon."

"OK. I figured out how to use the bequest your father left me."

"So?"

"That was it."

"That's it?"

"You want to know how?"

"As a little child, did you pull the legs off grasshoppers?"

Susan's cheeks puffed up, a mischievous grin spreading from ear to ear. "I'm going to have a room in the children's section of the hospital set aside for the kids, all decorated and filled with all kinds of stuff for them, and I'm planning to have storytellers, magicians, singers, musicians, science teachers, guys that make balloon animals, artists who draw caricatures, speakers from the museums and whoever entertain them. Some have already volunteered to come once a week, others whenever they could."

"That's it?" Jaime groaned.

"Don't you think it's a great idea?"

"No. It's a terrible idea," he grimaced.

Susan's face fell. She tried to hide her disappointment, but her eyes misted up. "You don't think it's a good idea?"

"No. If you were a child in the hospital, wouldn't you want to get well and go home?"

"Hey!" Jaime squirmed. "Stop poking me."

Susan grinned. "So. Are we going straight to your apartment?"

Jaime's brows waggled. "What do you have in mind?"

"Hey! Keep your hands to yourself and your eyes on the road!"

It was one of those rare days San Franciscans talk about in winter when the temperature is fifteen degrees cooler than across the Bridge in Sausalito and the sun carves through the low lying fog allowing a view of white crests curling in off the Pacific, terns and gulls swooping and diving, carrying off tiny fish in their beaks. As if, by unspoken agreement, they carefully avoided brushing against each other, savoring the eroticism, letting it build, aware even look a look would touch a spark to dry powder.

Chapter 3

They set off north over the Golden Gate Bridge, passing Sausalito, arriving at the Muir Woods where they hiked in the shade of giant redwoods a quarter as tall as the Empire State Building that had poked up eight-hundred years before Columbus discovered America. High over the Pacific, they watched surfers below braving the frigid waters in black body suits, seals sunning on a scarf of rock a hundred yards off shore and sea lions cavorting practicing back strokes.

"You've had a busy summer, haven't you?" Susan asked as they made their way around the trunks of trees larger in diameter than Jaime was tall.

Jaime nodded. "I did. It turned out different than I expected, in lots of ways."

"Tell me."

"I'm not sure where to start. I didn't want to go. The last thing I wanted to do was to meet the families my father...*cohabited* with... When I went, I decided I'd go and get out as fast as possible."

Susan tugged at his sleeve, her brow wrinkling a question.

"I know. I know. I think somebody in Philadelphia, Carlos Mutti maybe, the conductor of the Philadelphia Symphony, cast a spell over me with his baton."

Susan tugged his sleeve again, grinning.

"That's what I did everywhere else. The families my...father...preferred to...anyway...the strangest thing was...I can't explain it...in Atlanta, when this kid Sydney, who was acting a shit, mouthed off at me, I told the little fucker off, told him to use the fucking bequest my father left him to make something of his life and stop whining...I don't where I got the balls...and in New Bern, when I worked as a mate on a fishing boat for a day, trying to get all of it out of my gut, I told this young girl who was acting out because her father had brought his sons along from his new marriage, I told her I wished I was her, I don't know how I got off saying that, that at least she had a father, and she broke down and started to cry...and...you know...I guess I...did..."

They hurried back, after stopping at a chi-chi fish shack in Sausalito for crabs and a bottle of sparkling wine, fell asleep in each other's arms, Jaime still inside her, woke during the night when she stirred, made love again, this time more slowly, discovering for the first time that making love and having sex were as far one from the other as Jupiter was from the sun.

Chapter 4

"No dancing red and yellow rooster salt and pepper shakers!" Susan complained, retrieving her see through teddy from the floor and pulling it over her head.

"I made pancakes."

"I know. You have batter on your boxers…here, let me get that for you. Whoops…"

"Hey! That's my phone. Where the heck did I leave it?"

"On the chair with your whatevers. You missed some batter…"

Susan took another swipe. "I better take this."

'*Susan!* Why are you dressed like that at lunchtime! **AND WHO IS THAT WITH YOU?**'

Shit, Jaime mouthed, *I must have hit the wrong button.*

I forgot the time difference. Go! Put on some clothes. Susan mouthed back.

"I left a message," Susan apologized. "Didn't I say I was going to San Francisco?"

Susan shook her head. "Yes, Mother. It's Jaime. He had a medical emergency."

You little liar, Jaime mouthed.

Susan moued ferociously, waving him away with a free hand.

"I know, Mother. Tell Charles I'll call him when I get back. I'm getting a chill, I have to put some clothes on."

"Susan!" Jaime insisted when she punched off. "Who is Charles?"

Susan shrugged. "A colleague at the hospital."

"Another medical emergency?" Jaime snarked, heading for the shower.

"Hey," he demanded when he returned from showering and dressing, "have you been marking your territory?" The living room love seat was against the wall under the window, Chenny's hand-loomed Indian runner draped over the back, jonquils perkily prettily in a drinking glass on the end table.

Susan gave him a snarly look. "You can put it back when I leave…" she withdrew, insulted.

"You're teasing…aren't you? Were you ever tested for color blindness?"

Jamie screwed on his most ferocious face. "C'mere you," he demanded, wondering if weekend commutes were practical. At least it would reduce the number of conversations with her in his head.

"Whoa. I'm not here just to administer TLC. I set an hour-by-hour plan on your table. I left three hours a day for writing your book, an hour for reviewing the happenings in the classroom, and one for planning how to 'progress from Point A to Point B.'"

Jaime shook his head. "There's something missing," he complained, examining it closely.

"What? What did I forget?" Susan puzzled.

"Where are the hours for sex?"

"Don't be a smart ass," she shot back. "And don't get a swelled head…or anything else."

Chapter 5

Jaime's meeting with the Dean had been the morning of the day before. He had slept fitfully the night before, adding and deleting. At three in the morning, half groggy, he realized he'd deleted as much as he had written.

What, he wondered, rising early, was appropriate dress here in SF, home of tie-dyed, beaded hippies, for a meeting with a Dean? He put down his coffee and re-read what he had written. Shit. What looked like a superior piece of craftsmanship during the night now looked as limp as a dick. He checked his watch; it was too late to rewrite. Printing out three copies, he swiped toast crumbs from his shirt and set off for the admin building, a Frank Lloyd Wright look alike two short blocks from the Bart station. A uniformed guard checked his name, wanded him, pointed him to the end of the hall.

The digital clock up on the wall read 9:20, forty minutes early. He eased onto a long wooden bench along the wall planning to wait until 9:45 to announce his arrival so he wouldn't look too eager. Over the hum of voices coming from the open door, the voice of a woman floated: 'No, he has a ten o'clock appointment with that new instructor. No. It was a last-minute thing. Professor Van Bronson had a heart attack. The Dean had to find a replacement at the last minute or cancel the class. The only one available was an assistant prof who has been dropped by a tiny college in the boonies.'

His stomach rumbled. He stuffed his papers into his portfolio and headed for the men's room. It was the same feeling he had the first week of high school when a teacher in the crowded lunchroom pointed his finger at him, handed him a whistle, pointed to the public address system mike, and said 'blow it, get quiet.' He had stood in terror, afraid of he blew the whistle not a sound would come out. He'd look like an idiot.

It seemed only minutes later that he was gripping the arms of a leather-upholstered chair in the office facing Dean Gearhard.

Gearhard looked to be only a few years older than he was, smaller than expected, five-nine at most, the muscled body and shoulders of a weight lifter. Deep-set black eyes lent his face an intensity that didn't match his mocking, easygoing manner. Jaime took a breath, instantly aware he had chosen the wrong clothes. A crisply tailored blue on white striped shirt would have been appropriate. There was nothing he could do with his hair. The Dean sported an afro tipped with iridescent beads. He sat dwarf in a tall, swivel-backed, black leather chair. On the wall behind him was an Ashanti war mask. He had an image of a colonial English high-court judge in life and death deliberation. If not for his resume, lying open on his desk, and a framed photograph of his wife in a ceremonial dashiki with two children in similar dress, his polished ebony desk might have been for decoration.

As Gearhard's eyes started to scan his CV, Jaime interrupted nervously: "Dean Gearhard, I've put together a course structure to persuade students that the classics are relevant to their fast-paced lives." As he spoke he realized how pretentious he sounded, but he couldn't stop. "What I am proposing is an inter-active approach to engage students, ask them to open up, tell what rocks them, graphic stories, rap, hip hop, poetry, music, then lead them to discover the roots in the classics, encourage them to compare and discover if each does not have something to offer to the other."

When he not so much finished as tailed off, he looked to the Dean for a sign, but his face remained as fixed as Chief Tecumseh's at the historic moment in history when, his people dying, warned, 'Sleep Not Longer,' the picture Chenny had on the wall of her adobe.

Unsure if he was to continue, he reached into his briefcase, withdrew the one page course description he prepared, and laid on the desk in front of the Dean

Creativity Didn't End With Shakespeare
Each generation owns its own literature, music, and poetry.
What do hip hop, rap, and graphic novels have to offer from the past?
What does the past have to offer to hip hop, rap, and graphic novels?
An inter-active course in which students will present, and be prepared to defend, their points of view.

Gearhard lifted an impassive gaze from the proposal. "Can you expound on this bit a bit further, with a concrete example or two."

Jaime took a thin breath. He felt as had when he was a child, brought in front of the principal to explain his 'unfortunate' behavior. "What I propose," he offered, digging his fingernails into his palms, "is taking a cue from a rap, or graphic novel or song a student presents, selecting a single scene from one of Shakespeare's plays, not a whole act, just one scene, and ask the students to write a rap or hip hop or song encompassing it. The simplest would be the balcony scene from Romeo and Juliet. Or it might be Macbeth's scene on seeing Banquo's ghost at a banquet. 'Is this a dag, dag, dag dagger that I see. Come, come, come, come let me clutch thee…' Or I'd ask a student who plays a musical instrument to compose a parody on *Kiss Me Kate,* the musical version of Taming of the Shrew, 'I've come to wive it wealthily in Padua…' changing the words to make it politically correct. But there are other authors' works that would be thought-provoking, as well, that would excite animated discussion."

In the silence that ensued, Jaime struggled to keep still; keep himself from fidgeting. The Dean's face remained impassive, showing neither approval nor disapproval. He heard his own breathing, pressed his legs together fearing an accident.

"Shakespeare. Hasn't that been done, and redone?

"Well…" the Dean looked at his watch, indicating the meeting was over, "I guess we'll see how it goes, won't we?"

Jaime left the office with the Dean's – *I guess we'll see how it goes, won't we?* in his head, testing alternative meanings. He feared that if he told Susan, making a joke of it, she'd see right through it and try to buck him up with a 'pity' hug.

"What's this?!" she demanded the morning after she arrived when she came to breakfast. Next to her plate was what looked like a health insurance form in legalese, an uncapped pen alongside it, a space at the bottom for her to sign her name.

"It's a medical insurance claim form."

"Are you all right?" she asked, a look of concern clouding her face.

"It's for the house call."

Susan shook her head. "Maybe you do need a pediatrician."

"Hey! Didn't I see you coming out of the Dean's office a couple of days ago?" They had stopped at a near-by café for coffee and Danish before going to the Golden Gate Park. "You're the new English Lit guy, aren't you? Welcome to the Leper Colony. I'm Jack Treynor. Poly Sci."

Jaime jumped, shook Jack's hand. "Hey, join us. I'm Jaime and this is Susan, my pediatrician."

Jack had a shock of messy hair, a youthful edition of Albert Einstein's. There was a bit of devil in him the system hadn't yet beat out. His students no doubt looked at him as if he was the be all and end all, while he, just as surely had his eyes on one, or two, of them who he'd have before the end of the second month of the semester, not saying which, the chokingly beautiful young lad with the lashes that should have been given to his sister, or the heart-breaking girl in the first row who couldn't keep her deep eyes off him.

"Can only stop for a minute. If no one has already, I'll take you on a tour of the Colony. Did the Dean lay the meditative guru pose on you, folded knees, fingers laced under his chin, eyes on Alpha Centauri? Don't take it personally; he's balanced on a rolling pin atop the Tower. This is San Francisco the City where politically correct is politically incorrect. Like the present administration."

Jaime grinned, thinking this was how he'd describe him when he gets to write the book aching to get out.

"So how did it go?"

Jaime shrugged with a crooked self-mocking smile. "He said, 'I guess we'll see how it goes, won't we?'"

Jack shook his head knowingly. "It's from Genesis. Moses climbed down from the mount, stared at the vast desert stretching before the Israelites, and said, 'Vell, I guess we'll see how it goes, won't we?'"

"I gotta go," he said, loping off, dragging his eyes from Susan. "Call me. I'm in the book. We'll get together."

"I think he meant you," Jaime grinned at Susan once he was off.

"I wish," she grinned. "He's gay."

Chapter 6

If Susan noticed a difference in him as they took off for Lombard Street, the crookedest street in the world,' planning on Chinatown for dinner, he hoped she'd lay it to their last day. It was one of the end of summer days, fog rolling in from the Pacific, picturesque according to hardened xenophobes who see the positive in earthquake trackers listing seismic activity as 2.0, reduced by small recent tremors.

"Take a right here!" Susan directed.

"No, *no*! The *other* right!"

Instead of China Town, they found they were in North Beach, San Francisco's 'Little Italy.'

"It's your fault," Susan charged, ramped up.

"Mine?" Jaime objected.

"That's right! You know I'm terrible with directions. You shouldn't have listened."

Hand in hand they wandered in and out of the maze of streets, old grimy brick buildings toys in a children's fairy tale, storefront groceries, bakeries, restaurants, smells of garlic, fennel, thyme, windows filled with made pasta, angel hair, spaghetti, fettuccini, manicotti, lasagna noodles, parmesan, gorgonzola, ricotta, fontina, mozzarella cheese, wrinkled black olives, braids of pork sausages, haunches of prosciutto.

They chose Giovanni's, a tiny storefront restaurant serving dinner family style, families and strangers side by side at long twelve-foot tables, the restaurant large enough to hold only six.

Three couples, Pam and Andy in their late twenties, Goldman Sachs MBAs, Shelly and Peter, retired, eighty, married fifty-two years, just back from visiting their son in Texas, Mark and Tyrene, local Mercedes dealership employees, squeezed to make room for them, across from a family of eight, boys Tom and Christ, six and seven, daughter Marie, eight, 'Princess Meghan' four in a tutu and silver tiara, their mother Sherry in a simple cotton orange and green shift, more than a few pounds heavier than husband Tony, a mason, in work clothes.

Jaime filed them in memory for his novel: Tony, gray from heavy labor, eyes ghosts of what they were when he was his son Tom's age thinking of the glorious life that lay ahead, wondering if it's still too late for him, but when he looks at his little one who smiles back at him, he feels weak for the love of her, and then he thinks of kicking the ball around with his sons, and thinks, maybe it's all worthwhile.

And then Jaime thinks of Susan beside him and he's back.

Steam from stainless steel ovens behind the serving window in the back of the restaurant spreads a milky haze over frosted glass fixtures fixed three-quarters up the whitewashed walls. Waiters in white shirts with black, curly haired chests shuttle from the service window in the rear to the tables carrying steaming platters, refilling carafes, scurrying back with empties, their waists wrapped with white tablecloths.

He and Susan agreed they'd blend in, 'like natives,' but it was immediately obvious that they weren't *membri della famiglia* and found themselves obliged to give an account of themselves. Jamie looked at Susan, then at "Princess Meghan." "Do you know who this lady is?" he asked, waggling his fingers at Meghan.

Meghan's smile spread her fat cheeks. She looked at Susan, shook her head earnestly, sending a swirl of curls around her head. Her sister and brothers looked up from their electronics.

"Do you know the story, *The Cat in the Hat*?"

Meghan's shook her head 'yes,' her sister and brother's eyes widened.

"This is Doctor Suse."

Meghan's searched Susan's face, as if trying to recognize Susan from the picture in the book her father read to her. Her brothers looked skeptical, her older sister frowned.

"Not many know that the real Dr. Suse is really a lady doctor. Suse, show Meghan your ID."

Susan opened her wallet, pulled out her medical ID, and reached it across to Meghan. Meghan examined it, her mother, Sherry, read the words to her, she looked up at her mother, and her brothers and sister insisted on examining it as well.

Whenever he looked at Susan, Jaime felt as if he was breathing through his skin. Was this, he wondered, what people said love was? A shadow crossed his eyes; tomorrow at this time she'd be gone.

Dinner was arugula and red grape tomatoes dressed in virgin olive oil brushed with balsamic vinegar, platters of roast chicken, angel hair pasta in a fragrant red sauce sprinkled with grated aged parmesan cheese, string beans, chunks of crusty baguettes, for dessert tiramisu, demitasse for the adults, orange soda for the children. Each pair contributed their story. When Susan was called on, she asked Peter and Shelly the secret of a long marriage. They looked at each other. Peter was still vibrant at eight-four. He had a full head of gray hair. Shelly took a quick fond look at Peter. "There are no 'big' truths. I guess," she said, "but if I had to pick one thing, it's being able to hear your partner without your ears."

Peter looked at her as if he discovered a secret she had kept all these years but had never known. "I think people tend to assume that when we get old, we get wiser. What I've seen in the friends I grew up with is that they are exactly the same underneath the years they added as they were when we were boys. I heard recently, I think it was in a movie, that love is allowing your partner to love you back. Maybe that's it."

Chapter 7

The evening turned cool. Susan wore beige slacks, a black camisole, and the beige and black striped jacket she had traveled in; on her feet were frivolous tan sandals. Wisps of her blonde hair floated in the light breeze. Jaime dressed more carefully than usual, jeans, red polo shirt, navy and white sweater tossed over his shoulders. The streets were busy, grandmothers on camp stools, men playing bocce under streetlights, mothers nattering, teens in groups, boys posturing, girls pretending to ignore them.

They walked, making little jokes about the things they saw in the windows and on the streets, but Jaime's heart was no longer in it. When he looked at Susan, a wave of sadness overcame him; she was already gone, he already missed her. He stole looks at the hollows between her shoulders and neck where he nestled when they fell asleep, one hand under her bottom holding her to him, the other on her stomach holding her hand, her soft breath in his hair. When they made love, he would try to seal his mouth to hers so they'd breathe the same breath, breathe in what she exhaled, and return it to her. He could for a short time, but the seal would always break and he'd try again, wanting to sleep through the night that way, part of each other. At times he imagined, for a moment, that their skin disappeared and they shared one body – in time, he believed he could make that happen. What he liked least, after making love and falling asleep in each other's arms, was that time in the night when they'd pull apart, and fall back to sleep just holding hands. In the morning, if she woke first, he'd find her lying next to him watching him sleep. He'd pull her to him gently, they'd kiss softly and languidly, pressed against her he'd become hard again, but they kiss again and separate, wash up and have breakfast.

He could see in the light and shadows cast by the moon peeking in and out from behind a cloud that she saw he was struggling to say something. The temperature seemed to drop, the tenor of his voice, instead of playful and bantering, became toneless and unsteady. "Susan," he managed when he could put it off no longer, "I appreciate all you have been doing trying to help me. I can't put into words what I feel for you. You're warm and fun to be with and…you make me realize what I have missed all my life. I think I knew it from the first moment I saw you. That you would come here to be with me when I was down…I can't tell you how much it has meant to me.

"But…I don't know how to say this, feeling what I do for you…but I have to say it. I have…come to realize…I can't be your project. If I make it, I have to make it on my own. I can't walk in your shadow. If I can't do it, make something of myself on my own, I'd never be able to hold my head up, walk side by side with you, not one step behind. I'd feel like a queen's consort. Maybe I'll fail, fall flat on my face. I'm certainly not lighting up any skies now. But I have to try – and I have to do it on my own without your help. If I ever accomplish anything, I have to be able to feel that I did it, not that you did it.

"You have helped me more than I can tell you. You showed me that I did things this summer I never knew I was capable of, things I didn't appreciate until you pointed them out.

"I don't know if we can ever be what I hope we might be to each other, maybe I'll always regret it, but if it can be, it can only be as equals, if I don't feel that you made me what I became, that without you I'd be unable to function. I'd be no good to me – and if I'm no good to me, I'd be no good to you."

As Jaime struggled to find the words, he could see that Susan too was struggling, struggling not to keep from showing how his words hurt. She looked at him, looked away; her breath became shallow, it seemed she was processing what he said, running it over in her mind, she looked away again, her eyes misting, turned back. When her words came, they were little more than a whisper. "You want me to not say anything, not help," she asked. "Is that what you want? I understand. I can do that."

Jaime shook his head. He wanted to take back everything he had said, but he knew he couldn't. It felt as if his life was ebbing away. "It's not that easy. In court, an attorney said, you can't un-ring a bell. Once it's out there, it can't be erased from anyone's mind."

"I've thought and thought about this, trying to find a way, but it wouldn't work. Yes, we could *not* talk about what I do or fail to do, but it would always be out there, hanging over us, and I'd be continually uncertain, unsure, wondering would this be what you would have me do, or the other. I'd be continually second guessing myself, wondering if the decisions I made were mine, or what I thought would be what you'd decide.

"Can you see that?

"The more I thought about it, the more I realized that the only way it can work, and I hate it, is if there is a clean break. I have to have time to discover what I can do on my own. If I succeed, if there is still a chance for us at that time, if I can come to you as an equal, then…"

Susan shook her head, determined. "Jaime, isn't this what friends do for each other, take care of each other, help them through good times and not so good times?"

"Susan, let me tell you a story about Steve, the closest friend I had growing up.

"We had been like brothers, together so often, people who knew us thought we looked like each other. But we looked nothing of the sort. When he left college, he moved across the country, from New Jersey to California. I wondered why.

"One day I asked, did you move to get away from your mother? I loved both his parents. Steve's mother doted over him, wanted him to have friends. She was an excellent baker, stuffed Steve and his friends with her cookies and cake. But she could also let him know, with only a look, if he or his friends did anything she didn't approve of. I thought he found perfection hard to live with.

"'My mother!' Steve exploded, looking at me as if I lost it. 'Why would I want to get away from my mother? It was *my father* I had to get away from!'

"I was stunned. His father was the most supportive father anyone could have. No matter what Steve wanted, he supported. Go to engineering school, medical school, come into the business he had built, do something else, whatever Steve wanted he supported.

"'I had to get away from him. I knew where my mother was. She was here, I was there. But not my father. In order to be my own person, to know that my decisions were my own, I had to get away from him.'"

Susan took a deep breath. "You want me to go back to Philadelphia?" she asked, her voice ragged.

"Susan, the hardest thing in loving someone, Peter said, was letting them love you back."

"No." Susan shook her head resolutely. "The hardest thing was not letting them love you back."

Jaime looked about, searching for words. A group of young boys in ragged shorts, tee shirts, and expensive sneakers, knocking a rubber puck about in the street with hockey sticks, raced to the curb when a truck turned the corner.

"I don't want you to," he said at last, "but I need you to…I have to do this on my own. It has to be a clean break. For how long, I don't know. Maybe I won't make it, maybe I'll not do it all, but I have to see what I am capable of. If I don't, I'd not be any good to myself, not any good for you, I'd always be looking over my shoulder, wondering what you would do, or what you would have me do, never sure if it's my decision, or not."

29

Chapter 8

As Jaime watched Susan's plane lift off the runway the next morning, circle over the Monterey Peninsula and head east, his thoughts went to the twists and turns his life had taken that brought them together two months ago. It seemed his life had been a series of goodbyes.

It had been another scorcher the night before he left Nebraska, the sun singeing the arid mantle sending up mirages in heat waves. Chenoa opened the door to her adobe with a warm; welcoming smile, searching his eyes, circled him, stomping to the beat of an imaginary distant tom-tom, the greeting she invented to arouse her students, but that night the spirit was missing. He felt it and was sure she did, too. He was leaving in the morning, had set no plans when he might come back, if ever.

He would miss her. She was one of the few genuinely happy, uninhibited people he had ever know; she asked for nothing in return for the gift of joy she spread. Long ebony hair, tied in a braid down her back, framed her warm, heart-shaped face, her supple body moved to ancient tribal secrets, her quick mind played hob with shibboleths.

"Oh, superior one," she grinned the afternoon when they woke to late afternoon shadows, her dark oval eyes shining with après deviltry, "share your paleface's wisdom with me: how do others' rituals differ from those of our people of a lesser god?" He had teased her about tribal rites. "Pray name one that sect, ethnicity or religion whose rituals are not the equal of ours. Do Indians call it yoga, Hindus meditation, Jews davening, spiritualists – Christians, Buddhists, Islam, Sufis, Dervishes – *(and alcoholics)* – call it by other names. But as what's-his-name asked: What's in a name? Is not the object of each to excise demons, bring peace?"

Their short friendship had carried the poignant awareness that one day he would leave. "I have come this evening," he announced with a flourish of an imaginary cape, "to make amends, to offer a long overdue tribute to your people:

Murder on the Reservation

Be off, wise Chief Tecumseh ordered,
Determination in his eye,
'Tis in the bakery you'll find her
You'll Catch Her in the Rye!

"*Oy!* to quote your tribe.
"Quiet squaw. There's more."

When sadly she did not appear,
He turned to Pancho Villa,
Be off among the corn flakes search!
There'll be your cereal killer.

"It brings tears to my eyes."

Chenny's small, whitewashed adobe had fingers of scalloped cedar logs poking out below the eaves. Her home sat at the end of a clay road that turned soupy when more than a light rain fell. Her white plaster walls were hung with hand-loomed Indian runners and tribal totems, a tomahawk she found at a novelty shop, a bleached bison skull she found in the desert. The couch was covered with rawhide, there was a kiva in the corner.

The temperature would plummet once the sun fell behind then distant hills, but it was still warm enough to eat out back under the trellis inhaling the smell of the sweet honeysuckle vines and the pungent mesquite fire. Chenny tossed a pair of thick T-bones on the fire pit, arranged four husks of corn around the perimeter, tossed salad greens with olive oil and freshly squeezed lemon, he uncorked a bottle of red, filled two goblets and settled alongside her at the redwood table. The sun's slow descent over the distant hills softened the camel humps, prairie dogs poked their heads out of their burrows in search of food, owls slashed through the air after them, hummingbirds hovered over the honeysuckle, defying gravity.

As the light faded, he had look at Chenny and wondered if she meant more to him than he was aware of, or if it was the specter of being adrift without anchor that was haunting him.

Sparks flew up from the fire, flared into the night air, shadows lengthened, the edges of the hills turned umber. He felt a desperate need to find the words. They were used to sharing long stretches of silence, but tonight the silence hung heavy. None of the words and phrases seemed right. Uneasy, he sat quietly until, unexpectedly, his phone shattered the silence. Who would be calling him? He looked a question at Chenny, she shrugged, he started to click it off, another robo call, shrugged, lifted his cell phone to his ear.

"Yes," he answered, shaking his head, ready to click off. "Who?"

His eyes turned inward. "**NO!!!**" he roared. "**NO. I DON'T GIVE A FUCK!**" he turned away, clicked off.

Chenny's eyes were on him. "My…" he started, trying to get the word out, "my…father…"

"Your *father*?" Chenny paled. "You…you never mentioned…"

"No. Not my father. A detective. My…father…was found…dead."

Chenny sagged. "Oh no!"

Jaime shook his head, ran his hands through his hair, struggling for words. "I haven't heard a word from the son of a bitch since I was six. He left. No goodbye. Nothing. Took what money we had, left the bills. I'll never forget my mother's face."

Chenny's eyes unfocused. "Your father…"

Father! Don't call the son of a bitch a father! Shoving his dick into my mother didn't make him *a father."*

Chenny's lips became invisible.

Jaime shook his head, shook it again. He had felt like shit, like a shit. The wine he had drunk backed up, and his breathing became labored. He felt an overwhelming need to do something, say something.

"Whoever caught up with the prick deserves a medal."

Chenny started to reach for him, pulled back as if he was in flames.

Time slid by. The moon slid behind a rise, shadows became deeper. "The detective wants me to come to New Jersey, identify him."

They sat wrapped tightly together, their perspiration chilled by the night air. The fire ebbed, the sky grew black, the distant camel humps disappeared. In time he unwound, rose, shook his head.

"You're not coming back, are you?" Chenny asked. It was hardly above a whisper.

He froze.

"Are you?"

"Chenny," he managed…a vast emptiness overtaking him, "my dreams…my dreams are different than yours. I wish they could be different. You're the…the most realistic person I've ever known."

"Real? Am I?" Her listless face became animated. "Perhaps. You read your opinion of yourself in other's eyes."

His eyes fell. "Doesn't everyone?"

Chenny didn't answer.

"But haven't you," he asked, softening, "buried yourself in this remote corner of the world where there is no need to try and risk failing?"

She shook her head. Color rose in her cheeks. "Why is it so important to you how I choose to live my life? And how can you, who are afraid to put pen to paper, afraid you are not the equal of some long-dead woman, Willa Cather, the writer you wrote your master's thesis about, a woman who saw most of her life through a narrow spinster's lens, to pass judgment?"

His eyes fell. He breathed in an out. Moments passed. Slowly, she lifted his eyes to hers. "Why? Because I've had my share of rejections. Eventually, it becomes clear that your opinion of yourself is not shared by your peers."

"I think," she said, her eyes ringed with fury, "that you are better than you believe, that you have given up because you had a setback and are terrified of another."

"A setback? Is it that simple? Sometimes it's necessary have to face reality."

"So?" she demanded, "then what right have you to pass judgment on me? You don't really know anything about my life, the obligations that have kept me here. Do you think I haven't dreamt about New York, a life not exactly in the fast lane, but that, too?"

"What right? Because I see so much more in you. You've constructed your life around trivial things – I don't mean things that, in their own way, aren't delightful, but you have so much potential, you might be able to do so much more if you allowed yourself to meet the world."

Chenny glared at him. "Potential? Isn't that rather pejorative?"

He glared back, ready to snap, struggling for the words, until, unable to hold it any longer, they both began to laugh.

"It's not funny!" she insisted.

"I know. But you just accused me of taking the wrong 'P.'"

Chenny's eyes slid inward, her anger swept away in a freckled grin.

At the door, they kissed, kissed again. He didn't look back as he drove off. He didn't want his memory of her to be in her front door seeing him leaving.

Chapter 9

"Your first flight, young man?"

Shit. Jaime hastily covered his mouth, managed an embarrassed smile, pretended to have difficulty fastening his seat belt, his mind sixteen-hundred and fifteen point nine miles away in Surf Side, wondering what he'd have to deal with there. Climbing over her legs to his window seat, he buried his head in the in-flight magazine, drowned out the stewardess's instructions over the sound system – fasten your seat belts; bring your seat to the upright position, leave instructions for loved ones in the event of an of emergency – and tried to blank his mind, fastening it on the puzzle in the in-flight magazine.

It was no use. His mind refused to blank. For what seemed like the thousandth time, he tried unsuccessfully to wrench his thoughts from his father. All too soon, as the plane thrust up into the azure sky and reached altitude, the roar of the engines quieted.

"You mustn't mind me, but we meet such interesting people traveling, don't we?"

She might have been a chaperon for a girls' private school lacrosse team, a maiden aunt on her way home from her once a year visit with her nephew or a Norman Rockwell, cookie baking, grandmother offering homilies, tomorrow's a better day, after the rain comes the sun, look at the bright side, smile and… The brim of her woolen cap, knitted with yarn all the colors of the rainbow – red, orange, yellow, green, blue, indigo, violet – fell over her eye, and her wrinkled cheeks were overly rouged.

Hmm, he mumbled, hawking back over the puzzle, hoping she'd get the message.

"What's that, dear?"

What I said, Ma'am was, *There's nothing as annoying as someone nattering away when you're enjoying a good wallow in misery.* That would have been something his father would have said, loud enough only for him to hear. He smiled distractedly, and sunk his head deeper into the puzzle, back in Surf Side, his fifth birthday, the last day he ever saw his father.

"Filenkov the Fearless!" he roared. "This is the life for a pair of pirates." It was the adventure his father promised. "Hoist the main sails and pull up the anchor, me hearty. We're off on a voyage to find pieces of eight and doubloons and see far off lands."

The plane circled over the Atlantic, the throbbing of the engines muted, the pilot made a slow wide turn back over the coast on the final approach to Newark Airport, the bright lights of the Surf Side came into view below. The Ferris wheel fell away in the distance. The night before they boarded the enemy galleon armed with swords and pirates hats they rolled and folded from the newspapers.

They rode the bumper cars, brandished the swords at the lily livered Lilliputians who dared attempt to halt their treasure voyage, rode the Ferris Wheel, stood on their seats when they got to the top, like the couple in the Titanic, shouting 'iceberg ahead,' merrily ignoring the madly waving ants below, the ticket taker and starter. Filenkovs bow to no man or beast,' his father grinned as they dismounted and swaggered through a cheering crowd.

That was the last day he saw his father. The next day he was gone. He always wondered if he had gone off to find the doubloons and pieces of eight he had promised that they would go and find together.

Chapter 10

The Surf Side Police Department was a half mile from the Holiday Inn where he booked in, an unexceptional functional two-story, brick and cement building three blocks from the boardwalk he walked with his father. Detective Athena Christos, in her late twenties, a Helen of Troy in modern dress, tall, dark and slender, with small ears and large black eyes, met him at the door and led him up a flight of stairs to a bare conference room. Officer Mike Harmon Thompson and Intern Jim 'Parker' Merriman were waiting. The room was longer than it was narrow, the walls an uninterrupted sea of white except for a one-way mirror; along the side he entered and a copy of the Declaration of Independence centered on the other side. A soft shush of air flowed through vents in the ceiling. The wood chairs, however, were no more comfortable than they looked.

'Helen of Troy' was wearing summer-weight light gray slacks, a pale green blouse, and green button earrings that somehow combined to accent her business-like manner. Her long dark brown hair fell in a low ponytail. She looked to be twenty-seven, maybe a year or two older, wasn't beautiful, at least not in the usual sense. Thompson, in regulation uniform, with gun, badge, baton, was some twenty years older. He was six feet tall 10, trim, had jumbo ears, reddish-brown hair and mustache. Parker, who proved to be a Lodi High School gym instructor in winter, wore the summer parking uniform, khaki shorts, and blouse, with the insouciance of a five-foot-ten, twenty-two-year-old weight lifter whose badge jauntily displayed on the pocket of his shirt. He had sandy hair, light brown eyes, and a complexion that burns easily.

Jaime had expected the "I'm sorry for your loss." Christos didn't disappoint him. He didn't bother to respond. It fell into the category of the 'one stroker' Eric Byrnes described in *Games People Play,* an obligation by someone not obligated to offer 'two strokes.' 'Parker' stood rolling on one foot to the other, flipping quarters over, under and through the fingers of his one hand.

"Quarters for the meters," Parker tossed off with a *look* at Christos.

Christos ignored him. "You grew up in New Jersey, didn't you, Mr. Filenkov?"

Jaime nodded, wondering if this, too, was polite, or something more? The room had all the warmth of an abattoir – white cinder block walls, white acoustic tiled ceiling, three white fluorescent ceiling fixtures under frosted plastic, an eight-foot-long, heavily used mahogany conference table, matching ladder-back armless chairs along each side, one at each end.

"Were you in touch with your father?"

He shook his head grimly, wasn't sure more was necessary but managed, "He disappeared when I was five."

"Do you know where he lived since or why he chose to come to Surf Side this past December?" Christos handled the interrogation apparently, Thompson and Parker roles limited to looking official.

Jaime tightened. He'd want to ask the same questions. He shook his head.

"Everything we've been able to discover about your father is a mystery…as if he planned it that way."

Was this an observation or if he was expected to expand on it? Jaime didn't reply. His father had died as he lived.

"You knew he changed his name? It took a bit to find you."

Jaime reveled inwardly at the difficulties they had but struggled to look as if he was not enjoying their distress. His father had had his last laugh. He had always been able to jolt him out 'the mopes' with an absurd antic.

"Your father was found dead in his cottage by his neighbor, Mrs. Gregory," Christos continued. "The cause of death has not yet been determined. It may have been the result of a fall during a seizure – did you know your father was in the final stages of glioblastoma, an almost always fatal form of brain cancer?"

Jaime shut down. He stopped breathing. He didn't know how he should feel, but feelings he hadn't expected welled up he wanted to push back down. He turned away.

After a short pause, apparently to allow him time, she continued with no indication she had noticed his reaction, "How much do you know about Surf Side? Have you ever been here?"

He wasn't sure of the correct answer. He shook his head 'no'…then 'yes.' "Once. With my father. When I was five."

Christos nodded. She appeared to have reached a decision. "Surf Side is a community of eight thousand in winter, one-hundred thousand in summer when visitors come to swim, bathe, walk the boardwalk, and ride the rides. Most rent for one or two weeks to take advantage of the eight-mile strand of white sandy beach cooled by the Atlantic. Most of the cottages were built in the last century before the advent of air conditioning. Why your father chose to rent here offseason, and for only six months – his lease was up in a few days – is among the questions we are trying to find answers to." The expressions on Thompson and Parker seemed to indicate this was of some importance. "Where he was planning to go when his lease expired is unknown. He owned a 2016 Mercedes sports car, but we found no credit cards, bank statements, or sources of income. His name was Russian, but he changed it. Did you know he did?"

Jaime's head shot up. Everything about him was a mystery to him. Yet, somehow, none of it was a surprise. He lived the pirate's life he always dreamed of.

"Without answers," she went on, "no question seemed far-fetched, too fanciful. Was his name change connected with the Russian election hacking? Was he in a witness protection program? Was the gash in his head made by a wooden club in the hands of an enemy or a foreign agent? Or was it death by misadventure? Had he fallen? Splinters of glass found in the sole of his foot matched the broken glass from the globe that had been on the stand next to his bed?"

Jaime shook his head to clear it. *Death by Misadventure.* That was his father. He had promised that one day he'd write a novel, 'Death by Misadventure.'

Enough. Why was he listening? His father had lived his life the way he wanted to. He didn't give a shit for anyone. Why had he come? What the fuck was he hoping for? His father had written him out of his life twenty-six years ago. He had enough.

"Shit!" he exploded, pushing back from the table upsetting his chair. "I've heard all I want to hear. I don't know why I was asked to come. If I'm arrested, read me my rights. Otherwise, I'm leaving."

"Mr. Filenkov," Christos jumped up, "I can imagine…how this must have…been…for you…someone. I was very close to…my grandmother…passed…recently…"

Jaime stopped, stunned. His head spun. He felt as if he had entered a separate reality. What the fuck did she think, that he was grieving for his father? Like felt as though he was dealing with programmed robots.

"Please…Mr. Filenkov…Jaime… Don't go. Your father left something for you…left it with his neighbor, Mrs. Gregory. She refuses to give it to anyone but you. Everything we have learned about your father has us believe it must be…*unusual* –" *Unusual*? His father? If this…this…wasn't so pathetic, he would laugh, "…unusual…which may be why he chose to leave it with Mrs. Gregory. You'll see why when you meet her. When I met her, I thought of Red

Riding Hood's grandmother standing at the Dutch Door of her gingerbread house."

Jaime couldn't contain it. A mocking, sardonic laugh rumbled up from some deep recess within him. He felt as if he had lost it. Christos, Thompson, and Parker looked at him. He turned away, massaged his head. Everything he'd gone through the last few days, all of it that kicked in, assaulted him, the end of his career, his goodbye to Chenny, his father thrown back into his life, feelings he hadn't wanted, hadn't wanted to deal with, that he couldn't turn off, ravaged him. His head began to swim. He reached for the chair. Parker jumped up to steady him. Quarters dropped onto the floor, rolled around crazily.

Chapter 11

"Oy! Come in, darling, come in! Oy, like your father you look. I'd know you anywhere. The same face, the same dimples, the same twinkle. Come. Sit. You drink tea, coffee, Dr. Brown's tonic? Jaime, right? Athena, Mike, Parker, come, sit anywhere."

Jaime became aware of the sound of his breathing. He tried not to make his discomfort evident, but from the fragmented looks from everyone but Thompson, it was having the opposite effect. Thompson was the only one who seemed at ease. Christos had settled on the edge of the boutique-sized sofa that was covered in a brocade of wildflowers, pink, blue, white, orange and green between prickly shrubs with tiny round orange berries, Parker stood, he had chosen the chair farthest from them. Red Riding Hood's grandmother's house it was not. The small room was overwhelming, over-decorated, Dali-esque. Modigliani's *Recumbent Nude* hung on the wall directly opposite him, Kusama's *Boy at a Piano* on its right, above it Margaret Keane's *Big Eyes.* The smell of the lilac and verbena petals in a cut glass bowl filled the room, a red and gold enameled Chinese lamp with a matching silk shade was on the end table.

This woman was his father's *friend*? Meaning? Agnes had to be eighty but dressed forty. Teal skorts, white knit pullover, white sandals with gold clasps. What had his father seen in this woman…and the others he traded his mother for? Her large twinkling brown eyes seemed warm and genuine, her soft, golden brown pageboy was a far cry from the lacquered mannequin look he expected, she seemed anxious to make him feel at ease, but it would require more from him than he wanted to offer.

She was back, bubbling. "Come on, don't be bashful. Eat. Freshly baked. It wouldn't kill you. Oy, darling," she said, pushing a plate of rugula at him, "I can imagine how difficult this is for you. Your father tried to coat it all telling me stories of two mates, you and him, pirates, but I could see it was me he was trying to convince, or maybe himself. Come, a raspberry cookie at least. Prizes

I won for it. In the Bronx yet, tough customers the judges, but nothing like this they ever tasted.

"Look. That antique plate on the hutch. Old I maybe, but not yet senile. I bought it for $35 in a furniture store in SoHo. Black with soot it was before I cleaned it. They didn't know from the real McCoy. You watch the Antique Road Show? From the Ming Dynasty. Worth $10,000. Could be more. My daughter she don't want it. Maybe I'll leave it to charity. You have any favorite programs? I tell the time and day by my shows…"

Was this what Christos meant, an enchanted cottage? Getting old, living alone. The Hindustani novelist, Preeti Shenoy, wrote, *Life Is What You Make It*.

"*Dancing With the Stars*…I love the tight black pants the men wear, their tushes…"

"Agnes," Christos interrupted gently, "Mr. Filenkov's…"

"Oy. Right. Who wants to listen to an old lady? Come, eat up. There's plenty more. Where was I?"

Jaime shifted in his seat, willing this to be over. Agnes looked at him, grunted, and pulled herself up from the couch. "Oy. Hitler should have legs like these. May there really be a hell and he's in it." Hobbling to the hutch, she took a book from the shelf, slid an envelope from between the pages, hobbled back, and handed the envelope to Jaime.

"Go on, darling," she said, "open it. Your father's eyes weren't filled with the usual mischief when he gave it to me, asking in case…you know…in case something should… I could see his eyes knew… I should see you get it."

Jaime looked at what she was holding warily, as if wondering whether he wanted to know what was in it or not. What he wanted more than anything was to hold onto his anger, anger he carried with him all these years, wishing there was a way he could make his father aware of it. His father had charmed the old lady. Had he expected it would work its way through her to him? What would he gain by pushing the envelope back at her, an empty gesture, what would it accomplish?

Shit. He knew he was going to examine what was in the envelope, but…but stupidly, if he did, it would be as if he was forgiving him. It was crazy. He knew it. But it was the only thing he had left.

He became aware that the others were watching him. What? Did they believe they were witnessing a Hallmark moment? A father-son moment? Biting his lip, he took at the envelope, immediately aware there was something strange in it. He opened the flap and held it upside down. A key fell out and clunked to the floor. A single sheet of paper, folded in thirds, fluttered after it.

The others watched in silence. Agnes looked at him expectantly.

His breathing became ragged. A jumble of feelings he hadn't expected tumbled through him. Lowering himself slowly, he bent, picked up the paper, and unfolded it. Christos rose, Parker edged next to her to see it.

"Oy, darling, don't keep us hanging. An old lady my age, an attack I could have."

The sheet was his crayon drawing of two pirates with cutlasses, black hats, eye patches, boots and cutlasses, his father and him. His father had kept it.

"Oy," Agnes reached for Jaime. "Your father saved it." He shook her away. "Go on, dear. Look what else he left for you. A key. To his safety deposit box. Your father signed a card at the bank. Tomorrow, Monday, I'll take you."

Chapter 12

The room was warm, but Jaime felt a chill looking over the contents of the safety deposit box that was spread out in front of him on the table in the intimidating police conference room. What he was looking at was the sum total of a life. His breath came heavy. He rubbed his forehead and tried to sort it out, make sense of it. Despite the shabby existence his father appeared to be living, he was obviously not poor. In addition to a diary, there were over sixty thousand dollars in cash and a CD for twice that amount in the box, ownership papers for the Mercedes, and three stock certificates worth, in total, a good sum at current market values. His will named him his heir, but included the specific request that he personally deliver the certificates to the children the certificates were endorsed to.

Were the three children his father's? Did that mean he had blood relatives? Why had his father left them then certificates and everything else to him? Why had he left anything to him? He had never spoken to him, or made an effort to see him in twenty-six years. None of this made sense. A ton of emotions flooded through him. He sat there, staring at the contents, blank, unable to deal with it.

"Jamie. Jaime!" Detective Christos repeated.

Jaime lifted his head.

"Jaime. I'm sure this has hit you, wiped you out. But we have to move on. The cause of your father's death has not been determined; something here may help clear up questions we have."

Jaime sighed, hunched his shoulders in despair.

"When I first interviewed Agnes, she reportedly heard a to-do the evening the ME believes your father died. We suspect her hearing is impaired. She wasn't sure there were two voices. Your father's phone log listed a call to Amiable Escorts in Atlantic City that afternoon. Mrs. Gregory noticed that your father was often visited by '*nieces.*' Officer Thompson and Parker are on their way to there now to question the principles…"

Listening with half an ear, wrestling with the questions burning him, he was hardly aware of what Christos bad been saying until she mentioned his father's 'nieces.' At first Jaime boiled at the thought that there were still other blood relatives, then came fully awake…

"…I've tried to put the papers in some kind of chronological order, but I could find no obvious way to date most of them…" Christos voice went on, "…his diary seems to be partly written in a shorthand of his own…"

Jaime felt as if he was falling in and out of a bad dream. He began to flip through the photographs listlessly but couldn't keep his attention focused. "Can we take a break?" he asked, flexing his neck and shoulders.

Christos raised her head from the papers, watched him for a bit, then asked, "You grew up in New Jersey, didn't you?"

Jaime nodded disinterestedly.

"You're a professor of literature."

Jaime froze. "You had me investigated, Detective Christos."

Christos took a breath. "No," she insisted, shaking her head. "Your father knew. Agnes told me." Christos shook her head again, softened. "My name is Athena. No one calls me *Detective* Christos,' like that except my father. It's what he calls customers he'd rather have eat in someone else's restaurant."

Jamie came fully awake, as if he'd been doused with a pail of icy water. He had been shitting on the messenger. "I'm sorry," he owned. "I'm taking all of this out on you. I apologize. I had no right to. Please…your father isn't proud of you?"

Athena's face softened for an instant. "Proud? We're Greek. Greeks live their emotions. 'That's no job for Greek girl!' my father thundered, like Ares, the Greek god of war, when I told him I was taking the police exam. 'Find husband, get married, work in our bakery.'"

Jaime reluctantly began to laugh.

"I know!" I told him, "I know! It wasn't my first choice. We were at the table – my brothers, my mother, my aunt Penny, my uncle Stephen, and my cousins. Twelve of us. We fight, we argue, but we love each other to death. It's always a riot, everyone talking, shouting to be heard. But in that instant, everything stopped.

"'Your first choice?!' my father roared. 'What kind of nonsense is that?'

"I thought and thought, what is the right job for a Greek girl? Then it came to me. Launching ships.

"But then I looked in the mirror and said, 'Nah.'"

Jaime roared, "You didn't!"

"I did. He's a marshmallow. He pretends to be tough, but he melts. When he sees my daughter Sandy… 'Hurricane Sandy' he calls her…he gets all mushy. Agnes told me your father was like that, too. 'My son the Professor this, my son the Professor that.'"

The smile vanished. His words became hard. "My father abandoned me and my mother when I was six. I hadn't seen nor heard from him since."

Athena visibly faded. "I'm…I'm so sorry. I didn't know. This…this…this must be more difficult for you than I imagined. I shouldn't have…"

"Would you mind," Jaime asked, "if we leave the rest? I don't know any of this, who the people are, what I might find. Perhaps he wrote about in the diary. Could we just skim through it so I can leave?"

Chapter 13

For the rest of the morning, Jaime sat hunched over the diary with the detective, wrestling with the shorthand, slowly getting a sense of it.

Writing the story of a life, I realized after much thought, is far more difficult than I had imagined. Do you attempt to paint it with a kind brush, smooth the dips, put a sheen on the highs, do you scrape away the gloss, expose what lay beneath, do you strain to avoid choosing selectively.

Let me tell it as best I can and leave it to you see through the words to the real story that lies beneath.

Paul Bowles, in The Sheltering Sky, wrote, 'Because we don't know when we will die, we get to think of life as an inexhaustible well. Yet everything happens only a certain number of times, and a very small number really. How many more times will you remember a certain afternoon of your childhood, some afternoon that is so deeply a part of your being that you can't even conceive of your life without it? Perhaps four or five times more, perhaps not even that. How many more times will you watch the full moon rise? Perhaps twenty. And yet it all seems limitless.'

As words formed sentences and the sentences took on meaning, Jaime wondered if his father's purpose in writing this was to explain himself, or to tell of the life he fantasized, Captain Hook, roaming the seas of his imagination in search of treasures and adventure, following wherever the wind and the fates would take him.

It is time to downsize, rid myself of all I once thought important and focus on what is. Buddhists believe that life goes on, that we are all one with the universe, that when autumn leaves die and become compost, they return as flowers in the spring. Perhaps if I believed that, I might not be here today, spending what time I have left alone, without the comfort of family or friends, but to have the patience to sit cross-legged on a hard patch of dirt in a saffron robe waiting for rewards that never came, like my parents did, and as I once believed I could, was less appealing.

With the passing of time, memories grow hazy. So often I find it difficult to separate reality from fantasy, fact from fiction. What I remember of my long ago childhood may, over the years, have come to be idealized, but I believe I am not wrong in that I grew up secure in my parent's love, that my thoughts and opinions were listened to with the same respect that I listened to theirs.

I was born the only son of Avram and Bella, émigrés from Russia, who fled one step ahead of the Czar's soldiers, exchanging their ghetto in Minsk for one in Jersey City. The only possessions they carried from Russia, except the clothes on their backs, were a heavy aluminum food grinder. My mother used to make chopped liver for the Friday night dinner, and a brass mortar and pestle in which she ground spices for the roast chicken. After dinner, we sat around the kitchen table sewing bits of cloth on buttons for mattresses my father sold in the storefront as my father told of the lives and thinking of the great philosophers, Plato, Aristotle, Locke, and Descartes.

I suppose my childhood was a little different than most of my friends,' but even now I can't be sure if one of my earliest memories was real or one of my earliest fantasies. When I close my eyes, I can see the dingy back room of Schwartz's deli where I worked after school stacking crates of Doctor Brown's Celery Tonic on palettes above the wet cement floor, the rows of salamis hanging on hooks, the single hanging light bulb, I can even smell the dampness, and I remember the smell of Rosalie in the back room that afternoon. She was fourteen, two years older than I was. Perhaps I might have omitted this, save for what came later.

Jaime shifted uncomfortably in the hard wooden chair, acutely aware of Detective Spiros, seated beside him, avoiding his eyes.

I flipped when I laid eyes on Marci at the young folks' dance at the synagogue, I was sixteen, as old as her brother, she was not yet fourteen, the story of Rosalie had made the rounds. She refused to go out with me. When, after six months, nothing else would do, I showed up at her house one Saturday after services when she and her family were at lunch. On the dining room table was lox, cream cheese, bagels, sliced tomatoes and onions, seltzer. She, her brother, her mother, and father were still in the clothes they wore to shul. Without a word or a look at her, I went directly to her mother, presented her with a bunch of flowers. Marci turned red. Her mother's eyes went wide, her brother leaped up, glaring, her father looked amused, I then presented myself in front of her father and asked if I could have his permission to take his daughter to the dance at the temple the following Saturday evening as I intended to marry her.

Her father looked at me as if I was meshuggah, then at his wife, then at Marci. Do you know this fellow, he asked. Marci tried to hide, her father's eyes became so severe I thought he'd boot me out, but I caught a hint of the tiniest grin in the corners.

The next year, the best of my life, was torture. We were together every moment we could...except in the biblical sense. Our friends thought we were insane.

We laid plans to marry when I finished college but had to set the wedding forward when we discovered a child was on the way. I dropped out of college, Marci finished high school, her parents helped, and I went to work. We found a tiny one-bedroom apartment above a store in Hoboken.

We were in heaven, but I was in a dead-end job. We barely scraped by, even with her parent's help. When I came to her home that Saturday at lunchtime, I had promised her more.

Jaime got up from the table chewing on his lip.

"Hey!" Athena demanded, looking up at him, "I can go through this if you're not up to going on."

Chapter 14

Two roads diverged in a yellow wood/ I could not travel both…And that has made all the difference. Imagine one selected day struck out of a life, and think how different its course would have been. When someone seeks, then it easily happens that his eyes see only the thing that he seeks, and obsessed with his goal, thinks only about the thing he is seeking.

We celebrated Seder in Marci's mother's parents' new home the year Jaime was six, closing with the singing of Chad Gadya, thought to be a historical allegory representing a journey of self-development of the Jewish people. It tells the story of one little goat, which my father bought for two zuzim,' and continues, the cat came and ate the little goat which my father bought for two zuzim,' and on until the Angel of Death came and slew the slaughter who killed the ox that drank the water that extinguished the fire that burned the stick that beat the dog that bit the cat that ate the goat which my father bought for two zuzim.

Two zuzim was equal to the half-shekel tax upon every adult Israelite male. The price of a Jewish soul was said to be two zuzim.

Marci's brother had driven to the seder in his new Mercedes, his wife Rachel came in a luminous turquoise, gold-trimmed silk Dior dress. My value, as a husband and a father was two zuzim.

The side job I took as a fundraiser started our first real argument that went on without end. 'What kind of charity is Save the Child Foundation,' Marci exploded. 'I never heard of it. Who runs it? Are you sure it's legitimate? Maybe you should ask my brother.'

The idea of being away from home weekends ate at me. I'd miss Marci and Jaime. But my worth would no longer be two zuzim,

Temple Beth Yitzvak in Bryn Mawr, a western suburb of Philadelphia, was listed in the National Register of Historic Places, the first examples of 'Collegiate Gothic' architecture in the U.S. Homes there were priced by the inch, the Temple was not the bare storefront synagogue Marci and I attended. Light bulbs didn't hang on cords from the ceiling, congregants didn't sit on wooden folding chairs, unembroidered purple velvet didn't cover the Ark. Stained glass windows filtered sunlight, plush cushions covered the benches, the Ark glowed beneath the light of a cut-crystal chandelier.

I didn't fit there. Who was going to give a donation to someone wearing clothes bought on sale in Delancy Street, driving a six-year-old Dodge Dart.

I returned a week later driving a four-year-old BMW in a suit and tie from Brooks Brothers.' I told Marci my boss had advanced the money. He hadn't. I drained our joint account of wedding presents we were saving. It was the first lie I told to Marci. But I was doing it for her, I assured myself.

A synagogue never turns a newcomer away, but the smiles, as my aunt Bessie used to say, didn't stretch beyond the lips. By some inner radar, the members sensed I wasn't 'one of them.' I wandered around after the service wearing a forced smile, wondering if I would have to return the car and clothes and confess to Marci, cringing at the thought of her 'understanding' brother.

I must have looked what I felt for the next thing I found myself chatting with a woman who appeared as cut off from the others as I. Marsha Abramowitz was a few years older and a head shorter. Her soft blonde hair floated around her face, her eyes were shaded by long lashes; she had the eagerness of a young girl anxious to be liked. She had lost her husband six months earlier. After an initial outpouring of sympathy, long-time friends promised to call and get together but didn't.

If she suspected, she didn't ask. I let her assume that like her, I was unattached, that I traveled as a representative of the 'Save the Child Foundation.' We talked until the shamus began turning off lights. It seemed natural for her to invite me to come back to her home to continue talking.

It was the entry to wealthy donors I hoped for, but more; her home was a style of living I couldn't relate to. If the art on her walls was real, they could hang in New York's Metropolitan Museum of Art. We could fit our whole apartment in her living room. A concert-sized Steinway grand piano sat in one corner on a red and blue Persian rug, the couch was as soft as a featherbed, her coffee table was inlaid with mother of pearl. French windows looked out onto a flood-lit flower garden.

It was love at first sight, not with Marsha but with a way of life I'd only read about. It was perfectly innocent for Marsha to invite me to stay over – her six-year-old daughter was at a pajama party with friends – instead of 'returning to my hotel' at that late hour. Of course, I was not staying at a hotel but sleeping in the back of the car. I imagined how I would tell Marci all about this.

Of course, I didn't. Marsha introduced me to her former set, I received donations, my commissions, 5%, barely covered the cost of the standard expected of me, it became more and more difficult keeping the stories I told Marci and Marsha straight as Friday night sleepovers became more. The blow-up that followed came with an ultimatum.

It had been hell for me. I was miserable. I was deceiving the woman I loved. Worse, as Marci feared, the Foundation was a fraud. Marci had been right. Pictures of ragged African children, nurses in white caps, doctors with stethoscopes, testimonials, were fake. Other than for a few cents, the donations went into the pockets of the two principals. I was under investigation.

Marsha offered me a choice: I could return home with my tail between my legs, face our friends, our parents, Marci's brother, give up a standard of living I had lived for a jail cell, or I could live with her and her daughter Susan, who I had feelings for as if she were my own, she would bail me out if I gave up Marci and my son.

I can claim it was no choice, but I am less than proud of the choice I made.

Chapter 15

Jaime pushed the diary aside. Here was the woman and daughter his father chose over him and his mother, the reason he had spent so many nights crying himself to sleep. And now he was asked to deliver a stock certificate to the daughter who had replaced him.

He sat thinking of what to do for most of the rest of the day, trying not to let his eyes wander back over the remaining pages; hoping it all turned out badly but was afraid it would not be so. In the end, he knew he had to find out, turned back and resumed, becoming more and more familiar with his father's shorthand.

That Marsha clung to me wasn't only because she was grieving; she was struggling to break free from her mother who would never be seen, out or at home, without a hat, gloves, stockings and a back as straight as a rod. If I were to say claim that all I saw in Marsha was someone who could rescue me, I would be deceiving myself. I was not in love with Marsha, but I loved the child in her, the delight she took in little nothings. She taught an evening class at the local high school 'Where to Eat in Philadelphia,' knitted dolls she sold in a hobby store for pennies, was an enthusiastic member of the Garden Club.

Life is full of coincidences not always welcome. Six months before we met, an afternoon in late spring, Marsha felt a tremor run down her spine when over the radio she heard that a man had been killed crossing a downtown street coming back to his office after lunch. Somehow she knew it was her husband. He had been a heavy drinker. Not long after, her father suffered a stroke and was confined to a nursing home. When she started seeing me, she knew what her mother's reaction would be; she was not only dating a married man but taking him into her bed. Whatever warmth her mother allowed to escape her sculpted face would be her granddaughter Susan's alone.

It was an explosive mixture, for all of us, most of all for Susan who had lost a father and was being pulled in three directions.

Her friends were sympathetic at first, she had lost a husband and her father was sick, but the wealthy did not become wealthy by being soft-hearted about money, and though they had taken the tax deductions, that avenue closed, even after I testified on their behalf at the arraignment.

The situation was too explosive to last. As Marsha regained her equilibrium, the bond between mother and daughter strengthened and Marsha became a daughter her mother had wanted, in her image. The end was difficult for us both. Our feelings for each other were genuine, but I didn't fit the image Marsha now had of herself, nor did I want to, though not till then did I realize how deeply entrenched in each other's lives we had become in seven years, and how deeply I had come to care for Susan. I had felt wretched parting with my son; at six, he was already flexing his independence. But a daughter is all party dresses and patent leather shoes and beads and becoming a young lady, and I had been her dad for a while. Susan would always be her mother's daughter, but a hellion as well, what her mother once was. No one would ever be bored being with her. I would miss seeing her grow into womanhood.

Marsha and I made one determined attempt to restore the magic Francesca Zappa wrote of, 'Did you meet your soul mate? That always happens on the first day of school, right?'

I thought of calling Marci then, saying, 'Hi, how are you,' that kind of thing, I'd, ask how Jaime was doing in high school, did he go out for the basketball team. But I didn't. 'Forever' only sells made-for-TV movies.

Chapter 16

Susan, Marsha's daughter, would be about his age, Jaime assumed. A search for her phone number brought up: 'Number unlisted at customer's request.' A further search turned up a Susan Abramowitz, M.D., on the staff of the Philadelphia Children's Hospital. Was this her? He called the hospital and asked to be connected. A recorded voice said leave a message, the doctor would get back to him.

He had wanted to meet this young woman when he read what his father wrote about her, but his father's memory of her was of a girl six to twelve years old, and she was a doctor now, a grown woman with weighty responsibilities. He chewed on it during the ninety-mile drive to Philadelphia; wondering what kind of reception he'd receive if she'd even agreed to meet him. He would deliver the stock certificate and go.

Nothing about this was settling, including the Warwick Hotel he persuaded himself he was now able to afford for one night. Entering the thirty-foot, floor to ceiling glassed-in marble lobby overlooking Rittenhouse square, he experienced the seductive quality his father described the night he first entered Marsha's home in Bryn Mawr. Multiple panes of beveled glass threw off shimmering rainbows from reflections on passing cars. Jaime signed the registration, dropped his bag in his room, and set off for the hospital, leaving his car in one of the visitor's slots.

A work shift appeared to be over; women and men in green scrubs and sneakers were leaving as he entered. The receptionist at the front desk, a kindly looking grandmotherly type in her seventies, wearing a white hospital coat with a volunteer badge over a street dress, answered him pleasantly but unhelpfully. She was not permitted to give out personal phone numbers of staff members. Jamie took out his wallet, withdrew his Nebraska driver's license, and passed it to her. "I'm her half brother," he invented. "I've just been called from Nebraska for our father's funeral. Her phone number is unlisted. I've been attempting to reach Dr. Abramowitz or her mother for a week."

He could see that none of this was having an affect; the volunteer seemed anxious to be of help but was bewildered, there was nothing she could do. "Could you," he asked, refusing to give up, "let me speak to someone in the personnel department who might be able to help?"

It was another hour, when the woman and others she called could think of no other way to get rid of him, that she found someone in Human Resources willing to call.

"Dr. Abramowitz. This is Cindy Clermont at the hospital. No, no. It's not an emergency. I apologize for calling you at home, but there is someone here, Jaime Filenkov, who claims to be your half-brother, who says his father died and he has been trying to reach you. Would you be willing to speak to him?"

Jamie stood in front of her fenced off desk, shifting from foot to foot, wondering if Susan would. The last time she saw his father was twenty-five years ago, according to the diary.

Chapter 17

When Susan lifted the phone, she found herself listening with only half an ear. The personnel office? Her *half-brother*? What kind of scam was this? Son? He never mentioned a son. Half-brother? Like father, like son: A genial charlatan.

"Please," she heard someone speaking in the background. "Let me speak to her for just a second. Let me…it's all here in the diary my father left, a stock certificate for her in Pfizer, one of the leaders in breast cancer research – which my father apparently knew her mother has."

Susan heard the words, tried to absorb them. Aaron Fisher. Breast cancer.

Not until Jamie repeated himself three times did she realize what he was telling her, but even then she tried to think of excuses to brush him off. Had he really left stock in a drug company conducting research on breast cancer because of her mother's cancer?

Susan didn't tell her mother of the phone call, unsure of her reaction, unhappy she agreed to meet him for breakfast. She would listen to his father like son pitch, cut, and leave, claiming she was on call, she'd get back to him, in the same way his father did, never.

Chapter 18

Jamie chewed on it for some time on the way back to the Hotel. Chenny was the one solid thing in his life. He didn't want to lose her, not when he was struggling with so many emotions.

He had thought many times of what it would be like for Chenny to leave Red Plains, unable to escape the thought of Shangri-la, the idyllic lamasery atop a peak in the Himalayas James Hilton described in his novel, *The Lost Horizon*. It is to the lamasery that Conway finds his way after his plane crashes in the mountain peaks, discovering a place where people age slowly – he guesses that the High Lama is 250 years old. But also learns that if they were to leave, they age quickly and die. He falls in love with Lo-Tsen, a seemingly young lovely Manchu woman. When he falls ill and their medicine fails him, Lo-Tsen carries him to a doctor out of the valley, and soon dies. 'Most old of anyone I have ever seen,' the doctor reports. She had aged drastically departing from the lamasery in Shangri-La.

He could call Chenny. She would still be awake. It was two hours earlier there. But email would allow him to delete words that strayed unwittingly.

To: Chenny125@aol.com
Cc:
Subject: Travels of the Pirate's Son.

Hi:

It seems that, at no wish of mine, I am destined to spend my summer traveling. I expected, when I found this to be so, that it would be an opportunity to write *An Innocent Abroad,* only to discover that a fellow by the name of Mark Twain already used that title. Just as well. It seems the fellow never became a success.

The London Saturday Review, 1870: Lord Macaulay died too soon. We never felt this so deeply as when we finished the last chapter of the above-named extravagant work. Macaulay died too soon – for none but he could mete out complete and comprehensive justice to the insolence, the impertinence, the presumption, the mendacity, and, above all, the majestic ignorance of this author. The book is absolutely dangerous…considering the multitude and variety of its misstatements, and the convincing confidence with which they are made.

I believe I made it evident when I was asked to come east to view the remains of a man I had neither seen nor heard from for a quarter of a century, that I had little interest in ever seeing him again, alive or dead. I had expected that I would arrive, shake my head, 'No, I don't know the son of a bitch,' and get right back on a plane. Instead, I found he saddled me with the obligation to personally deliver bequests he left to members of families he had live with, families I had not known existed.

Instead of dwelling on the pain it will be to meet families he chose in preference to me, I think instead of blazing hot afternoons spent skinny dipping, a cloudless baby blue sky, the nip of the sun on my skin, diving, splashing and swimming about like a pair of daffy porpoises, hardly what I expected when I found I was to spend a year in a place that time forgot. Ah, were I there now…

It occurs to me that I am not the first one in my family to have been pleasantly surprised in his travels. My grandfather – this was a good many years ago – sent to call on a prospective account in Texarkana, Arkansas, was touched when he learned that Mr. W had driven to a delicatessen in Dallas the morning of the day he arrived – 180 miles each way – and returned with a corned beef sandwich on rye for him. Mr. W had never before met a Jew, and didn't know what a Jew ate.

Naively, perhaps, I might not have been surprised when I arrived that I came under suspicion of having had a hand in arranging to become my father's heir. Fortunately, the police settled instead on Cherry Sweet, '*sociable*' young woman and her mentor, Roberto di Valenciago.

And so, what I expected would be a quick in and out became rather longer, a bunch of legal matters to attend to, a need to prove that Aaron Fisher, the name my father went by, and Allan Filenkov, were one and the same, the need to probate his will, and the need to make plans to deliver certain bequests to who he lived with in Philadelphia, Charleston and Raleigh Durham.

Fortunately, finding an attorney these days is not difficult; there are plenty of highly regarded attorneys who have ads on the sides of buses.

So much has happened in the few days since I left I hardly know where to begin. Why my father kept a diary in his bewildering shorthand is as mysterious as much I have discovered about him. That he left the balance of what he owned to me would seem an expression of remorse, but is it, or is it quite the opposite, a final affront visited upon me from beyond the grave to make evident that I may be no better than him, for I was offered with the choice of rejecting the inheritance, or facing the families he chose to spend his life with in preference to my mother and me.

I agonized over this at length and decided he was right – I must be his son. If he can send me a message from the beyond the grave, I have one for him: I'm keeping the inheritance.

So much I have learned in the short time I've been here. Did you know that every state has a different rule regarding probate? If it is a small estate, as is this one, an in-state executor has to file the will with the Probate Court for the funds or property to be released to the next of kin, which also requires filing a small estate affidavit. In the case of a larger estate, an ancillary probate case must be filed in order to get an order of adjudication as to the rightful owner and then an order of disbursement. I expect this information will be useful the next time you play trivia.

All this seems…so trivial, my mind keeps drifting back to that morning lying on my back on the bank of the lake, the hot dry sun sucking the few remaining drops on my stomach and chest, and elsewhere. It is odd, is it not, that the Kama Sutra and sex manuals allot so much space to intricate positions, to whips and chains and other toys, with little mention of what anticipation plays.

Before I stray any further, I'll sign off. Hope all goes well with you. I make my first visit in the morning, ninety miles from where I started, in Philadelphia.

Ciao.

Chapter 19

Susan looked at the calendar and cringed. June 30th. This was the weekend she and Jonathan were to have left for two weeks in France. The dull ache that had slowly begun to fade welled up again. She wanted to hold on to it, hold it close, didn't want it ever to go away. It was all that she had left of him.

She looked around the room and out through the French windows into the garden. The early sun was slanting down casting lights and shadows on her mother and her husband Hermann having breakfast in the gazebo. She could picture them in on the lawn on the south shore of Long Island in a scene from The Great Gatsby, her mother in a lavender and lemon yellow silk tea dress, Hermann in a white shirt, stiff high collar and brown tweeds, she sipping tea, he eating his boiled egg in an egg cup.

July was more than a hint. The irises in the border of the garden were losing their purple petals, the tulip bulbs the gardener replanted in beds in the fall were pushing up green shoots, the tea roses had filled in around the blue green lawn, tiny yellow-throated tits were sipping nectar from the wisteria trumpets wound round the lacy gazebo.

What had seemed a haven when she was growing up no longer felt like home, not the home she had dreamed of. It was just a year ago, in Evian, on the balcony of a hotel room in the Ermitage, halfway up the mountain, overlooking the town on the edge of the lake, the shores of Geneva visible in early morning mist on the other side of the lake, where Jonathan had proposed.

Only two images, burned into her mind, had remained with her since then, Jonathan on his knees beside the small white café table on the balcony, their bed clothes strewn across the room behind them, and coming awake on the hard operating table, a bright light streaming down into her eyes, everything fuzzy, asking for Jonathan, not wanting to hear their reply.

Since then, once she was discharged, only for work did she leave the newly gentrified one-bedroom loft on Constitution Avenue, three blocks from The Philadelphia Navy Yard, which was to be their home.

"It's only speed that kills," Jonathan insisted, with that shameless quirky smile and innocent face that had her knees too weak to hold her up from the first moment she met him. "It stands to reason. The National Safety Council has it backwards. The faster you're off the road, the less the chance for an accident."

"Oh, Jonathan."

She remembered repeating that, making a stupid joke about it when she was in the hospital, doped up, still in shock. The airbags had saved her life, but not Jonathan's. The semi, barreling along from the left through the light, stove in his side of the car.

It was only to stop her mother's badgering that she agreed to go to Temple with her to say *Yizkor* for Jonathan's *Yahrzeit,* the one-year anniversary of his death, and stay over with her. When her phone rang in the evening, she jumped.

"Dr. Abramowitz. This is Cindy Clermont at the hospital. No, no. It's not an emergency. I apologize for calling you at home, but there is someone here, Jaime Filenkov, who claims to be your half-brother, who says his father died and he has been trying to reach you. Would you be willing to speak to him?"

Susan listened, shocked. The last time she had seen him was twenty-five years ago. *Half-brother*?

"Please," she heard, a man's voice, just give me a second. "I've been trying to reach you for almost two hours. It was the only way they would call you. My father left a stock certificate for you in Pfizer, a leader in breast cancer research – which he knew your mother has."

Susan heard the words, tried to absorb them. Aaron Filenkov. Breast cancer. Stock in Pfizer. Why would he leave stock to her? She last saw him when she was twelve, twenty years ago. She had come to love him when he came to live with them after her father died, but there was a scam he was involved with, she was told, and her mother sent him away. She tried to think of excuses to brush him off. Had he really left stock in a drug company conducting research on breast cancer because of her mother's cancer?

She woke early after a sleep troubled by the crazy quilt pattern of dreams that had haunted her for what seemed forever, with the added torment of coming face to face with the son of the man who had filled a hole in her life after her father died and then left her too. She hadn't told her mother who had called, afraid of her reaction, agreed to meet him for breakfast, listen to his father like son pitch, cut, and leave, claiming she was on call, she'd get back to him, in the same way his father did, never.

Chapter 20

Jaime sat waiting for Susan to arrive, wondering if she'd show up, only vaguely aware of the posh, glassed-in, historic two-story lobby overlooking Rittenhouse Square, a restoration from an earlier gentler time when chauffeur-driven jeweled clientele arrived in formal clothes. Checking in, he did not feel the thrill he had thought it would be. He felt torn, pulled in more directions than there were in the compass. Shutting down, turning off, was the only relief he had been able to find from dealing with the emotions tearing at him; how he felt about his father, being thrust into a mix of strangers he was both curious about and jealous of. As unsettling as that was, allowing himself to enjoy, for the first time in his life, the ability not to stint and not to pinch pennies, instead of being exhilarating was tearing at him even more.

He often wondered if it would have made a difference if he had a more romantic name in keeping with the literary career he hoped would one day would make him famous, a name he'd borrow from his Russian heritage, Feyodor, or Constantine, or at least Petrov, and he constructed a story that having been exiled to Red Plains, and sentenced to live under such conditions, further added color to the tales he'd tell about what went into making him the author he had become, and he'd finish the talk introducing his book, with a wry, self-deprecating moue, of how he had been denied tenure, leaving it to his audience to surmise that 'they' had failed to appreciate the talent that had propelled him to the top of the New York Times bestseller list.

The habit of a lifetime, watching every cent he spent, searching out the least expensive restaurants, wearing clothes bought in discount stores long after they should have been discarded, persuading himself that now that he could afford it he had a right to spend money on himself, that he was not being profligate, would be long gone. Checking into a hotel like this, even though it was little more expensive than less central motels, would no longer be the thrill it once was, but now seemed the height of wastefulness.

He would laugh remembering his mother's great aunt Sadie who had grown up in poverty, but who, even after her husband became wealthy, saved rubber bands and string and bundled newspapers to sell for pennies.

Even from a distance, when the dining room hostess led her from to the table in the breakfast room, he saw the hesitation. He rose when the hostess brought her to the table, but seemed uncertain whether to extend his hand. He felt as if a trap door had opened beneath him and he had fallen through. He had never been good at hiding his emotions. This was not the girl his father described in his diary, a young girl full of life, perky, bursting with fun. Lowering himself back down, he tried to keep what he was thinking from his face. It was twenty-five years since his father left her, she was no longer a girl, but what happened to her in the years since? She was a doctor, an internist at a leading children's hospital. She would have a life he could only imagine, everything going for her. But everything about her was dull. She refused to make eye contact, her body language was one of despair, her clothes seemed of less than no interest, a dun-colored, mid-calf skirt that might have come from a bin of Salvation Army, a faded gray cotton turtleneck sweater that hung on her thin collar bones, her hair, what he could see of it not tucked into a lifeless brown knitted watch cap, was blonde. The only thing that could suggest the girl his father described was the depth of the blue in her eyes, that and her clear complexion. Was it she, not her mother, who was being treated for breast cancer?

The way she settled tightly on the edge of her seat, the set of her lips, the story he read in her eyes, made it evident that she planned on keeping this short, that she had no interest in him or what had become of his father after he left her. If he said the wrong thing, she would jump up and race off.

"I feel I'm intruding, bringing back unpleasant memories," he began, unsure what to say. She lifted her eyes briefly, looked at him curiously, then let her gaze fall back on her coffee. "I guess," he continued, "my…father…I once called him that, but that was long ago…"

When she continued to remain silent, avoiding eye contact, he grew still more uncomfortable. "Schiller, I think it was," he half mumbled, "who said, 'It is not flesh and blood but heart, which makes us fathers and sons.'"

He'd hardly gotten it out of his mouth when he wished he could stuff it back in again, certain it sounded as if he was trying to sound as if he was a pedant. It had so seemed to startle her that he stopped talking and shut down, forgetting what he had rehearsed to say' furious that he had allowed himself to be persuaded to make these calls.

When the silence extended for what seemed like several minutes, she lifted her head from her coffee cup. "You weren't fond of your father?"

"Fond of him? I didn't know him. I was six when he abandoned my mother and me. I hadn't seen him until last week when I was called – I was teaching in Nebraska – to identify his body. Like him? I don't think he gave a damn about me…"

"…but he adored you."

For an instant his eyes widened, but quickly changed to disbelief.

"He left a diary," he hurried on, afraid he was going to lose her again. "I have a copy, the police in Surf Side have the original. He talked about how badly he felt when he was forced to leave you, but I suppose you know that.

"Anyway, he left you shares in Pfizer – he learned your…mother…" he searched her eyes for confirmation, seeing it, plunged ahead… "your mother…has breast cancer… Pfizer is working on a drug that had promise. Here…" He took a manila envelope out of a folder and held it out to her.

Susan seemed to consider the envelope, tore her eyes away. Jaime held for another moment, and let his hand drop.

"He was my father…for a while, too," she said, a tear clouding her eye, warily taking the envelope from him. "Do you have to leave right away, or could we talk for a while?"

Chapter 21

As they sat, awkwardly edging into conversation, he was startled by the metamorphosis taking place before his eyes. At first they both picked their way over splinters of glass, but as it slowly became easier, she removed her cap letting her blonde hair fall free. The melancholy in her face gradually dissolved, replaced by animation that had been hidden, and she began talking about her life, about her mother, the pain he had seen in the irises of her eyes earlier appearing less and less often.

"You know," she admitted, "I can see the resemblance between you and your father, the shape of your face, the same mischievous eyes, as if they were laughing at me, didn't take me seriously."

He felt as if she had doused him in a bath of ice water. He was afraid to respond. He didn't know how she felt about his father. If he said the wrong thing, he might shut her down. He had hoped mention of him could be avoided, though it was inevitable. The last thing be wanted was to hear was that he was like his father.

She seemed to sense she had touched a button and immediately shut down. Jamie feared she'd sink back into the former melancholy state. "It is your mother…I mean…is it she who has…breast cancer?" He tried for something to say.

"Stage two." He could see how she was hurting. "She had a lumpectomy six years ago, the cancerous lymph nodes were removed, she had radiation and chemo. The oncologist said that if it didn't recur within four years it wasn't likely to. We thought she had it beat, but it metastasized."

As she talked, Jaime wondered at the transformation taking place. She was not the young woman who approached his table in frumpy clothes less than an hour ago. He could see her in bright colors, in becoming dresses. "Did you…" he began with no clear idea of what he was going to ask, "… always…want to be a doctor? A children's doctor?"

She seemed to consider this before she answered, as if it was important to explain, make it clear. "I'm not sure what I always planned to be," she finally answered. She seemed to be looking inward. "I think part of it is the pressure I felt, the Jewish mantra: education…education…education. Did you have that? Had you always wanted to teach literature?"

"Always. Absolutely!" he answered seriously, but the look on his face belied his words.

"Absolutely?"

"Yeah. I never thought of it that way. I had no idea what it was I wanted to be. If I had to put a label on it, I would say – I had 'aspirations.'"

Susan searched his eyes. "Aspirations?"

"I guess I sound like…like the cow told of in the Bahá'í Library that imagined itself in a lofty station…"

"The cow…? You wanted to write '*Moo,*' the novel Jane Smiley's wrote about characters in *Moo U,*" – she flicked the second and third fingers of both hands – "the *Great American Novel.*'"

Jaime felt the wall he had wrapped tightly around himself crumble. A broad smile spread across his face. He shook his head. "No!"

"No?"

"No! Only for a start."

"Got it. How much of it have you written?"

Jaime shook his head.

"How much?"

"I have a working title."

"*That* much."

Jaime tore his eyes from her for a chance to breathe, to not say too much. Through the 20' high, floor to ceiling panes of glass that enclosed the lobby, the world outside still looked as he remembered it. The world hadn't changed. He hadn't wanted to be here and now he didn't want to leave. "It's a beautiful day outside," he found himself saying. "Is there any chance we could walk a bit? I've always wanted to see some of it. Isn't Philadelphia the Cradle of Liberty?"

"You don't want to do something corny, do you, like going to see the Liberty Bell?"

Was she teasing him? He was beginning to see that she had a million expressions and switched from one to another so smoothly he found himself continually wondering which was the real one, keeping him off balance. His face turned a deep reddish umber. "Yup." It was all he could manage, like Luke from Dubuque.

"OK," Susan said as they rose from the table, shaking her head in mock irritation. "Follow me. I'll head you to the Chamber of Commerce." Turning to go, she said, "Oh, what the hell, it's the least I can do for someone from Nebraska."

Chapter 22

It was a ten-minute walk from the hotel in Rittenhouse Square along Market Street to the Liberty Bell in Independence National Park. "Didja know," she asked as she led him along, "that Philadelphia is 6th in the U.S. in the number of sites listed in the National Register of Historic Places?"

"Didja?"

"If you don't want to learn I don't have to take the trouble to broaden your horizons."

"Sorry."

"Would you like to guess which cities have more?"

"Red Plains, Nebraska?"

"Close. It was edged out by St Augustine, number one, followed by Santa Fe, Boston, Annapolis and New Castle."

"New Castle? New Castle Delaware?"

"Please don't interrupt. If you have questions, wait until the end of the tour. If you will look to your right now, you will see one of the wonders of the modern world, Wanamaker's Grand Court, now part of Macy's."

Jaime opened his mouth to toss back a quip, but it caught in his throat. To call this a 'Court' was to call the Sistine Chapel a dome. The Wanamaker court rose seven-stories high to a gabled ceiling. It was the width of a football field and built entirely of tan marble. But what made it so breathtaking was the organ at its rear. Seated over three marble arches extending the width of the Court, through which visitors could reach the mall beyond, was the world's largest organ, 28,604 gold pipes housed in a series of domes, three on each side, rising in height, from the far walls to the center dome which was topped by a statue of winged victory to all but touch the seven-story ceiling.

A bronze plaque on the wall on the side offered some of the details:

The Wanamaker Grand Court Organ is the largest fully functioning pipe organ in the world. It is played at least twice a day Monday through Saturday, and more frequently during the Christmas season. The organ has 28,604 pipes and the console has six keyboards. The string division has eighty-eight ranks of pipes forming the largest single organ chamber in the world. The organ is famed for its orchestra-like sound, coming from pipes that are voiced softer than usual, allowing an unusually rich build-up because of the massing of pipestone families. Two curators are employed in its constant and scrupulous care. The organ, with its regular program of concerts and recitals, was maintained by Wanamaker's throughout the chain's history, even as the company's financial fortunes waned.

There was only one 'luxury' Jaime had ever allowed himself, music. As they waited for the organ recital to begin, the talking and laughing and shuffling about in the Court slowly died, and as the first quiet notes of the organ stole from the tiniest pipes, a hush fell over the room. Jaime stood, transfixed, rapt, in a world of his own, as if infusing, absorbing, ingesting every note, making it a part of him, from the highest register, the flutes and chimes, to the midrange, the cellos and oboes and horns, to the deepest of the bass, the violins and contrabassoons and tubas, feeling it enter the walls of the giant court until the whole room seemed to throb and vibrate and pulsate.

The recital began with Irving Berlin's 'America' – Jaime could hear Ray Charles singing it – the organist moved smoothly to Justin Bieber's, 'Let Me Love You,' and after a pause for the court to take a breath, it followed with the encompassing, grand, intense Toccata and Fugue in D Minor by Bach.

When the final notes died, it was as if the audience began to breathe again. Not until he and Susan were a half block off on their way to the Liberty Bell could Jaime break the mood. "Those women," he asked, indicating with a nod the direction from which they came, "you don't care for them?"

Two smartly dressed young women of about Susan's age, entering the Court as the two of them were leaving, rushed to Susan and embraced her. Susan seemed embarrassed, anxious to escape as quickly as possible.

"I…I apologize. I should have introduced them. It's…"

"Me?"

"No. No. They mean well, but I…they're…no, they're…" she shook her head, throwing away what she was saying, switching abruptly, making it obvious she wanted to change the subject. "I watched you…" she tried for a grin. "Were you conducting?"

Jaime tried to hide his embarrassment. "I know, I know," he responded limply. "I'm I…I can't explain it. When I hear music, I…I have to move to it. It's as if I was born with internal Wi-Fi. I can't understand how others cannot move to it. How can anyone listen to…Sousa's 'Stars and Stripes for Ever'…and not even tap their feet or… How do I explain it? As an infant, I remember pulling myself up in my crib, holding on, and bouncing to music when my mother turned on the radio or stereo. It's like…like music turns a switch in me, it becomes part of me, or I of it, the way Wi-Fi energizes a computer or iPad and…I can't explain it. You're in medicine. Maybe you can explain it."

Susan looked at him as if he was…odd, or worse. "Did you ever want to make music your career?"

Jaime shrugged. "You need to have perfect pitch. I don't. I have what's called 'relative pitch,' but that's not good enough."

"Relative pitch?"

"Someone with perfect pitch can read a sheet of music and hear it in his head, or hear a note played or sung and identify it as 'A sharp,' or 'B flat.' I can't do that. I can hear a piece of music and whistle it, I can hear if a performer is off by even a half note, but it's…let me tell you a true story. Herbert von Karajan, the legendary martinet, the former imposing, great conductor of the Berlin Symphony Orchestra, was rehearsing a piece for an upcoming concert. Furious, he stopped, raised his hands for quiet! The harpist had played a G minor instead of a G. With a sharp word, he raised his baton, started again. Again when they came to that point, the harpist played that wrong note! Von Karajan, in a rage, climbed down from the podium, stomped over to the harpist, took a penknife from his pants pocket, sliced off all the strings in the harp – except the one she was supposed to play."

"You wouldn't do that, would you?"

All Jaime could do was grin. "I noticed that Justin Bieber's 'Let Me Love You' did something…"

Jaime stopped abruptly. It was as if Susan imploded. She looked…defeated, beaten, spent… a tear formed on her lower eyelid. He had seen it when 'Let Me Love You' was played during the performance. Her eyes teared up suddenly, and just as quickly she looked away so as not be noticed, brushing at the tears with the back of her hand. He had noticed it earlier at breakfast, the shifting of her eyes and the movement of her mouth, as if her emotions were so close to the surface they threatened to spill over. He had wondered then if she had had a deep emotional relationship with his father, that his visit reminded her of it, if, God forbid, she had been scarred by him in some unimaginable way, and why the playing of that piece should have aroused that.

They walked on in silence, Jaime wondering if he was imposing, dragging Susan away from things she had planned, people she wanted to be with, whether she saw this as an obligation. For the first time since the phone call came summoning him to New Jersey, he had begun to feel the tension in him beginning to melt away, replaced by a different kind of tension. Maybe it would be common courtesy to ask her. She was, after all, taking her time to show him around.

"Uh…" he sort of muttered, when they got in line to see the Liberty Bell.

Susan's mobile face now changed to still another expression, one he hadn't yet seen. "Is that Lakota Indian language, like 'Ugh'?" she asked when he broke off abruptly. "Or is that Lakota ebonics?"

"'Uh' means, me heap hungry for roast possum. Would you join me for lunch after this?"

Susan grunted, "Ugh, kemo sabe."

The line for the Liberty Bell didn't seem to grow any shorter. As they were waiting, two little girls, sisters, the older about ten, the younger six, broke into line in front of them. "Hey," Jaime called, "did you just sneak into line?"

The younger one giggled. "We did!"

Jaime grinned. The older one tried to look serious but couldn't keep a smile from her face when the younger one giggled even louder. Save for the obvious difference in age, they might have been twins. They were in matching yellow shorts, white tees with green slogans, 'Save the Planet,' 'No Nukes,' had round chubby faces, striking red hair and freckles on the bridges of their noses.

Jaime looked at the pair with mock anger, lips pinched, nostrils narrowed, brow creased. "Hmm," he exhorted.

The lines of pain in Susan's face minutes before were gone. There now was a wistful smile, almost bliss.

Chapter 23

Jaime bit into the Philadelphia cheesesteak sandwich Susan insisted he had to try. They were sitting on a bench opposite the lawn in the Independence Center. Around the perimeter, bees were at work diving into the pink and yellow azaleas. One and two-parent families nearby were chatting in a polyglot of languages – French, German, Italian and, possibly Ukrainian – and he heard the distinctive argot of Shaw's Londoners.

"Why can't the British learn to speak English?" Jaime demanded through a mouth half full.

"Yeah!" Susan insisted, with a serious moue as emphasis.

Jaime lifted his eyes, studying Susan thoughtfully, beginning with the hair framing her face to her brow, then going to her eyes, her cheeks, her nose, her lips and, finally, working its way down to her neck and breasts.

Susan reddened.

"Benjamin Disraeli was right," Jaime observed.

Susan reddened further. "Disraeli? The British Prime Minister?"

Jaime flushed. He lowered his eyes to his sandwich, shook his head.

"How was Disraeli right?" Susan insisted.

Eyes fixed on his sandwich, Jaime mumbled, "What we anticipate seldom occurs: but what we least expect generally happens."

Had he looked up in the silence that followed, he'd have seen Susan's face transform through several more expressions.

The background hum rose and fell, children's laughter floated like tiny bubbles over the voices. A trio of pre-teen boys that had been racing and jumping playing Frisbee on the lawn were laughing and hooting as they were being chased off by a uniformed National Park Ranger.

"Probably from somewhere uncivilized, like Red Plains," Susan observed, following them as they ran off.

There it was again, the rapid shift, the tone of voice, the expression, Jaime saw. It was as if she was…*fragile*…it was the only word he could think of. Was it him? Had he brought back hurtful memories? He wanted to ask but didn't know how. The friends he had always seemed to want to be closer to him than he cared to be to them. If a guy was troubled, he'd lay it out. Not women. He had to wean it from them. When he allowed himself to look at her again, he saw something there he couldn't interpret and didn't know if he should ask.

Susan seemed to be studying him without appearing to. What would it have been like, she wondered, if he had been her brother, if Jaime's father had told them he had a son, if he had brought Jaime to live with them, if they had grown up together, if she had someone who was always there for her when she was down, or in pain?

After a while, she turned to him: "You know, I keep looking at families, like the ones we've seen here today, and it makes me sad. How often do I see two parents with their children, not one? Even then I wonder if the parents were their birth parents, or if this was another patched-together home – and if it was patched together, I wondered how the children felt about it if they had been scarred by the arrangement forced upon them…if they were even asked."

Jaime sensed Susan was talking about herself, about feelings she had when she lost her father, when her mother forced someone on her, brought his father into her home at a time when she was hurting so badly, later when his father was wrenched from her after she had come to be close to him, and then again when she was forced to accept still another man in her home. He ran his fingers through his hair and let his hand fall limply. He looked around and studied the families sitting at the tables near them, trying to sort them out. One family of four, two boys in slate shorts and white tee shirts, stiff, well-behaved, the mother in red, a short-sleeved blouse, a deeper red pleated skirt that swirled around her ample hips, the man, dark, rugged, the veined nose of a drinker, at another table, Americans, five of them thumbing cell phones or small hand-held games, even the three year old.

And then his thoughts shifted to his life; if he would have had it any better if his mother had been happier; if she hadn't been forced to hold two jobs; if he had had to live with a man who was not his father.

There were so many 'ifs.'

"Hey!" he erupted determined to salvage the fragile connection they established that now seemed in danger of going limp, "Didja ever think of the paradox the electronic age has foisted upon us, how it has brought people closer together…and further apart?"

Susan frowned, beetling her brow; she tilted her head down to look at him over the top of her sunglasses. "Closer together and further apart? You must keep your classes on the edge of their seats."

Jaime tilted his head down, looked over the top of his sunglasses. His eyes sparkled. "You don't see it? Sitting here, talking to each other? We're so…out of it…so retro. Face to face talk seems to be for dinosaurs. Look at them all, the families, the couples, everywhere, sitting at tables, eating with one hand, emailing or texting with the other, snapchatting, viewing photos, playing games, talking to friends, anything but talking to whoever they're there with, even couples on dates."

"Hold on a sec," Susan interrupted, pulling out her cell phone. "What's your number?"

Chapter 24

As they bagged their garbage and disposed of it in a nearby barrel, Jaime tried to keep his thoughts from drifting in the direction they were headed. He could understand now why his father had adored Susan. He had done a number on her, and now, what was he thinking. He didn't want to leave, but he didn't want her to think like father like son. He was afraid what might happen if he didn't go.

"I guess," he began uncertainly, hoping she would correct him, "I'm keeping you from…from…whatever…"

"You have some other of your father's…'loose ends'…to tie up?" Susan slowed, turned so as not to look at him, as if she had let it slip out and was embarrassed.

Jaime felt the sting of the words, drew in a sharp breath. He hadn't realized it, but Susan wasn't the only one whose emotions were so close to spilling over.

When he didn't reply, Susan hurried to catch up to him, "I'm sorry," she said. "That was a horrible thing to say. I don't know…I guess…this must be… must be difficult for you as well."

Jaime slowed his step to hers. He shook his head. "I…I hated doing this. I wasn't going to do it at first. 'Cleaning up after my father' – father in name only – is exactly what it is. *I*…I guess I…I should leave, not keep reminding you of what you want to forget."

They walked on woodenly in silence in the direction from which they came, not looking at each other, neither having anything to say but reluctant to break it off and leave.

As they neared the Warwick, Jaime experienced a flush of such overwhelming anger he was afraid if he were to open his mouth to speak, to say *'Goodbye,'* something would come out that would make him even more…abhorrent…than she must already think of him. He tried to force a smile, but he was sure it was like the one he had pasted on his face when he and the others of the 'Round Table' were aware he was not getting tenure and was leaving the college, and was sure she would see it as one more piece in the person she thought him. He just wanted to hurry off and escape.

He turned and started toward the entrance to the hotel when he heard her voice from what seemed miles away. "Jaime. I'm so terribly sorry. I accepted your kindness and returned…unkindness. I don't know why I said that, maybe I…this has not been a good year for me, and I dumped on you. Please, let me…let's…I mean could we…could we go somewhere and talk…I'm sure you have other places you have to be…but…"

Jaime was too overcome to answer. He wanted to turn, reach for her hand, take it in his, but he stood there dumbly.

"It's all right, Jaime. I just wanted to say I'm sorry before you leave, and –"

Jaime shook his head. "It's…not been…been…a good year…?"

Susan stood numb, eyes lowered. She looked so abject, if he felt it was allowable, he would have reached for her to comfort her.

Susan nodded miserably. "Jaime, would you…I mean…there's a little café two blocks from here. If you don't have to rush away, could we have a cup of coffee, or a drink or…? I'd like to…you never knew…I mean, did you ever hear from your father after he…"

Susan ordered a bottle of red wine. They settled awkwardly into the plastic and wire chairs around a tiny table that might have been ordered for an ice-cream parlor, tiptoeing carefully, wary of straying into any subject that might be painful. Only two tables were occupied at this off-hour. At one, a middle-aged man with a shadow of a beard, dark hair and prominent cheekbones wearing dark suit trousers, a white shirt and a tie with regimental stripes sat hunched over a laptop, at the other, two young women with carefully coifed brunette hair, mid-thigh length dresses, one a solid navy, the other a floral print on a white background, were in intense conversations on their cell phones. There were six unoccupied tables, a glass counter ran along one side of the café, and hidden soft spotlights in the low ceiling illuminated maroon walls.

Jaime's eyes narrowed as if he was looking inward. He tried to make light of what it had been like for him and his mother after his father left. "With my father out of the picture, I became head of the house. 'King Jaime IV,' my mother called me."

Susan face seemed to say how hard it was for him. "I had 'interchangeable' fathers," she offered in the same vein, "like plug-in components," both keenly aware of the pain that lay beneath the attempt at humor.

It was not until near the end of the first bottle before Jaime worked up the courage to follow up what Susan had hinted at. "This past year…wasn't…so… *good?*"

It hadn't come out as gently as he intended. Tears welled up in Susan's eyes. She shook her head, turned away, shutting down as she had before.

Jaime's face turned the gray of Susan's. Women, he believed, rarely opened up to men as they did to women. Men were left to guess, but he somehow had an inner compass, an ability to sense, from a look in their eyes, from their body language, if something was off, or when he had been unintentionally insensitive.

"It was…it was…a year ago this weekend," Susan finally managed. "My…fiancé – we were going to be married in September the week before Rosh Hashanah. There was a Yizkor service in my mother's synagogue last night."

Jaime spread his hands soberly in a gesture of futility.

"No. No," she insisted. "I let it all fall on you…But…it's been…I…my friends, my mother…I…I never talked about it…to anyone…it's…I buried Jonathan, I tried to bury his memory…I… "

Jaime looked away, picked up his wine glass, stared at it, watched the remains of the wine swirl around, and set it down again, unable to think of anything to say. He had never confided in men and always closely guarded what he said to women, biting off impulses to say anything he knew, from experience, he'd desperately want to reel back in the morning.

"I've been a recluse," Susan continued. "Except for work. My friends have tried to coax me out of it, asking me to join them, but I couldn't be with other people. Other than for my mother, her husband, Hermann, the people at work and my patients, you're the only one I've said this to. My mother… I was with her before synagogue last night when you called. She wants to meet you…but if you don't want to…"

Jaime tried to gauge what he had been hearing, how much of what Susan was saying was needy, how much a desire to spend time with him. "Is…that…" he asked cautiously, "what you would like?"

Susan nodded through her tears. "But only…" she looked up at him earnestly, "if you want to. I mean…" she hurried on, "the Kimmel Center here is supposed to have the finest acoustics of any hall in the world, even compared to Avery Fisher and the Met in Lincoln Center."

Jaime felt as if he had just been lifted from a dark place into the sunlight. He tried to think of words to frame his answer in a way to say what he was feeling without saying too much, but before he could, Susan looked around as if embarrassed to see if anyone here was watching or listening, and added, "I… I might run into…friends."

At quickly as his mood had soared, so quickly did Jaime feel he'd been doused with a pail of ice water.

"No. No," Susan hurriedly added, as if wanting to take back her words. "I didn't mean it like that." She stopped, studied his face, and raised her eyes earnestly. "Oh God. Jaime, I feel like everything inside me is crying. Please don't take it like that. My friends have been nagging at me, begging me to join them but I've been avoiding then, everyone. It's not just that I wouldn't face them alone, it's not just that you're my sort of…stepbrother…but…"

But? It wasn't reassuring. It could have a dozen meanings. Air seeped slowly back into his lungs. "Susan, I feel privileged that you asked me."

Susan's raised her face to his. "It's not too much? You wouldn't mind?"

Jaime drew in a deep breath and held it, afraid he would say too much. He felt as if a switch inside him had been turned, that his insides had become attuned and were vibrating with hers, like two strings of a single instrument. What he needed to say was that this was the first moment since he was called from Red Plains that he didn't want to turn around and run back, what he would have said if he knew how she would take it was 'You want me to be your eunuch, your beard?' but all that he allowed himself to say was, "No."

Susan lifted her eyes hopefully to meet his. "We could," she began, "have brunch with my mother tomorrow – I can look on my iPhone and see what's scheduled – we could get tickets for the symphony for tomorrow night or – how long would you be able to stay?" reddening, as if she was afraid she was babbling.

Chapter 25

It was almost four when they left the café on foot. The sky had a cast like the eye of Sam High Foot, the Lakota Indian with the broken nose and the sad countenance who shuffled into Red Plains on Saturday nights from the Indian reservation for a six-pack, his gray-streaked black hair falling half over his good eye. With rain threatening, they set off at a brisk pace for Susan's flat, three blocks along South Broad Street, the second floor of an oak-timbered, red-brick remnant of the once flourishing textile industry vacated and in disrepair when mill owners fled south for lower non-union wages. Saved from the wrecking ball by developers, the building was now part of a hot neighborhood for Yuppies and young couples within walking distance of the Naval docks further south.

By the time they reached the brightly lit entry, the rain was slashing down driven by a chilling northern wind that ripped through the streets soaking them to the bone. The historic hydraulic cage elevator, installed when the building was erected in 1802, used to raise the burlap-wrapped bales of Georgia Sea Island cotton as they arrived from the docks on horse-drawn wagons to the fourth floor, where it was carded and combed before it was sent through a chute to the spinning frames on the third floor, was temporarily out of order, according to the frayed sign tacked to the overhead cage. "Shit," Susan grumbled under her breath, racing up the stairs two at a time, Jaime at her heels.

Unlike the apartment doors in high-crime districts, Jaime had known growing up that had locks running down the jamb side of the door like studs on bikers' leather pants, Susan's door opened with a single digital lock with a key override that she disabled remotely. He had barely time for a hasty look down the long, softly lit room before Susan dragged him into a shining marble bathroom, tossed him an oversized terry towel and ordered him to strip, toss out his clothes and shower, in the voice of someone used to issuing commands in somewhat more extreme situations.

Jaime stripped off his sodden clothes, 'as commanded,' noting the seemingly simple touches she had added to poke fun at 'The Bold Look of

Kohler,' four-by-six inch black silhouette cutouts, bathers, strollers and bicyclers of the ragtime era.

"Pass me your clothes," she commanded. "I'll put them through the dryer and have them for you after you shower."

Jaime grinned, caught himself in the mirror looking like a hairy baboon.

When he stepped out of the bathroom, showered, toweled off, and dressed in freshly dried and pressed clothes she had slid through a crack in the door, he found her sitting on a soft brown and tan couch in the long living room under a wide picture window in a peachy-colored, short-sleeved blouse and yellow shorts, her bare legs tucked under her, sipping a glass of wine, her damp tawny hair brushed and combed and tied into a ponytail that fell to her waist, her cheeks burnished and glowing. Through the window could be seen mushy lights from the masts of ships in the Navy Yard three blocks from the building. Under the low, multi-hued glass coffee table sitting in front of the couch, on which was a waiting goblet of red wine, lurked a crouching tiger, bright orange with black and white spots, with sly, grinning hungry eyes.

Hand-axed oak ceiling beams that once supported the heavy cast iron spinning frames on the floor above ran the width of the room. On the wall to one side of the window hung a hand-loomed purple, red, and yellow table runner that might have sat under a tin milk pitcher on a long wooden Amish breakfast table. On the other side hung a framed sepia Daguerreotype of this building as it was in the eighteen hundreds, bales of cotton being unloaded from a horse-drawn wagon; the horse munching on a tuft of grass growing on the side of the dirt road, small boys in suspenders and tweed caps playing catch, dogs nipping at their feet.

Jaime smiled, the strain of the last few days beginning to catch up with him, the continual need to be 'on,' to be 'bright,' to 'fit in,' the apprehension he felt coming here, the urge to show he was not his father, and now, in addition, the sexual tension, the intimate setting, the inappropriate feelings he begun to have for Susan. In that instant, his thoughts went to the quiet peace he remembered with Chenny when there was no need to be anyone but himself. A wave of exhaustion swept over him. He longed to stop acting, playing a role, to let himself fall limp, feel the weariness ooze from him. She seemed spent as well, exhausted. He hesitated, didn't know whether he should sit or stand, searched her eyes, her body language for help, finding none, edged tentatively onto the far end of the couch, leaving as much space as possible between them.

The rain slashed down. There was a low, constant drumming on the window, a smell of freshly brewed coffee. She looked up at him briefly with a hesitant smile, looked back on the glass of wine she was holding as if this was conversation enough. He felt grateful there seemed no need to talk, to make conversation.

He thought he remembered the rain still drumming on the window when he stirred, stiff, feeling wedged in. He lifted his eyelids carefully, found Susan sleeping next to him, her head on his shoulder, let his lids close again and fell back to sleep.

When he next awoke, Susan was curled against his chest breathing softly, smelling slightly of toothpaste. He became aware his hand was holding her small bottom, of the tiny silky blonde hair on her long bare legs, of her slightly parted lips. He had no idea how late it was, but only of a feeling of peace, the first since he left Nebraska.

He longed to draw her tighter against him, brush her hair with his lips, but when he stirred she started to come awake, saw where she was and pulled away, unwilling to catch his eyes.

He didn't know what to say; nor did she. His hand lingered lightly on her shoulder. She didn't seem to notice. They sat in silence wondering if something had happened between them. After a while, she began to speak, shyly at first. "This is the first time in…forever…that I felt…rested."

"Oh my God!" she blurted, her eyes lighting on the watch on her wrist, "It's seven twenty. You must be hungry and stiff. Why didn't you wake me?"

Jaime reached, brushed the hair from her eyes, let his hand linger on her face. "I have…a step-sister."

Susan's eyes fell, embarrassed, unwilling to find the meaning behind his words. "We can still make dinner with my friends," she offered instead, "if you'd like."

Jaime rubbed sleep wrinkles from his forehead. "Would it be embarrassing if you were expected and didn't show up?"

Susan took a breath, considered this. "I can dress in a sec," she promised. "We can grab a cab to your hotel for you to change…I mean," she added uncertainly, "if you're really willing."

As she raised herself from the couch, her eyes went to the book on her coffee table. She stopped midway, seemed to shrink. Her eyes began to tear up. "Jonathan gave me that," she said miserably, referring to the book: *Illnesses You May Not Have Considered You Could Have: A Hypochondriac's Guide.* "He was always…"

Jaime felt the air go out of him. He longed to draw her into his arms, comfort her, but knew it was the wrong thing to do. He reached for her hand, and when she didn't pull it away, laced his fingers with hers. She began to sob softly. He sat, holding her hand, not knowing what else to do.

"I'm sorry," she said at last, wiping her eyes with the back of her free hand. "You must be going through enough without this."

Jaime reached his hand under her chin and lifted her head. "That's what a 'stepbrother' – once removed – or is it twice removed," he grinned, "is for."

Susan tried to smile through the mist of tears. "I hold the world record for quick change," she said, racing off.

He saw it now, the instant changes in emotions he had seen all day, how really fragile she must be. For the first time, for as long as he could remember, as difficult as he knew it was going be, he had to restrain what was tugging at him.

Chapter 26

The mood at the table was bright, expansive, the chatter an invisible force field hovering over the group at the table, an evening dedicated to fun and laughter, a tableau from a scene from the roaring twenties a century earlier when the fun, the partying, the good times, were expected to go on and last forever.

As they approached the table, there was an awkward change in the rhythm of the conversation as the group gathered around Susan offering welcome, but after introductions, it picked up again in small pockets that quickly spread to the group.

Susan was the center of conversation; Jaime saw the effort she was making to be part of it, not dampen the merriment, but if the others noticed it, it was as if they agreed not to see it. But for all of her efforts to make him feel comfortable, he felt an outsider, as if he was observing the group from a distance.

There were ten at the table, five couples, or so he assumed. As he attempted to follow the conversation and sort out who was with whom, he was aware of Susan next to him, and how her hand came to rest on his arm reassuringly from time to time.

Shawna and Jaylin, he quickly grasped, were a couple. She was the manager of Jangles, a local restaurant in which she and Jaylin, the chef, were part owners. They had met in high school, and except for years when they both went away to college, had been together ever since. "My mother warned me I could do better," she sighed with an air of helplessness, "but I felt so sorry for him, 'cause no one else would have him."

"She followed me like a sister of mercy," Jaylin agreed.

Shawna shook her head. "Hopeless."

They were the same height. She had perfect blue-black skin, large perky breasts, an inner glow and the body of a runner, one of the things they did together as a family with their two children, Marcus eight and Destiny six. He had been quarterback on their high school football team, his wiry frame dwarfed in shoulder pads and helmet, she, head cheerleader, might have stepped out of an old movie from the 1930s in a pleated red skirt that pinched her tiny waist and covered little else, and a cable-knit white sweater that needed no padding. Jaylin had gone on to the Culinary Institute in Hyde Park, FDR's summer home, after college, Susan filled in. They were leaving in the morning, a couple of days before the 4th, for two weeks on the Jersey shore with their kids, their boogie boards, their bikes, their barbecue. "…with North American Van Lines," Jaylin added, "hauling enough stuff to sink the destroyer my father served on. He was with Special Forces in the Middle East on a Kill-for-Peace mission."

Chrissie, a perky, freckled brunette, five-foot-ten physical therapist at the V.A. in Philadelphia, glowed, poking Stefan and waving a brimful carafe of pinot noir. "Stefan and I are stopping in D.C. to visit his brother, a minor muckamuck at the Greek Embassy, and then we're off to Athens." Both divorced, they met, began dating a year ago, split up, got back together just a month ago – the impression Jaime got was that it was a summer cost-sharing hook-up that might or might not remain hooked up.

Stefan, it turned out, was a partner in a small law firm that specialized in bump-and-dent accident cases which they usually settled without trial. He looked long suffering, his curly dark hair falling over his coal-black eye. Susan whispered that he should be able to suck ouzo up from the cleft in his chin through his nose. Jaime bent down behind her to pick up the napkin he dropped. "A nice person wouldn't say something like that," he whispered into her hair. Susan lifted her napkin to her lips to hide a mischievous grin.

The exchange didn't miss Chrissie who turned from Stefan to Susan with a look. Susan shrugged her shoulders in an innocent '*What?*'

"He's free." Chrissie picked up after a moment. She was, Jaime divined, referring to his nine-year-old son Nicky who normally spent weekends with him. Nicky lived with his mother, a paralegal in New York City, but was spending the first month of the summer at a boy-scout camp in the Adirondacks. "We're stopping for a couple of days in D.C., then we're off to Athens where I'm dancing the bouzouki – is that the dance or the instrument they play, I can never remember. I bought a sheer yellow dress with a ragged hem made from about three inches of fabric priced at $1,000 an inch. If that doesn't put a smile on Stefan's face, or some other part of him…" she pushed up from her seat, tousled his hair and began performing her version of the Zorba-the-Greek dance, accompanying it with come-hither hands – "and then we're taking a boat to Santorini where we are going to ride the donkeys to the top, lay out on the white sand beaches during the day, eat grilled octopus in olive oil fresh from the sea, drink ouzo, and when the sun goes down, and if the yellow dress doesn't work, I'm gonna find a curly dark-haired sixteen-year-old Adonis with laughing black eyes who'd rather do something with his nights than haul up fishing nets."

"She's incorrigible," Susan whispered.

Jaime shook his head in mock despair. "You were in high school together?" he replied, proving a failure as a ventriloquist. "And who's that," he mouthed, tilting his head in the direction of a thirty-ish auburn-haired woman at the end of the table with Cupid's lips who had a possessive hand on the arm of the man sitting next to her. "Nancy," Susan mouthed, "the fellow's Bob Ellis." There was something obvious but indefinable in the little ways they were with each other that seemed to say they were more than friends. "They're engaged," Susan whispered.

Bob had a ready, amiable smile, broad cheeks, and looked buttoned-down, happy to leave the conversation to Nancy. She was an assistant director of the Walnut Street Theater, a company that produced Broadway-run shows and, occasionally, originals. She had grown up in Brookline and following graduation from Emerson with an MFA degree, interned with WBZ Boston before coming to Philadelphia. "Her first assignment," Susan whispered, "was to do research for an original play the director was staging, 'The Alchemist,' an accountant, who turned wood scraps and lumber mill leavings into dollars with magic accounting. She went to Bob, who was then a junior accountant, to find out if it really could be done. It was obvious he didn't know she wasn't serious, and when he asked for a date, she chilled him. Fast-forward seven years. They meet again at a party. She's in a relationship, Bob is up for partnership and engaged to the Head Partner's daughter."

Jaime raised his eyebrows. "And…?"

"Let's just say, he's an accountant. He *figured* it out."

Jaime hadn't known what to expect when he met her friends, unusual people, he assumed, formidable, special, accomplished, but as he studied them, he saw they were ordinary, not ordinary in that sense, but ordinary in that they were no different from people he knew. Still he remained quiet, grateful that they had held off questions.

That now seemed to have given way to curiosity about a life that was foreign to them. He had told Susan enough that he was sure she could infer the rest, but to air it here, he feared, would reflect not on him but on her, that she would elect to bring him with her.

He found it curious that they would think living near an Indian reservation was adventurous, and cautiously began feeling comfortable enough to tell them what it was like living there, but it soon came to him that they could sense what he was not saying, and shut down.

"It took courage," Susan jumped in, as if daring the others to challenge her, "not to let yourself be defeated."

Jaime felt something inside him give. He had come to prop Susan up, give her support, and here she was propping him up, supporting him.

Earlier, when they had approached the table, the noise level, the easy laughter, made it clear that these were good friends with no need to impress each other. Once in a while there was talk of the country's political mess, or of daily problems, finding parking places in downtown Philadelphia, the scarcity of good, moderately priced restaurants that have been crowded out by cookie cutter franchises that offered good, but not great food, the relative merits of different health clubs and workout venues, but mostly the talk was about summer vacation plans.

He was aware of the brief looks her friends shot at each other when they thought Susan wasn't looking, judgmental looks, as if they were surprised she wasn't the grieving widow they expected. It was as if she was on trial and could do no right; if she appeared happy, she would be condemned for not being true to Jonathan, if she was not, she was judged unable to move on. Once during the evening, two of the women, whispered together shooting intermittent looks at Susan, as if appraising her. He saw that she saw it and reddened. "It was very brave of Susan," he blurted out, as if out of the blue, "to come tonight. It took more than a little persuasion to overcome her reluctance."

Susan sent a quick grateful look at him. He had no idea how he came up with those words. It wasn't like him. It was as if, without realizing how, the words moved through him by their choice at that exact moment.

The uneasiness he felt coming here, meeting her friends, turned 180° – he no longer sat longing for the evening to end, though he knew that like a stand-up entertainer whose repertoire was markedly limited, once drained, he had nothing more to offer. But Susan appeared to be impressed at how he fielded, or deflected their questions, though he wondered if it was simply that she was grateful that the attention had been shifted from her, that she no longer had to pretend to be thankful for their well-meaning but unwanted awkward assurances that with time she would heal and love again.

When they broke up at 10:30 and stepped outside the restaurant, as everyone else left, Jaime stood there awkwardly. The rain had ended, the night had turned clear, there was warm, dry wind coming from the south kicking up papers in the street and whirling them around. Susan pushed the hair out of her face. "It's been a long day," she observed shyly. He heard the indecision in her words and the way she avoided his eyes and shifted the tiniest bit from one foot to the other.

If she was any other girl, Jaime would have picked up on it and run with it. But she was not any other girl. An annoying inner voice nagged at him, reminding him of the promise he made that he now didn't want to keep. He stood, making no effort to leave, trying not to look as miserable as he felt.

Susan raised her eyes and looked up at him timidly. "We could watch television…for a short while…" she added uncertainly, "if you want to."

When they returned to her apartment, Jaime determined to do nothing more than watch a movie and leave. Self-consciously, he followed Susan into her bedroom, and as she cleared the stuffed animals from her king-sized bed, kicked off her shoes, propped herself up on one of the pillows and plumped one next to her for him, he lowered himself onto the very edge of the bottom of the bed, his back to her, facing the large screen wall TV, determined to remain focused on the screen, keep his thoughts from straying to the long legs partly hidden beneath the silky black sheath, and leave all the space between them the arrangement allowed.

In minutes, the tension, the thoughts that stubbornly refused to do as he ordered, the mesmerizing flickering light of the television wormed into his pores, melting his bones, weighting his eyelids, testing his determination to remain awake. The last thing he remembered was the flickering light on the screen. When he opened his eyes again, the bedside clock read 1:30. The TV was still flickering – Susan was lying beside him, eyes open, watching him slowly come awake.

Gently, she leaned over, kissed him softly on the lips, clicked off the TV, wiggled into him, and immediately fell back to sleep. In the morning, when he woke, he found the covers over them. Sometime during the night, they had removed most of their clothes. He tried but didn't remember any of it, or if anything had happened. He lay quietly, listening to her breathing, holding himself still so as not to wake her, tracing the curve of her lashes, the swell of her breasts, and the gracefulness of her long slim neck.

When she awoke some time later and saw him studying her, she lowered her eyes shyly. *If he could lie there forever watching her,* he thought, *he'd want nothing more.*

Chapter 27

Even before they reached her mother's house, something Susan said – perhaps not said – made him fear the visit would be uncomfortable. He sensed she had issues with her mother – but then, didn't everyone? But it was more than that. She wasn't any other girl. It was idiotic, he knew, to feel the way he did – they had spent so little time together – but he felt it important that this visit went well.

They were expected at 9:30 but found things that had to be done before they left: the mirror in the bathroom had to be cleaned of steam, the bed had to be made – and remade, the clothes Susan had planned to wear were too casual, or too formal, it became important to stop at hotel desk in case there had been messages, Jaime's wardrobe offered few choices, but even those took more than a little consideration, and all the while, there seemed an agonizingly acute awareness of each other and the fear that a casual touch would undo the restraint that had been so difficult.

They played with the idea of calling to say they couldn't come, something came up, a medical emergency, a call from the detective who had summoned him, but none seemed realistic. When they could delay no longer, they set out, the morning sun behind them, Susan seeming to notice things for the first time along the familiar road, the traffic, the flowers, the shops, the side streets she had never explored.

Jaime knew from what he read in his father's diary that when his father left Bryn Mawr, there had been a tide of ill feelings. The invitation to brunch, he assumed, was more from curiosity than any desire to meet him. And then he was his father's son, not much of a recommendation. The fears he had when he was trying to decide whether to meet the families his father chose over his own came roaring back with a rush. And wouldn't Susan's mother be anxious for Susan, that she could be preyed upon, as she was, particularly at a time when she was as vulnerable as she had once been. Were Susan to deny it, would have the exact opposite effect.

From what was written in the diary, he had formed a picture of Susan's grandmother, formidable, stiff-spined, correct, proper, a woman for whom breeding was the be-all and end-all, overshadowing all else, as long as all else wasn't evident. Susan's mother rebelled in tiny, little ways, finding kooky things to become involved in that were not outrageous, but not quite 'correct.' When her mother died, the reason to rebel was no more, and he had the impression from remarks Susan made that her mother had slowly become what her grandmother had wanted her to become, a 'correct' lady. It was there in the many books he read, *The Nest; Letter to My Daughter; Redeeming Love; The Daughter's Walk; Mother Daughter Me; Walking on Eggshells*: mother-daughter relationships were more subtle and complex than any writer, and certainly he, could ever fully understand.

"I don't want him here," Marsha insisted. "I don't care what I said, or what kind of guilt payment the man left for Susan, he was a sleaze, and you can bet the son didn't fall far from the tree. I wouldn't be surprised if he had designs on Susan the same way his father had on me."

Hermann watched her in the mirror slipping her dress over her head. "You're all tensed up, Marsha. C'mon over her, and let me un-tense you."

"Herman! For God's sake. They'll be here in no time. Put some clothes on, stop acting like it doesn't exist, and help me get through this."

"If you didn't want him here, why did you tell Susan to bring him? You know how vulnerable she is now, saying Yizkur for Jonathan only two nights ago."

"I know. But I also know Susan, how she digs in her heels when I try to tell her what to do for her own good."

"You mean like you did when your husband died."

"Hermann! It wasn't like that at all. I have to do it in a way that she sees him for what he is. C'mon. You want me to tie your tie?"

"How about something a little lower."

"Christ, Hermann, quit it now. I'm serious."

The scent of tea roses and impatiens enveloped them as soon as they opened the doors and stepped out of the car. Susan's mother was at the door, a smile of welcome on her lips, the crunching of the oyster shells beneath the wheels of the flower-bordered, circular driveway announcing their arrival. The welcome was so warm, so generous, so 180° out of sync with what Susan had intimated that he wondered if a mother-daughter love-hate relationship was at work here.

He had come prepared to act as if the starched proprieties of a former era added a luster missing from his daily life, to ignore the 'look' he had been warned of that might suggest he had been shown to the wrong door, but the greeting was so gracious, he was annoyed that once again he had done something he vowed he wouldn't do, made a pre-judgment.

If her mother had had cosmetic surgery, it had been performed by an expert surgeon; her skin was flawless. If she was wearing makeup, it was so sheer and had been applied so artfully that it was unnoticeable. She appeared to be at least ten years younger than the age he knew her to be. She wore her hair, which had the luster of a L'Oreal model, in a modest sweep over her right forehead, she came to the door in a printed silk, high-necked afternoon dress the color of sweet cream strewn with scatterings of tiny fall brown and amber leaves, sheer stockings, and cream pumps.

Was he expected to dress for brunch? Susan hadn't. Her mother's husband, Hermann, came to the door behind her in a dappled brown Irish tweed jacket, white shirt, golden brown tie, knife-edged brown slacks and polished oxfords. Susan 'accepted' his light kiss on her cheek, Jaime's hand was gripped so heartily, he assumed it was to convey a suggestion of 'we men.'

"I expect you must be hungry," her mother offered with a barely noticeable meaningful glance at her diamond-encrusted wristwatch. "Everything's ready."

Jaime stifled an all but overwhelming urge to respond, 'Hungry? No, not really. Susan and I had breakfast in bed this morning,' but was unable to keep a grin from escaping.

Susan sent a silent, 'What?'

Jaime lifted his shoulders a tiny fraction feigning innocence.

French doors in the richly appointed living room led out to a rock-edged path through the manicured lawn to a white-roofed gazebo with intricately carved beaded corbels on each side of the six uprights supporting the cedar-shingled roof. "Will everyone have mimosas?" Susan's mother offered, reaching for a frost-covered carafe and motioning for everyone to join her at the table set with Waterford, Limoge and Reed and Barton, a spread from *House and Garden*.

Once the tumblers were filled, her mother solemnly raised her glass. "I was so sad to learn of your father's passing," she offered. "There is something I want you to know. I had no idea that your father was married, or that he had a child. If I had…I never would…I never would have…"

In that instant, all sounds seemed to be swallowed up. The birds circling the gazebo stopped chattering, the wind died, the grass stopped growing. Hermann reached for his wife's hand, Susan sat stiff, Jaime deflated. Her mother was stiffly erect, yet just then she didn't seem like a marble statue at all.

All of a sudden, Jaime felt out of his element, out of his comfort zone. He couldn't immediately put his finger on what it was. He didn't have the feeling that he was with his kind of people, '*heimische*' people, folks with whom he there was no need to pretend, with whom he could be who he was, folks with whom he could be comfortable, where there wasn't the feeling that he was on trial, folks to whom he could tell bawdy jokes, with whom he didn't have to watch his every word.

Even the words he had been speaking sounded stilted to him. "It is I," he said when he found his voice, "who should…apologize." All of them, her mother, Hermann, even Susan looked at him strangely. He shook his head. "I know you didn't know. My father left a diary. Until two weeks ago, when I received a phone call in Nebraska to come to New Jersey to identify him, I didn't even know he still existed. The last time I saw him was when I was six years old. I knew nothing of my father's life since then, but I did know you didn't know he was married, or of me, because he left a diary. I brought a copy for you – if you would like to have it – but if you would forgive me, I would like not to talk about him today."

Susan's mother seemed to have stopped breathing while he was speaking, as if she was having difficulty showing emotions that intruded on the demeanor she was intent on maintaining, unlike Susan who appeared to have unveiled a well of sorrow she had stored behind her eyes. Hermann shot a quick look at his wife, sent an almost imperceptible message, rubbed his chin as if to rid it of unwanted thoughts.

It was Susan's mother who broke the silence. "Is it the Chinese who said that happiness and unhappiness are two sides of the same coin. Susan had said as much when she called."

"Lao-Tse, I think it was," Jaime suggested.

"Please," Susan's mother offered to suggest nothing more needed to be added, and it was time to get on to something else, "help yourself to whatever you wish from the sideboard, or if there is anything else you would prefer, don't please ask."

On the sideboard was cold, poached glazed salmon with wedges of lemon and dill mayonnaise dressing, sliced, pressed cucumbers, German potato salad, generous slices of whole-grain seeded rye bread, and chilled, fermented Amish apple cider.

When their plates and goblets had been filled and they were back at the table, Hermann wiped a sliver of poached salmon from his lips and turned to Jaime. "Susan tells us that you are a music lover. She said listening to the Wanamaker organ, you seemed transported. You embarrassed the life out of her."

Jaime sucked in a breath. He turned to look at Susan. Her eyes were wide, her mouth open as if she had been betrayed. Before she could object, Hermann apologized. "Please forgive me. Perhaps my command of English colloquialisms is poor." If he was teasing, there was nothing to show it save for a glimmer in the corners of his eyes.

Everyone began talking at once, throwaway things, small talk. Jaime thought he was off the hot seat until he caught the implication when, with no preparation, Susan's mother asked about Red Plains, and how soon he was planning to return after he and Susan attended the Side-by-Side Concert tonight, Rachmaninoff's *Symphonic Dances*, Tchaikovsky's *Capriccio Italien*, Aaron Copland's *Fanfare for the Common Man*.

He shrugged it off, but Hermann persisted. "You don't have that kind of thing Red Plains, do you, free concerts?"

"Free!!!" he tossed back. "Susan! You told me the tickets were $125?"

"Yes. Free to us. But not Nebraskans."

"You are a professor of literature at Red Plains College in Nebraska, where Willa Cather, the writer, came from, I understand," her mother persisted. "I expect you're anxious to get back to prepare for the fall term. It must be different living and teaching there?"

"It is lovely in its own way, but in another way, it lacks what you have here. It's small, only 2,500 in the College, it's seventy miles from the nearest major city, Lincoln, which is not all that major, so it's fairly isolated. But the people are real, self-reliant, friendly, they go out of their way for you, and like people everywhere, I guess, mostly decent, a few not. Television and the internet have brought the world closer, it's not crowded, but at night you can see that there are still really stars up in the sky."

"Is that why you chose it?"

Jaime paused to consider this, how to answer. How his father had misrepresented himself was a burr under his skin. He had the sense that Susan's mother was not as warmly welcoming as he had first thought, that she believed that, like his father, he was an amiable humbug who was able to confuse fact and fiction when it suited him. He had been judged. He would live up to what he was expected to be, confirm her expectations.

"I think," he owned, with no hint of satisfaction, "that I've given you a false picture of me. The people in Red Plains are real, and there is a peaceful quality to life there, but I would not be there if I hadn't failed. I failed at my job I believed because I believed it was to '*teach*'– to force feed students. It was *me against them*…not *me with them*…or still better, *them with me*. I know that sounds puzzled, but I believed the process began with *me; I* see now it must begin with *them*."

Hermann looked at him curiously. *"Begin with them?"*

"What I see, or believe I see, is that I have to begin by exploring what excites them, what turns them on, what interests them, what they relate to, and when we become engaged in that conversation, gradually broaden it, lead them into new ideas, works of literature, expose them to opportunities they hadn't considered, open their eyes to realize that literature has something to offer them. But that is not the greatest mistake I made: I have allowed myself to believe that the failures I've had were not mine, but the failures of others to realize my worth."

"Wow!" Hermann exclaimed. "You make failure sound like an advantage I wish I could have had."

Susan's mother threw a look at him.

"You won't miss Red Plains?" Susan asked, with a mischievous grin, "switching to the University of San Francisco instead of going back at the end of the summer."

"I will." Jaime squashed the irritation. The serious expression on his face faded. In its place was a broad smile. "Of course, Red Plains does not have your 'free' Philharmonic, but on alternate Saturday nights I whistled and on the others Carrie Hepplewood played the musical comb. And we *never* charge unsuspecting Philadelphians $125 a ticket for the concerts."

Chapter 28

"Why so glum?"

They had left Bryn Mawr, the affluent homes, pampered lawns, sculptured gardens and manicured boutiques along Lancaster Avenue had given way to graying wood-framed, clapboard houses and storefront shops, faded coats of paint with occasional splashes of what once might have been yellow or blue.

"I feel like a prize idiot." Jaime responded spiritlessly, keeping his eyes glued straight ahead.

"Believe me," Susan insisted, "that's not so...*entirely*."

"Thanks."

"No, no. What I meant was there was no need for that word."

Jaime's brow scrunched up. "That word?"

"Prize."

Jaime turned his head to examine Susan. She was taking tiny bites on her lower lip, her eyes sparkling mischievously. Freckles appeared on the bridge of her nose in the slanting light reflected off the hood of the car. "Did you mention that you were a former cheerleader?"

"See. You're better already."

How could such a small person, he wondered, so petite, so young, a woman so bright, so in command of herself, able to make decisions that could mean the difference between an infant or a child enjoying a normal, healthy, fulfilling life, or a stunted life with a disability, if it survived at all, one who had the grit to face its parents to explain what the choices were, want to become involved with a loser.

They had entered Bala Cynwyd, a town settled by immigrants with names like Alwyn, and Maachathi, and Uaid, who came from Wales in the 1680s to form two towns, Bala and Cynwyd, now thought of as one, Bala Cynwyd, in the way Buda and Pest came to be known as Budapest. Like towns in New England, settlers came to work in the factories that sprang up along the rivers to power looms and spindles and other machinery, and moved on, with the mills, when low-cost, efficient electric motors no longer made it necessary to rely on not always dependable rivers to power equipment.

He wondered if he was going down the same endless, frustrating road again, ready to believe he had found her, the one, the one he saw in his head when he went to bed at night, the *Blue-Eyed Devil* Lisa Kleypas wrote of...

I no longer believed in the idea of soul mates, or love at first sight. But I was beginning to believe that a very few times in your life, if you were lucky, you might meet someone who was exactly right for you. Not because he was perfect, or because you were, but because your combined flaws were arranged in a way that allowed two separate beings to hinge together.

...but the reality was that when fireworks light up the night sky, in the morning, when he next opened his eyes, he saw they also left the ground covered with ashes.

"Do you really think you can get students on board in the way you said?" Susan asked, darting a look at Jaime.

"I'm going to try. What I have been doing hasn't worked. One or two, or a few at times, respond, but it's a downer to see the sea of glazed eyes staring back at me. I'm not sure I blame them. They can't see the relevance of 18th and 19th and even 20th century literature to their own lives. Whatever interest in poetry they have begins and ends with hip-hop."

"Isn't a failure someone who has given up? It didn't sound as if you've given up. Edison tried a thousand experiments before he got the light bulb to work."

They had entered Wissahickon Valley Park and would soon be at his hotel. Jaime swallowed up Susan with his eyes. "What do you wish for?"

"What do I wish for? When I was a kid, my friends and I would talk about what we wished for when we grew up. Some of them were from broken homes, some one-parent homes, one shuttled between two homes and had a brother and two stepsisters. My mother seemed unable to come to peace with herself; she needed someone after my father died. She loves me. I've heard it say that a mother will sacrifice her life for her child. Who knows? Maybe there are some, but I saw her pushing your father away and it wasn't for me. I lost the first man in my life, then she pushed away the second. And now the third. It's funny what sex does to us. I decided I was never going to marry or live with a man when I was growing up, that I'd be completely into myself. But then I met Jonathan. I have friends that say they only need a man for sex. Jonathan and I were more than sex. Did you notice at dinner last night what the couples had in common? Each was a combination of a left-brained person and a right-brained person. Was that a coincidence, or was it that 'opposites attract.' Does a doctor have to be left-brained? I don't think I am."

"You know," Jaime confessed, "I think I'm in the wrong body. I don't mean that I'd want to have a sex-change operation. That's not it. I'm really a left-brained person in a right-brained profession. Maybe what I need is not a sex-change operation but a job-changed operation. But I like what I do. I guess what I really wish…" Susan looked up from the road and found him staring at her…

"What? What do you wish?"

"I wish… I had a sister,"

"A sister! You had wanted to sleep with your sister?"

Jaime blushed.

Seconds later, the blush registered. Her cheeks turned red. "Me too."

Susan's eyes remained fixed on the road straight ahead as they neared the Warwick Hotel. "I guess you'll want to…to get on your way…I mean, after the concert tonight."

Jaime sat, reluctant to move, to get out of the car. "I'm…I mean… I'm not on a time table."

Susan looked at him shyly. "You could stay on a while?"

One day, he thought, when he wrote the book he had always planned to write, he would write about how difficult it was for people to say what they really wanted to say for fear that it was not what the other wanted to hear.

"Don't you have to work?"

"I have vacation time coming. I could take off a few days. I guess, I mean I always wanted to visit the Amish country, the fireworks display over river on the 4th is spectacular, I read, and…"

It was all Jaime could do to keep from leaping from the cab before it came to a stop when Symphony Hall came into sight, a venue that drew musicians from all over the world to immerse themselves in the Hall's acoustics. Even with the time, effort and money devoted to discover the exact combination of materials, structure, placement of musicians and instruments, achieving the 'sound' such as heard here remained as much an art as a science.

"I feel like I've died and gone to heaven," Jaime exulted, feeing in danger of losing the struggle to appear sophisticated, someone for whom attending symphonies in world-class halls was an everyday event. Throwing back his shoulders, he lifted his chin, strained to his full 6'3", and stepped onto the walk in front of the concert hall.

Susan eyed him with amusement. "All you need is a set of shades to look like Charles Schulz's Joe Cool," she observed, "and maybe a shorter nose."

"No, no," she rushed to add when Jaime's mouth opened to object, "it's refreshing to see someone who can enjoy a high without the need for drugs or alcohol."

"I *was* on a high without the music…" Jaime grinned, shooting a look at Susan, "…until a moment ago."

From what he had seen of the Hall as they drew up, it looked like a three-layer mocha birthday cake, but in place of candles on top, there was a tree-lined atrium enclosed by a towering sparkling glass arch ∩ that ran from the front to the rear forming a tunnel into the beyond.

Until they approached the building, Jaime had been having the damndest time to keep from touching Susan, determined to savor it all until later, continually put to the test by Susan who hadn't been on board with the plan.

"If music means that much to you," she charged as they pushed into the crowds on the sidewalk, "why didn't you make it your career?"

Jaime shook his head, screwing up his cheeks. "I would have loved to if I had the talent. I often wonder what it would be like. How many people do you know work at what they would love to do instead of at what they can make a living at? Do you?"

Susan halted before entering the Hall, moved aside to let others through, considering the question. "I'm not sure how to answer that. At times I get a good deal of satisfaction from what I do, but even though it's – she put up two fingers in each hand – 'medicine' – much of it is routine. I'm not sure I could stand living on a continual high. It would tear me up. There was a morning last year in which a mother brought her son in to see me, a little boy, Dennis, a child two and a half years old. She, the mother, seemed to be having difficulty explaining why she brought him in. All she was able to say was, *He's not right*.

"Parents are often overly concerned with a slight change in their child's behavior. The child looked healthy, none of the tests I ordered came back positive. Normally I would have released the little child and sent him home, but something… I don't know what had me… 'concerned'…is the best way I can put it. It's hospital policy to release a bed, but I went against it and insisted on keeping the child overnight. Thank God. That night the little boy went into convulsions. There was a blockage none of the tests showed. If we hadn't been able to act immediately, he might have died."

Jaime felt something inside him go. It was a moment before he felt able to respond. "The highs I get from music," he confessed when he felt settled enough, "seem so trivial when I hear something like that. A few times in class…" he began, but he tore his eyes from Susan and his words trailed off.

"What?"

Jaime shrugged his shoulders.

Crowds going by milled about, chatting animatedly, greeting friends, most dressed casually, slacks and knit shirts, dresses and sandals, here and there a few that that looked as if they shopped in the Salvation Army discard bin. One couple in their eighties drew looks as they walked in. They came dressed from the silent movie era to attend a premiere at Gruaman's Chinese Theater, he in a tux, starched shirt, top hat, bow tie and patent leather shoes, she in an ankle-length black dress, white bolero rabbit skins jacket, a two-inch headband with a loopy feather, and a rope of pearls long enough to lasso Roy Roger's horse.

"What?!" Susan persisted.

Jaime shook his head, turned away.

"Jaime, if I promise not to go online and tell everyone of your innermost secret, will you whisper it to me?"

Jaime tried to keep from breaking up, but he couldn't hold it in. Concertgoers passing them looked to see why he was laughing so.

"Well?" she persisted, ignoring the stares.

Jaime shook his head. He felt as if he was floating and drowning all at the same time. "Once in a great while," he answered, bending to put his mouth close to Susan's ear, "when a student grasps the sense of what lies behind a poet's or author's words, I get a feeling like that." He thought of Martin Littleton who struggled so at first with Frost's, '*A Road Not Taken.*' "But compared to what you do…it seems so…inconsequential. If I'm lucky, I get through to one in a class of twenty. What you do helps them all."

Susan shook her head in exasperation. She walked on, leaving Jaime hurrying to catch up, handed their tickets to the attendant, and headed under the loges into the 2,500-seat theater. Three layers from outside became three tiers of loges and box seats inside on both sides of the auditorium, forming a ring around the two-thousand orchestra seats.

"Jaime," she protested when the usher showed them to their seats, "why do you make what you have done sound inconsequential? Why are you so hard on yourself, not give yourself credit? If you've made one person's life better, don't you see you added something special to someone's life?"

Jaime sat back in his seat and stared unseeingly at the program the usher had handed him, unable to respond, struggling to make sense of this. Did Susan really believe that, that he made a difference? Was she just being kind, or was it more than that? Each time he decided, absolutely certainly, that anything more than a casual friendship made no sense, she made him think he might be wrong.

Why was he tearing himself about it, he wondered, rather than just enjoying it? It had been a perfect day, he was with a delightful woman who seemed to want to be with him, who made him feel good about himself, they were about to listen to world-class musicians in a world-class hall playing his favorite music, he would be spending the next few days with her, making love, visiting places he'd always wanted to visit, the entire day had been foreplay, why was he overthinking it, not just letting it happen.

Even this, the concert, was foreplay. It was the first time he realized it. He had never thought of it that way, but now he saw it, what concert and opera goers must have long known, that the foreplay begins even as they enter an auditorium as rich and seductive as a siren's boudoir, that it then builds, layer upon layer, titillation upon titillation, as the musicians enter from the wings, file across to seats arranged to an arcane plan, discordant sounds of musical instruments are heard, all at once a hush falls, out of the wings appears the Concert Master, the first violinist who strides purposely to a reserved seat, raises his bow, nods to the oboist, the oboist sounds an A, the discordant notes begin to sound like they belong to an orchestra, a hush falls once more, applause swells as from the wings the conductor makes his entrance, the musicians stand, the conductor bows to the audience, bows to the musicians, raises his baton, then with the fall of the baton, the first notes of the orgasm the concertgoers had been primed for is heard.

Jaime reached for Susan's hand. As the concert began, she laced her fingers into his.

Chapter 29

The three days flew by. Jaime never remembered being as happy. It was the honeymoon he always planned, the one he dreamed of, the one he hoped he'd have one day. That evening, almost before the last note of the concert faded, almost before the conductor and the musicians acknowledged the thunderous applause, even before they were across the threshold, Susan was on him, entwined like a boa constrictor, legs locked in a death grip around his middle, the key dangling in the door, her toes digging into his bottom, spurring him, her hands pulling at him, her breath his, his breath hers, her tongue everywhere, sucking his tongue, his lips, fumbling with his buttons, his zipper, fingers everywhere, his hands searching under her skirt, lifting her, carrying her pressed to him into her bedroom, one more arrangement, then another and another, the bed sopping, beneath her, beneath him, still another arrangement of limbs and then another and another, trying to get it right, just right.

She pulled him to her, he pulled back searching, one more place, one more crease, one more fold, to kiss, to taste, to feel, again and again she cried now, again and again, almost there, he pulled back, finding one more place to taste, to lick, to suck, to bury his tongue, please, please she moaned, but still he pulled away, wanting this to go on, be their forever, what they would always have, again and again, time and time again his tongue searched, returned to places that caused sparks, time and again she answered, with her tongue, with her fingers, places he never imagined, between his legs, behind his legs, again she cried, begged, pleaded, it was becoming harder to hold back, harder and harder, but still he held himself one more time, refusing, tantalizing, denying until there was no more, was no more holding back, and when he began to surrender, entering her slowly, she would not allow it and pull him into her with a strength he couldn't credit and at once the ripples began, growing stronger and stronger she spasmed, the air whooshing out of her, her nails digging painfully into his back, severing the skin, and when there seemed there could be no more, still she would not release him, and with her insides she set the rhythm again, and he felt himself becoming harder than he believed he could ever be, and he knew the need to go deeper and deeper to depths he'd never reached, and with every thrust she pulled him deeper, or maybe he found places she didn't know she owned, and all of a sudden he felt fingers inside her, as strong as those in a milkmaid's hand, gripping him, and he exploded, in pain and joy, and collapsed on her sweet breast drenched in their fluids.

Once, during the night, Jaime remembered, he awoke, still inside her, kissed her hair, slid out, and still in her arms, fell back to sleep, but when he awoke in morning to the smell of coffee and reached for her, in her place was a note, 'Gone for croissants. Be right back. S'

"Just like a woman," he griped, hiding a grin when she returned, bent over him, planted a kiss on his nose and artfully slid away before he could pull her back into bed, "discards him once she had her use of him!"

"Just like a man," she insisted, "overestimating his abilities," planting another kiss on his nose and heading into the kitchen. "Coffee and croissants and shower await, not in that order," she called over her shoulder. "While you were idling the day away unproductively, I was productive. I lucked out, I got us a last-minute cancellation at the French Manor B&B in the Poconos. You'll probably want me to drive so you can try to restore your energy in case you get lucky again, so I'll take an energy bar for you. No, better make that two."

Susan drove, Jaime lay back, lulled by the hum of the tires on the road, the soft whoosh of the air running over the windshield, watching the lush countryside go by, the meadows and hills and valleys and streams. It was that half-way state between awake and asleep, aware of everything, Susan beside him, the pattern of the trees in full leaf, the yellow center line of the road, the signs of honeymoon hotels and inns, the change in the rhythm of the hum of tires whenever the pavement changed from concrete to macadam and back to concrete, the smoothness of her cheeks, the hidden tendons in her arm when she turned the wheel, the delicate way her fingers held the wheel as if it was made of feathers, and even the absence of music beating from the radio, and how everything seemed so simple now, and more complicated than ever, how easy it was to imagine what a life could be like with this woman beside him, and yet how difficult it was to construct an image that didn't fall apart when he tried to see it as real. It was like so many things he looked for in his life, the prestige he would receive one day, the book he would write, the recognition that would be heaped on him as an educator, all the things that were real only in his imagination, and yet without them, his life seemed meaningless, without hope, and so he forced his mind back on Susan and told himself that this was reality, that she was here with him, that why was he not enjoying the moment, and it occurred to him that he had never been really seeing Chenny, really seeing and appreciating her, that fantasy and reality could actually be one and the same, that perception altered reality, and when he tried to sort it out, he found it all jumbled up, and he tried, once again, to turn his focus on the reality of what was now, and enjoy that he was here with Susan even if…

"Where were you?" Susan smiled. "You seemed to be…off somewhere."

He thought of what to answer, how to answer. Susan's long chestnut hair falling halfway down her back was the shimmering in the sunbeams slanting through the window. "I was counting the hairs on your head. You interrupted me. Now I have to start all over."

Susan's brow crinkled. "Weird."

"Weird? Ha. Did you ever think that everyone you ever met is a bit 'weird' in some ways – that abnormal is normal?"

Jaime watched the creases around Susan's mouth gather as she smiled, as she would if enjoying the efforts of a child to understand the world around him, and realized how pleasant it was to believe that people were uncomplicated, that they were as he chose to see them without looking too deep. Unconscious that he was saying the words aloud, words he remembered from long ago bubbled from his lips:

"How oft I've wander'd by the Clyde, When night obscured the landscape near. Far from my friends, far from my home, I wander on a distant shore."

"What is that?" Susan asked, taking her eyes from the road for an instant. For the first time since he met her – was it only a few days ago – she seemed at peace, her face relaxed, almost wistful.

He felt her presence alongside him physically, without looking at her, as if they were actually touching. The words that had spilled from his lips were a window into a piece of him he kept hidden that frightened him.

When he didn't reply, she seemed to sense it and wouldn't let it pass. "What was that?"

"*Mary,* by Daniel Weir, one of the 'Songs of Scotland.'"

"Is there more?"

Jaime nodded. He felt all jumbled up inside.

"How dear to think on former days,
And former scenes I've wander'd o'er
They well deserve a poet's praise,
In lofty rhyme they ought to soar.
"How oft I've wandered by the Clyde,
When night obscured the landscape near,
To hear its murm'ring waters glide,

And think upon my Mary dear.

"Far from my friends, far from my home,
I wander on a distant shore,
Far from those scenes I used to roam,
And scenes perhaps I tread no more."

When he finished, he sat looking straight ahead, afraid to let her see him.

"You really love what you do, don't you?" Susan asked, darting a look at him, sensing his embarrassment.

"Ummm," Jaime admitted, realizing that he really did. "I… I guess I would love it more if I could transmit it to students."

They drove along in silence. After a while, Jaime asked, "Is there anything inside you…I don't know…I mean do you ever have feelings…wanting to get out?"

They had left I-380 and were climbing the secondary roads through the rolling hills past kitschy hotels with heart-shaped signs advertising heart-shaped beds and hot tubs and honeymoon cottages.

"I guess I do," Susan admitted, straining to keep a smile from completely disappearing, "but…I buried them when…"

Jaime's stomach dropped. He'd known Susan only two days, didn't really know her, didn't know if what he sensed this morning since he woke was real, but he sensed something different as if she had been holding on, trying not to drown. He had been thinking of himself and it came to him that, insensitively, he had opened a window she had been trying not to look into, painful memories.

It was not something he did, thinking of someone else's feelings. He hadn't done it when he was with Chenny, concerning himself with what she might be feeling, even wondering if she had feelings, and now it hit him, how unfeeling he must have seemed to her, to someone who deserved more. It was all mixed up in his head. What were his feelings for Chenny? What were his feelings for Susan? He was not used to fathoming below the surface and was uncomfortable doing it now.

"More heart-shaped signs," he pointed out abruptly, brightly switching gears, "than in *I ♥ New York.*"

Susan bounced back with more elastic than he had, bubbling away again, about everything and nothing except anything personal, keeping her attention on the road ahead.

"Wow!" Jaime exclaimed, wide-eyed, when the French Manor drove into sight.

He hadn't expected anything that could live up to Susan's description. As stunning as Wanamaker Hall was with its great organ, so too was the Manor in its way. Commanding a 500-acre site, with twenty-mile panoramic views of the surrounding hills, and valleys, the maples and oaks that would draw thousands on leaf tours in the fall when the greens turned to reds and yellows to meet with the greens of the pines, the Manor was constructed of native fieldstone, with cone-shaped, ant-hill like roofs of imported Spanish slate, windows of leaded glass, and an arched Romanesque entranceway. It had been two years in building, using lumber and fieldstone from local quarries, the work of 165 German and Italian craftsmen and artisans imported from abroad during the Depression when dollars went a long way by a mining magnate awash in money.

They entered through rooms of native woods with vaulted ceilings, a Great Room where they would have dinner beside a massive stone wood burning fireplace presided over by an award winning chef famous for his cuisine, an in-house spa, tile-lined pool with exquisite views of the outside gardens, and found their way to their bedroom of pecky cypress and cedar, arched ceilings, four-poster canopied bed, and an ensuite marble bath with jet fixtures.

For the first time in his life, Jaime felt like giggling. He caught Susan's eyes. She seemed to be trying to match his excitement, but tears were clouding her eyes.

"Would you rather not stay," he asked, sensing what had been accompanying them. "We can go somewhere else."

She shook her head sagging. "I'll be all right in a moment. Could you just hold me a bit?"

Jaime took a step to her and drew her into his arms as if she was fragile and might break, and felt what she was feeling slowly drain from her.

A few minutes went by. Slowly she lifted her head, kissed his cheek, "I'm all right now," she said, her hazel eyes sparkling through the tears. "Want to go hiking?"

They returned hours later, their skins smarting from the afternoon sun, their muscles aching pleasantly from the rocky climbs and steep descents, from picking their way over rocks fording streams, rounding hundred-year-old trees, climbing boulders. Except for one young couple they met on the trail better dressed for hiking, they had the planet to themselves. They showered together, anointed each other with soothing balm Susan had brought, lay down alongside each other, hand in hand, on top of the bedspread with the ceiling fan cooling their naked bodies, and fell asleep.

When Jaime awoke, the room was in darkness, save for the light from lanterns among the trees outside creating shadows on the wall. The illuminated dial on the bedside clock read 7:42. He leaned over, kissed Susan's hair, waking her. She smiled shyly at him. "Should we go to dinner?"

Candles were burning on the table reserved for them next to the massive fieldstone fireplace, the woody smell of burning oak filling the room. They ordered a bottle of Pommard from a vintner in Rheims, started with a small, green salad sprinkled with extra-virgin Spanish olive oil and juice from a lemon, followed by quail seasoned with a light sprinkle of salt, dash of pepper, fennel, shallots and touch of garlic sautéed in a skillet at the table to a pale golden brown, accompanied by fingerling potatoes and a mélange of fresh vegetables in a balsamic wine reduction. Dessert was a soufflé with a dripping of Calvados.

The temperature dropped swiftly from the seventies into the fifties as the sun lit behind the western mountains, and the sky came alight with millions of stars. They donned sweaters and walked beneath the lanterns in the gardens, and then along a path bathed in moonlight under the 360° sky of summer stars listening to the serenade of amorous tree frogs, crickets at their nighttime work, and sounds from the underbrush of night-prowling animals. By eleven they were back in their room, washed, shyly now, wanting only the comfort, the peacefulness of each other's arms, but sometime during the night, when Susan stirred, they found it was not enough, but this time their breaths were soft, there was time to explore each other slowly, with their eyes, with feather touches, with tender kisses and soon they fell back to sleep wrapped in each other's arms, without orgasm, Jaime inside her, thinking this is how we will always fall asleep, this is the way it will always be.

Chapter 30

"Shit!"

"Oops. Pardon me."

"Damn!"

Susan wedged her eyes open and levered her head around to squint at Jaime. "Hi," she managed shyly, yawning. "What is it?" she asked snuggling against him. "Is your arm numb?"

"No," Jaime scowled. "Do you smell it?"

Her brow crinkled. "Smell what?"

Jaime's eyebrows went vertical. "Eggs, bacon, Danish, coffee...*breakfast.*"

Susan blinked uncomprehendingly. "So?"

"It's a...a damn plot, a conspiracy."

"A conspiracy?"

"I wasn't done here."

"So just like a man," she noted. "Stomach comes first. Come here, you."

"Hey," Susan erupted, eying the bedside digital clock. "If we don't hurry, we're gonna miss breakfast."

"Ha, the pot calling the kettle black. C'mon."

"Hey!" he added. "Didja read what it says here. They ask guests to save water. C'mon, let's save the planet, let's shower together."

Still damp, in not quite matching shorts and tees, Jaime's on the order of a 'day on the farm,' Susan's on the order of a 'day at the mall,' they set out to track down the source of the 'conspiracy' hand in hand. As they made their way along the hall and were about to enter the main room, Susan paused for a second. "You look downright knackered, as the Brits say, and before Jaime could protest, as he looked about in embarrassment, she sang –

'Auntie Mame and uncle Able, Fainted at the breakfast table,
Which should be sufficient warning, Not to do it in the morning.
But Ovaltine has set them right, Now they do it every night.'"

106

Seated around the table, also as fresh laid as the eggs, were three couples. "Hi," Susan bubbled, the universal ubiquitous greeting that could mean 'hello,' 'shit, not you,' or a dozen other things as they slid into cushioned wood-backed chairs along one side of the long oak table. Floating over the pungent odor of cold oak ashes in the hearth, remnants from of last night's dinner, were the welcoming smells of freshly squeezed orange juice, bits of pulp floating on top, warm blueberry muffins, dark roast coffee, giant strawberries with heavy cream, orange cranberry nut loaf, churned sweet butter from a neighboring dairy farm, a crock of orange marmalade, raspberry jam and quince preserves, and on the sideboard, scrambled eggs and a joint of cold country ham.

"Where are you from?" the distaff side of what looked like a pair of bikers asked, adding, "I'm Nancy and this is Ray." Nancy was an appealing looking blonde in a raggedy sort of way with football shoulders, a butterfly tattoo on one muscled arm, a Coptic Cross on the other. She was wearing gray denim cut-offs, a biker's belt with a buckle in the shape of the great seal of Massachusetts, and a sleeveless flower embroidered blouse with just enough décolleté to allow the edges of her sports bra to peek out. Ray had a broad, sun-burned forehead, a two-day buzz of facial hair, ears that would shield Nancy riding tandem from the wind, and tufts of elm brown shrubs that could nest blue jays sprouting from both ears.

Immediately the chatter began: Where from…you? Philadelphia? I have a cousin there. Do you know Marty Unterman? He's in insurance. We're on our way to…

Ingrid and Ziggy, from Munich Germany, took a while to thaw out, struggling with heavily accented English, he with lidded, gray eyes, square jaw, and pepper and salt hair, wearing a forest green Alpine jacket, tweed hiking trousers, and ankle-length boots, she was a rosy-cheeked, ample-breasted, blue-eyed kewpie doll with bangs in a short-sleeved, calf-length day dress.

"Munich!" Ray chimed in. "My uncle Lou was in Munich buying motorcycle castings years ago. It was the first time he was out of this country. The night he arrived, he was wandering around near his hotel and passed a shop that sold paintings and thought he might bring home an old master at a bargain price. He wrote down the number on the door, then went to the corner and wrote down the name of the street. The next day he was being shown around by the factory owner, Karl Peters, and the foreman Hans, and asked them if he knew anything about the shop. He had studied a bit of German before going and wanted to show it off. 'I have the address,' he said: *Ein-un-funfzig Einbahn Strasse,* reading what he had written down. Karl and Hans looked at him and erupted in laughter, not what he expected. Ingrid and Ziggy seemed to have trouble stifling giggles. 'You don't know what you wrote?' the factory owner asked when he and Hans were able to stop laughing. '*Fifty-one, One-Way Street.*'"

Bobby, a barracuda in her fifties with a wandering, assessing eye from the Virginia beltway around D.C., allowed a hint of a smile to mar an almost perfect example of cosmetic surgery. She had chin-length blonde hair, lizard green eyes; was wearing tan, knife-edge knee-length shorts; red striped shirt, and a modest gold chain. Her husband, Dan, an attorney, 5'11", trim, with close-cropped gray hair and rimless glasses, was in tailored navy shorts and a polo shirt, and a navy cable-knit sweater draped casually over his shoulders.

As he and Susan headed back to their room to close up their suitcases and prepare to leave, Jaime sensed Susan was becoming a different person. It was hard to exactly put his finger on it, but the not quite visible tinge of sadness that seemed to lay behind her smiles had gradually melted away and she had become relaxed, bubbly. The edge of sadness that had been there was mostly gone. Unlike the dinner they had with her friends, at breakfast it seemed that the chains that had her in irons had been cast off, that she was free to be herself; he could see a Susan emerging that was there all the time, like a chrysalis emerging from a cocoon. Less and less often did he see sudden shards of pain in her eyes, and with that, he had become freer too, more relaxed, and could almost allow himself to believe there could be a future for them.

"I could get used to this," he said as they headed for the desk to check out.

Susan beamed. "The French Manor?"

"That too."

Susan blushed, avoiding his eyes. "You were so funny at breakfast."

Jaime's brow creased. "Funny?"

"The way you sort of ducked, pulled away when Bobby put her hand on your arm."

"That woman is a piranha. I hate being pawed by someone like that. It bothers me when I see women, men too, touched like that, even on TV."

The change from day to day was all but extraordinary. On the drive to the Manor, they had driven in silence for some time, following the winding road, observing the signs boasting heart-shaped beds, in-room spas, massages, tennis, eighteen holes of golf, Broadway entertainment, lawn bowling, putting greens, and on one, stock quotes, when Jaime ventured beyond the safety of the impersonal. "How," he asked, "did you meet Jonathan?"

Susan seemed to consider how to answer. "My friend Maxine," she admitted after a while. "She had been after me, wouldn't let me alone, and wanted to set me up on a double date. I kept making excuses. I'd gone on enough of them. Besides, I was studying for my boards. I finally gave in. That night when I got home, she called: 'So?' "'I'm going to marry that man,' I said. "Jonathan was…he was caring, he was my best friend, he was funny, you know how two people can live identical lives and one is always upbeat and then other is always down, Jonathan was always positive, cheerful. He'd surprised me with little nonsense gifts, a single Hershey's kiss, a perfect stone he found, I couldn't wait to see him when I came home at night, for the first time I even thought of what it would be like having children – we wanted to wait, but now I'm sorry we did, I'd would have had a little piece of him. I'm sorry for going on like this, dumping on you – I don't know why I am, maybe it's because you're easy to talk to, or because you'll be going off. It's the only way I know to preserve his memory. I've been keeping it bottled up inside me. You must live the life you planned, and I know it may not work with mine – you'll be on the west coast, I'll be here, maybe something might work out between us, but I want to have these days with you, I want to thank your father for the chance I've had to know you.

"I'm not saying Jonathan was perfect. He did things that drove me nuts. He never picked up his clothes, would forget to buy milk for breakfast. 'How can you sit there at a time like this and not worry?' I asked furiously one morning. We were in danger of losing the deposit we had put down for airline tickets. 'Why do I have to have to worry?' he answered maddeningly. 'You're doing it for me.' I was…furious… I was ready for a knock-down-drag-out fight, but a minute later we were laughing."

He had sat beside her watching her as she spoke, watching her lips move…watching the flickers of pain shoot across her face, aware of how much she was hurting, of how close she was for her emotions to spill over, how fragile she was, how she could break and fall at any time, and it came to him that when Susan complained about Jonathan it was in the way that a mother complains about her son, how disobedient he is, or how impossible he is, how she can't do a thing with him, but what it really was an excuse to talk about him, what she really was saying was I adore him, he's my life

"You really loved him," he'd said.

She didn't answer right away. When she did, all she said was, "Mmm."

Jaime stretched to work out the kinks when they pulled off at an overlook where the road crested a mountain. Down below, the river wound peacefully through the broad sweep of lush countryside, a scattering of tiny houses along its bank placed like tokens on a game board. Weeping willows bent deeply tasting the water, the morning sun flooded over the mountain rising from its opposite bank, silhouetting the sentinel oaks and elms along its ridge. What they had expected would be a two-and-a-half-hour drive now looked like three and a half, the road streaming with holiday traffic.

Chapter 31

It was another hour before they came to the sign 'This Exit for Lancaster County.' Route 380, a four-lane, sunbaked, grass-verged secondary road became a two-lane road under a canopy of giant oaks rich with the smells of summer, manure, fresh-mown hay. The secondary road meandered lazily past fields of ready for picking, corn tassels flagging in the light breeze. Coming out the other side of an old, weathered covered wooden bridge spanning a tinkling stream they came abreast of an Amish farmer in traditional dress, broad-brimmed black hat, open-collared white shirt, black trousers, guiding a wooden-handled, steel-bladed plow, one hand on the wooden handle, the other on the leather reins of the gray mare pulling the plow. A quarter-mile later a dirt road lead to Ringlehoff's, the B&B they had booked in, a two-story, cedar-shingled farmhouse with one-story wings sprouting from each side. On the left, a chicken coop, on the right, a red barn with hayloft, youngsters in shorts and tees petting a sheep and feeding goats and a pony in a fenced-in grassy area.

"I had an image," Jaime said, with a wry smile, after signing the register and being shown to their room, "when we booked into a farmhouse, of painted iron-rail headboards, straw-stuffed mattresses, kerosene lamps, wooden planked floors and flaking paint, pegs on the wall for clothes, a cracked mirror on a sideboard over an earthenware pitcher, a bowl and bar of soap, the toilet down the hall, a Farmer's Almanac calendar on the wall. We could be in the Four Seasons, canopied bed, en-suite marble bath, Jacuzzis, air conditioning, French doors leading to our private garden with lounges, umbrella, and table. It's like coming upon a muddy mining camp in the foothills of the California mountains during the 1840s gold rush, expecting Bret Harte's *Luck of Roaring Camp with Heathen Chinee,* and finding yourself at the Ritz Carlton with a Jacuzzi and an in-ground pool."

"I thought you'd want a change from…where was that again…Red Plains?"

"Hey! Don't badmouth Red Plains. Last year they put heaters in the outhouse, and this winter they're going to turn them on."

"C'mon, you," Susan beamed, "let's leave the bags where they are and explore."

They left through the French doors, followed the path through the garden around the wings of the house drawn by the shrieks and laughter of children. Jaime was amused at how the reverse of rustic the farmhouse actually was despite the apparent effort to make it look authentic. On close up, the cracks in the shingles and the holes in the wood looked to had been added, the iron rings hung from the posts along the path added to suggest settlers once tethered livestock here, the weathered appearance of the barn from the outside at odds with the spotless, freshly painted stalls.

I'm having an out-of-body experience, he thought. On first look, everything looked...finished, but when I looked a second time, there were cracks in the walls, seam lines in the wood, flakes in the paint. He turned and peered closely examining Susan.

"What?" she asked, wrinkling her nose.

He shook his head. "C'mon," he said, walking on.

Ahead, riding on the back of a pony led by a young Amish girl in a blue ankle-length dress and white cap, flaps hanging down both sides covering her ears, was a serious, three-and-a-half-year-old cutie in pink shorts and a white tee, painted adorned with a picture of a fairy princess. She was biting her lips, concentrating on holding tight to a leather strap cinched around the pony's middle; her blonde, ringlet curls bouncing with each step of the pony. An anxious mother followed close behind, the father's hand never far from the little one's bottom.

In a stall in the barn, a little girl seated on a wooden stool tight against a milkmaid's side squealed with delight each time a stream of milk she squeezed from the bored cow's udders squirted into the metal pail.

Further off, a five-year-old hell-raiser in blue shorts and a Dungeons and Dragon tee was pulling on the tail of a bleating sheep trying to escape, while his mother yelled, 'Tommy, stop!' with an apologetic expression that said, 'I can't do a thing with him.'

It was the same look Jaime had seen on Susan's face when she was talking about Jonathan, but now Susan's face was alight. "What?" he asked, in what had become their verbal shorthand.

"Do you know why Jewish children aren't named after a living relative?"

He shook his head, suppressing a grin at the non sequitur.

"So the angel of death won't be confused and take the child instead of the older relative. And it's why Jews are hesitant to sing their child's praises: the angel of death is selective and only takes good children."

Jaime took in a sharp breath, wondering if they were beginning to read each other's thoughts. "I'm not superstitious," he agreed, working to keep a straight face. "Pooh! Pooh! Pooh!"

Susan grinned. Spitting three times was what was needed to scare the devil away. "Me neither," she insisted, "but as the rabbi says 'how does it hoit?'"

They continued around the perimeter, a dozen or so football fields in length, coming to a vegetable garden lush with cucumbers, tomatoes, string beans, and peppers, and squash, radishes, lettuce and cabbages in neat rows along the ground, then headed to the in-ground pool at the front of the other wing where young children were splashing about in the shallow end under the watchful eyes of their parents, and a pair of teenage girls were stretched hedonistically on chaise lounges texting and working on their tans.

They took off their shoes and laid back on a pair of chaises, relaxing in the sun, watching a dark-eyed, six-year-old in a two-piece yellow bikini showing a three-year-old in a matching bikini how to do the dog paddle. "Children are more resilient than adults believe," Susan sighed wistfully. "When my younger cousin Amy was six, she couldn't get organized in the morning, so my aunt drew a chart and tacked it up on her corkboard with a list to check off each morning: brush teeth, wash face and hands, dress, make bed, feed fish, and take school books. One night, before going to sleep, she went into Amy's room, as she did every night, checking to see that Amy was covered. The last goldfish was floating on the top of the water, curled in death. Amy was a bundle of little ones' emotions, sometimes on the top of world; skipping, dancing, whirling around; other times reeling from the day's tragedies. The next morning, her mother slipped softly into the room wary of how Amy would handle the loss. On the blackboard, a heavy black line was drawn through 'Feed fish.'"

Jaime laughed, but stopped quickly, stealing a look at Susan, sensing that the story was more about her than her cousin.

"I feel like we're in Disney Land North, All the world's a stage, and all the men and women merely players," Susan beamed. "I find it hard to wrap my head around an image of the Amish embracing plainness, no electricity, no modern conveniences, but PayPal, internet ads for B&Bs, restaurants and house tours."

"As they say at Sotheby's in London: 'Speak British, But Think Yiddish. Business is business.'"

"You're a cynic."

"Hey," Jaime whispered with a wicked grin when they passed a strawberry-red sign in the window of Yoder's bakery-restaurant: 'Annual Strawberry Festival.' Inside the bakery, customers were lined in front of a glass display counter filled with fourteen-inch strawberry pies topped with three-inches of swirly whipped cream. "Lunch! How about one of those pies, a knife and a fork, sit outside and make it our lunch?"

For answer, Susan grinned guiltily, discovering an unexpected competitiveness, pausing only to wipe whipped cream from each other's lips and return to the pie.

"Oy!" Jaime groaned, filled, struggling to get up, "no more."

"You're leaving this last piece?" Susan prodded, following him.

"I feel like a traitor."

Susan looked at him curiously, "A traitor? To who?"

"Myself."

She was beginning to become used to how Jaime would go from joking and kidding around to earnestly serious in the same breath. She searched deeply for something in his eyes or in the curl of his cheeks, a giveaway, but could find nothing to suggest it was some mischief, that he wasn't serious. Groaning, joking at being unable to finish off that last piece of the pie, they had set off to explore the town, trailing in and out of shops after swarms of shoppers buzzing over Amish handicraft, buggy whips, home-made cheeses, wood furniture, home-loomed table runners, leather sandals, tee shirts, and refrigerator magnets, signs and bumper stickers with Amish homilies: 'Those who had no children know best how to raise them,' 'Marriage may be made in Heaven but man is responsible for the upkeep,' 'If at first you succeed, try not to look astonished,' 'A word to the wise is unnecessary,' 'A happy memory never wears out.'

"How are you a traitor to yourself?" she asked, becoming aware that he was serious.

"I've mocked and poked fun at 'The Great American Pastime,' shopping. And now I've joined them. I feel…*"*

"Human?"

Jaime recoiled, grimacing. "That's a terrible thing to be accused of."

Susan screwed up her face. "C'mon," she said, grabbing his hand, feigning deep sympathy, "let's go to Bird in Hand and join a tour of an Amish home and working farm."

Amity, a nineteen-year-old Amish woman in traditional dress, white bonnet, high-necked black dress, and black grandma shoes, met the tour group at the door of her home and led them into a room measuring approximately twelve by fifteen. "This," she explained, waving her hand, fluttering her fingers to show the extent of the room, "is my family's dining room, sitting room and the room in which our Church services are held when it is our turn to host them." Save for a long wooden table and eight wooden chairs in the

114

center of the room, the room was bare There were no pictures on the walls, no decorations to indicate that a family lived here.

"My day," she continued, her clear blue eyes sparkling, her cheeks burnished by the sun, "begins at 4 a.m. when I milk the cows while my two younger brothers do chores in the barn and my young sister gathers the eggs the chickens in the coop laid during the night. It is my job, on alternate days, to help my mother prepare breakfast – oatmeal, griddle cakes, and thick slices of freshly baked whole-grain bread with great slabs of freshly churned butter. There is coffee for my parents and me, and milk for my brothers and sister."

Members of the tour, six adults and four youngsters, a three and five-year-old brother and sister, an infant in a father's stomach sling and a boy of eight, followed her into the kitchen in which was a cast-iron a wood-burning stove, a refrigerator powered by propane gas, a zinc sink, a stack of wood cut to size for the stove and a wood work table and chair. "We don't use electricity," as you see, she continued. Standing before them, in the modest traditional Amish garment, she gave an impression of being far taller than her five foot ten inches, in the way Marc Chagall depicts women in his murals and paintings. Looking closely, auburn hair could be seen peeking from under her white bonnet, but nothing else, not a pin or even a comb was there to call attention to her.

"Careful," she warned the older dark-haired boy who scooted from his parents to examine the stove, "it may still be warm."

"The reason we don't use electricity," she explained, keeping one eye on him, "is that we believe that if we come to depend on power generated by an electric company, we become tied too closely to the world and open ourselves to influences that run counter to our values. We are careful of the temptation television, radio, and the internet can bring into the home, and believe that reliance on labor-saving devices may deprive children of character building opportunities to work."

"Do no Amish use electricity?" one of the women on the tour asked.

Amity brought her hand to her mouth. She looked a little embarrassed. "There is," she admitted, "a more *liberal* local group, the 'Peachey' Amish, but Lancaster County Amish banned public power in 1920, considering it a worldly luxury."

"I wouldn't mind living this way," Jaime whispered as they followed a young couple to the stairs, "if I could have TV for Monday night football."

The woman in front turned and grinned.

"Yeah," Susan agreed, "and a hairdryer."

"And a dishwasher," the woman added.

Amity pretended not to have heard them. Leading the way up the wooden staircase, she took the group through three small bedrooms, as bare of

115

decorations, save for a picture of Jesus, as the rooms below. "Our lives are centered on our family, our community, our land, and the worship of God. I'm betrothed," she blushed shyly. "Jacob and I are to marry in the fall after the harvest. In Amish communities, it is a custom for the parents to give a parcel of land to the new couple, but because there is no more land to be had, to further subdivide our farm would leave too little land to farm to support a family, so Jacob has taken a job in a factory in town and I will make jellies and jams to sell. We will live in a house near my parents that our community will help us build. It is Jacob and my choice to remain in the community," she explained as she led the group outside to the barn where animals were kept in the winter. Over the door of the barn hung a large Amish pie-shaped hex sign, a green three-leafed clover, on each side a mystical bird with a long bushy tail. Tools hung on the walls inside, scythes, plow blades, a spare buggy wheel, and other farming implements. "We are free to leave the community, but if we chose to remain, we are expected to conform to our ways or risk being ostracized, 'shunned.' Please feel free to explore the barn and the implements before you leave," she offered, stepping outside, saying goodbye and wishing them 'Gute Reise,' good journey.

Chapter 32

"Still up for a balloon ride at sunset?" Jaime asked as they climbed back into Susan's car and turned on the air conditioner. It was coming on to four, the temperature had risen well into the eighties, but the evening was forecasted to be cool. In the distance, the sky was a lighter shade of blue, but high up, tiny orange and aqua vapor trails shot across the sky. Susan had switched from tan shorts and tee shirt to a burgundy mini skirt, yellow knit top with two buttons open and brown leather espadrilles, and had let her blonde hair fall loose in a ponytail. Jaime couldn't keep his eyes off her. She looked like a lollipop on a stick.

Susan eyed him cautiously. "Is it something you really want to do?"

Jaime took a breath before answering. "We don't have to if you'd rather not."

Susan hesitated. Jaime wondered if she was thinking of him and didn't want to disappoint him, but he sensed something else as well, that like him, she was keenly aware that their time together was rapidly coming to an end, that in a matter of hours, a day and a half at most, he would be on his way and she would be back in the hospital, that the idyll they shared would be over, that all the ever after fantasies, the promises they would make, that they would see each other regularly, that they could make a long-distance relationship work, were just that, fantasies. He could not keep from hearing in his head Chenny Breitman's bittersweet 'Time to say goodbye.'

"It says here," she said, unaware of his thoughts, 'on the 19th of September 1783, Pilatre De Rozier, a scientist, launched the first hot air balloon called *Aerostat Reveillon*. The passengers were a sheep, a duck, and a rooster, and the balloon stayed in the air for a grand total of 15 minutes before crashing back to the ground.'

"It also says," she added, smiling weakly, "that the balloon pilots are licensed, FAA trained, and that according to statistics, it is actually safer than riding in a car, that you have the sensation you are standing still, taking in breath-taking views, that everything else is moving slowly."

"I'm sure that must be so," Jaime agreed.

"Why?" She looked at him dubiously. "Why must it be so?"

"Read the fine print on the bottom."

Not politically affiliated. She screwed up her brow. "Why should that give us confidence?"

Jaime bit his lower lip, said nothing, a hint of a smile leaking from the corner of his eyes.

Susan's eyes widened. "Oh!" she exclaimed. She attempted a weak grin. "OK."

From a distance, as the van approached the clearing in the field in which the balloon was tethered, it looked like a giant ice-cream cone standing in a bed of shimmering green Jell-O surrounded by Martians in white jumpsuits. As they drew nearer, the base of the ice cream cone resolved into a wicker basket tethered to a partially inflated huge balloon with a hungry open mouth at the bottom. Tiny winged insects drawn by the reflection of the sun on the surface of the balloon were flittering about. The sun, still high enough to cast a short shadow, began to lengthen as they came nearer, a gentle breeze trembled the taller grass, ideal conditions, according to the pilot, a man of forty with buzz-cut hair wearing Ray-Ban sunglasses with a , selected for his sharply planed face and professional manner.

As Jaime helped Susan out of the van, he caught the splinter of concern in her eyes. Ducking his head so the others couldn't hear, he whispered, "Are you sure you want to go?"

"Mmm," she grunted through compressed lips.

"We can just watch," he offered.

"We paid already," she reasoned.

"So?"

"No! We're going!" she insisted.

"If we die together, you may have to spend eternity with me."

"Are you trying to talk me out of it?" she demanded, pulling him toward the balloon surrounded by young Amish children in traditional dress, bonnets, and hats sucking on lollipops the crew was handing out.

There was a sense of shared restrained joviality as they and the young couple who joined them examined the balloon and gondola, which appeared to be sitting, like an obedient dog, straining to be let loose, to soar, waiting only for its master's command.

Before climbing into the basket, the other couple introduced themselves. The young fellow, Tom, had a shock of wheat-colored hair that fell over his right eye, smooth full cheeks, traces of acne, and shoulders not yet fully developed. His companion, Carrie, had the look of a high-school cheerleader, high breasts, pinched waist, and large brown eyes with sweeping lashes. As the pilot explained what to expect, they seemed to have trouble keeping their hands off each other.

Almost immediately, the pilot made a last check of the fuel canister, the levers that controlled the length and strength of the bursts of flames that heated the air inside the balloon to give it loft, and the harnesses that held the gondola, delivering a running description of what he was doing.

Susan eyed the burner worriedly. The flames that would shoot out to heat the air were less than18" above their heads. Jaime grinned, imagining the pilot would end his pre-flight orientation with, 'Thank you for choosing Delta,' as he opened the valve shooting flames into the waiting mouth of the balloon. At once, the ground crew untied the ropes, their link to stakes in the ground, the air over their heads became heated, there was a small jolt, and as the basket lifted, Susan gripped Jaime's hand nervously with one hand, the rim of the basket with the other as the Amish children danced about waving them off.

Seconds later they were hovering over the ground, climbing slowly, squinting at the sun quartering in the azure sky, holding tightly to the side of the basket, looking down at the children and ground crew growing smaller and smaller. Two long hot bursts of flame from the burner lifted them to 'cruising' altitude, a thousand feet above the ground. At this height, streaks of gold and silver splintered from the lowering sun, the ground had a look of a giant checkerboard, squares divided by long narrow furrows, one square of rich, freshly turned black brown earth awaiting seed, another capped with tawny wheat, a third a sea of green, lettuce atop corduroy mounds.

The light breeze took them above a winding river, a necklace twisting by toy farmhouses, trees that looked no more than shrubs at this height. Jaime waved back to the children small as black ants below, as Susan, wide-eyed, clung tightly to his hand. From time to time, they heard the hiss of short bursts of flame and felt the heat as the pilot lifted them higher after allowing them to slowly descend. From this height, they could still see the sun which had yet to dip behind the low rise in the west, but soon all that remained was an afterglow as star by star popped out in the inky sky, like tiny diamonds placed there by a Tiffany sales associate.

They floated along in quiet for a while when the burner was shut down and the insistent hiss of the flames was no longer heard, engulfed in a deep, profound silence, below only the silhouette of trees and a single twinkling light of a farmhouse. As Jaime turned his gaze up into the vast, endless canopy, the millions and millions of stars winking back at him, an epiphany he had once and tucked safely away returned, the insignificance of man in the universe. It had been in shul, on Yom Kippur, the Day of Atonement, the holiest day of the year in the Jewish calendar, the Day in which it is Decreed *How many shall pass away and how many shall be born, Who shall live and who shall die,* and when the rabbi read from the Torah: *'Oh Lord, what is man?'* he had a feeling he hadn't known he possessed.

As the night lengthened and a feeling of endless peace came over him, Susan nestled against him, safe enough now to peer straight down over the side of the gondola, then all too soon they began their descent. With a light thump, the basket kissed the ground, white jumpsuited ground crew had them safely tethered to stakes, the few stalwart Amish youngsters who had stayed, greeted them in English and Pennsylvanian German watching them disembark.

At once, as the balloon was deflated, folded and stored in a large giant sack, the rigging dismantled, there was a shared joviality, the young couple, the pilot and the ground crew, congratulated each other, agreeing on what a serene experience it was, but Jaime was subdued, aware that Susan was strangely quiet, wary that making much of it would cheapen the intense experience.

As they had climbed from the gondola with Tom and Carrie, in the light from the lantern on the nearby aluminum folding table set with a white table cloth and napkins and a magnum of champagne cooling in a silver ice bucket, Jaime spotted a look in Susan's eyes he couldn't decipher. She would look at him quickly and quickly look away, as if assessing him, appraising him.

"They don't look old enough to have learner's permits," Jaime whispered nervously into Susan's ponytail, as they had handed her a flute of champagne.

"I don't think they need a permit," she whispered, "for what they'd been doing. Did you notice where Tom's hand was when we were up in the balloon?"

"Wasn't that…like awesome," Carrie gushed, holding tight to Tom.

Susan smiled, darting a quick look at Jaime. *"Like…awesome,"* she grinned, tugging his hand.

Jaime's cheeks grew into a smile that didn't fully reach his eyes. Susan was…*different.* Had the balloon ride released something in her? She was listening to Carrie who was flirting with the pilot passing chocolates but stealing looks at him. She tugged Jaime's hand: "Let's walk back," she whispered. There was an unusual edge to her voice.

"In the dark?" Jaime whispered. "We could wind up sleeping in the fields."

"Yeah," Susan grinned evilly. "C'mon," she said, pulling him after her.

They hadn't quite reached the end of the field, the balloon one hundred yards away, when she stopped, looked up. "Let's count the stars," she urged wickedly, wriggling back into him. "One, two, a million, two million," she counted, pulling his arms around her.

"One, three, four million, wait, I think I missed one," she giggled, wedging her hand between them.

Jaime gasped. She was naked under her skirt. "They can see us."

"Let 'em," she giggled.

Jaime looked wildly over his shoulder. "Susan," he objected.

But it was too late.

Chapter 33

He didn't know how much later it was. The moon had already risen, the cool night air was stealing in, nipping at them, biting their skin as they separated and set off in the direction the van had taken, holding on to each other in the lingering afterglow.

It was almost ten when they found their way back, guided by an Amish farmer they came across in nightshirt and boots waving his arms wildly shouting *Gadverdamme Küh.* The cow lifted his head, its round eyes shining in the moonlight, and went right back to grazing on his wife's lettuce patch.

"Maybe the cow doesn't speak Pennsylvania Dutch," Jaime observed wearily as they continued along the path the farmer pointed to.

They slept late the next morning, set off for Paradise under a balmy sky for brunch, pancakes, farm fresh eggs, country sausage, pan-fried scrapple, grilled sticky buns and coffee, finding things to make much of along the way into town, a three-year-old in a granny dress, a weather-beaten sign 'This way to Paradise,' anything to keep from letting on that they had taken on a passenger, the fear that it all had been make believe. A joke Jaime attempted fell flat, Susan reached to touch Jaime's arm but didn't. The enthusiasm and banter of the day before had given way to awkward politeness. Jaime ached to go back to where they had been, to break the spell that had seized them, say to Susan all the things he had wanted to say before, all the words he had held back, but he couldn't, wary of Susan's response, wary of whether what he had been feeling had been real, wary that whatever Susan was feeling might be no more than a rebound from the loss she suffered, wary of whether Susan was froth, icing on the cake while Chenny was real. And in those moments when Susan's attention was diverted and he was able to observe her unobserved, he wondered if her feelings were any different than his.

Before setting off for Philadelphia, they spent another hour poring over Amish handicraft at an open-air market, grateful for the diversion, made much of whether they should have a picnic dinner while watching the Fourth's fireworks over the Delaware from Penn's Landing, a few blocks from where the Battleship New Jersey docked and about as far from Susan's apartment, and spent another forty-five minutes choosing whether a 24" long baguette was too long or an 18" too short, selecting four cheeses from an assortment of several dozen, plus one of the shriveled wursts from a wicker basket, three ripe beefsteak tomatoes, a funnel cake sprinkled with powdered sugar and hard apple cider.

By the time they got on the road, traffic along I-76 was picking up. "So much for Map Quest," Jaime bitched, his usual bantering muffled, "some hour and a half drive."

"Look on the bright side," Susan offered, aware of how strained their conversation had become, "we have an in-depth look at bumpers."

As they drove along listening to *Don't Wanna Know* on the local A.M. station followed by Justin Bieber's *Let Me Love You,* Jaime knew what was burning in his gut was not the traffic, not the post-sex let down, but the impossibility of long-distance relationships, how slim the odds were of any relationship lasting more than a few months, and words ringing in his ears from *The Portable Henry Rollins:*

It hurts to let go. Sometimes it seems the harder you try to hold on to something or someone the more it wants to get away. You feel like some kind of criminal for having felt, for having wanted. For having wanted to be wanted. It confuses you, because you think that your feelings were wrong and it makes you feel so small because it's so hard to keep it inside when you let it out and it doesn't come back. You're left so alone that you can't explain. Damn, there's nothing like that, is there? I've been there and you have too. You're nodding your head.

They would both make promises when he left he knew they'd never keep. Susan was not moving to San Francisco, he was not moving to Philadelphia. They'd promise to keep in touch and that they would see each other often; San Francisco was only five hours by plane. But they both knew long-distance relationships faded. She had a life here, he had to make a life there. They would always be friends.

The same feeling of melancholy he had when he was summoned from Nebraska to New Jersey overcame him, but now it was so deep it seemed bottomless. He had kept it casual In Red Plains, fun and games, a diversion, he assured himself, to keep him afloat in exile, but here he had allowed himself to believe that it could be more. But if only that were all, if he was free to choose Red Plains or here. What of the obligation he had to find two more of his 'families?' And what of the obligation to himself, to make something of himself; how easy it was to imagine how he would become teacher of the year in San Francisco and a famous author. But he still hadn't entered the classroom, nor had he put one word of his book on paper.

"What's the matter?" Susan asked. "You look like you lost your best friend."

Jaime lifted his head. Cars were slogging along in each direction. He had been staring straight ahead unseeing. He took a deep breath, trying to decide what to say, how much to say, keeping his eyes fixed on the road, unwilling to find Susan's. "Am I that transparent?" He fixed a smile on his face. "It feels as if I'm about to."

If Susan heard what he said, he didn't know. She continued driving, following the bends in the road. Miles went by with no response. With effort, he forced himself to turn his head. She looked forlorn, miserable. If she hadn't been driving, he would have drawn her into his arms and kissed her tears away. He had been thinking of himself but hadn't realized what it had to be like for her, going from a lost love to one that had no future.

He thought of all the many books and poems he had read. So much had been written, but he could think of nothing that helped. Everything that was written, prose, poetry, songs, attempted to express the exhilaration of falling in love, finding a soul mate, or the end of an affair, losing a love, falling out of love. None of that seemed right, none of that could ease their suffering or the guilt he was feeling. He cast about, trying to find words that fit, but none came.

"Have you ever watched the Hallmark movies on television?" he asked at last.

Susan blinked away a tear, turned to look at him for a split second, curious at what must have seemed a non sequitur.

"You must have. They begin with two people in high paying jobs in long-term loving relationships about to be married, but circumstances force each of them to spend a week with someone they despise. While, their fiancés are in Nepal, or someplace less exotic, like Chicago, he discovers that the woman is not the ball buster he had originally thought and she discovers that the guy's not the bastard he seemed at first after he confesses, in a touchy feely moment, something that indicates that he has a feminine side, and at the end of the seven days, each tells his or her fiancé that they had found their true soul mate, were giving up New York City, their penthouse and Mercedes sports cars for pickup trucks, that she always dreamed of living in a small town with a Starbucks and opening a shop selling cookies she'd bake, and he always dreamed of making wooden end tables, and that they are going to live the happily ever after lives they always dreamed of."

Susan's brow furrowed. For a second the melancholy seemed forgotten. She darted a quick look at him as if he had lost it. "Is there more to this?"

Jaime shook his head. "Had you any doubt? I've come to a decision where my future lay. I'm going to write stories for television like those with a twist."

The furrows in Susan's brow vanished along with the melancholy. She turned fully to look at him, with a look that said, *What kind of nonsense is coming now?*

"Hey! Watch the road."

"OK," she allowed. "What's the twist?"

"My movies are going to end the way the stories really end. He looks at her, she looks at him. Are you for real? They both demand. You want me to give up a six-year relation with a great guy/gal, my penthouse, my Mercedes and New York City to come live in Dubuque? You must be out of your fucking gourd. And as the credits roll, we see the two saying their vows in front of a shit-load of guests in the Grand Ballroom of the Waldorf Astoria before their private jet heads off for two sun-filled weeks in Tahiti and Bora Bora."

An artificial brightness hungover breakfast the next morning. The night before, in bed, after the fireworks, they lied to each other, Jaime would head for Charleston in the morning, find his father's families, take up his position in San Francisco, Susan would head for the hospital, they'd see each other as often as possible, the time apart would be a test of their feelings, give them time to work out what had to be worked out, but in the morning, sitting across from each other, with the time to leave less than a half-hour away, the lies they told each other the night before caught in their throats. Without saying it, they knew. They were looking at the end, the end of the balloon ride, the time in the ride when the air comes out and there is nothing to keep it afloat.

They rose from the table together, put the milk and butter in the refrigerator, stacked the dishes, Jaime gathered the canvas sack he packed the night before, Susan picked her car keys from a pocket in her pantsuit and reached for the doorknob.

"No! God damn it!" she insisted, turning. "It's not going to end like this, like someone died!"

Jaime gasped. The thought, the inference caught him in his chest. *Jonathan.*

Susan stood, back to the door, feet set, shoulders braced, defiant, tears slipping down her cheeks. "We can make this work… if we want to."

In front of his eyes, as Jaime stood there and watched, Susan's defiance seemed to crumble and her bones seemed to melt. She looked up, shrunken. "Can't we?"

Jaime set down his canvas sack. He reached for Susan, gathered her in his arms, pressed her to him, kissing away her tears, and his own.

"We can," he said miserably, wanting everything to change, but knowing nothing had.

Chapter 34

Post-holiday traffic was already on the road when Jaime joined I-95 going south, the road that would take him through Delaware, past Baltimore, the District of Columbia, the Capitol into Virginia, which he always thought of as the northern extremity of the South. The flow of cars and trucks sped along at ten miles above the speed limit for short stretches, only to grind to a virtual halt at the whim of puckish Loki, the Norse god, up to his old tricks. Jaime drove along mindlessly, unaware of the traffic, Indy-500 drivers jiggling in and out of lane, usually to little or no advantage, mindless of the families returning from vacation, the roofs strapped with luggage, boards, canvas tents, bicycles riding on racks strapped to the rear bumper, kids glomming him from the rear window, and workers returning to jobs in the Beltway after the holiday, struggling with a thought that refused to leave him in peace, was he running away from something, running to something, or just running. Equally unsettling, he was unable to shake the feeling in his gut that it wasn't just curiosity that was drawing him along on this errand for his father but a force he couldn't explain.

He had a name, Sydney Goldbloom, and a city, Charleston, but a search of the internet for the boy, who by now would be eighteen or nineteen, or his mother, Leonora, came up blank. Exhausted, needing to recharge his batteries, he checked into a Hampton Inn in Virginia, showered, had dinner, returned to his room, turned on a rerun of 'Sweet Home Alabama,' intending to rest a bit before re-reading his father's diary, but the next time he looked at his watch, it was 12:30. He had missed watching Melanie deck Candace Bergen, the Mayor of New York City.

He had dinner at Ye Olde Virginia Eatery, a cutesy gingerbread restaurant a half-mile from the motel the desk clerk recommended, a shingled gabled bungalow with frosted windows and a curved brass handle half the height of the door, how, as a child, he imagined Little Red Riding Hood's grandmother's house. The waitresses, young girls, all had painted red lips and rouged cheeks, checkered red and white gingham waitress uniforms pinched at the waist with short white sleeves and collars, short ruffled skirts and red frilly aprons. On the walls were floral prints, roses, tulips, and lilacs. Hand-stitched samplers were lit with small, cut-glass hanging lanterns.

The special southern fried chicken came with buttermilk biscuits, pickled veggies, mashed potatoes and gravy, and a fresh vegetable which turned out to be boiled carrots. The chicken and mashed potatoes, seasoned with a spice he couldn't recognize, coriander possibly, were delicious, but the sight of the carrots touched a memory, his mother demanding that he eat his carrots if he wanted dessert. Thinking of it now, he grinned, remembering his dilemma, whether to leave the carrots as long as possible and hope a good fairy would come and make them disappear or stuff them down as fast as he could to get to his dessert. It seemed amusing now, but it wasn't then. If he pushed them away to the back of his plate, they seemed to sit there staring at him, but the time he gobbled them down, he was afraid they would come back up. One time, when his mother's attention was elsewhere, he pushed them under the mashed potatoes and smushed them all around. When his mother looked back, he tried to play innocent. She didn't say anything, but she looked at him with that disappointed look making him feel that she was disappointed in him. Like the carrots, he had been putting off tackling the next pages of the diary, dreading what he would find in Charleston, though the visit to Philadelphia, which he had also dreaded, turned out so much better than expected.

Leave the Goddamn diary for tomorrow after breakfast, he decided, heading back to the hotel, not anxious to read more of how the son of a bitch fucked up, and how he blamed it on everyone but himself.

If this were a child's fairy tale, somehow during the night the diary would climb out of his backpack and fly out of the window. But the fucking windows were bolted shut.

In the watery slurry of thoughts that tumbled through his brain at night as he drifted off to sleep, in that short interval before sleep blanked whatever was on his mind, he relived his day, congratulating himself on his 'triumphs' and badgering himself about his failures – which he thought of as 'un-triumphs,' then went on to the paradox of how everyone was unique, yet everyone was really the same, and then it seemed a long time went by and he found himself with Chenny on a reservation near Red Plains, but the Lakota Indian talking to them introduced himself as Seneca, advisor to Nero, and said, "We suffer more often in imagination than in reality…" and he objected, You're thinking of Susan's mother who turned out to not be the gargoyle I expected, aren't you? *"And what of Susan?"* Seneca demanded, and before he could answer a light shined in his eyes, and when he squinted, he saw it was the sun streaming through the window and the time on his cell phone was 8:20.

128

"Shit," he muttered, pulling the covers off and scrambling to the bathroom to relieve his bladder.

The freebie continental breakfast was in a room off the lobby indistinguishable from rooms in hundreds of motels that line the interstates identified by tiny dots on Google satellite maps. He pushed in and found an empty table on the far end. A pair of cheaply framed eclectic prints hung on the off-white wall at either end of the sideboard above the toaster, but if it had been with the intent to give the room a personality or homey touch, it fell woefully short. 7-11 sweet rolls under two red heat lamps filled the room with the aroma of cinnamon and raisins, Folgers' coffee dripped from a percolator, large glass jars contained corn flakes, Wheaties and Cheerios. Except for an errant Cheerios hiding behind the toaster, the room was sparkling clean.

The business day had begun. Businessmen in freshly pressed suits, women in jackets and slacks were eating a Danish or drinking coffee with one hand, tapping iPhones or laptops with the other. He selected corn flakes, juice and coffee from the buffet, settled into a seat at the back, pushed the diary, like carrots, as far away as the table allowed, and turned his thoughts back to Susan.

Every cell in his body seemed to be craving for every inch of her, from the sparkle in her eyes he had kissed, to the tiny toes he had sucked on, and everything between. During the night, he had sex with her in his dream. She wasn't one of the fizzy drinks he'd had one-nighters with nor one of the soft marshmallows either. At the brunch, her mother told how hard it was to get Susan organized in the morning when she was six or seven. She was always busy with something or dreaming who knows where. 'When nothing else worked, I made a list for her and tacked it up on her bulletin board: Wash face and hands; Brush teeth; Dress; Feed fish; Make Bed; Take backpack; Eat breakfast; with a column to check off,' her mother said.

The goldfish story Susan had told was about her. 'One night,' her mother went on, 'before I went to bed, I came into her room to see that she was covered and kiss her. The last one of her goldfish in the bowl was floating on top of the water, dead. Oh God, I worried. I had no idea what to do, how would she handle it? The next morning, I tiptoed into her room, not knowing what I'd find. There was no indication she had even noticed, except for a line drawn through the words, *Feed fish.*'

"What did you expect, Mom," Susan grinned, "that I should have given the goldfish mount-to-mouth resuscitation?"

Jamie had often wondered how a doctor, particularly a children's doctor handled the death of a child.

He laughed to himself at the thought, took a last sip of coffee and looked around the room reluctantly, and reached for the diary, unable to put it off any longer.

At a distance you fool others, close at hand just yourself. In the mirror everyone sees his best friend and his worst enemy. God had blessed me, brought me to Marsha with one hand, punished me, had Marsha banish me with the other.

Such were the dark thoughts that followed me that fall as I headed south feeling sorry for myself, with no plan, no direction, no destination. Sholem Aleichem said, "Life is a dream for the wise, a game for the fool, a comedy for the rich, a tragedy for the poor." That was the specter staring me in the face.

I drove along for miles, eating myself up, seeing the early morning traffic streaming by, men and women on the way to work with a destination, gainful employment, a loving home awaiting them at the end of the day, the joyful sounds of children. Even bickering, arguments seemed appealing, even desirable to the sterile motel rooms I faced.

I was wallowing in self-pity, drowning, promising God that if He gave me one more chance, when I heard a voice in my head, 'It's not whether you get knocked down, it's whether you get up,' words I remembered I heard Vincent Lombardi, arguably the greatest football coach of all time, speak.

Had God heard? I had forgotten Him. Did I now have a commitment to Him? As it turned out, it would have been better had He not.

Jaime lifted his head, looked around. The breakfast room had begun to thin out. A young red-haired waitress was cleaning off a table in the back just vacated. Shit, he muttered under his breath. The merchant of menace, the devil quoting scriptures for his purpose like a villain with a smiling cheek. He took a breath, rubbed the distaste from his mouth, and turned back to the diary.

The Charleston of Harper Lee's To Kill a Mockingbird, a city of wealth and contrasts, has the second oldest Jewish settlement in the United States after Newport, Rhode Island, the outpost where a Sephardic Jew, a member of a Portuguese trading family, settled in the early 1700s. Known for gracious historic mansions with hangings of Spanish moss, Charleston is also home to tumbledown shacks with drippings of flaking paint, a Mecca for marble and tiled modern shopping malls selling Gucci and Godiva, corrugated roofed wooden bodegas selling beer and lottery tickets, a repository of deep-south charm and Yankee horse trading, and as everywhere, as I was to discover, a city of jealousies, hatreds, ambitions, greed, fidelity and infidelity.

The scents of roses, chrysanthemums, and verbena filled the air when I arrived, carried by gentle winds blowing off the river, mixed with coriander, sage, and thyme that seemed to cling to the trees and buildings. Labor-day tourists had departed, hansom carriages idled at the curbs of hotels, liveried drivers in morning clothes and top hats chatted as they groomed their mares as I went off in search of suitable accommodations. A small furnished brownstone in a respectable, still fashionable, section of the City that boasted of old-fashioned charm, with decorative rosette medallions on the ceilings, tall windows looking out over grass-verged neighborhood streets, seemed better matched to the image of dignity and permanence I had in mind – as well as my pocketbook – than modern high rises – aware that up north I knew I could be patted on the back with one hand and have my pocket picked with the other, whereas here I didn't know what I might expect.

Kahal Kadosh Beth Elohim, a reformed temple and a National Historic Landmark, the country's second oldest synagogue, established in 1749, has an Ionic façade in the style of classic Greek temples. It was designed by New York architect Cyrus L. Warner and built by congregation member David Lopez.

I was delighted, soon after I arrived, to find myself welcomed enthusiastically by unattached women in the congregation, though, admittedly, their choices were limited. I might have been the bachelor Sholem Aleichem described as the man who came to work each morning from a different direction, but for all its cosmopolitan ways, at heart Charleston was a small town and I didn't want to get a reputation as a player. In truth, however, if I didn't want to fall back into my old pattern, I might have risked it, for I noticed that for most women it was more a turn-on than a turn-off. But Lennie was not most women. For the first time, I began to wonder if, for her, I could keep my promise, be more than I had been, if in time, she might come to want to spend the rest of her life with me.

Lennie, Leonora Goldbloom, had, appropriately, been named after the Leonora Overture to Fedelio, the single opera Beethoven composed, her name chosen, in part, because Beethoven wrote and rewrote that overture until he felt he 'got it right,' which was what her parents must have said when first they laid eyes on her when she was born. It was the same response I had the first time I laid eyes on her that Friday evening after the services at the synagogue. It wasn't that she was beautiful; she wasn't. She was perfect.

To me, beautiful women, Ralph Lauren mannequins, always seemed bloodless, lifeless. Lennie was nothing like that. She was alive, exciting, five-six inches tall, with a shy smile that I'd feel I earned when it stole from the corners of her eyes and spread across her face, lighting the tiny freckles on the bridge of her nose and widening her cheeks. Her hair was the color of the rusty ink scribes, working deep into the night in abbeys, dipped their quills into copying sonnets. If she used makeup, you never could be persuaded she had. When I first saw her, she was in her early thirties, but I saw the young girl who once climbed trees and raced boys.

Leonora's husband Ben died in a yachting accident two years before leaving her with a son not yet two and a home in a gated community at the top of a nearby hill overlooking the bay where their modest yacht, which she refused to go near since the accident, was still docked. It was two months before she agreed to go out with me, and then only to Tony's for the best pizza in Charleston, and not for another month or forty five days would she talk of Ben, who she said she loved, though he had been something of a 'rascal' – which I understood to mean, when I began to understand her often understated sense of humor, he 'stepped out on her.' 'Never,' she insisted, locking onto my eyes, the tips of her perfect teeth biting her lower lip, would she ever allow that again, no matter how much in love she might be. It was, I sensed, a warning meant for me, and it emboldened me that night to ask if our evening might end with more than a chaste kiss.

From that evening on, there was never a day in which we weren't together, and within another month we were living together. When I came to Charleston, I had been hoping to find someone who could take Marsha's place. 'Take' was the operative word. Now I wanted to give. I wanted to be the one she would rely on, someone she could be proud of, someone she would want to live out the rest of her life with, to believe in fairy tales.

Jaime looked up from the diary feeling vaguely uncomfortable. When he read, he usually found himself becoming enmeshed with the characters, trying to get into their skins, to understand them, where they were coming from, making them real, but he couldn't do that with his father. To do that, he would have to accept him as a human being.

He dragged his eyes away, took another look around, aware he was putting off reading, filled his lungs and reluctantly turned back to the diary.

Tamara Beauvier, the Human Resources Director of the Charleston office of Barclay, Goodman & Seiden, B G & S, settled behind a desk stacked four inches high with applications in manila folders, indicating a seat with something less than enthusiasm. She was six foot two, had dark eyes and the high cheekbones of a Cajun Indian maiden, but was built in the shape of a bowling pin, a small round head matted with white-blonde hair cropped close to her skull in a pixie-cut topping a body that tapered to its widest point at her hips. The stock market had been booming and there was a line of applicants in the reception room eager to cash in like a line of cockroaches streaming out of the woodwork after ripe carrion.

She scanned through my scores on the broker's exam, raised her eyes with a look that seemed to say 'Thank you, we'll call you,' when something caught her eye: "High net-worth individuals?" She stopped, inhaled, took a deep breath, inflated like the blow-up dolls in the windows of 42nd Street Sex Shoppes, her eyeballs adding $s. The donors I listed weren't Baron Rothschilds, but they weren't supping at soup kitchens either.

Tamara passed me along to Selwin D'Amico, head of Client Relations, an olive-skinned, dark-eyed fellow young enough to still be breastfeeding, with a smile so innocent. He had a desk the size of Manhattan and the knotty muscles of a runner. The wall behind his chair was hung with heavy maroon drapes that sucked all the sound from the office, designed to give a feeling that anything said there was as private as in a confessional. Selly, as he told me to call him, with a 'just-between-the-two-of-us look' intended to elicit confidences, leaned back, laced his hands over his ridged belly, ran his eyes over my papers, peppered me with questions that seemed to have no purpose other than to set in stone our relative positions in the company ladder, but it was a formality. If I accepted the job, he allowed, after a four-week training period I would be assigned to a broker's desk.

I left his office on air, beaming, bursting the buttons off my shirt, anxious to tell Leonora – until I was introduced to Lyndon St. Pierre who had a job similar to the one I would have. He had been given the title of vice president and a small list of accounts once he was allowed to meet clients. "It's all window dressing," he confided, running his hand in front of his lips as if he was revealing a secret. "The job's only one step up from a mailroom clerk. B G & S doesn't pay more than scale until you create something that brings in big bucks, and," he added with a wink, "isn't overly fussy how you do it. Think Used Car Salesman."

I received further education on afternoons after the market closed, batting it around with Carl Devereaux, a foppish retail account manager who affected a goatee and a wardrobe out of a Bond Street catalog, and with Madeline LaFontaine, our gravelly voiced, cynical fiftyish institutional account manager. "Not 'Used' Car Salesman, Lyndon," she corrected. "Pre-owned." She lifted a frosted stein of Red Stripe. "Here's to Sharks-peare," she added, mixing metaphors, "Dreck by another name smells as sweet."

"What's the best swindle you've ever seen?" Carl inveigled. Carl would have tongue-kissed a leper to get a shot at the institutional side.

"How about," she asked, lowering her stein after considering the question, "Contrarianism?"

"Contrarianism?" I wasn't familiar with what she was talking about.

"David Dreman dreamed that up. He said he was a contrarian. He would buy stocks out of favor when no one wanted them and they were cheap, and sell them when everyone wanted them. What a great idea! Why hadn't I thought of it? Translated, what he said was he'd Buy low, sell high."

"Of course, it was what every other money manager promises. David's fund didn't do better than others. But it made David wealthy, a millionaire many times over."

"Do you have an all-time favorite?" Carl fawned.

Madeline scowled, hardly fooled. "Hard to pick one, but of them all, I'd have to pick zero-coupon convertible bonds." She smiled enigmatically.

Zero-coupon convertible bonds. What the hell were they?

"A Merrill Lynch salesman," she went on, "invented those. Overnight they took over the multi-billion-dollar convertible bond market. No one thought to ask how Merrill could afford to pay the salesman who invented them a bonus exceeding $500 million year after year... until it all collapsed."

I hadn't wanted to look green, so I didn't ask then what the scam was, but years later, in his book 'Nothing Personal,' Mike Offit, senior trader at Goldman Sachs wrote: 'If nobody understands it, it will probably make you rich.'

'Zero-coupon convertibles' were one of the scams that fit square in that category. I looked them up. Thousands of the brightest money managers bought them, but I was forewarned. If it seems too good to be true...

Shit, he fumed under his breath. The son of a bitch...

After a two-week orientation, forearmed, I was set loose on the mortgage desk. It was early days, before the debut of sub-prime mortgage debentures. I was detailed to visit banks to buy, at discount prices, quality mortgages the banks had written, freeing up capital to allow them to earn money writing additional mortgages. B G & S then resold the mortgages at a profit to clients seeking to add quality interest paying instruments to their portfolios.

It was profitable, legitimate, the chance I had asked for when I made that promise to God. I was on my way. My career had begun.

I was on the mortgage desk three weeks when I met Phillippe de Montaigne who had a small comped office but no apparent job tied to B G & S, like a high roller at Las Vegas' MGM Grand Hotel. He was balding, stout, a florid face that receded into a weak chin, and smelled more like a delicatessen owner rather than a French nobleman – understandably: I rarely saw him at his desk without a corned beef sandwich while he traded options nonstop. I had heard of investors earning a fortune in options, so I was anxious to wet my feet.

Fortunately, Philly came along when he did. "Son," he warned with a twinkle, "watch it, Options are a 'zero-sum game.'"

Philly had started thirty-five years earlier, fresh out of Stanford, with twenty-five thousand dollars of family money, ran it up to a half-million in six months, lost almost all in three. He was now working for a hedge fund. The words 'hedge fund' raised images of yachts and the lifestyle I hoped I would one day offer Leonora. What the fuck was a 'zero-sum' game?

I offered to buy Philly dinner at the New York deli on the corner which had black and white floor tiles that looked to be from the time of the Ark, an after-hours hangout for traders. He showed up at the quiet corner table in the back, for which I tipped the waiter a fifty, in his Zegna shirt and Salvatore Ferragamo loafers, wide-brimmed planter's hat with an almost as wide red and white ribbon circling the base, chewing on an unlit black cheroot. I told Leonora that night he was the only person I ever met who could talk non-stop while eating a six-inch high corned beef on rye without taking a breath.

I sat through a few of his stories before I could switch him to options where, he confided, the big bucks were made. But, he warned, for no one but brokers.

I didn't want to believe that. It was like being told there was no Santa Claus. "What most people don't understand," he continued, holding his sandwich in one hand and his cheroot in the other, "is what a 'zero-sum game' is."

He wiped a blob of mustard from his chin and continued. "Ask option traders, even those who should know better, and you'll find them convinced that if they select options scientifically, or set up the right spreads or butterflies, or other complex arcane combinations, they can turn a few bucks into millions."

He looked around to see if anyone was listening, dipped the end of his cheroot into his beer, slurped it up, and continued, "What they don't realize is, boiled down to its simplest state, an option is a bet, just like one you place in a casino. Bet a dollar on Number 5. If the little white ball falls into that slot in the roulette wheel, the casino pays you $32.

"In a casino, it's the casino that covers your bet. But when you buy an option, it's not a casino that covers your bet, it's another options trader. For an option to exist, there must be a buyer willing to buy and a seller willing to sell at terms both agree to. Think, if there is another investor on the other end of an option trade, why would he be willing to agree to be paid a small payment, called a premium, to cover a bet that could cost him millions?

"For example, with IBM selling for $50 a share, if you wanted to bet its price would rise, you might offer to pay $2 to buy shares at $50 for a period of, say, six months, and look for someone willing to sell that option to you. If IBM rose to $60 within that period of time, you would have the right to buy the stock from the one who sold the option for $50, sell the stock on the market for $60, and make a profit of $8, after allowing for the $2 you paid for the option. That's a profit of 400%.

"It seems complicated, but in truth it's not. Years ago, if you had wanted to buy that option, you would have placed an ad in the newspapers offering to buy it, hoping to find someone willing to sell it. In 1973, the CBOE, The Chicago Board of Options Exchange, set up to put buyers and sellers together – for a small fee – and option trading became easy. Billions of contracts now trade each year on the exchange.

"The question to now ask is why anyone would want to take the other side of that bet? The answer, of course, is that the seller believes that $2 a share is more than that option is worth.

"What you see then is that option trading is a 'zero-sum game.' If an option is 'perfectly' priced, neither the buyer nor the seller has an advantage."

I had looked at him. What fairy tale was this?

Philly drained the last of the pitcher. I was tempted to look under the table to see if beer was leaking from a hollow leg. He caught the look and his wide mouth spread even wider as he chuckled, spraying foam on the table and me.

"Perfectly priced? How can there be such a thing?" I asked skeptically, blotting my face with a bar napkin.

"That," he went on, "is what quants, statisticians, spend their full time trying to determine. It's all based on probabilities, how volatile the stock and the market is at the time, not on crystal balls, not on an attempt to predict whether the stock, or the market, is likely to rise or fall. It's no different than in the casinos. The odds casinos offer have nothing to do with the future, whether you are on a hot or losing streak.

"But...and it's a big but! Here's the 'gotcha.' If an option is perfectly priced, not only has neither side an advantage, but both sides are at a disadvantage.

"Imagine. All the millions and millions – even billions – of options bought and sold each day. Both sides smelling roses, but the only one always smelling roses is the broker. It's no different than in a casino; the house always wins. The broker collects commission from the buyer and the seller... AND earns interest on the cash, stock, gold or what have you, the seller must post to cover the potential loss he could incur.

"What is amusing is that brokers offer sophisticated mathematical algorithms without charge to allow you to select option combinations, spreads, butterflies, strangles and others, in which you both buy and sell options on the same stock that offer the advantage that if one side of the combination doesn't pay off, the other side will. Which, at its common denominator, is like betting head and tails on the flip of a coin–and paying for the privilege to do so."

"Hey, young fellow," Philly grinned, waving to the waiter for another pitcher of beer and a side of French fries, *"you look like I just told you there's no Santa Claus."*

Jaime laid the diary aside, got up, stretched, and lingered at the sideboard, refilling his cup. The room was thinning out. The father and his two children were gone, in their place a couple who didn't look old enough to vote, the fellow a stringy six feet, with a narrow bony face, three-day beard and unkempt black hair hanging unevenly over the collar of his black leather jacket. The girl, a foot shorter, so thin there was hardly a bump in her Madonna tee shirt for breasts, was looking at him through innocent green eyes as if for approval.

Christ, he wondered, *were they runaways?*

He let out the air he had been holding in a gust of disgust, looked around again, anything to keep from considering the dark thought that had been nagging him as he read his father's journal. Afraid to let it form, to recognize it, he went back to his seat determining to blank his mind on anything but what his father had written.

Desire, wrote Thomas Merton, an American Catholic, born in France in 1915 and died in Bangkok in 1968, a poet and mystic who lived as a Trappist monk in the Abbey of Gethsemani in Kentucky, leads to a fulfillment whose limits extend to infinity. Confucius said, "Desire to succeed, the will to win, the urge to reach your full potential… these are the keys that will unlock the door to personal excellence." "Human behavior," Plato said, "flows from three main sources: desire, emotion, and knowledge." Epictetus, born a slave in Greece in AD 50, wrote that when a person achieves his proper place in life, he does not desire anything beyond it. Why then, he asked, would you strut before us as if you had swallowed a ramrod?

I can tell you desire is none of that: Desire is a monster that devours you.

Leonora and I were like two kids, in bed and out of bed. We had friends, we traveled, we discovered off-the-beaten-path eateries, sampled exotic cuisines, surprised each other with little kooky gifts, Every Day is Valentine's Day, a calendar with a giant ♥ in each day, a gift-wrapped nighty For Naughty Girls, an illustrated Bed Time Menu. At night she might be a virgin in a convent clutching her thin chemise close, a one-eyed pirate in black boots, cocked hat, and saber, a hippie in mini-skirt, boots and ponytail, a high school cheerleader with pompoms, her imagination boundless. I was her mustachioed lothario, bold adventurer, sweaty circus roustabout, favorite uncle on her mother's side. But beneath the play-acting, there were genuine feelings. We had become a family, her imp of a son Sydney, infuriating at times, maddening at others, a little rascal that had only to let his lopsided mischievous grin loose could melt us. By four he was a skilled negotiator: we'd look daggers at him but the little beggar knew we were grinning behind our hands.

I was going to be Leonora's Mr. Darcy, her lover, her hero, a financial advisor to her friends in the synagogue in which she was Sisterhood President, in which I was now a member of the finance committee. It was the promise I made, the promise I was going to keep.

B G & S, Bellingham, Gottschalk & Sullivan, was small potatoes, a pygmy next to Merrill Lynch and Bear Stearns which were coining money in the booming real estate market selling sub-prime real estate debentures to its clients, along with firms as reputable as Goldman Sachs, whose top executives included a President of the World Bank, and others who sat on the President's Council of Economic Advisors. Debentures are rated AAA to D. Ratings of B+ or better are considered 'Prime,' or 'Investment Grade,' suitable for investors seeking acceptable risk. Lower grades, offering proportionally greater interest income, offer greater risk. 'Sub-prime' is a Wall Street salesman's invention that focuses investors on the word 'Prime' or 'Investment Grade,' without defining how far below the quality is.

Madeline LaFontaine, our cynical fiftyish institutional account manager likened it to 'Contrarianism' and 'zero-coupon convertibles.' I stood forewarned, as did the rest of our guys, but if sub-prime debentures were suited to be sold to clients of Goldman Sachs and others, how could we have expected they weren't worthy of ours.

...but as Fanny Price said at the end of Mansfield Park, "It could have turned out differently, I suppose."

"But it didn't."

***

Could I have known? Was there a sign I could have seen? When I think back now, so many years later, at how I had lived my life before I met Leonora, living solely for myself, in denial of any obligation to others, my wife, my son, even to Marsha, could I have foreseen that when I did what I promised, turned my life around, became a man Leonora could be proud of, a respected member of the congregation, when everything I dreamt of was falling into place, it was *too late, that as Plutarch had warned The mills of the gods grind slowly – but grind exceedingly fine.*

Squirreling back down in his seat, putting the cup aside, feeling himself growing more and more pissed, he turned his attention back to the diary thinking, *What a fucking world this has become.*

It had been a heady feeling, working not only for my good but for the family I loved, as well as for our friends and neighbors. I hadn't been able to wait to get home at night, to feel that at last I was no longer the drone I once was.

At work, we believed we were pretty fine fellows, congratulating each other with a 'low five,' a secret handshake, Robert Redford's side of the nose, forefinger flick. Everything we touched turned to gold. Our shoes barely touched the ground when we walked.

It's funny now when I look back, the different perspective I have, how I see what I should have seen approaching the year 2008, my eighth anniversary with Leonora and Barclay, Goodman & Seiden. I thought I had learned so much.

If I am to be accused of being bitter, I believe I had a right to be. I thought I understood it. We all did. But as we discovered too late, nobody on Wall Street did.

The signs were there, but by the end of that summer of 2008, when the heat had broken and children were going back to school, the smug, congratulatory winks we exchanged were no longer there. Nobody really understands stocks, we knew, except for the vague notion that prices relate to earnings. But bonds had been our business; we did our homework and believed we understood bonds. And certainly if not us, Goldman Sachs, Bank of America and Morgan Stanley.

The afternoon it all came down we sat around, trying to find some way to dispel the gloom. The shades were drawn, more from letting anyone see us than for us to see them. Someone lit a cigarette, quickly snuffed it out, though no one objected, even seemed to care. We were already dead. How did it matter? Someone else attempted a joke, but it fell flat. Even the twisted digs we zinged at each other that could always be counted on to get a rise fell flat.

As we sat in the gathering gloom, Nathaniel Seiden, the senior managing partner, came to tell us what we already knew: the firm was shutting its doors. He had helped start the firm fifty years before, working from the kitchen of the tiny two-room apartment he shared with his wife Evelyn and his infant son Robin. His personal fortune, which he put up as collateral as prices of the sub-

prime debentures slid to almost zero, was wiped out. As he made his way to the table in the trading room, hunched over, robbed of four inches of his five foot ten, gone was the undaunted spirit that had always been in his eyes, the ruddiness in his cheeks, the image of a southern gentlemen he projected from a more civilized era. Never before had we seen him, even on dress-down Fridays, minus the crisp white handkerchief in his jacket, his tie in a perfect Windsor, his suit knife-edged fresh.

The five of us sat silently, barely breathing, aware that for all our pain, what he faced was worse. He looked his age; he didn't have the energy to start over. We didn't know if he had come to say something to us, or if he had numbly followed his footsteps to those responsible.

For a full five minutes he sat with us in that wake, head down, staring unseeingly at the tape, fingering the table's polished mahogany surface, imprinting it in his memory before saying what he came to say.

When the words came, they were so low we sneaked looks at each other, not sure if they were meant for us or were a product of exhaustion.

"J'accuse!"

We stole looks at each other. It had been our department that had taken positions in the sub-prime debentures, bought and sold them, inventoried them.

Mr. Seiden shook his head again. "J'accuse," he uttered once again, staring unseeingly at some indistinguishable pattern in table, not in fury, not in anger, but in exhausted resignation.

As he spoke, the walls echoed his words, the vapor in the room rose, perspiration dripped from under our arms, just as he had seen it drip from under the arms of ten old men swathed in taluses in a minion reciting the prayer for the dead.

He looked over us with weary, unfocused eyes, shook his head, began to gather himself up, like a marionette pulled up by invisible strings, started disjointedly for the door as if in pain; turned back to take it all in for the last time, and left.

I wondered, as he headed off, head down, eyes vacant, if he heard Pagliacci cry out in fury and despair as his young wife fell dead at his feet, his knife in her heart, "La commedia è finite." ("The comedy is over.")

Had he thought how like us that opera was, a traveling troupe of actors, how the leading character, a clown, learns it had all been an illusion, that it was not an act, that in real life he had been deceived, and with the audience looking on, as the curtain falls, he cries out in rage and despair, "La commedia è finite."

***

It was some years later, when it was too late to do anything but mourn, that I would have liked to tell Mr. Seiden that he had been indeed correct.

J'accuse! We had thought he had meant it for us. He had not. Nor had he meant it for the thieves who colluded in the mortgage swindle, though he might have included the robber barons who ordered underlings to raise credit ratings to enable lenders to write worthless mortgages, nor was it meant for those who purchased the worthless mortgages, shredded them, reassembled the pieces into unrecognizable packages, sprinkled in shreds of investment grade bonds, like con men of old salting worthless mines, and coined the term 'sub-prime' to mislead the unwary, nor had he meant the bond rating agencies, Standard and Poor's and Moody's, who were paid to award the bonds inflated ratings, though they deserved it too, nor had it been meant for those who knowingly sold those bonds to unwary clients even as they bet they would fail, though they deserved it too.

As we discovered later, what he saw was rather more diabolical. White-collar crime was tacitly sanctioned; it was a profit center for the U.S. government. Not one of the principals who had a role in the scheme was subsequently prosecuted. The government had no interest in turning the spigot on a lucrative source of revenue. In the year 2000, the Securities Exchange Commission collected fines $490 million; during the next twelve years the annual take grew steadily reaching $3.1 billion in 2012, an annual rate of growth of approximately 17%; during that same span, the Commission's operating budget grew from $380 million to $1.4billion, an annual rate of over 11%. The Justice Department, not to be outdone, played an identical game.

***

I was left thinking where it had begun: my father bought a goat for two zuzim.

I had lived without regrets during the years before, but when I tried to stand up and be counted, I betrayed Leonora. There was nowhere for the two of us to hide. People who had once been our friends smiled politely as they passed us, but I had become persona non grata.

The pain I saw in Leonora's eyes when we went to services dug into me like a cancer. Friends she had grown up with, whom she had known her entire life, were too polite to shun her. Being tolerated was worse.

Her home was sold out from under her, her son Sydney, who I once believed had grown close, turned on me. "What do you need him for?" I heard him. "You don't abandon someone because he's down. He's not evil, it wasn't his fault." But what we had could not be recovered.

I thought of all the uncaring things I had done in my life, and much as I would rather not, I saw that for once it would be better for Leonora and her son, who I loved as a son, if I was cut out of their life, so she'd have to make excuses for me no more. When there seemed no other way, after a sleepless night I told her. It was the one decent thing I could do in my life, to take myself off. In the few months she had aged thirty years. Neither of could staunch the tears. I would try to find work somewhere, and as soon as I was settled, I would call for her and Sydney to join me. We would take him out of school and start over.

But as I stowed my things in my car that morning and hugged her awkwardly saying goodbye, I think we both knew it was the end for us.

A large part of the money she had received from Ben's insurance that she had put away for Sydney's education would go to pay off debts we had run up this past year when my earnings crumbled, her circumstances would be greatly reduced; Sydney would have to be taken out of private school.

I was miserable, leaving misery in my wake. I had been born under a black cloud. I tried to do good, succeeded only in bringing misery. No more would I try.

As I said before, if I am bitter, I believe I have a right to be. In 2016, Mike Offit wrote the book Nothing Personal based on the sub-prime mortgage debacle. He may have taken the title from a line in the movie You've Got Mail. When Tom Hank's discount bookstore drives Meg Ryan's small bookstore out of business, he tells her, "It wasn't personal."

"It wasn't personal to you," Meg replied, "but it was personal to me."

What went down in the sub-prime debenture market may not have been personal to Offit. But it was personal to me, and to a lot of people.

***

When I think back now, so many years later, at how I had lived my life before I met Leonora, living solely for myself, in denial of any obligation to others, my wife, my son, even to Marsha, could I have foreseen that when I did what I promised, turned my life around, became a man Leonora could be proud of, a respected member of the congregation, when everything I dreamt of was falling into place, it was too late, that Plutarch had warned the mills of the gods grind slowly – but grind exceedingly fine.

Chapter 35

Exhausted, emotionally spent, Jaime pushed the diary from him, barely registering the homogenized, impersonal breakfast room in which he was sitting. The anger at his father he had worn like a cancer all these years turned into fury, a fury so intense, so searing, he consciously shut down, unable and unwilling to deal with all the emotions pressing in on him, suffocating him. Worse, for a brief moment, he had been conned. When he read of his father's arrival in Charleston, and the pledge he made to turn his life around, to stand up and be counted for, to be there for the people who were supposed to mean something to him, he had begun to see him not as a two-dimensional cardboard cutout, a stick-figure devoid of character, devoid of conscience, devoid of decency, a man who never had a thought for anyone but himself, but human, a three-dimensional figure with all the qualities humans have, good and bad, only to find himself even more furious, furious at himself, furious for allowing himself to be taken in, to believe that underneath, deep down, his father had qualities he could be proud of. But in the end, he turned into the man he believed him to be all along, blaming everyone but himself for his failures, for the unhappiness he left in his wake, blaming fate, kismet, karma…and even the government, and for leaving him to clean up after him, so he could die with a clear conscience.

He let out the fetid air he had been holding in a gust of disgust, looked around again, desperate for anything to keep from recognizing the dark thoughts that had been nagging him. What of his father had become him? Had the acorn not fallen far from the tree? Had he given a thought to Chenny when he left? Had his promises to Susan not been empty?

His breath caught in his throat. He raised his head, caught his reflection in the window. The irises of his eyes were black pinpoints. He was shaking. His face was dark, his hair disheveled. He looked like a wild man.

"Are you all right?"

He spun around, wondered if he imagined the words. He had been tearing up packets of sugar from the bowl and emptying them on the table. The young

143

waitress was staring at him, her eyes wide, alarmed, as if wondering if he might be having a seizure; if she should call someone for help.

He gulped an involuntary gasp of air, realized his fists were clenching and unclenching. He forced a deeper breath, pried his fingers open, stretched the muscles in his face, and twisted his neck. "I'm…*O.K,*" he managed, pushing the diary away as if it were toxic.

"You sure?" she asked, her eyes going uncertainly to the diary then to him.

He realized how he must have frightened her. Everyone in the room had left. She was alone with him, probably waiting for him to finish cleaning up. She looked so concerned, he tried to smile to assure her, but it came out pained. Her eyes went from him to the diary again.

He worked at getting his breathing under control. He wanted to thank her, she looked so compassionate, so caring, but he didn't know how, or think it appropriate. "It's…" he tilted his head toward the journal. "…my father's diary."

She blinked in understanding. "Is he…?"

Jaime nodded, wiped at his nose with the back of his hand, the compassion he saw in her eyes triggering a response deep in him he didn't understand.

"If you want to talk about it…"

It startled him that she was grieving for him, that a stranger could feel like this for someone not close to her. She was wearing a fresh, starched pink and white waitress uniform, a white ruffled apron tied around her waist spotted with bits of the morning's breakfast. White, gum-soled shoes added a half-inch to her five foot six. Her red curly hair was tied neatly in a ponytail, she was slim, had green eyes, a snub nose, a blob of freckles, a wide generous mouth. Tiny crow's feet in the corners of her eyes belied the age of twenty-two or three he guessed at first, but she looked as if she should be out playing sandlot baseball.

She seemed unsure if it was appropriate to return the smile he attempted. When she did, the transformation was startling. Tiny lines fanned out from the corners of her eyes and swelled her cheeks, creating a glow of goodness he remembered seeing only once.

It had been in the army, a young Catholic nurse, five foot five, slim, but contradictorily, when he looked at her, he imagined someone as soft as a marshmallow. She had never given him the feeling, as he had with a Jewish girl he had dated, that she paraded her beliefs, but several times a day she would stop into church. When I asked why, she said, "To say hello to God." He had been afraid he could easily fall in love with her, but he had been at that foolish time in his life when he was concerned with what his mother and his aunts, her sisters, would think if he brought home a shiksa. How foolish he had been, and how he had kidded her: "If you really believe in Jesus," he teased, "how come you don't adopt his religion?"

"Oh, Jaime," she replied exasperated as if he was hopeless. In some ways, Chenny reminded him of her, someone he would always feel comfortable with.

He wasn't sure if he wanted to talk about it, but he desperately wanted to spend time with her. He peered up into her jade green eyes and felt the tension begin to ooze from him, the strain ease. "If you have time," he offered, hopefully, "I'd," he tilted his head in the direction of the coffee remaining coffee in the Silex coffee maker on the sideboard, "buy you a cup of coffee."

The smile on her face was all he hoped for. It was eleven fifteen when they looked up, the room was being prepared for lunch. He had told her something of why he was here, what he did, where he was going, but not till they had been talking for almost an hour did he feel comfortable enough to tell her of all that had happened in the ten days since he left Red Plains, his anger at his father, and even then, not for some time was he able to tell her of his fear that he had inherited his father's worst traits.

She listened so caringly, was so positive and upbeat, he was amazed when he discovered the life she had led. "I have loving parents," she said when she began to tell him about her life. "I grew up feeling safe, cared for...we respected each other, attended church together, talked about almost everything, what was moral, what wasn't, the difference between moral and ethical, how we are told God wants us to live our lives. All that ended when I was starting my senior year, the night, I awoke up and went downstairs to get a glass of milk."

The beatific expression on her face faded. "I was barefoot," she continued, her eyes haunted. "The stairs were carpeted. As I started down, I heard noises. Our neighbors had dinner with us. I thought they had left. I was in my pajamas and didn't want to be seen. I edged to the bottom of the stairs and peeked in. The living room was dark, but the light was coming from the dining room. I thought my parents and they were playing cards. The stereo was on softly. I remember the tune, a song my mother sang to me when I was an infant, 'My Funny Valentine,' My mother was in the living room, on the couch, naked...*doing it*...with our neighbor, my father was on the floor, next to the couch, with our neighbor's wife. I can't hear that song without seeing that."

The breath caught in her throat for a second, then, unexpectedly, she smiled. I couldn't understand how she could. In a way, she had been betrayed just as I had been. But she seemed undisturbed, at peace. Hadn't she felt deceived? To me, it would seem too awful to contemplate.

145

She must have seen it in my eyes, for she nodded, "I know. All the strict moral rules my parents and I talked of seemed…a sham, a fraud. I felt as if I was drowning. What was worse, I had to live with them, knowing what I knew.

"I handled it the only way I could. I shut down. 'What is it,' they asked, 'what's troubling you?' I forced myself to act as it was nothing, stuff in school. They were sure it was puberty, teenage stuff. I couldn't even tell my best friend Jessica.

"I began to sneak out at night when my parents were asleep. I'd climb down the trellis outside my window and spend the nights partying with boys. I got a reputation for being easy. One night, right before the end of my junior year, there was an end-of-the-term party at a lake, but when I went to climb out the window, it was nailed shut. I pretended I wasn't aware of it. So did my parents. But I no longer had the feeling I was their little girl as I'd pretended I was. When it was time to think of college, I told them I was sending off applications, but once I graduated high school, I announced that I was going to take a year off before college to travel with the money I had earned working after school that was supposed to pay some of my college expenses. There was a big to-do; arguing, pleading, yelling, but I just packed a backpack and left.

For the next three years I backpacked all over, by myself, with friends I met along the way, sometimes living on beaches, sometimes sharing rooms in hostels, sometimes sleeping under the stars, staying in one place only long enough to make a few dollars, enough to get me to the next place. In winters I headed for warm places, the Costa del Sol in southern Spain, I visited the Alhambra, one of the Seven Wonders of the World, went to Casa Blanca in Morocco, visited Lake Maggiore in northern Italy in the summer, saw the little mermaid on a rock on the waterside in Copenhagen. At the beginning of the third year I trekked across Europe to visit the Taj Mahal in Agra, the white marble mausoleum the emperor, Jahan, built in memory of his favorite wife, climbed the Great Wall in China, and ended up in a Tibetan Buddhist monastery in a tiny town in Nepal in the foothills of the Himalayas. I planned to stop there out of curiosity for a day or two or three, but I stayed six months, working and living with the monks in the ashram after the others I traveled with left, meditating and practicing Ashtanga yoga. It was there that I came to understand the Hindu philosophy dharma that changed my life."

Jaime couldn't keep his eyes off her as she spoke. Every part of her was alive, radiant, as if she was in the places she was describing, visiting them all over again. She had adopted the Hindu name, Arushi, which means first ray of the sun, and he imagined her sitting cross-legged in the asana yoga position in a field of yellow and red wildflowers in a lush valley in the Himalayas, facing east, waiting to greet the sun when it peeked over the mountains. Watching her, he had the sensation Carlos Castaneda wrote about, of 'seeing' someone, not their outer physical self, but their inner being, her compassion, the inner peace he saw when he first looked up from his father's diary.

"Dharma?" he asked. "It changed your life? How?"

"It was a process. I began by studying Ashtanga yoga. The monks, at first, were reluctant to accept that I was serious, not a dilettante, that I was willing to put in the effort to try to reach *satori,* 'enlightenment.' It's popular for westerners to come professing to want to become 'enlightened,' thinking of it as going to a restaurant and ordering a serving of the local specialty. Rarely will they accept any who hadn't already immersed themselves in the disciplines, that hadn't taken courses, had made it evident that they were willing to put in the work to achieve enlightenment, seeing one's true nature and the nature of the world.

"But I refused to quit, and eventually they agreed to help guide me. The road to enlightenment begins with this method of yoga, which involves synchronizing your breath with a progressive series of postures, a process that generates voluminous internal heat and profuse sweating with the intent of detoxifying the muscles and organs, improving circulation, and creating a lithe strong body and calm mind.

"Dharma, which means righteousness, morality, and ethics, in accordance with the Hindu scriptures for accomplishing material and spiritual goals and for the growth of the individual and society, as you might imagine, spoke to me. Its principles encompass all duties, individual, social, and religious, as well as adherence to the laws of the land. Not until I became immersed in it did I become aware of the contradiction, that 'moral' and 'social standards' varied from place to place, as well as from time to time.

"I questioned my teachers, but none could give me a satisfactory constant. Even 'Do unto others as you would have others do unto you,' the golden rule, failed the test, for what is moral to one may be immoral to others. I am sure I need not cite specific examples. You can think of many for yourself.

"It wasn't for some time until I could come up with one, the physician's creed, 'Do no harm.' But then I saw that even that was unsatisfactory. Would I not do harm to some by not doing harm to others?

"And in the end, I saw that enlightenment gave me the obligation to try not to judge, to 'see,' to understand that my parents weren't gods, that they weren't born parents, that they had compelling needs, but that they had always been there for me as well.

"In my mind, 'seeing,' understanding, was more important than the vapid concept of 'forgiveness.' I found that I could lose the anger that had weighed on me for all those years when I realized what was important, all the love that they had heaped on me. I had been loved but thought of nothing but the injury I believed they had done to me."

They sat a while in silence, each thinking his or her thoughts. The clock over the sideboard read 11:20. "How old are you?" Jaime asked.

Arushi looked at him, puzzled by the question. "Twenty-four."

"Could we talk some more?"

Arushi was ten years younger yet wiser than him.

"Are you waiting at lunch, or could you have lunch with me, or spend the afternoon or evening with me?"

Chapter 36

They spent the afternoon in Fredericksburg Alum Springs Park hiking wooded trails, climbing rocks, picking their way along a winding creek.

"I feel like I'm playing hooky," Jaime said. They had had separated themselves from clusters of hikers they passed on the trail. They made their way around huge boulders, fallen trees, debris and thick stands of oaks and elms that thinned as they reached the top of the mountain, left the cover of leaves behind, and were now stretched out on their backs on a flat rock on the top of a mountain, shielding their eyes from the hot afternoon sun beating down on them.

"Hooky? From what?"

She had changed into a pair of yellow shorts that fell just far enough to keep from chilling her essentials, had let her hair fall freely down her back, brushing wisps from her face stirred by the breeze, and wore a tee shirt that had been painted by disciples of Guru Shirashti, her spiritual guide. It showed him sitting cross-legged atop a rugged mountain in Nepal gazing into the beyond, his wrinkled skin polished mahogany. "The ashram sells these tees in a gift shop to 'nourish his body as he nourishes the acolytes' minds."

Kicking off her pink sneakers and lining them up with his on the rock, "As everywhere, as in Nepal, business is business."

"I'm not used to being unin-something," Jaime sighed. "I don't think I could sit quietly meditating for longer than sixty seconds."

Arushi levered herself up on one elbow and grinned at him as she might a young child building a fort with blocks. "You must accomplish an awful lot."

"Huh?" Jaime rolled on his side to look at her.

He wondered what was going on. Was Arushi just being herself, bantering, or was she flirting with him? She had changed into clothes that had him calculating, recalculating and recalculating again the driving time between Fredericksburg and Charleston. Women, he once heard, dress for women, but he wondered if whom they really dressed for was men. He was wearing tan shorts, a brown and tan knit shirt, sweat socks, and sneakers, the same clothes he wore at breakfast that morning.

"I've always wondered," he offered, a bit puzzled, "about the difference between men and women. I mean," he added hastily, "in the way they dress. Women always seem to put their best... *foot*...forward, so to speak," running his eyes up slowly, from her bare toes, lingering along the way, "but I've always felt that if a woman could take me when I was at my worst, I had a better chance."

Arushi made a show of thinking this over. "You mean, sometimes you're even more sparkling than you were this morning?"

Jaime grinned and lay back in a companionable silence, light breezes stirring the leaves on the trees on higher mountains in the west. Far below, the stream meandered peacefully on its journey, leaves and small branches hung up on rocks and fallen logs, eventually working free and floating on.

Late in the afternoon, when they made their way back to the car, Jaime ventured a thought that had been troubling since their talk this morning, "I've been trying to do what you did," he struggled, "but I can't see how."

"You mean how I scampered over the trail leaving you lagging way behind?"

Jaime made a show of opening the door for her. "That was chivalry."

"Aha!"

He shook his head. "No. What I meant was, I can see how you can...understand...accept...that what your parents did, were doing, they were not doing to you, but I can't see what my father did in the same light."

"I think," Arushi observed after some thought, "that the feelings that each of us has about our parents are so complex, and so difficult to sort out, that even a slight affront can overshadow everything they did for us."

"*Slight?*" Jaime balked at the word. He turned to Arushi awaiting a response, but when there was none, realized he hadn't said it aloud.

On the road heading for Charleston early the next morning, Jamie felt at ease for the first time since the phone call from Detective Spiros. He and Arushi had had dinner together and talked deep into the night. He wanted to spend the night with her and sensed she wanted it too, but somehow he felt it would trivialize their time together. It had been an odd experience in so many ways. Everything about Arushi was alive, exciting; yet with her, he had a feeling of deepest peace, as if he was in the presence of Guru Shirashti, her spiritual guide in Nepal.

What Arushi had said when they returned to the car yesterday afternoon, after they climbed down from the mountain, touched a memory, one he had pushed away, covered over, of the weekend when he was six, the week before his father had left and hadn't returned. He and his father had set off by themselves early Saturday morning heading west on Route 80 for the campground at the National Recreation Area at the Delaware Water Gap at the western edge of New Jersey near the Delaware River. Driving along now, down I-95, with mile after mile of concrete road streaming by, trees and rocks and shrubs bordering both sides, he remembered how excited he had been, a weekend camping, just he and his father. It had been a beautiful spring day. The sky was cerulean…they had made up rhymes, cerulean, shoe-lean, fool-lean, the temperature was edging up to eighty, they had a two-man pup tent, a hamper packed with ice, steaks, beans, beer, soda, bread…but when they arrived discovered that all the campsites had been reserved.

His father waggled his eyebrows, "No problem, mon!" he grinned, "for a pair of pirates – *like us*. C'mon, we'll find a place on the mountain away from everyone, like Black Bart, and pitch our tent. Campsites are for sissies."

They drove as far as road went, left the car, grabbed their stuff, he took what he could, his father took the rest, climbed halfway up the mountain and pitched their tent on a patch of level ground, cleared away rocks, pebbles and twigs under the tent, spread leaves for a 'hunter's' mattress, dug a trench around the tent to channel water away in case of rain, dug a pit, a 'woodsman's refrigerator,' lined it with rocks, stored the meat, soda and beer in it, laced branches and dirt over it to keep animals away, built a circle of rocks, gathered branches, roasted a steak for each of them over a fire of branches, the open can of beans on the fringe of the fire bubbled, all the time laughing and joking, just like pirates.

It was the best steak and beans he ever ate. They toasted marshmallows, his father started a story about a pirate ship, he continued it, then his father – it went back and forth. The stars were twinkling when he crawled into the tent and went to sleep while his father stayed up tending the fire.

In the middle of the night, his father roused him from a sound sleep. "C'mon Me Bucko," he laughed, "we gotta vamoose." A raging storm had hit. Rain was pouring down the side of the mountain washing over the trench they built, streaming under the tent. Our 'mattress' and blanket were soaked, it was dark as pitch, all the stars that had been there earlier disappeared. They grabbed their flash lights, blanket and tent – left the pegs, the food, sodas, the beer in the woodsman's 'refrigerator' – wondered if anyone ever found them – scrambled down the mountain, sliding over rocks and limbs in the pouring rain, wet and miserable.

It was the happiest time he ever remembered.

He drove along, reliving it, awakening feelings he didn't want to awake, turned on the radio to a talk station that faded in an out, tried to concentrate on what the DJ was saying. The happy mood Arushi left him with faded.

It was almost ten hours after he left Fredericksburg that he checked into the Jasmine House Inn in the heart of Charleston's historic district after breaking for a lunch of barbecue, hush puppies, and beer in Fayetteville, North Carolina.

Chapter 37

When Jaime finally found his way through the maze of streets in the historic district to reach the Inn on Hasell Street, he thought he might be hallucinating; somewhere on the way south, he had made a right turn instead of a left. He'd only seen it in pictures and photographs, but instead of Charleston, he was in New Orleans. The Inn, three-story, cream-colored brick, with a large, white double-door entrance, had tall, floor to ceiling windows on the second level leading out onto delicately scrolled wrought-iron balconies.

His large brass room key opened on a room with a pale blue motif with a step-up, queen-sized four-poster bed between tall bedside lamps. The floor to ceiling French window he'd seen from the street opened onto the wrought-iron balcony, there was a pale cream brick fireplace with an ornate-carved marble mantle, a dark blue upholstered Queen Anne armchair comfortable enough to daydream in, and on the wide-planked wood floor, a hooked scatter rug in a concoction of blue tones Monet might have imagined.

He laid his overnighter on the antimacassar on the dresser, dug a pair of swim shorts from the bag, shucked his clothes in a heap on the vanity chair in the marble bath, slid on the slippers waiting next to the glassed-in shower, tossed a warm terry towel over his shoulders, and headed down to the pool behind the Inn. Stretching out on a lounge at the pool, he ordered a mint julep —worked his muscles, unknotting eight-hundred miles of stiffness and fatigue, and considered how best to begin the search for Leonora or her son Sydney.

It had been ten years since his father left Charleston. Leonora's son Sydney, two years old when he met her, would now be twenty-one, old enough to be out of high school and in college. Leonora would be in her forties. In the intervening years, she might have remarried or moved. The place to start, he thought, would be in the high school, but if that failed, the rabbi – or possibly an older member of one of synagogues – might have kept in touch with them, or would know where to find them. A high school, and the largest synagogue, Temple Kahal Kadosh Beth Elohim, mentioned in his father's diary, were only a few blocks away in the historic district.

Weary from the drive, reliving the day he spent with Arushi, he considered sitting cross-legged on the lounge chanting *Om,* decided he'd skip the cross-legged bit and chant *Om* in the room in his shower. The clothes he'd worn failed to pass the college 'sniff test,' but a look at prices on the Inn's laundry list prompted a less demanding 're-test' and he set off for Waterfront Park, a ten-minute walk.

It appeared to be girl's night out. Bars and restaurants were elbow to elbow with women, most so young, in outfits du jour, sundresses that left little to the imagination, he felt like a grandfather. One young woman was in lace, see-through shorts and tiny top suspended with spaghetti straps. A couple of young women eyed him and turned back to chat and gossip. *Damn*, he thought, shrugging. *I'm either losing it – or I should have sprung for the laundry.*

More tired than he realized, he found an empty table overlooking the water on the patio of the Fleet Landing Restaurant, a glassed-in cross between the Palace of Versailles and a waterfront dive, ordered a pint of the local craft beer and the house specialties, Low Country Seafood Gumbo with Andouille Sausage, okra and rice, followed by Crispy Whole Fried Southern Flounder with Apricot Glaze, looked over the dessert menu, skipped it, and headed straight back to the Inn.

With the money his father left, he could now allow himself an occasional indulgence, but at the prices the Inn charged, he couldn't bring himself to use their laundry. Instead, he stood wearily over the sink, washing enough underwear, tee shirts, and socks to last a day, or possibly two, until he could find a Laundromat – then blow-dried the clothes with the Inn's hairdryer. It made no sense, but he couldn't bring himself to spend the money, even remembering how the family laughed the Sunday his aunt's parents, his great aunt and uncle, Rosie and Hymie, flew home from Miami Beach.

Born in Europe, dirt poor, they immigrated to the States as teenagers, met, married, and with hardly a penny between them, began life living in the back of a store on Bathgate Avenue in the Bronx, working into the night sewing bits of cloth on buttons for mattresses they sold in the shop in front. In time, their storefront business grew, becoming the largest bedding manufacturer in New York City.

Both now were gray and wrinkled. Rosie walked painfully on legs gnarled with varicose veins hidden under heavy tan cotton socks rolled at the top over her heavy thighs. Hymie's shoulders were knotted from years of hard labor. They had learned English, but flavored their speech with Yiddish. Rosie called her grandchildren *Dollink,* Hymie, feisty as he must have been in his youth, would stand in front of his TV ranting at the posturing *meshugenah* wrestlers.

That Sunday the first buds of spring were just showing on the trees when his mother took him on a bus across the George Washington Bridge to welcome them home from Miami Beach. Their apartment was on 189th St. and Fort Washington Avenue, one block south of Fort Tryon Park, the highest point in Manhattan, a fifteen-minute walk from the bus terminal. Hymie was raging, going on and on at Rosie, a Yiddish rant that was somewhere between an *Oy* and an *Oy Veh*. The airline had charged them more than a hundred dollars overweight. When he opened one of the suitcases, he found six quart cans of orange juice. "They were on sale," Rosie explained righteously.

We all had a good laugh, but two years later, on a sweltering day in July, she schlepped her full wire shopping cart up the long hill from Broadway, suffered a stroke and died. The supermarket had run a sale. Saving pennies was a habit that had once had given her life meaning.

Jaime awoke exhausted after more than eight hours of sleep, his roller-coaster days exacting a toll. When he was six, after his father left, he had shut down, determined to never let anyone in again, never again feel anything for anyone. He never had but for that brief moment, when he met Susan. It was a mistake. He saw the message in her eyes the morning he left. It was one more disappointment in a life of one long series of disappointments. Since he left, he felt like he was going through the motions, putting one foot in front of the other. All the people he had met since leaving Red Plains had been intent on giving him advice, telling him how to fix his life. He felt like he had been watching a continuous stream of TV commercials, deliriously happy families, black, white, yellow, smiling, laughing, beaming at the camera having discovered the secret to a supremely happy life, Kellogg's Corn Flakes, Preparation H, Tide washing detergent, a drug with an unpronounceable name with thirty-seven side effects you shouldn't take if you are pregnant, believe you might be or planning to become pregnant.

Doggedly, he dried a few spots on the shorts that were still damp, put on the freshly cleaned clothes, had breakfast in the dining room, eggs, grits, and biscuits, and set off heading into the slanting morning sun for the nearest high school, the North Charleston High on Montagu Street, a ten-block walk under a sparkling blue sky.

North Charleston High School proved to be a yellowish brick building with a covered portico leading from the curb to double glass front doors that opened with a push bar. A young monitor seated inside, after a few questions, pointed him to the office down a long empty hallway stacked with green lockers along the walls. Classes were in session, he could hear voices behind the wood doors on both sides.

Jaime stopped behind the waist high island trying not to look pushy. Three minutes, or a bit more passed, until the woman flicked her hair from her face, let out an exasperated sigh, and turned to him with a harried look. Turning on his most hopeless smile, he began, "Ms. Wilkerson? I wonder if you can help me locate a boy who may be a student here or might have been in the past. His name is Sydney Goldbloom, his mother's name was Leonora Goldbloom. The last information I have of them was ten years ago when Sydney would have been eleven. It's possible that his mother since remarried and that both she and her son took her new husband's name. Sydney would be twenty-one now," he added unnecessarily, realizing he was babbling.

The woman began to rise from her chair in obvious pain, slid back down, and rubbed her brow. "I'd have to check our records. I don't know anyone by that name, but it's possible he may be in our files. Why are you trying to locate him?"

Jaime wasn't certain how much information he should give her, but he didn't see a need for secrecy. "I'm Jaime Frommer. My father lived with Sydney and her mother ten years ago. In his will he left something for Sydney…it's sort of…I don't know, it's a crazy story…if you have time, I can tell it to you but in his will, he designated me as his executor and asked me to find Sydney and give it to him. My father's name was Aaron Frommer, but he also used the name Allen Fisher, and may have used others."

She seemed to consider this, but the uncertainty in her gray eyes was evident behind her oversized lenses. "I'm not sure I can give out that information without authorization."

From the way she said it, Jaime sensed she wanted to but, because of some vague rules, couldn't. "I have a copy of the instructions my father left in his diary," he offered, pulling the translation from a folder he had with him, "if you'd like…"

She pushed back in her chair, eyed the document as if afraid it might burst into flames.

"Do you have records that go back that far?" Jaime tried. "If you do, if you could tell me if he was ever enrolled here and transferred out, it would help… By the way…" Ms. Wilkerson shifted about, making it clear she was anxious to get rid of him – "…I was, I mean I was going to say that I'm a teacher, an assistant professor, at Red Plains College…in Nebraska…I mean if you want to verify…who I…"

Ms. Wilkerson swiveled in her seat, pushed her hair back from her forehead, and then looked up at the clock on the wall. "Could you come back…"

Jaime started to edge away from the counter but stopped, determined to give it one more shot. "Would it take very long, I mean to do a quick search?"

She looked up at the clock again. "I guess," she conceded reluctantly. "We computerized our records five years ago. They go back only a dozen years."

Working the mouse on the desk, she clicked a desktop icon. "What did you say his name was?"

"Sydney Goldbloom. Sydney spelled S-y-d-n-e-y."

Ms. Wilkerson lowered her eyeglasses, peered over the top of the frames, studied the screen, typed a few letters, and ran her eyes over the screen that came up. "Sydney Goldbloom?"

Jaime took a breath. "Is he there?"

Ms. Wilkerson nodded. "Yes. His record shows that he was a student in his freshman year in 2010. But there's no record of him returning for his sophomore year."

"Does it show if his records were transferred?"

"No. Someone, apparently his mother, picked up a copy."

"Does it show his last known address?"

"1121 McCantes Drive. I believe that's out near Patriot's Point."

Chapter 38

"Hi," Jaime called. "It's the peri-pathetic traveler."

Chenny was bending over her computer, her face alive. "I've been wondering how you're doing. By the way, the word is *peripatetic*."

"No. Not in my case. It's peri-*pathetic.*"

Chenny's brightness faded reflecting his tone. Her eyes swung about, as if searching for words of comfort, widened as they settled back and peered more closely. "*Hey!*" she demanded. "Put something on. You'll catch a chill."

"Oh shit! I didn't think they had Skype in Red Plains."

The delight leaped back into Chenny's face. "It's hard to keep up. I know. Last week the icemen went on strike when the appliance store put in electric refrigerators… So?" she asked, "what have you been up to?"

"Up to? Up to my ears. I feel like I've been playing Pokémon GO, traveling between the real world and the virtual world of Pokémon. I just came from the Oneg Shabat, the coffee and Danish shtick after the Friday night services at the Synagogue here in Charleston. It's almost an exact scaled down replica of the Acropolis… I could have been in Greece, but the reception was so frosty it felt like the Arctic Circle."

"Charleston? Greece? The Arctic Circle? I thought you were heading for Philadelphia."

"Call me Gulliver. Been there. Done that. I've been all over… *Hey!* What's what? You're all gussied up. Did I call at a bad time? It's seven there now, isn't it? On your way out?"

"It's OK. I still have time. Noah's picking me up at eight."

Noah. The high school PE teacher and football team coach. BMOC. *Do they still use that term, or is it antediluvian?* He called him Chief Tomahawk. He had the sharply planed features of his ancestors, bronzed skin, zero-point-two ounces of body fat, wide evenly defined cheekbones, inset dark eyes under ledges, was an inch taller and a couple of years younger than him. Why should it bother him?

"Noah?" he repeated, mugging. "You're going to a powwow?"

Chenny's eyes sparkled mischievously. "Perhaps," she tossed back blithely.

"So," she picked up after allowing time for him to play with it, "why Charleston…and what became of Philadelphia?"

Jaime cursed mentally, rearranging his face. He should not have skyped. He should have stuck to e-mail so he could edit his words and his expressions. Chenny's eyes were boring into him. The conversation wasn't going the way he saw it in the script. There was an edge to her voice he'd never heard. Where was the easy-going, comfortably compliant Chenny he knew and the TLC he expected. He rubbed his chin with his open fist, using the short time gap to rearrange his face once again. "Hey!" he demanded, switching gears, turning the page in the script he rehearsed, "hold on. Your mom. How's she doing?"

The mischievous smile disappeared from Chenny's face as quickly as it had appeared. Her eyes turned sober. "She's…upbeat…" she conceded reluctantly. "She… she doesn't let on. But I can see that the chemo gets to her. She tries to hide how tired she is and smiles through the pain. Her oncologist is in Omaha, but there's a clinic in Lincoln I take her to for tests every other Friday. They have oral chemo now. It's a blessing…otherwise I'd have to take her to Omaha for treatments and she'd have to have a port in her chest to administer it. She has another four weeks of chemo to go, then five weeks of radiation at the radiological clinic in Lincoln. My mom complains she'd have been better off going to Sam Mahonatac, the Lakota medicine man…I know she says that to get a rise out of me… 'you mean,' I oblige, 'if he took insurance,' and that sets her off. 'You young people think you know everything. Let me tell you, Ms., I've seen things hard to explain. Call it what you will, the mind's healing powers, positive thinking, spirits of our ancestors. Sam believes that there are objects that possess spiritual or prehistoric powers…like the medicine bundle, a sack carrying items the owner believes important, rocks, feathers, a picture of parent, a child, whatever.' And for a minute, she forgets the agony she's going through, worrying about what will become of me rather than for herself."

Jaime smiled. He could visualize her lined face and white hair…he was afraid to ask if she still had her hair. She was of old, pioneer stock, raw-boned, wide hips, feet planted flat on the ground, wore boots, had startling clear, pale blue eyes that lit up and came alive when she spoke about those days as if she could still see them. How much was gospel and how much actually happened he was never sure for her stories included bits and pieces Tom Sawyer wrote about in mining camps, gold strikes, jumping frogs in Calaveras County, but he listened wide-eyed – he had pointed out once that Tom Sawyer wrote that same thing, but she just nodded, ''Course he did, I told him of it,' and went right on about how '…her grandpa and ma, young and hopeful, headed west on a wagon train intendin' to sell breeches and shovels and supplies to the miners in 'Roaring' camp, but the brace broke two miles from right where I'm standin', and before we could spit, the heathen Indians surrounded the wagon train, intent on murder, for all we knew the heathees was cannibals, but the Chief's daughter got a gander at the wagon train leader and…'

"Please tell her I'm thinking good thoughts for her. I don't know if you follow golf, but Phil Mickelson, one of the top golfers in the world, a real crowd favorite and a devoted husband…when his wife got breast cancer, he dropped off the tour for nine months to stay home and care for her…and she's pulled through. I hope your mom will too…"

As he was speaking, Chenny's eyes had teared up. "…oh gee…" Jaime sighed, "I'm…sorry…"

"I know…thanks," Chenny said, swiping at her tears with the back of her hand. "Please…go on, tell me what you've been up to. My mom's been following your…peregrinations… It sounds like they haven't been all that much fun either."

Jaime stifled a grim expression, wondering if his travels and the things he'd seen had been woven into her grandmother's adventures. He rubbed his forehead, not sure how to answer. "It's…it's hard to put into words," he finally allowed. He had wanted to tell somebody, had really wanted to tell Chenny – but didn't want to say anything that might hurt her. There never had been any talk of a commitment – but don't-ask, don-t tell to him seemed…what you'd expect from a politician.

"I've," he began when he found the words, "I've been on an emotional roller coaster, one minute up, the next minute down. I felt as if something was compelling me to go on with this, but I didn't really want to."

"Maybe," Chenny interrupted, "it was because it was a way to get to know your father, to get an understanding of why he did what he did."

Was that why he was doing it, Jaime wondered, chewing on his lip. If it was, what the fuck had he hoped, to confirm that he was the son of a bitch he always believed him to be, or that there was a real reason for what he did and that he had always really loved him?

"I don't know," he allowed reluctantly, not wanting to think if it might be so.

Jaime went on, trying to pick and choose what to say, what to leave out, in a way wanting to relive it all with Chenny, who he saw, what he did, how knotted up he had been when he set out fearing the reception he'd receive from families his father preyed upon.

He told her about the visit to Philadelphia, how awkward he felt at first, of his meeting with Susan, a neonatal pediatrician, how in time the awkwardness melted, the visit to the Liberty Bell, the wonder of the Wanamaker marble Grand Court seven stories high the width of a football field housing the world's largest an organ with over 28,600 gold pipes, the dinner that night with her friends, the awkward brunch the next morning, Sunday, with her mother and stepfather, the free concert they attended that same night in Symphony Hall, a hall renowned for its acoustics, their visit to the French Country Inn in the Poconos, the day they spent exploring the Amish country, the shops, the restaurants, hot air ballooning at sunset over the farms, watching the spectacular 4th of July fireworks over Delaware from Susan's apartment.

As he spoke, he studied Chenny's face, searching for signs that she might suspect that during the four days he spent with Susan they had been more than casual companions. Hurriedly, he went on to tell her about Arushi, the waitress in Fredericksburg, how, at twenty four, she had already backpacked halfway around the world on her own, and had spent six months living in an ashram in the Himalayas in Nepal meditating and practicing Ashtanga Yoga, and finally how ragged he was feeling after the tough day he had in Charleston attempting to locate the woman his father lived with and her son Sydney.

"The high school wasn't exactly helpful and the synagogue was worse. When I asked around, after the Friday night services, it felt as if the Great Wall of China had been erected, as if I was contagious. People turned away when I approached them. Instead of the welcome as a newcomer I experienced elsewhere, there was a chill.

"I eventually found a seventy-five-year old woman, a Mrs. Edelman, who would admit she knew them. She was less stylish than the other women, not frumpy, but her hair hadn't been coiffed in a salon, there were no four-carat diamonds on her fingers or hanging from her ears, the one piece of jewelry she wore was an antique cameo pinned at the opening of a no longer fashionable dress that must have been an heirloom passed down to her. I brought her a cup of coffee from the urn on the side table and a cinnamon Danish and we chatted in the far corner out of earshot of the others. Memories were long there. It's a big city but a small town. Leonora, the woman my father lived with, had left under a cloud after wealthy members lost scads of money on sub-prime mortgage debentures my father assured them were gilt-edged. It made no difference that Leonora did as well, and that the biggest Wall Street names went down in the same fiasco. It was she who had brought my father to them, testified to his bona fides.

"She became persona non grata. Though she had been born and brought up here, it had become so uncomfortable she had to leave. Mrs. Edelman said she believed Leonora moved in with her sister in a run-down suburb of Atlanta."

As he talked, the delight and brightness in Chenny's face slowly faded, becoming somber and darker.

Jaime stopped abruptly. "What's the matter?"

Chenny shifted about uncomfortably, avoiding his eyes. The brightness Jaime had been working to keep in his face began to pall. "Chenny," Jaime repeated, "What is it? What's the matter?"

It was a few moments until Chenny gathered herself and was able to speak. "Jaime," she demanded, "You have an interesting life. What is it you want of me?"

Jaime felt as if a black empty hole had opened inside him. "Want of you?" he replied lamely.

"Yes. What exactly is it that you want of me?"

Jaime wondered what had got into Chenny. Never, in all the time he had known her, had he ever seen her like this, confrontational, not the usual amiable supportive friend. It was a side to her he had never seen, hadn't expected. At first he thought that something he said set her off, but the more he thought about it, the more worked up he became. He had made it clear from the beginning that their relationship was just one of friends but now she seemed angry as if blaming him that it was nothing more. The more he thought about it, the more incensed he became.

"Want of you? I thought we were…friends. What would I want of you? You sound as if I want something of you. I'm not a taker."

"People take in different ways."

"I've been taking things from you?" Jaime replied, growing angry, feeling himself losing his cool.

"You've covered your feelings so deeply, I don't think you know if you have any anymore. Does anything ever upset you, thrill you, except some piece of music? I'll bet when you met Susan you allowed yourself to feel something, aware that in a few days it would all be over, you could sigh, comfortable that you'd be free to do whatever you've always done in a matter of days. Your father did a number on you. You don't feel you're worthy of being loved and so you don't allow yourself to."

"And you!" he found himself heatedly snapping back. "Look at you. Buried in a town where nothing is expected of you so you don't have to feel you've failed."

"Have you even started writing, or have you relied on finding one excuse after another. Is that why you wanted a friend, to validate your excuses, make

162

them seem real, valid. Is that what it was that kept you with me? That you felt 'at peace' with me, because I let you believe your excuses, the lies you want to believe? I've always sensed that you've never really been at peace. I sensed it from the time I met you."

"What gives you the right to criticize me, my choices?" Jamie snapped back. "And what of you? Haven't you settled, taking the easy way? What risks are you willing to take? Have you ever even allowed yourself to think about what it would be like living somewhere else, where there are opportunities to explore, to get a taste of cultural events, sports, music, art, able to pick and choose?"

"Maybe I have. But not any longer. Maybe we both have. But I'm not willing to live my life that way any longer."

"You mean that you would be willing to leave Red Plains, live somewhere where life is more than just one day following the next, where there's more to life than eating, sleeping and breathing?"

"Is that all you felt, Jaime, while you were here?"

"What I feel is that you have changed the rules."

"The rules? Jaime. What rules? Those in your head that tell you what you want to hear? I have to go. I want to wish you the best. I hope you find what you're looking for."

Chapter 39

The haunting, unsettling feeling of having been set adrift, of being unconnected, settled over Jaime like a dark, stultifying cloud as mile after mind-numbing mile slid by on the wearying five-hour drive from Charleston to Atlanta. When he shut down his computer last night, instead of the feeling of comfort he had looked forward to after the difficult, frustrating day, he felt he had been kicked in the stomach. What the fuck brought it on? What set her off? *Women!* Had he made some promise he failed to keep? Some obligation he hadn't fulfilled? When they parted, she said, "Keep in touch." Well, *hadn't he?*

He caught sight of his reflection in the mirror on the windshield. His eyes were raw, dark narrow slits. Shit, shit, shit.

Nor was he likely to find a Brady Bunch reception in the home he was headed to. When he located the address, he found it in 'Cabbage Town,' the second poorest area of Atlanta, an unpleasant come down from Leonora's privileged neighborhood in Charleston. As a reminder of the man responsible, he could hardly expect a hearty welcome.

He rehearsed and reworked what he would say when he phoned again and again, but everything he came up with sounded lame. "I'm calling on behalf of an anonymous donor." It sounded false and pretentious, even to him. The pause on the other end of the line when he phoned hardly surprised him. "I've been searching for you and your son," he hurried on – not giving his name, fearing she'd hang up – "at the last address I had for you in Charleston where I am now. A Mrs. Edelman, a member of the Kahal Kadosh Beth Elohim Synagogue, told me you had moved to Atlanta. I have a bequest that was left for your son I've been asked to deliver in person. I can leave first thing in the morning and be at your home at eight in the evening, if that would be convenient. If your son could meet me there…"

He heard the hesitation in her voice, the obvious wariness. He fended off her questions, told her the minimal he needed, promising that all would be made clear when he arrived. Her reluctance was palpable, but in the end she agreed. He could hardly believe it was his persuasiveness; how could she not? Whether her son would be there or not she wouldn't say. Was it because she wished to spare her son, or him?

The miles went by agonizingly slowly, much of it on secondary roads under the scrutiny of predatory Ray Banned constabulary with quotas to fill. He made Aiken shortly after noon, stopped for lunch at Willie Jewell's Bar-B-Q Heaven, bypassing Italian, Mexican, Japanese, Chinese and Thai restaurants, shattering his image of the south as backwater.

"Y'all new in town?" the well-endowed thirty-ish, redheaded waitress asked, bending well over, raising, among other things, a suggestion that may have served Erskine Caldwell, author of *God's Little Acre*. What is it with these southern girls, he wondered, lifted for the moment from his funk. Putting aside any further speculation, selecting the special, ribs and hush puppies, he opened his phone to Wikipedia and read up in on Cabbage Town.

> Site of one of the first southern textile mills, Cabbage Town recently enjoyed a modest renaissance as yuppies, chi chi restaurants and art galleries followed artists to the area in search of lofts available at depressed prices long lying empty. The cotton mill, built in the latter part of the 1800s by a German Jewish immigrant, employed Scottish and Irish workers he brought from Appalachia to live in one and two-story shotgun and cottage style houses he erected on a grid of narrow short blocks surrounding the mill. According to one of several legends, the name 'Cabbage Town' came from the odor of cabbages mill workers grew in their front yards.

It was gathering dusk when Jaime found his way through the warren of narrow streets to the address two blocks off Carroll Street, the main thoroughfare along which shops, restaurants, and galleries had sprung up. It proved to be one of the wood-shingled cottage style houses the cotton mill owner built with windows of the type once common, an upper and lower sash, each with six panes in a wooden frame, the lower frame counterbalanced with lead weights suspended on clothesline rope over pulleys set in the frame above. Small window air conditioners, protruding from front rooms, disturbed the profile, chugging away, spewing heat into the muggy air trapped in the crazy quilt warren of narrow streets.

When the door was opened for him, Jamie tried to see behind the map of hard years on the face of a woman his father said wasn't beautiful, but perfect, the woman she had once been, alive, exciting, a young woman whose shy smile stole from the corners of her eyes and spread across her face lighting the tiny freckles on the bridge of her nose, a young woman who had once climbed trees and raced boys. But even softened by the dim light hanging from the ceiling fixture in the room behind her, the change was there, the strands of gray woven though the rust of her hair, the weariness not quite hidden in her dark eyes. But there, too, he thought he saw, or maybe he wanted to see, a fighter, tired, but determined to continue her battle with time.

He tried not to give way to the ache he felt in his gut at what he saw had become of the woman his father described, but he could see in her expression that he failed. He didn't really understand why his eyes became watery, but he knew why. She was, worse than he, a victim, a victim of his father. He was sorry he had to see what he did, regretted he agreed to come here…but was glad that he did, that he might do something in a small way to help atone for the man whose seed he bore.

He had an inkling she guessed who he might be and had taken extra care dressing. She was wearing a white and gray, knee-length, wrap-around cotton dress with a V-neck and low-heeled white Cuban pumps that showed years of polishing, a style that had once been in fashion, perhaps clothes she wore on summer afternoons to parties she gave on the lawn of her house overlooking the bay and the yacht club in which she and her husband were members.

The fading yellow walls of the room into which she led him held what must have been vestiges of a former life that she brought from Charleston, an Oriental rug now almost threadbare, a Stiffel lamp on which the shade had been replaced, a Belle Èpoque sofa upholstered in tired gold damask, a coffee table of heavy glass set on curly wrought iron legs, and a pair of stiff-backed French Renaissance chairs with carved legs. Out of place was a small flat screen TV on the wall opposite the sofa.

"I can see the resemblance," her sister Gabriella who was with her said, when the introductions were complete, furthering his embarrassment. It was evident that neither they nor he knew what there was to be said. Leonora seemed nervous, not only about what to say or ask, but what she should feel. Gabriella's eyes went from her to him and back repeatedly. She was the same height as Leonora, but at least seven years older. Age had brought broader features, the brown dye from the bottle failed to reach the roots of her wavy hair. She tried to put both of them at ease several times, but she was so nervous it was obvious it made it worse. Jaime sat on the edge of the overstuffed chair imagining that Leonora and her sister must be holding their tongues, not saying what they had to be thinking, that his father, the man Leonora had placed her trust in, was trying to earn salvation, that his son was no more than a toady errand boy.

166

He wondered what Leonora really thought about his father but didn't ask her. In his diary, what his father wrote of their lives ended when the price of sub-prime mortgage debentures crashed and he left Charleston in disgrace. They had been deeply in love at one time, but relationships fade with time. Did Leonora go on believing in him even when he left? Would she have if he had not left? Had she defended him to her friends, her sister, her son until no one would listen any longer? Or did she finally see him for what he was, a man who stayed for the good times, and cut and ran when they ended, a charming adventurer, an amiable rogue, the kind that casts a spell and is adored for all his faults.

Was it the story of Gilda in Verdi's opera Rigoletto based on Victor Hugo's play *Le roi s'amuse*, Gilda, the treasured innocent young daughter of the humped-backed court jester who was debauched by Rigoletto's master, the licentious Duke of Mantua, and who, in the final scene, to save the Duke, throws herself on the knife her father sent with a messenger to kill the Duke? Was it the spell his father cast on women, an old tale brought to life?

Or did she see him for what he was and accept him, remembering the nine good years she had with him as the gift he gave her?

Talk was awkward, of trivialities in which no one was really interested, offered sufficiently in earnest to suggest that it was, indeed, of much interest, though all were embarrassed, aware that it was only to fill awkward silence. It was the propriety that ate into him, the kind of polite meaningless drivel he despised that allows people to feel they fulfilled an obligation for which they had little desire, as so exquisitely pricked in an off-off Broadway play by Gertrude Stein. Jaime didn't remember the name, but the dialog was unforgettable. The setting was an indoor-outdoor garden party, the guests and host animatedly conversing, as guests and hostesses do at such parties, on topics guests and hostesses discuss at such parties, with degrees of interest appropriate to each topic, but all of it in but two words: *Saw wood.*

Saw wood. It summed up Stein's take on vapid conversation.

It was evident that all of them felt the burden of trying to keep the conversation from flagging, longing for Sydney's return so they need pretend no longer. Jaime felt the need to give a sketchy idea of what brought him here, that Leonora knew his father under a different name, avoiding anything that might suggest how little he had accomplished, ashamed of wanting to be admired. But as the hour grew late, the silences longer, attempts to fill them became increasingly awkward, Jaime had the feeling that compared to what his father did to him, he had gotten off lightly.

"My son Sydney," Leonora apologized nervously several times, "works until nine. He wanted to be here earlier," she offered with a tilt of her head with a 'you understand' smile. Gabriella nodded in agreement, kneading her hands, as if to add support to the inference that it was important business that delayed him, but when Sydney did arrive almost two hours later, the smell of drink was obvious, the top buttons of his shirt were open, his shorts were wrinkled and stained, the laces on his high tops hung loose. Following him through the door was a gangly, heavily mascaraed seventeen-year-old girl with magenta-streaked black hair and an assortment of cheap rings through her pierced nose and ears. She was wearing black shorts, a black tee shirt with a picture of the Grateful Dead, and walked balanced on 4" stilettos.

Leonora started to rise from the sofa to reach for Sydney's but shrunk backward in the wave of invective that gushed from him, her wrinkled cheeks and heavy eyebrows attempting to form an embarrassed half-smile, as if it to make it seem it was all a joke. The young woman reached for his shoulder, but he brushed her off angrily and she backed away to inhabit another world.

"You're such a fuckin' hypocrite!" he spat, his liquored eyes and swollen veined cheeks fixed on his mother, "sittin' here with this prick, entertaining the fuckin' crook's son as if he was la-di-da fuckin' royalty."

Gabriella jumped up to keep her sister from falling backward, but Leonora shook her off, reached for Sydney again as if to placate him, tossing away hair that tumbled over her eye with a worried wave of her head.

Sydney snarled. "Get ya fuckin' paws away from me. Ya never had nothing for me, making excuses for that son of a bitch who had you hanging over him like he was fuckin' God – even after all he did to you, to us. Not his fault! *Not his fault!* Who's the fuck fault was it, tell me."

Jaime edged backward in his chair, as if to escape the solid blast of venom. If it wasn't obvious before, it was now: What he was seeing was the legacy his father left. He thought of pulling the stock certificates from the envelope from his pocket, hand them to Sydney and flee, but he feared that in the state Sydney was in, he would grab them and shred them into bits and pieces, and that fleeing he'd look like a thief fleeing the scene of a crime.

"Get him the fuck outa here!" Sydney screamed, his eyes boring into Jaime, moving into his personal space, his jaw jutting out, gobs of saliva dripping from his lips. "I don't know what the fuck you have, but the man who fucked up our lives is not buying absolution from the family he fucked up."

Jaime first instinct was to retreat, get distance between them, but his knee-jerk unthinking reaction was one he later was never able to explain. Sydney's fury became his, multiplied. His temples grew heated, his fists clenched, his jaw set. He had not found his way here willingly. He had no personal interest in helping this foul, vulgar prick who abused his harried mother making her a target for his bile. He was no less a victim that this loud-mouthed lout.

Grabbing the edges of the cushion, he levered himself up to the full extent of his height and pushed forward to stand eyeball to eyeball with Sydney, his nose so close not even the thin edge of a playing card separated them.

"Go ahead you shit, show your girlfriend what a big fucking man you are, beat up on your mother who probably has done more for you in your miserable fucking life than any one of the dead beat fucking friends you dick around with, but first, go on! Take a swing at me, you little prick, why don't you?"

Jaime remembered having been in only one fight in his lifetime. It occurred late one night on the boardwalk in Ocean City. He had been fifteen, alone. Rumbling teenagers, anti-Semites, a year or two older than he, had come down then boardwalk looking for trouble, looking to beat up Jews. One of them grabbed him, spun him around, punched him in the gut, began pummeling him while the others jeered and cheered him on. Without knowing how or what he was doing, a wave of red-hot fury came over him. Adrenalin pumped, transforming him. Shoving his chin in his chest, his feet working, he charged the son of a bitch, swinging with a strength and fury he hadn't known he had possessed. His second punch caught the son of a bitch's nose, split it sending blood streaming down his face, routing him and the others in his wake. Afterwards, he stood where he had been in the dark night air shaking, sick at what he had done, and sick at seeing the blood streaming down the kid's face. He had never hit anyone again. But he never backed off from anyone after that either.

He didn't remember much after that. It seemed that he and Sydney stood there forever, nose to nose, Sydney, challenging him, daring him, his mother and aunt holding their breaths, eyes wide, frightened, waiting for the explosion. "You fuckin' cock sucker!" Sydney blasted, blowing spit into his face, so furious he was shaking. "You think you're so fucking much because you're bigger than me, that I couldn't wipe the fuckin' ground with you. Where do you get off puttin' a foot in this house, the house of the woman that son of a bitch used, took the money my father left and left, leaving us living like this, one step better than the fuckin' homeless. Look around you, you son of a bitch. Look at what you see here. I bring down every curse there ever was on you. Swing at you? Hit you? I wouldn't waste my fists on a prick like you. Take whatever it is you brought with you and get the fuck out of this house. I don't want anything of his. Ever! If I ever see even a glimpse of your miserable fuckin' face again, I'll come after you with a bat and beat your fucking brains out. Consider yourself warned. Get out!" Sydney screamed, backing off only enough to allow Jaime to move off and leave. "Now!"

Jaime stood stock still, trying to hide the trembling in his gut. He took in a deep breath, trying to steady himself, recover his balance, set himself, the smell of alcohol overwhelming.

"Look around me! Look around me. I'll tell you what I see, you miserable son of a bitch. I see a home that's a hell of a lot better than the one that man left my mother and me without a penny when I was six, when my mother had to go out to work two jobs to support us. And you know what else I see, a whiner, a miserable prick that would rather blame someone for the mess he's made with his life than do something about it, who doesn't even have the guts to. Do you think I was left better than you? Do you? I worked from the time I was seven; delivering papers, running errands, anything I could find because I was damned if I was gonna let that son of a bitch keep me from doing something with my life. I struggled, put myself through college, but I did it instead of lying around whining. Go ahead, you son of a bitch. Throw the rest of your life away. I've come with something for you that's a damned sight better than he ever gave me at your age, an opportunity to go to college…and even beyond if you want to turn your life around. Who the fuck ever told you the world owes you anything? You want to be furious with him. Do so. Be furious with him. But don't allow yourself to use it as an excuse for failure. So. What is it to be? Take what I've come to bring you, piss and moan about your fuckin' life as you piss it away, or sit right down now, know that this is the first day of your life and plan to make something with it."

Sydney wiped at snot running down under his nose with the back of his hand, glaring at Jaime, not saying a word. His mother and aunt sat on the edge of their seat, fear and hope in their faces in equal measure. Harmony, the young woman sat shrunken in on herself, her face devoid of expression.

"You were left, too?" It came out as half inquiry, half challenge.

"Worse. Far worse! No one offered me money. I worked my way through school, summers, vacation, after school. When the other kids were out partying, I was working. But I was determined. I made it through and now teach college. Everything I see around me today is young people doing amazing things, thirteen-year-olds starting business that are sold for a billion dollars, eight-year-old musicians performing, doing all kinds of things. It's a young person's world. I've gotten only so far, but I'm nowhere near where I'm going to be one day, even at my 'advanced' age. So?"

As he stood, facing Sydney, his mother and aunt holding their breath, Sydney's spine seemed to melt, the piss going out of him. His mother lifted up from her seat, seemed to want to go to hold Sydney, thought better of it, and announced that she was going to make a pot of tea. His aunt followed, Sydney seemed undecided, softened and followed, as did Jaime. Harmony looked lost, unsure what to do, started after Sydney, stopped and returned to where she had been.

The three sat down at the kitchen table in silence, waiting. Jaime took from his pocket the envelope and handed it to Sydney. He looked at the envelope for a minute before opening it and examining the contents as if unsure at what he was seeing.

"If you sell this stock and use the money sparingly," Jaime told him, "you may have to supplement it working as you go, but there is enough for four years of college, and possibly more. If you choose, you can do more with your life, knowing that before the man who did this to you died, he cared enough to leave this for you. It can't change the past, but it can change the future."

There was much to be said that wasn't said. They drank more tea, made awkward conversation. It was almost two in the morning when Jaime left. At the door they shook hands. Jaime saw new life come into Sydney's mother's eyes and, he imagined, new spring in her steps. Sydney's aunt kneaded the handkerchief sodden in her hands, Harmony, the young girl, seemed to have softened or fallen into a daze. They exchanged numbers, promised to keep in touch. *Perhaps*, Jaime thought, *someday they will.* He left believing that Sydney saw he had the love of the father he never had.

As he stepped into the night air and climbed into his car, Jaime felt as if his limbs had dissolved, his spine had melted. He had done a thing he had never done before, stood up and fought instead of backing down. He grasped the wheel tightly with both hands to steady himself, afraid he couldn't control the car.

It had been exhilarating – and terrifying.

Chapter 40

The sign on the dock in New Bern read 'Deck Hand Wanted.' A vision of young women in bikinis, or nothing at all, sunning on the deck of one of the yachts, far out at sea, away from it all, under a serene azure sky, a light, summer breeze in his face, hooked Jaime like a gaffed fish. It was two days since leaving Atlanta, wasted and depressed, unable to rid his mind of the grief his father had left behind him, or of what misery his father visited on the family in North Carolina he was still to see that turned him back north to Ocean City to die. Why he chose the scene of his youth to die, or why he retraced his path, turning north from Charleston to go to North Carolina, was a mystery. Nothing in his diary offered a clue. There was a mention of stopping off to visit the Tryon Palace in New Bern in his notes, but nothing more to explain it, or why his next destination came to be the Raleigh Durham triangle in North Carolina.

Jaime stood on the dock, unable to take his eyes off the sign and the luxury yachts tied up in the marina. The drive to Raleigh Durham from Charleston via I-95 would have taken less than half the time it took driving north along the coast, but he had been in no hurry to meet another of his father's wounded. On the drive north, passing tiny towns nestled along the Atlantic, he wondered if his father had taken the same route, or if it was just a coincidence. Or was it that his father, who grew up in Washington Heights, a few blocks south of Fort Tryon Park, was drawn to visit Tryon Palace, the former headquarters of Major General Sir William Tryon, the last British Governor of colonial New York City, for whom Fort Tryon Park was named. Fort Tryon Park was where he had met the woman he married who became his mother. As far as he was concerned, Fort Tryon Park had a lot to answer for.

"Interested?"

Jaime swung around to see who it was.

"Hi." The man had an easy, broad smile, a crop of curly blonde hair drifting untidily over his right ear, and a face burnished by the sun that said nothing was worth taking seriously. "I don't think this is for you. You look…as if you spent most of your life behind a desk. Name's Ben."

Half a head taller than Jaime, he had a grip like a vise and stood evenly balanced on his two feet like a mariner on the deck of a rolling ship. His denim shirt was cut off at the shoulders, his shorts an inch below the crotch, both of his arms and legs were matted with thick swaths of the same sun-bleached hair on his head, on his left shoulder was a tattoo of a sea chart, on his right a sextant and compass.

Jaime gave his grip back with interest. "Ben? As in 'Ben there, done that?' Jaime–as in Jaime!"

"Y'all sound like a Yankee or a furriner. Welcome to paradise. Just visiting?"

"Paradise?" Up close, Jaime saw a tiny web of fine lines radiating from the corners of his eyes. The sun-bleached knots of muscle were affixed to an older frame than he imagined. "I think I took a wrong turn. This isn't New Bern?"

Ben let go a good-natured laugh. "Yup."

A feeling swept over Jaime, one he'd experienced rarely: he liked this man. He was someone he'd want as a friend. He had had that experience only two or three times in his life and didn't know how to explain it. When it happened, it came over him like the warm sun changing something in him. If he had to put it into words, it would embarrass him. It was as if it opened the shell he kept around him in the way the sun opens the petals of a flower.

"Is one of those boats yours?"

Ben's eyes sparkled. "Yup. Ever been out fishing?"

"Yup," Jaime grinned, impishly batting the word back like a badminton shuttlecock.

"You up for it?"

Jaime shrugged, delighted. "What the hell," he found himself saying, with no idea what he was agreeing to.

"You OK with youngsters?"

Youngsters? Baffled, Jaime almost lost it, stopped just in time. Not young hot chicks? *The Old Man and the Sea* popped into his mind and with it, Hemmingway's philosophy, 'The only value we have as human beings are the risks we're willing to take.' Not play it safe? Maybe it was what he needed.

"Like the Pied Piper."

Chapter 41

Jaime awoke to the alarm on his phone, checked the time, 5:00 a.m., and grinned, remembering the day's fishing he'd once had. The school tuna run was late that spring, the Sachem, a converted WWI mine chaser party boat, took only twenty when it went for tuna, first come first served. He had risen at 3:30 that Saturday morning to be among the first. The last on board were three twenty-ish beefy guys from the Midwest wearing cutoffs and sneakers. It was there first time out fishing. They had come to party with loaded Styrofoam chests and hampers, belting out off-key ribald doggerel about Charlie the Tuna.

The boat left the dock at 5:45 heading east out into the Atlantic, straight into the sun just beginning to peek up over the horizon. The three bavants, already on the second of the Buds they took from the chest, began chomping their way through overstuffed foot-and-a-half Italian hoagies, salami, bologna, provolone, mozzarella, and Italian peppers slathered with spicy yellow mustard. Old-timers on the boat had already settled in. They'd attached hooks and light shot to their monofilament lines; tied their rods to the iron pipe railing and were laying back on the bench running alongside the cabin, eyes closed, catching more than forty winks for the three-plus hour run to the fishing grounds. But he had been too excited to miss a minute of it.

At the signal, the mates untied the mooring lines and the captain eased the 30' boat from the slip as gently as a mother easing a newborn from its bodysuit. He felt the throb of the engines, gloried in the thrill as the Sachem headed off around the breakwater to the cut into the open water of the Atlantic. Until that moment, unable to sit with excitement, he hadn't noticed, over the chugging of the engine and rush of spray, that the three revelers were no longer singing. All three were hanging over the side, spewing hoagies and beer. It turned out to be their fishing for the day.

It was an agonizingly long three plus hours before he heard the throbbing of engines slow and, finally, stop altogether. Before the captain reached his hand through the window of the pilothouse to ring the brass bell mounted beside the window, the signal for 'Lines Down,' his line was already down.

174

And there he had stood, three frustrating hours waiting for a strike, afraid to break to use the head in fear it would be just then when a tuna struck. They were more than sixty miles from shore, drifting, the Atlantic as calm as a lake, so clear he could see his bait dangling thirty or forty feet in the water below. And there he stood, anxious, alert, waiting,

It had to be an hour later, his attention wandering, when looking down, he hardly believed what he saw below. Tuna, some the size of beer barrels, some even bigger, circling the lines. And then, in seconds, it was mayhem, everyone screaming 'fish on, fish on,' 'hey, watch it,' 'move your line,' 'get over there,' line sloughing off reels thirty feet a second, running in all directions, crossing, tangling, knotting, the mate racing up and down the deck, cutting lines, untying knots, freeing lines, battles with the fish raging, arms knotting muscling rods up, reeling in a few feet of line, muscling up more, reeling another few feet, again and again and again, forty, fifty, sixty, seventy-pound tuna, smaller albacore, hoisted over the side, the race to bait up again, and then again, lines back in the water, straining in another fish, and then another and another.

An hour and a half later, he remembered, the frenzy was still underway, the captain came by. "Get up! Get up!" He ordered, standing over him. "There's more fish."

He had lain there, sprawled on the deck smelling of fish, exhausted, done in, thrilled, two tuna and one albacore, one hundred and sixty pounds in the burlap sack tied to the rail, too tired almost to answer. "Uh uh." He shook his head. His shoulders felt as if he'd been lifting hundred pound sacks of cement all afternoon, the tendons in his legs felt like knots, it hurt to turn his head. "No more. I have enough."

It had been the greatest day fishing ever, the only time he remembered quitting when there were still fish to be caught.

Chapter 42

They met at the dock at six the next morning, Ben, Jaime and the family of four that had chartered Ben's *Morning Glory,* the time of morning when the air is fresh born, innocent, and screams of what is yet to come. In place of the bikini-clad model Jaime had hoped for was a sulky twelve-year-old Lolita who made it clear she didn't want to be here, her father Hank, and her half-brothers, Bobby eight and Peter six. As a youngster, Jaime imagined it would be fun to work as a mate on a fishing boat, spending the day under the open sky, inhaling the clean smell of the sea, balancing on the deck in a rolling sea, racing back and forth baiting lines, scrubbing the deck of fish guts, unhooking fish from lines, living his day on the water and being paid for it.

Ben's 29' Morning Glory wasn't the kind of boat Jaime had ever been on, one whose amenities were more than a foul-smelling pull chain head the size of a broom closet and narrow five-foot wooden pallets in the hold for sleeping on overnight fishing trips, or for the seasick who didn't choose throwing themselves overboard as the better choice. He had never been seasick, but he had seen it and never forgot the early December morning under a winter sky blanketed with evil gray clouds as he and his cousin Ted, teenagers, eagerly climbed onto a grizzled forty-foot party boat leaving Sheepshead Bay with their rods, reels, tackle and the lunch his aunt, Ted's mother, packed the night before. From the moment the boat left the harbor, it bucked and yawed from side to side. At the fishing grounds, it was impossible to fish. Everyone hung onto the railings to keep from being thrown across the slick water-swept deck. There was no respite, no relief. On board was a young girl. It was her first time out fishing. From the moment the boat left the dock at six that morning until it returned to the dock at four that afternoon, she was violently sick, so sick she would gladly have thrown herself overboard if it would have ended her misery. She threw up her guts continually. Everything she ate went over the side, and when there was no more, she dry heaved. Everyone felt her agony. No one laughed, no one made fun, not even the old-timers who would usually joke at the expense of the 'greeners.'

But this was a party boat, the captain was paid, he promised a full day's fishing, even if the boat rolled from side to side until the deck almost touched the angry sea. It was impossible to fish holding tight to the rail with one hand and trying to manage the rod with the other. No one pulled up a fish. Even the old-timers who paid their hard-earned money were willing to quit, but there they stayed, absorbing the full force of the Atlantic at its worst. He had only been able to imagine what it had been like for that young girl that day, but a half dozen years later, in the army sick bay with hepatitis he lived that sickening experience day after day as his eyeballs turned yellow. He fervently hoped no one in this party would succumb, or that he'd have the job of cleaning up after them.

The *Morning Glory* was far removed from any fishing boat he'd ever been on, a diamond to a rhinestone. It had a flying bridge, a fully equipped cuddy cabin fitted with a sink, refrigerator, table-top stove, fold down bunks with mattresses and fitted sheets, a sunroof over the deck chairs, and a pair of fighting chairs at the stern equipped with harnesses, plus twin 175 Yamaha outboards which, at top speed in a calm sea, could make the sixty mile trip out to the Gulf Stream where marlin and sailfish fed in an hour and a half.

He had met Ben at 6:00 a.m. when the sun was just rising over the Atlantic in the east, the sky was clear, seagulls and terns circling, and went with him to buy live bait from a dock ten minutes away. Sand eels and shrimp were stored in the live well in the stern which had circulating seawater, frozen ballyhoo and squid were refrigerated, the live bait would be for game fish, thawed frozen bait for the smaller reef fish the kids would be delighted to catch. The coolers were stocked with bottled water, sodas, beer, and sandwiches. The fuel tanks were topped off, the electronics checked.

It quickly became apparent to Jaime when the family showed up that this was the father's summer weeks with his kids, that his efforts to find a rhythm with his daughter hadn't yet succeeded. Wendy was at the awkward long-legged pony stage age, her breasts just little bumps in her Madonna tee shirt. She had braces on her teeth, was no longer a girl, not yet a woman. Young girls were cute when they were pouting, but Wendy was intent on testing her father's tolerance. She made a show, almost as if imitating a B-picture actress, of flopping onto a deck chair, stretching out her long golden legs, kicking off her sandals and rubbing suntan lotion all over.

Her half-brothers, Bobby and Peter, exploded onto the deck from the dock, Peter, the younger one more intrepid in the lead, racing about, exploring every inch of the boat, from the harpoon platform jutting out from the prow, to the bait well in the stern, climbing up onto the flying bridge to pepper the captain with questions. They came dressed in denim shorts, caps and deck sneakers,

Bobby in a Red Sox tee, Peter in a Bruin's, buckled on orange life jackets. No GPS was needed to locate their home: *Bahston.*

Wendy scowled, bucked at the life jacket, buckled it on at the captain insistence, a coast guard requirement, went right on texting. But when the twin Yamahas fired up with a roar and the boat jumped ahead like a tethered puppy straining at its leash, her melon ball eyes went wide as seagulls and terns swooped and dove for fish, snails, and flotsam in the wake stirred up from the muddy bottom by the screw propellers of the powerful engines.

Captain Ben either liked kids or else had a hell of a lot of patience, answering a barrage of questions and explaining the function of each instrument on the control panel, compass, tachometer, radar, GPS, fish finder, depth finder, UHF and VHF radios. He showed the boys how he set their destination on the GPS and described how, just as a car turns corners, follows roundabouts, he'd follow the route marked through channels, around sand bars, reefs, and shallows to the open water.

"If you've been out in the ocean before," he finished, "and I can see from your grins you haven't, you should be aware of what experienced sailors say: 'There are old sailors…and there are bold sailors…but there are no old, bold sailors.' Our number one priority when we're on board is safety. The weather forecast is excellent, sunny skies, temperature in the low eighties, a five to ten-mile offshore wind, a two to four-foot sea. But that doesn't mean a rogue wave can't hit with a force of ten, so keep both feet planted on the deck, and once we're underway, no climbing on the catwalks, and if you use the ladder, hold on with both hands."

He told Jamie he didn't want to frighten them, but he never forgot a day that looked as calm as this, so calm he might have been sitting in an easy chair in his living room. The Atlantic had a slight chop, but hardly more than he'd have in his bathtub. As he headed into the cut that would take him from the bay into the Atlantic, blinded by the glare of the rising sun, with nothing on his mind but whether to shoot straight out to the fishing grounds and go for marlin, or go for stripers inshore…his gut lurched; when next he looked, the boat was heading into a solid wall of water, a rogue wave half again higher than the boat, something he'd heard of but never experienced. Before he could react he was inside a wave coming over the top of the wheelhouse with a force that could flip the boat. In that instant he knew, instinctively, if he tried to turn, go back, get clear of it, he'd take the full force broadside and the boat would flip. There was nothing to do but hang on, hold tight to the wheel with all his strength, muscle the rudder, trying to keep it straight, keep the boat going right on, hoping it would make it through the cut into the Atlantic.

He told the kids none of this, was amused that what most captured them, what they repeated over and over, was 'R R R,' the three 'R's,' Red Right Returning, the international channel and buoy marking system, red buoys on the right returning to port, the green buoys on the left, and reversed leaving port.

The resemblance of the boys to the father was easy to see, the same hazel eyes, narrow brows, sun-streaked brown hair, ears like conch shells pressed flat to the sides of their heads, full lips, and his strong, confident chin. Despite their similar appearance, the differences between the boys were marked. Bobby, the older one, was cautious, serious, testing each step of the shiny stainless steel ladder when he climbed up to the flying bridge, holding tight to the railing beside the catwalk when he made his way alongside the side of the cabin to the prow. Not Peter who scampered up the ladder like a monkey, sure of his footing, hung far over the prow, he could imagine his 'I'm gonna live forever' assurance. Bobby was the one who wanted to know the workings of every instrument in detail before touching anything, Peter was sure he could run the boat, begged for the chance.

The resemblance with Wendy, their half-sister was harder to see. She had hair several shades darker, full cheeks, a button chin and a scattering of sun freckles on the bridge of her nose. She tried to hide her superior amusement at their child-like antics, how it niggled at her, how unconcerned they were at how they appeared to others.

Jaime untied the lines cleated to the stanchions on dock, Ben eased the boat out of the slip. As they cleared the harbor to the cries of circling terns and squawks of swooping gulls, Ben ramped up the engines, the prow leaped, the boat surged ahead, quickly reaching cruising speed, thirty-three knots, three-quarters of the speed the Yamahas were capable of delivering. In minutes the boat was off beyond the spit of land now painted gold by the slanting sun climbing above the horizon, the salt mist spray coming off the bow on both sides sweeping away the smell of fuel oil that hovered at the dock. The light chop was hardly noticeable as the boat sliced through the water.

The boys were wound up, unable to stay still, racing from side to side, searching for dolphin, watching terns swooping and diving, goggling at trawlers draped with fishnets, sports boats with splayed outriggers on their way to the fishing grounds, dogging Jaime's heels as he set boat rods into stainless holders cut into the sides of the boat, tied hooks and sinkers on the lines, tested the drags on the reels, cut squid into strips for bait, and showed them how to set the drag to allow line to slough off the reel if they hooked a fish large enough to snap the line. Hank, their father, watched with fond amusement from

179

the comfort of the fighting chair as the boys asked questions nonstop, ever so often turning a wistful eye on his daughter whose eyes remained glued to her phone.

As they went along, the chop picked up, Ben eased back on the throttles to tame the bucking and heaving keeping a steady course. Wendy's color faded, but she remained fixed on her phone, Peter seemed to be handling the motion. Some twenty minutes later, Ben throttled way back, one eye on the icon in the GPS, the other eye on the fish finder. At his signal, Jaime climbed along the catwalk to the anchor well in the bow, dropped the anchor over the side until it hit bottom, let anther ten yards of line slough off, tested that the anchor was holding, and signaled Ben on the flying bridge who cut the engines.

No longer underway, the ocean's roll no longer muted by the forward thrust, though the sea was light, no more than three feet, the boat bobbed like a cork in a bathtub. Peter clenched his jaw, breathing through his nose, determined not to give in, took the rod from Jaime after Jaime let the line feed to the bottom and set the drag on the reel. Bobby fumbled the line at first, but managed to feed it out, holding the rod, jaw set, concentrating, ready, waiting, not certain what to expect. Hank's line was down almost as soon as Ben gave Jaime the signal, but Wendy shook Jaime off, gritted her teeth, and kept her eyes fixed on her phone. Not three minutes later, Bobby grunted excitedly, motioning to Jaime who immediately was at his side. "Keep his head up," Jaime urged, "that's the way, lift the rod, feel the fish fighting, reel in as you lower the rod, don't worry that the line is sloughing off the reel, you have a big one, lift the rod again, don't yank it, lift it, try to keep the fish from running all over, tangling the other lines, keep your line tight, lift, reel in, lift again, reel in, that's the way, it's coming up, there it is, I can see it, its' a beauty, when he breaks the water, don't jerk or yank him, but smoothly lift him over the side. That's it. He's still on, one more time."

As a red snapper came over the side and flopped on the deck, a grin as wide as his cheeks replaced the look of intense determination on Bobby's face. Jaime took hold of the struggling fish from the underside slipping a finger into the gills on each side and brought the fish up for Bobby's inspection, showed it to Peter and their father. Wendy shrunk away with a disgusted 'ugh' under her breath as Jaime unhooked the terrified fish, opened the hatch over the salt water well cut into the boat's side and dropped it in. Minutes later, Hank brought a calico bass over the side, and then Peter had one too. "C'mon," Jaime coaxed, offering Wendy his rod, "I have one on. Take my rod, bring it in. C'mon try it." Wendy barely looked up, shook him off.

Hank tied his rod to the rail, came over to Wendy, kissed the top of her head and whispered something in her ear. She looked up briefly, her eyes watery, shook her head.

Chapter 43

By eleven o'clock, the well more than half full, Ben said, "What say we go after a big one? There's enough here for dinner. The restaurant in town, The Impudent Oyster, will cook them up for you for dinner. How 'bout we put the smaller ones back in the water to let them grow for another day, take a break, have a soda, something to eat, and then take a run way out and see if we can scout up a marlin or sailfish?"

"What do you think?" Hank asked, turning to Peter whose teeth were set, his smile strained and a bit lopsided. Wendy avoided his eyes. "Or those who want can spend the afternoon on beach swimming while the others fish. What say?"

"Fish!" Bobby insisted, snaring a piece of cold fried chicken from a plastic container and washing it down with Coke. "Fish!" Peter agreed through clenched his teeth, shaking his head up and down.

Hank grinned, then sobered. As the boys ate, he scrabbled across to Wendy. "Honey," he proposed, hardly above a whisper, "if you'd rather go to the beach, the boys can go off, and you and I can spend the afternoon on the beach…or shop for shoes."

Wendy blinked, her eyes popped doubtfully, a smile starting to sneak out before she could squeeze it away. "You want to go shoe shopping? You… *Oh!*" she stopped, comprehending. She snuffed in a breath, swiped at a tiny tear forming over her lower lid. "No," she shook her head sharply, unwilling to be courted so easily. "Even fishing would be better than watching you watch me pick shoes. I'll fish."

Hank grinned. "You sure honey?"

"Yuh."

She was not an attractive kid, but strangely Jaime felt he knew her. She made it clear she had been deliberately acting like a shit, and he sensed why. She wanted to punish her father, make him suffer as she had been suffering in the only way she knew how. He had been everything to her once, before he left. She waited at the door for him, hardly able to wait until he came home at night from work. In the summer she waited outside on the walk. Her mother loved her, she supposed – mothers were supposed to love their daughters – but fathers were different. They had had a secret language all their own, a wink, a scrunch of the nose, a wiggle of the ears, each meaning something different. And it had been all hers. Her mother was jealous. They fought all the time. But if her parents split up she hadn't worried. A lot of her friends' parents split up. But she knew her father would never go without her. If they separated, he'd take her with him.

But he hadn't.

And now he had a new family and she was nothing, an add-on, his four-times a year duty. She hated him. Screw him. Let him hang if he thought she was going to put on an act to make him feel like he'd done his duty. He'd tried the old wink, thinking it would make up for it all. Fuck him. She wasn't going to play that game with him anymore. She'd begged her mother not to make her go, but her mother didn't want her either. She was flotsam, wanted her out of the way for two weeks so she could play kissy-face with her boyfriend, the fucking balding orangutan that comes on to her with a sickeningly phony smile. She had to grit her teeth when he came near, making her feel crawly, afraid he'd try something.

Jaime knew that if his father came back when he was alive, that's the way he would have acted; he would have made him as miserable as he possibly could. The difference was that at least Wendy's father was trying to make up for her abandoning her while he was alive. But what her father did to her, his father did to him in spades; and he'd left him to deal with the wreckage of families he screwed, like the one he just left in Atlanta. How many more, he wondered, had there been in addition to the three.

As Ben set the *Morning Glory* on course for the gulf stream where marlin and sailfish fed, Bobby, Peter and their father climbed up onto the flying bridge passing Ben's binoculars back and forth searching the horizon, leaving Wendy sitting where she was, while Jaime, stripped to the waist, busied himself cleaning away leavings and empty bottles, and washing down the deck and railings of scraps of bait, fish scales, and slime. Wendy pretended not to notice him skirting around her; Jaime pretended not to notice the glances that came his way when she thought he wasn't looking.

"You know," Jaime said, leaning against the railing near Wendy's chair after stowing the hose and mop, "I wish I were you."

Wendy's brow, shades darker than when she came aboard, darkened further. She swung around, scrunched in on herself, looked up at him in alarm.

Jaime recoiled, terrified at what he'd said, at what she might be thinking. "I…do," he offered softly, trying to defuse her fear, wishing he had never said anything.

Wendy tightened still further in horror, pushing back as far her chair allowed. "Are you…" she cried, frightened and mystified, at a loss for the right word, "…*LGBT?*"

Jaime blinked, fell backward, running his hand over his mouth in horror. "OMG!" he exhorted. "I…I forgot. We're in North Carolina. No, no. No. It's…it's something else entirely. Is that what you thought I meant? I'm sorry. It isn't that at all. It's just that…in some ways…seeing you with your dad, I thought…we're not so different."

"You and I? Me and my dad?"

Jaime shook his head, aware Wendy had no idea what he was talking about. "No. No. What I meant was that the one good memory I had of my father was…of him taking me fishing…"

Wendy stared at him, the tendons in her neck easing the tiniest bit. "Your father took you fishing too?"

"Mmm…" Jaime's head fell, his shoulders feeling too weak to support it. "He did…once…years ago…" He ran his fingers through his hair and shook his head. "I… I apologize. I really shouldn't have said anything. I didn't mean what I think you think I mean. It wasn't that at all."

Wendy's face softened. She looked at him searchingly. "What happened…to *him*?"

Jaime shook his head. "I never knew. He left."

Wendy's head swung back and forth, puzzled, "And…and that's why you think we're alike?"

"I'm sorry," Jaime apologized again, his eyes still fastened on his feet. "I spoke out of turn. I shouldn't have said anything, It's only that you seemed…unhappy…and I…"

Wendy continued shaking her head. "I don't understand…"

Jaime raised his head, saw written in Wendy's face that she hadn't understood what he had tried to say. "I never had the chance…to say the things I wanted to say to him."

"You never saw him again," she asked sensitively, beginning to tear up.

"No. Not till three weeks ago."

"Did you tell him then?"

"I couldn't. He was…he wasn't…he was…dead."

Tears began running down Wendy's face, she remained frozen, sitting where she was, Jaime stood frozen where he was, afraid to look at her, afraid he would tear up, afraid not to look.

The boat sped on its way, neither saying a word, neither wanting to say what they were thinking. A tern circled the stern eying a bit of bait Jaime missed, dove at it, at the last second veered away and flew off, following the boat hungrily.

"Did you…" Wendy began, only to let the thought slough off in the wind. Jaime shook his head in answer.

"Did you…" she tried again, not willing to let it go, as if his answer was important to her, "did you…love him?"

Jaime wiped his eyes on his shoulder looking away, shaking his head. "I hate him." He pulled a cloth from his pocket and blew his nose.

Wendy held his eyes, refusing to let him turn away. Tears were running down her eyes. Seeing something in his eyes, she turned. Her father was standing beside, his face filled with concern. "What is it, honey?" he keened.

She shook her head silently, her tears now streaming freely. Alarmed, her father reached for her tentatively, as if in fear she'd recoil. All at once she was in arms and was holding him to her with all her strength, sobbing into his chest, her tears soaking his shirt. "Oh honey," he cried, kissing her head, "Oh honey," he cried, again and again and again.

Jaime felt it all, as if it was he in his arms, confused, unwilling to allow himself to feel what he was feeling. He watched, wanting to be a part of this, knowing he couldn't, silently slid away, furious, castigating himself for allowing himself such feelings.

Chapter 44

The Double Tree Hilton fronts on the dock on the Bern River. Physically and emotionally exhausted, Jaime trudged to the hotel and took the elevator to his room. He had had his dream, a day as a mate on a fishing boat. Now he was sorry he had. When they went far offshore to the edge of the Gulf Stream to troll for marlin, Wendy was a different child. She stood over her father, with her stepbrothers on either side, as he muscled in a three hundred twenty-five pound marlin. For an hour and twenty minutes, the line screamed off his oversized reel as the magnificent fish, its round black eyes spewing defiance, put on a stunning aerial ballet, leaping and twisting, battling for its freedom against heavily weighted odds. Time and again the marlin seemed near to surrender only to turn and race off again, until at last, exhausted, when it seemed it had no more to give, nearing the boat it gave one last mighty shudder and dove again only to surface and look up at them as a king for whom it was beneath his dignity to plead for its life.

As Jaime leaned far over the side preparing to gaff the fish, Wendy wailed, "No, please. Don't. Let it go back, into the sea where it belongs." Her father looked at her, then the boys. The looks in their faces said what they knew. The planet belongs not only to us, but to all. A fish like this, that had such courage and character, deserved to live free, and with a nod to the captain, seeing the children's eyes, the captain leaned far down over the side with a pair of pliers, carefully extracted the hook from the marlin's jaw, steadied the majestic fish, and when it recovered enough, they bid goodbye to it as it swam off to the sea, looking back at them in what they knew was thanks.

Jaime watched them walk off the boat when they returned not as they climbed on that morning, but as a family. Wendy said goodbye to him shyly, the boys gave him high fives, and their father pumped his hand. But her father ruined it all by insisting on tipping him. He knew it was to express his thanks, but it made clear to him that he was not one of them.

Tired, sweaty, smelling of fish, he should shower, but he couldn't face his own company. Shucking his tee on the desk chair in his room, he shrugged on a fresh shirt, left the room, trudged down the stairs to the lobby, found the bar, climbed onto a stool, ordered a beer, caught sight of himself in the mirror behind the whisky and wine bottles on the ledge, and hunkered down, turning off the sounds, the clink of glasses, the background chatter, the blast of ships' horns on the way into port, trying to still thoughts niggling at him, to not think what he was thinking. He had promised himself he'd never feel sorry for himself, and he wasn't now, he insisted. But it was impossible to escape the misery heaped on him his father left in his wake, and what might yet await him when he found his way to the last family. Facing him too was the promise he made to inspire students, write, allow himself no more excuses, and apologize to Chenny…

…but not tonight.

Christ, he moaned, what kind of spineless wimp have I've become, wallowing like a…

"What's that, young feller?"

Shit, he thought, *had I said it aloud?* He snapped his head up to see who'd spoken. An old geezer two seats away nursing a beer, wearing a captain's hat over a scraggly mop of white hair that looked like it hadn't seen a comb for some days. A week's worth of stubble sprouted on his creased sunbaked face, eyes like marbles peered out from under a shelf of shaggy eyebrows that had lost all illusions.

"Been out on the water, I'd wager, from the smell of fish and the sea on ya. Names Ed. Cap'n Ed they call me, not that I ever owned a boat, mebbe cause of my age."

"Christ," Jaime grumbled to himself, hunchin' up further to get shot of the garrulous old coot ready to chew the ear off anyone who'd listen…and buy him a beer.

"Jaime," he sort of mumbled, regretting it even before it escaped, keeping his head in his beer to deliver the message.

"What's that you say young feller? You say yer English?"

He was wearing a seaman's sweater that once would have been brown that had seen heavy weather at sea. Christ. *English?* What's with this old fart? "Uh uh," he muttered, preparing to move off.

"The English, as most know," he went on, needing no encouragement, "are famous for their fantastic desserts, though they disguise 'em with names designed to put you off."

Shit, the guy's senile. He set a look on his face to suggest they were from different planets, which didn't seem to put the feller off at all.

"If you ain't among the initiate," he continued smartly, "the only way y'll ever know about them is to hover out of sight behind a table in which English are seated, and hope they won't detect that yer eavesdropping. Or if you happen to be seated at a table with one, pretend to be fully engaged in conversation so you can catch 'em orderin' unaware."

Jaime couldn't decide whether to make his escape or follow the fellow's tale, his prose so much a contradiction to his diction.

"I had just such an opportunity one day," he went on, apparently taking Jaime's failure to hop down from the bar stool and make his way out of the bar as an indication of interest, "takin' a chance I wasn't bein' led down the garden path (a metaphor the English are partial to), I ordered the 'Eton Mess,' soon fearin' I had been had, after all, when the fellow who happened to let slip the name, instead chose from the menu overflowing with a scattering of dishes with equally off-puttin' names, a dish of fresh fruit."

Jaime was sure he'd heard that story before but didn't know where. He considered the possibility that old guy had heard or read it as well and, by means of introduction, told it to anyone who would listen, hopin' to swap it for a drink. The room was filling up, the bar was becoming busier. A young woman with hair the color of the setting sun, wearing a lime green micro mini that made clear she had legs up to her whatever, who had been eying him, had a keen eye on the empty seat between them, but by some inner radar, the old fellow cut her off and took possession of the seat himself. In his present depressed state, and considering his aroma, Jaime wasn't sure he should be pissed, or if it was just as well.

Later that night, when he tried to reconstruct exactly what took place, he was unable to decide whether he made up the whole incident, a product of his state of mind, the drinks he had and the exhausting day, or it had actually occurred. He had been half out of it when he sat down at the bar, in a filthy state. But the fellow had him despite himself, even so far, before he ran out of stories, as to consider calling Chenny later, taking into account, considering the two-hour time difference, when that Indian feller might come.

"Yer from Noo York, ainchu, young feller? No, no need to answer fer in my travels I've studied speech patterns and can tell from yer pure diction, unlike fer instance, folks from Boston, that you are. Spottin' that foxy young lady comin' our way that I headed off, bein' in a bar and all, it recalled to mind an evenin' I had when I visited yer fair city. I'll tell yer about if y'd kindly stake me to another beer as I've gotten kinda dry and all tellin' about the Eton mess.

"The trouble I discovered being naïve, young feller, is that no one believes the things that happened to you actually happened. But on my mother's grave, what I'm about to tell ya is the God's honest absolute truth. First off, as yer no doubt have already seen, I'm not as sophisticated as ye might first have thought. In fact, as I pointed out, I'm a bit naïve. So imagine my surprise one Friday evenin' when I was in Noo York on some business matter and stumbled not exactly accidentally into Maxwell's Plum. Now as you may know, Maxwell's Plum's is a fancy waterin' hole on upper Madison Avenue, up where the swells live, a clone of the original in San Francisco's Ghirardelli Square overlookin' the bay, at the place where the cable cars turn about for the run back up their steep hills. Bein' as I am from a small town, I was curious to see fer myself a bit of the mischief I heard tell of that goes on in the Big Apple, so I run my eyes over the sweet young ladies about as I set down at a circular bar that is the size of an amusement park carousel. Mind ya, this was end of the workweek, and everyone there, comin' from their offices and places of business, was dressed in suits and ties, men and women both, so I fit right in. I order a Manhattan, believin' that bein' where I was, it would make it seem I belonged, take a healthy sip and all but choke, it being sweet as cherry coke.

"Anyway, as I said, I'm a bit naïve, fer soon after, as I head fer the men's room, a foxy young lady in conversation with a pair of apple-cheeked young fellers, gives me the eye. The only reason I could think of – (I didn't always cut such an unattractive figure, mind you) – was she was bored by their juvenile antics and anxious, after a hard week, for conversation with someone a bit more mature. So, on the way back, after havin' taken care of what I had to take care of, I eased over and fell in with the three of them, and soon had her winnowed away, pleased to believe I still had it as she followed me to the bar where we were soon in meaningful conversation.

"Now, as strangers on first meetin' might, she asked into the kind of work I did. I told her, and turned the talk to her, asking same question. She was rather shy, I expect, for she sorta fluttered her lashes and said 'guess.' Well, I said, after studyin' how pleasant she was and the smart way she was dressed, ya seem to be very sociable. 'Sociable,' she says, 'I couldn't be more sociable.'

"Well, as I said, not being sophisticated from the big city and all, and given that I'm naïve, but not that naïve, as the sayin' goes, the penny dropped, and I guess right the first time. But then everyone's entitle to a night off, I expect, so I figured she was here for a bit of conversation, and being up for a bit of conversation myself, as you might no doubt discovered, I asked how much she was paid for her services, just, you know, to be up on general information having no interest to pay for what ladies have always been pleased to offer so freely. $250, she admits straight out, as a shop girl would give the price of a pound of peaches.

"Now by this time, I'm startin' to figure that she had gotten the idea that I might be interested, so to set her straight, just so she knows where I stand, I say, I don't believe my lady friend would be comfortable with that, attemptin' to get across the idea that I had no need to pay for what she might be offerin,' but she didn't catch my meanin' I suppose, and comes back, 'if there's to be two, you and your lady friend, it would be $500.'

"Well by then, lookin' at me, she gets the idea that this is nothin' but talk, so she squares up and looks me in the eye, kinda miffed, and sez, 'Yer a business man, aintcha?' When I nod, havin' no idea yet what she has in mind, she adds, 'You get paid for your time, dontcha?'

"Well, you can imagine my jaw dropped, fer I see she ain't so sociable after all, believin' I might be willin' to pay for spendin' a bit of time chinnin' with her. But as you might expect, were I to make a similar request, it could embarrass her financially something fierce, so gettin' my meanin' without so much as a by your leave, she ups and heads off.

"Now getting' back to Eton mess, which is a traditional English dessert consisting of a mixture of strawberries, broken meringue, and whipped heavy cream…"

But having had all the conversation he cared to have that evening, Jaime excused himself and headed off, first buying the old fellow one last drink.

Chapter 45

Jaime woke muzzy, disoriented, attempting to remember exactly what had happened in the bar, wondering if he imagined the whole thing, if he had tried to call Chenny when he returned to the room, and if he had, had he spoken to her, or had she hung up on him again. He blinked, breathed in, smelled fish guts and salt spray, took another breath, realized the smell was coming from him, shook his head trying to clear it of the annoying reminder that he'd been putting off what he should have been getting to. Pissed, feeling like a child scolded for not doing his homework, he reminded himself that he was an adult, no longer a child, didn't have to account to an authority figure, like his mother or a teacher, and turned his thoughts instead to play with the possibility that the smell he smelled might be more appealing than the smell of cloying, syrupy sweet after-shave lotion, or the 'manly' scents in locker rooms, and when that ran nowhere, decided that not putting off what he had been putting off, reading the final pages of his father's diary, and braving Chenny's anger might be better. Squinting, shading his eyes from the sun streaming through the window, he peered at his watch on the night table. If he didn't get his ass out of bed now, if a shower was mandatory, he'd barely be on time for the hotel's complimentary continental breakfast.

The diary on top of his clothes in his carryon stared up at him like an accusing monitor as he raced into the shower. "OK, OK!" he yelled, *I'll get to it!* Shit! Give me a break! I'm up to here. *It's been one thing after another.* Christ! He fumed, looking at himself in the bleary mirror, I'm arguing with a fucking diary. I need a rest, peace of mind. Jumping into the shower, he yowled. The fucking water was freezing. Fuck. Give me a break.

"OK, OK!" he yelled again, climbing out and grabbing a towel and wiping the steam off the mirror. I'll get to it...*but not this morning.*

He hung over his coffee in the alcove until the wait staff's 'coughs' could no longer be ignored, pushed his cup aside, clumped back up to his room, changed into his Spandex running shorts and shirt in Montclair State's colors, red and white, his padded Thorlos and extra wide New Balance sneakers,

191

tossed a towel around his neck, took the elevator down, and in the muggy humid air in the lee of the building shaded from the sun, he began his cardio warm-up exercise routine, knee-to-chest stretches, bending palms to floor and jumping jacks, feet spread, arms wide overhead, getting a kick out of a little five-year-old tow-headed boy in short pants and his little three-year-old sister with eyes as large as saucepans mimicking his routine. With droplets of sweat beginning to drip under his arms and down his chest, he high-fived the kids and set off for a five-mile run up Front Street along the river.

It was not yet mid-morning but the temperature was heading into the nineties. The offshore breeze from the Neuse River provided scant relief, and even that only at street corners where the breeze wasn't blocked by Cape homes built tight along the shoreline. The sun was already well up in the sky burning a haze over the ocean; Captain Ed was probably long gone, well out to sea. Several blocks further on, on a launching ramp at the water's edge, catching sight of a fellow that looked to be about his age winching a 16' Boston Whaler into the water from a boat trailer tethered to the back of a panel truck, set him thinking of the life he fantasized about as a youngster, spending his days out in the ocean in his own boat, living off his catch, the sun beating on his face, salt air in his lungs, the tug on his line that would have him instantly alert, net in hand, ready to lean far over the side to scoop up a keeper from the ocean, living one day at a time, without pressure, with no need to become a 'something.'

Why the heck not, he wondered, as he jogged along. Where was it written that there was only one way to live a life? Why must life be one long struggle with the constant feeling of being driven? How did it really matter what he might ever become? To who did matter? Was anyone keeping score, or even care whether he made a contribution to the world, or if he left something behind – except him? Why did it have to dream?

He ran along keeping to his measured pace, six-miles an hour, savoring the image, embellishing it, the minimalism, the women who'd swarm around him, good-bye alarm clock, so long nine-to-five, farewell routine. It was some twenty minutes into his run, the heat and humidity beginning to get to him, when he was jolted from his reverie by the clatter of skates and the sound of laughter as a trio of sun-burnt, tousle-headed, bare-chested ten-year-old boys in cutoffs and Pumas hot dogged by him on skateboards, tossing snarly grins back over their shoulders as they sailed by. Instantly, all else forgotten, he ramped up, pumping, pressing his elbows close to his chest, pounding the macadam, intent on showing them he was still up for it, they being on skateboards more than twenty years younger making it all the sweeter. Before the end of the block he was abreast and raced past, tossing the 'look' back over his shoulder.

Exulting, the race was on. Almost before he knew it, the boys were back in the lead and he pumped harder, clenching his teeth, tightening the tendons in his neck, calling for another ounce of reserves, exulting at the feeling, mining a fountain of energy he hadn't known he could call on. Within seconds, he was up with them again about to shoot into the lead when, in an instant, a pain like the stab of a stiletto dug into his right calf and, immediately, he was struck by a sack of cement exploding in his chest.

Panicking, fearing a heart attack, but refusing to allow the kids see his distress and sail on sniggering at him, he forced himself to stay upright, told himself relax, breathe in, work the calf muscles and turned to hide the sweat streaming down his face. Struggling for breath, each painful breath rattling in his chest, he prayed they'd not see him being taken away in an ambulance.

Not until he was sure they were gone, out of sight, did he allow his knees to give way, slump to the ground, wondering if he were to collapse, would he be found lying here. He looked up, startled, a short squat figure bending over him, limply shook him off. Cars slowed, continued on when he managed a sick smile and a faint flick of his head. A gray-haired woman stopped, feeling concerned, opened her window, called, and drove away when he shook her off.

He remained there, hunched over, his muscles like water, straining for breath, aware of how ridiculous he had been, yet stubbornly buoyed, glowing, elated that he still had it in him.

Not for some time, until he was able to suck large gulps of air into his lungs without wheezing, until his heart no longer sounded like a bass drum booming in his chest, until his legs no longer felt that they'd not support him, did he struggle to his feet and test whether he'd be able to walk at even a measured pace. Awash in a sea of perspiration, as limp as a marionette, the towel around his neck sodden, hanging like a hod of bricks, what had been a twenty-minute run had become an hour under a blazing sun in humid air, the specter of the two decisions still awaiting him.

As he came up within a few blocks of the hotel, he looked down the intersection to the boat ramp where he'd spotted a fellow launching his boat, and thought again of his boyhood fantasy, living his life like that, free of worry, free of daily pressures, with nothing to prove, free of challenge, and saw it as a dream, a wonderful dream, but realized that someone who responded automatically, without conscious thought, to challenge, someone whose competitive juices could be ignited by playful boys' taunts, would never live a life without the rush of an occasional jolt of adrenaline. It would be a wonderful way to live, a delightful fantasy for someone who could live that way, for someone who had the temperament but, regretfully, he could not.

Chapter 46

What had happened that morning shook him more than he expected. He made his way back to his room, shucked off his sodden clothes, let them fall to the floor along the way into the shower, struck by the sight of his ashen face he saw in the mirror. It wasn't that he had come face to face with his own mortality, an awareness that he wasn't going to live forever, that a third of his life was over with nothing to show for it. No. He had never expected, or even wanted to live forever. Nor did he see himself in the role he and his friends played at as youngsters, living as Nick Romano, 'Live fast, die young, and leave a good-looking corpse.'

The thought of dying never bothered him. He had no illusions of an afterlife, believed, as the Bible, from dust he came and to dust he'd return. But deep down, secretly, he'd always yearned to feel he had done something worthwhile in his time on earth, left something behind – even knowing that once gone, he'd never know if it was. No, it wasn't that. It wasn't dying that bothered him. What did bother him was what those young boys made clear, that he was no longer the equal of what he once was, that without becoming aware of it, he had become diminished.

Shaken, not fully aware of how much the morning had taken out of him physically and mentally both, he dragged himself out of the shower, dried off, picked up the diary, opened it to the place marked where he'd left off, read 'The Moving Finger writes,' exploded in a fury of scalding, ballistic irritation, in no mood to read more of his father's self-serving bullshit excuses, slammed the diary shut, pulled his bathing suit and a top from his valise, headed down to the pool, lowered himself onto an empty lounge under an umbrella, ordered a BLT and a beer, and by the time it arrived, was asleep.

It was late in the afternoon before he opened his eyes. He became aware of the sounds of laughter and shouts, then looked around and saw bodies of different ages, sizes, and shapes lounging and playing in the pool. The sandwich, cut into wedges skewered with olive topped toothpicks, lay on a folding table at his elbow along with the bottle of beer, now tepid. Ravenous, scolding himself for the waste of money, he bit into the soggy sandwich, scowled, washed it down with the beer now flat, decided he was not up to tackling the diary or calling Chenny. Casting about in his thoughts, he wondered how to spend the evening. Nothing seemed remotely appealing, another evening in a pickup bar, the need to make bright conversation, pretending interest, drinking shots in order to spend the night with a warm body, all of it paled.

Three hours later, back in his room, after a dinner of fried oysters, french-fries and slaw on a worm-eaten driftwood table in the Blue Grotto, a kitschy restaurant several blocks along the waterfront hung with glass globes filled with colorful liquids, fishing nets and buoys, stripped to his jockeys, after a desultory search on the TV, he settled for 'The Boys from The South,' a spy thriller on HBO in which a sultry stripper befriends a shy thirty-five-year old bookkeeper who uncovers a plot to blow up Lincoln Center during a production of Carmen at the Metropolitan Opera in order to divert attention from a megalomaniac Ukrainian submarine commander in the Hudson River preparing to launch an ICBM at Wall Street's raging bull in a plot to topple Brazil's coffee economy and scuttle an alliance with the British. As the film climbs to a climax, the henchmen of the evil Dr. Mayhem unwittingly locks the meek bookkeeper and the stripper in a room in an abandoned warehouse, empty save for a discarded sheet of paper. Without watching, Jaime was willing to bet that in the final scenes it will be revealed that the mild-mannered bookkeeper's hobby is origami, the Japanese art of paper folding, and in his hands a single sheet of paper is a lethal weapon, and that in the mano a mano scene that follows, when the evil doctor returns to the room, drooling with the intent to have deviant sex with the terrorized stripper, the mild-mannered bookkeeper, after a furious struggle with the Doctor, that teeters this way and that, kills him with a fatal paper cut, at which point he rescues the stripper, saves the Brazilian economy and the European Union, President Gilberto of Brazil hangs the Medal of Honor around his neck, the stripper, who had heretofore totally despised him, has an epiphany, realizes that she had her fill of hunks with six-pack abs and jutting jaws, that she had secretly dreamed of someone touchy feely who preferred cuddling, and in a defining moment, determines to give up the tantric sex she'd been having on a trapeze in the Park Avenue penthouse apartment of a hunk, played in the movie by Mel Gibson, and give up for all time the ritual cult sex she'd been having using psychedelic oils with another hunk, a scion of a house of Scottish Royalty, played by Colin Firth, for the mild-mannered bookkeeper, her one true love, played by Woody Allen. And in the final scene, when she tears off his clothes and whips him with a tongue that would be the envy of a ravenous anteater, we discover the mild-mannered bookkeeper had been neutered as a lad by a near-sighted surgeon who removed what he mistook for tonsils, but to her delight and his joint surprise, and to the amazement of the senior staff at Johns Hopkins, they find that with dedicated effort the neutering was reversible, and Ebert and Siskel gave the movie five-stars at the Cannes Film Festival.

As the closing credits roll, Jaime was roused from his reverie by the chirping of his computer. Puzzled, he checked his watch, noted it was a few minutes before eleven, wondered who'd be calling at this hour, decided it had to be Susan. Opening the screen, expecting to see her face smiling back at him, inevitably, as always, it wasn't who he'd anticipated. Surprised, he hardly expected it to be her after the way she left last time.

He tried to make out the expression on her face but couldn't quite. He thought he knew them all, but obviously not. What he thought he saw in her face was an apologetic twisting of her lips, not the smooth way they usually spread when she was pleased, tilted up when she was delighted, neither up nor down when she was pensive, tilted down a bit when she was bothered, a tiny uncertain grin lurking, peeking out from the depths in her brown eyes, and a wide-eyed stare, as if surprised at the sight of something or someone not expected.

"Hi," Chenny managed uncertainly.

"Hi," Jaime returned, wondering what might be coming. He knew she'd been seeing Noah. "Hold a second. Let me turn off the TV." Scooting over, he reached for the remote, shut it off, and returned. "I…wanted to apologize –" he began.

"*No*. Let me," she interrupted, cutting him off. "I need to. I'm sorry the way I left. I had no reason to…"

"No." Jaime shook his head. "I've been wanting to call and kept putting it off. I was sure something I said was the reason and then…" he struggled to find the right words, "…what's been happening here…"

The tiny trace of a grin that had been lurking behind Chenny's eyes broke out evilly. "Like most men," she chided, with an obvious look at his crotch, "I've noticed, you think more clearly with your pants on."

"Chenny!" Jaime exploded, realizing he was sitting at the computer in his shorts.

"What?" she grinned, all innocent.

"What happened to the innocent young woman I knew… I thought I knew?"

"An Easterner debauched me."

"And enjoyed it, too."

"What's going on?"

"No. You first. How's your mother?"

"Her doctor is hopeful that the radiation will kill the tumor in the node in her neck, but they won't be sure until six weeks after it's over when the radiation dissipates and she can have a PET scan. Have your *visits* been tough?"

"The one in Charleston was really…only it wasn't in Charleston," Jaime realized he had had it all locked away and been hoping for an opportunity to tell Chenny, but didn't know if she'd want to hear it. "I…I don't… I'm not sure…"

"It's not been…" she offered, letting it fade off.

Jaime's face drained. His jaw hung listlessly, shaking his head.

"It's been pretty gruesome, hasn't it," Chenny sympathized, sensing his pain.

"I guess." Jaime shook his head. "But I wouldn't use that word. I feel like…like my father returned from the grave to rub my nose in shit. I know that sounds horrible, but that's how I feel. He did a number on me as a boy and returned to finish the job. He was a fucking selfish son of a bitch. He lived for himself, insensitive to the feelings of anyone else. He didn't give a damn for me. I wonder what he thought having me do all this would accomplish."

All of a sudden, Jaime realized he was raging and yelling across two thousand miles of the country, spewing the poison that had been burning in his throat, vomiting up the bile bubbling in his stomach.

"I'm sorry, Chenny. I apologize. If I ever have children, they're going to know what a parent is, that it's not a self-aggrandizing son of a bitch who pissed on the people in his life and then, after he used them, makes a grand gesture from beyond the grave intended to show what a good guy he was. Too bad the bastard didn't do any of it while he was alive."

Jaime ducked his head from the screen in fury, caught sight of himself in the mirror over the desk. His face was flushed, livid, enraged. He knew he was going on, that he should stop, but he couldn't. It had lain inside him for too long. He had to get it out. He told her of Leonora and Sydney, the feelings in the pit of his stomach, of inventing reasons not to go on, leaving nothing out.

"Shit. Chenny, I'm sorry. It's just that when I think of all this, I feel sick. It's like I've been frozen, unable to move on, do what I have to do so I can get on with my life. I've wanted to tell you, but not like this. I apologize." He had seen the shock in Chenny's face when he began and thought he'd blown it.

As Chenny listened to the words spew from his lips, his vehemence hit her like a blast from a furnace. It was a side to him she'd never seen, the vitriol, the rage, the anger. But then it occurred to her that this was the first time she'd ever seen Jaime express deep feelings, real emotion. Their relationship had never delved below the surface, as if nothing was hidden there, or the fear that their relationship couldn't handle anything deeper. In that instant, she felt a desire to be there in the room with him, to hold him, comfort him, and let all of his poison drain out. She had often wanted to tell him of her deepest hopes and fears but had been afraid she'd scare him off. Perhaps one day she would. As he went on, she tried to crystallize her feelings for him, decide if he was the person she could be happy with, decide if she understood what it was that drives him, and how his needs could mesh with her own. She sensed all along, that he was a needy person, but that he also had the capacity for great caring, the capacity to attempt great tasks, but underneath, unknown to him, he needed someone who could always be there for him when things didn't go well, and she wasn't sure, as much as she wanted it, she was capable of giving him that. He needed her, perhaps more than she needed him. She saw that, but he was not ready for that, she felt. He had things to prove for himself before they could be more than good friends. He needed to go off and find out what he was capable of. If he failed, he probably would be no good for himself or for anyone. If he succeeded, he might not want her, but at least there'd be a chance for them. He was his father's son. He'd be no good as a failure.

Chenny listened carefully to all he told her, where he'd been and what he had done, she asked questions, offered suggestions when he asked for them until, at last, they ran out of words.

They sat in silence avoiding each other's eyes for a while, neither wanting to hang up. At last, Jaime decided to risk it.

"There's something I've been wanting to ask you," Jaime added lightly, enigmatically.

Chenny looked at him curiously, as if wondering if it was some bit of nonsense, then saw his eyes shift nervously, as if it was something he'd been afraid to ask, or afraid of what her answer might be. She found herself growing nervous and tried to hide it, wondering what it was he wanted to ask, and what her answer would be.

When Jaime didn't continue right away, she lowered her eyes, not sure she'd prefer he didn't ask it, or if he would.

Jaime studied Chenny's face but found he couldn't read it. When the silence went on, there was nothing for it but to just ask.

"Chenny. After I finish up seeing this last family in Raleigh Durham, I was wondering if you would…consider…I mean, would you spend a week with me, or two weeks, I mean…I thought we could meet at the airport parking lot in Omaha, drive across the country, stopping at the national parks or wherever, ending up in San Francisco for a time, maybe you could help me find a place to rent, and you could fly back from San Francisco to Omaha to pick up your car."

In the silence that followed, Jaime was sure he'd blown it. He was unable to read the expression on Chenny's face and wondered if she might have been expecting him to ask something entirely different, and instead of being pleased by his invitation, was hurt by it.

"I'm sorry…" he began, wishing he could unsay what he asked.

"Sorry?" Chenny's face glowed. "I was only trying to think how I could arrange everything. I'd love to."

"You would?" Jaime's face metamorphosed into a huge grin. "And there's one other thing."

"What?" she looked at him curiously.

"I seem to be the only one right now who is dressed appropriately,"

"Jaime! You're a dirty old man," Chenny insisted, as she began to strip off her blouse.

Chapter 47

Jaime woke early, feeling refreshed for the first time since the ghastly phone call that sent him on this fucking journey. There was still one more visit to make it through before forgetting the whole fucking thing and setting off cross-country for Chenny. Sitting up, he yawned, stretched, looked out the window. The sun glinted off the masts of the boats in the marina beckoning and taunting him. A thirty-two foot Hatteras with a flying bridge, its outriggers set, was just now clearing the breakwater on its way out to a day on the fishing grounds. Why the fuck do I want to go through another of these fucking charades, he muttered to himself on the way into the shower, his stomach telling him it's time for breakfast, when I could be out in the ocean fishing, or on my way to Chenny? It's not like who's gonna know.

The more he thought about it under the hot tingling spray of the shower, the more attractive forgetting the whole fucking thing became. Shit. He swiped at the mirror, watching his face materialize through the mist. And why fucking bother to shave? He blinked, took another look at his face. Hardly anything there. Shit, he grimaced, disgusted. He'd had that same fucking argument with himself almost every morning since as long as he could remember. Why fuckin' shave? It's was so stupid. Shit. He knew why. The nagging. He'd be conscious of it eating into him all day long. He'd look like a fuckin' old geezer from skid row.

Shit. What he really needed wasn't a shave but a lobotomy to cut out the fucking nagging. What a great idea. No more nagging. He played with it as he toweled off. No more nagging, no more. He could sell it. A hundred down and a hundred a month for life. They line for it would be longer than the line for the Christmas show at Radio City Music Hall in Rockefeller Center. He'd be as rich as Stephen Jobs and Mark Zuckerberg combined.

He knew who implanted the fucking nagging in his brain: his mother. He could see her, bending over him just before he went under, her eyes gleaming above the surgical mask, a hypodermic syringe with a twelve-inch needle in her hand, in the syringe nagging serum. When he came awake, he'd been programmed.

Shit. Why don't I just read the rest of his fucking fairy tale and...whatever.

I had someone else entirely in mind, Melissa Boudelaire, the day I entered J. Peete's, the haberdashery that catered to the city's swells. Melissa, a client of Richelieu and Sons, the small brokerage house where I was employed as a customer's man, had come in to enquire about adding municipal bonds to her rather considerable portfolio, and I had set out looking for an outfit that would make it seem I was in her league for our coffee date. The two-piece off-the-rack Ralph Lauren knockoff I wore wouldn't have paid for the tax on her Jimmy Chloos.

It was rare that I took notice of my surroundings, and even rarer that I had the desire to chronicle them, but what happened that day was so over the top, I couldn't have rested that night if I hadn't made note of it.

Bruce, 'my J. Peete fashion consultant,' eyed me up and down with a smile Joe may have turned on Marilyn the day he caught her with her skirt up around her waist. He spared me the hand rubbing, but I saw it in his eyes.

He showed me to a six-sided mirror and proceeded, with a flounce of his wrist, to tape me, shoulders, chest, waist, sleeve to wrist, crotch to toe. Up close, there was a slight but definite scent of Brut, a manly scent. Bruce had a soft oval face, with just the edge of pushiness poised ready to spring from behind his speckled brown eyes. He was just a fraction over five-foot-ten and managed to walk without bending his clothes, a conservative three-piece midnight brown suit woven through with almost invisible threads of bubble-gum pink and canary yellow, and a yellow tie with emerald green sprinkles. A fresh forest green handkerchief hung sassily from his jacket pocket. High polished oxfords completed his wardrobe. He was in his late thirties but looked older, the result of acute tendonitis in his calves from walking on the balls of his feet.

Neither a rack nor a collection of clothes were on display on the floor, the equivalent of the living room in the presidential suite of the London Ritz. I had the impression when I entered the store that he decided I had lost my GPS and had wandered in by mistake, but recalling the scene in Pretty Woman when Julia Roberts is snubbed by the sales women on Rodeo Drive, ever since waited in hope lightning might strike a second time.

The cerulean blue Italian silk jacket, burgundy Savile Row slacks and Pierre Cardin regimental striped tie, Dash, his assistant brought from the back, at 'only' $3,400, he assured me, were what was being seen at tea in Covent Gardens. 'Notice,' he urged, 'that for a lot of guys, pastel colors *conjure up the Preppy Handbook, but what you see here is a smarter shade of pale.'*

I checked myself up and down in the mirror to see if I could see it. Standing behind Bruce in the mirror, close enough to overhear, a woman dressed as if she had just come off a fifty-mile cross-country dirt bike ride grinned, scrunched up her nose, shook her head 'uh uh' and mouthed 'He's color blind.'

I did my best to suppress a smile, but I fear a tiny one escaped. Bruce turned to see the cause. The more dressed down shoppers were, the more affluent they were likely to be these days. "Exquisite, isn't it," he nodded, assured.

There was nothing usual about Gerry, including the way I met her. If not for a color-blind 'consultant,' I might never have. That we ever came to hook up, I with her, she with me, surprised the hell out of me.

How do I describe her? She told me when I came to know her, she wasn't taken seriously when she started as gofer in the small local ad agency. She was too…timid…too little womanish. She had ideas, but the Pukka Sahibs in the agency ignored them, so she decided she had to out-kook the kooks. She assessed herself, decided that she had no unusual features she could exaggerate, nothing that would make her standout – she's actually pretty in an ordinary way, sexy even – but she didn't want to trade on sex, at least not obviously, so she took to showing up in the office in combat boots, safari shorts, and shirts with cut off sleeves, spiky hair with purple tips, purple eyeliner, triple pierced ears, long dangling earrings, and a tiger tooth necklace, bought a musket and took up target shooting, and drove around like a Tanzanian safari guide driving a cross-country jeep. But for formal evenings, she chose eye-popping long slinky gowns slit up the side with combat boots.

The Raleigh Durham Research Triangle is a Mecca for doctors and scientists, no-nonsense people dedicating their lives to finding drugs and medical procedures to help mankind. You can imagine, she told me, the reception I had at first. If I was going to stand out, I quickly realized, it wasn't only my image I had to change, but I had to capture the attention of those who make burnt offerings to Madison Avenue and would offer their first-born to nail an account.

'The first commandment of adverting in Advertising 101 is Sex Sells (as was the second through to the tenth commandments). Every ad I wrote henceforth had the underlying theme, Madam (or Sir), are you a good lay?'

Gerry's first real success was a twenty-second TV spot she wrote for a Mrs. Springer's cupcakes.

Scene: A Swiss-born, bearded, Freudian psychiatrist, middle-aged, seated at his desk, a gorgeous thirty-ish, trendily dressed woman on a leather couch alongside.

(Woman in despair): It's my husband, Doctor.

(Dr. nodding sagely): Yezz?

(Woman, teary): When he comes home in the evening, he has dinner and falls sleep in front of the TV. And in the morning...he has to rush off to work!

(Dr.) Ach zo, tell me Mizssus Jones. You haff children?

(W, mystified): Children? Why...yes.

(Dr.) You giff your little ones Mrs. Shpringer's cupcakes?

(W, tears drying): Why...of course.

(Dr.) Your children, zay are lively?

(W, enthusiastically): Oh yes, I can't keep them down.

(Dr.): My advice ist give him Mrs. Shpringer's cupcakes. Put a shpring in his step.

(W, a light bulb goes on): Oh. Of course!

(Dr.) Dot vill be $300 pliz.

Overnight, Mrs. 'Springer's' cupcakes went national. Gerry received 20% of the franchise fees as payment and opened her own agency. When she was in character, she was a combination of Tug Boat Annie and Aunty Mame, swearing like a sailor on shore leave, but when we were alone, she could be as soft and cuddly as a kitten. She taught me, but I never could shoot a musket like she did, and it was wild and hair raising hanging on for dear life when she tore over foothills of the Carolinas in her two-by-four. She drove at only two speeds, fast and stop. Thank God for roll bars and reinforced seat belts. We came close to tipping several times but somehow she was always was able to right us. But I ached for days.

As I came to set down the events of what I now see will be the final days of my life, I find I am able to see things more clearly than when I was living it. I guess it's not unusual to try to make sense of one's life, especially when you are facing the last remaining days. There are parts, I admit, I am less than proud of that I do not care to dwell on, for recriminations serve no useful purpose, and certainly not at a time like this. But there have been joyful events I had the good fortune to have had. I have loved and have been loved. If life is a journey, let it be for the joys one remembers. It may be selfish to do so, but after all, are we all not selfish in our own way.

As Doctor Dunton, a psychiatrist, once said to me, "We do what we have to do." What could be more selfish? If it is to bring joy to others, is it not that it brings joy to us? If it is at our expense, is it not because the pain is the lesser? Is acting so not simply evidence of being human?

Perhaps what has brought the most joy to me are the children whose lives I shared for even a short time, Jaime, the son I abandoned to do what I had to do, Susan, Marsha's daughter, who I abandoned when, had I not, it would have been painful for her mother, Sydney, when my presence would have been a daily reminder of the life I innocently condemned him and his mother to, and finally Leslie, Gerry's lovely imp, with whom I lived until my last days, whom I abandoned rather than allow her memory of me to be of someone who was once her 'daddy' whose body abandoned him.

> *'The Moving Finger writes; and, having writ,*
> *Moves on: nor all thy Piety nor Wit*
> *Shall lure it back to cancel half a Line,*
> *Nor all thy Tears wash out a Word of it.'*

Omar Khayyám

Chapter 48

Jaime closed the diary and pushed it as far away from him as the breakfast table allowed. Feelings tumbled through him he hadn't expected. He thought he had buried them all the night of his bar mitzvah when he realized, finally, his father was never coming back. Day after day at first, then month after month, then year after year he waited for him, certain at first, later hoping. But when he didn't come to his bar mitzvah, he stopped hoping and buried all the feelings he had ever had for him, keeping only the anger. Now, the feelings he thought were buried came rushing back. He saw now that the reason he had put off reading the last of the diary was that it would be the last contact he'd ever have with his father. A sense of profound sadness he couldn't explain filled him, and a profound disappointment that he would have such feelings.

He shook his head to clear it away, swallowed the lump in his throat, blinked away a tear in his eye, laid the remains of his father, his diary, to rest beneath his dirty clothes at the bottom of his suitcase. He would do what he had to do, that's all, and move on.

Jaime had no difficulty finding the phone number of Gerry's agency in Durham, but had to wait for some time before the secretary could put the call through. When he told Gerry who he was, and explained the reason he wanted to meet her and her daughter, she was both delighted and saddened, delighted to meet him – she hadn't known his father had a son – and saddened to learn of where he had been living and of his death. This rather puzzled him. He was aware his father didn't tell the women he'd lived with he had a son, but from what he surmised from the diary, he and Gerry had been close and lived together for some time until he left Durham a year ago. Why had he left, and why hadn't they been in touch since. There must, he was sure, be more to the story than let on.

When Gerry discovered he was in New Bern, less than two hours away, and that he was hoping to meet her and her daughter, she urged, "Can you find your way to my office? My daughter Leslie is enrolled at UNC's summer music workshop in Chapel Hill, about ten miles south of here. We could meet here and drive to the camp together. If you'd like to stay over, I have plenty of room."

Jaime hung up, leaving the invitation hanging. She sounded gracious and welcoming, but something didn't fit, the meetings, even with Susan's mother, had been awkward. The reception he'd find when he actually arrived was unsure. In any case, a short fifteen or twenty minute drive both ways from Durham to Chapel Hill and an hour dinner and he'd be off.

"What's that letter on wall in the reception room?" Jaime asked when he was shown into her office later that afternoon. He had timed his arrival at 4:45, a quarter hour ahead of time. On the walls of the reception room, in addition to framed ads for dozens of accounts, was a Photostat of a letter Gerry sent to the CEO of General Motors in Detroit.

"It's the letter I sent demanding royalties," she answered smartly. "They are trading on my name."

Nothing his father had written in his diary about Gerry had been an exaggeration. When he stepped into the reception room, his eyes popped. The décor was elegant kook, over the top. Ads for clients hung in a psychedelic array on purple and orange walls alongside bleached cattle bones, crossword puzzles, a photo of a sunburned woman with wild fuchsia-tipped hair sitting on the back of a Jeep at the top of rugged outcrop of rocks, odd bits of desert flotsam, Coca-Cola bottle caps in honor of Coke's birthplace, New Bern, and assorted what not illuminated by hidden halogen lights.

The stunning young redheaded receptionist who rose to greet him was wearing a Stetson, a red denim cowgirl's jacket, a ruffled embroidered ranch blouse, a black string tie cinched with a turquoise Hopi Indian ring, and the rugged hiking boots his father's diary mentioned. A scent hovered in the air he couldn't quite identify, woodsy, possibly the trademark of an account hawking aromatherapy or, more prosaically, scented candles. The range of accounts the Agency handled appeared even more eclectic than the diary suggested. A once over of the walls showed everything from Mrs. Spinger's Cup Cakes, camping equipment, freeze-dried rations, the local Ford dealership, Carolina Grits, Horner's Health Spa, Jacks's Southern Style Ribs to *Randy's* BBQ Sauce, '*It won't let you down.*'

Between phone calls and ad-checking, he noted that the receptionist found opportunities to steal cute glances his way. He pretended not to notice, chalking them up to his curse, how women lusted after him – he'd joke about it, as if deep down he didn't really believe it to be so, but it also occurred to him there was a possibility, a slim possibility, that it might be reserved for special clients. There was something in her body language, the way she moved, that suggested she would not be averse to an in depth discussion of the weather. He could imagine her spontaneously whooping: 'Saddle up ye bronco!'

The way she greeted him with 'Gerry's expecting you,' made him feel that his visit was the reason the Agency originally opened its doors. 'It'll be a minute or two. She's with a client,' she smiled, leading him to a camp chair in an alcove arranged for intimate tête-à-têtes, offering him coffee, Coke, biscuits, and Mrs. Springer's cupcakes. Jaime smiled, hearing coffee, tea or me?

It was but a few minutes later, hardy enough time to sample one of Mrs. Springer's chocolate cupcakes, when she came for him and showed him into Gerry's office. He knew, when Gerry rose to greet him, that she had to be well into her fifties, but was surprised how youthful and trim she appeared and the energy she radiated. There was an indefinable magnetic quality about her he couldn't quite identify, but one he wished he possessed, a quality that made him want to know her. He had read a bit about her from articles on the web and expected someone rather formal and imposing, considering the size of the agency she built and headed, but surprisingly she seemed as delighted as a child to meet him and have the opportunity to show him about.

Had he not read his father's description of her and several articles on the web that made much of the rags to riches theme, how she had grown up in poverty in a home with a mostly absent father, leaving the support of her, her brother and two younger sisters to her mother who clerked at a Piggly Wiggly, he might have been unprepared when he was brought in to her office. Instead of scaring her, one writer prone to hyperbole penned, it had forged her into a resilient and upbeat woman, hardly, Jaime expected, the kind of woman to have taken up with his father. He wondered if, as Marjorie Kennetton, Montclair's Dorothy Parker of the Round Table, would ask, what's a story without a little exaggeration?

"General Motors is trading on your name?" Jaime blurted out in response to her earlier answer, wondering if the sparkle in her eyes was some kind of mischief, or what made her a success. Her office could have served as a set for Bonanza, driftwood furniture, hanging cowbell lamps, knotty wood-plank flooring. He had never read anything of a GM settlement, but he didn't follow business news closely.

"Absolutely. GMC Advertising. It's for Gerry Marino Inc. I offered to settle with GM for a small royalty on each car they sell."

"The letter is dated seven years ago. Did they settle?"

"Not yet. I'm waiting for their reply."

If he knew from the way she was sizing him up what she was thinking, he would have been embarrassed. She saw his eyes grow wide drinking in everything in her office. A shadow in her eyes said she sensed there was something missing in him she couldn't put her finger on, beyond an awareness of the difference between them.

"You're not interested in the nuts and bolts of advertising, are you?" she inquired. "You're looking at these ads as if they were a black art."

Jaime blushed. "I guess what…what's the word…what *gets to me –*"

"That's three words," Gerry corrected.

Jaime reacted stiffly, as if chastised, then caught Gerry's mischievous grin. He was hers. "I know," he began again, "how hard it is to create something out of nothing. But what you have done from scratch is amazing."

Gerry laughed, hiding a blush. "You're looking at me as if I was an alchemist, a practitioner of black arts. If I told you I could sum up everything you need to know to be a marketing and advertising expert in one sentence, and that you could leave here equipped to open your own agency, create powerful ads, or unlock the key to motivating people, would you be amazed? I shouldn't admit this, but it's like everything else. Reduce a magic trick to its simplest elements and you find it's bloody easy. It took me four years to realize that, but once I did…"

Gerry's hazel eyes seemed to search for something from her past. She pushed a wisp of spiky hair from her sunburned brow and bit her lower lip. "I struggled in high school," she admitted. "I tried to memorize everything my teachers tossed at me and wound up with my head so filled with stuff that when it came to a test I panicked, trying to sort through it all. But somehow, when I entered college, it came to me. I found the secret."

She paused, a speaker's practiced effect, before continuing, "I sailed through college, doing hardly any work. But…if I were to tell you the secret… I'd have to kill you."

Jaime wondered if this was at part of the mystique, the magician's trick, never allow a peek at what was hidden behind the curtain, or if Gerry's mind was a steel trap, absorbing everything and making it sound easy. He rubbed his jaw, imitating Rodin's 'The Thinker.' "If I sign a non-compete clause, and persuade GM to ante up, would you reveal it?" He had begun to see what his father saw in Gerry, but wondered what she saw in him.

Gerry appeared as pleased as punch. "Some see what at an ad agency does as mysterious as an alchemist turning lead into gold, but…reduce it to it down to the two P Quotients, and it's as simple as…"

When she let the idea hang, Jaime caught on. She had a fish on the line and was waiting for the hook to set. Unwilling to disappoint her he cued, "Two P quotients…?"

"Let me show you around the offices here, and if you're still interested," she tantalized, "I'll explain."

For the next twenty minutes, Jaime could hardly think of anything else as she took him around the agency, the creative staff, 'the *bull* pen,' she mimed, the art, time and space buyers, production, ending with the billing department (*agency income is primarily from 15% of ad costs rebated by the media, but clients may also be billed for the cost of commercials, which can run into the millions*).

"Boiled down," she summarized, screwing her face into a moue, Madison Avenue gets the glamour – think *Mad Men* – local agencies do the same for local products, but we also do the ground work for National products – think *work*. We create point of sale pieces, improve shelf space, set up impulse displays, prepare tie-in ads.

Back in her office, she led Jaime to a pair of leather camp chairs set around a faux campfire, offered him a Coke, and when comfortably settled, added, a grin stealing out of her signature impish gleam, "Let's see, was there something else?"

"You mentioned something about 'two Ps,'" Jaime responded. "Would that be a shortening for the six Ps we stress in the classroom?"

Gerry's brow furrowed. *"Six P's?"*

"If I told you, I'd have to kill you."

The sprinkling of freckles on the bridge of Gerry's nose merged, her long tapered fingers beat a tattoo on her knee and she lifted her Coke as a salute. "OK, podner, fair is fair."

"I warn you, I'm playing with your mind." Gerry ran her hand down over the length of her face, like a mime, changing her mobile face from sad to happy. "Do not underestimate the value consumers pay for a products' emotional or Prestige Quotient. Take a pair of sneakers, for example, one pair sells for $40, the other with Magic Johnson's endorsement sells for $240, six times the price. Both pairs' Product Quotient may be identical, but the Prestige Quotient for Magic's might be 10 versus 3 for the other.

"Nike trades on this. It makes none of its products. Its budget goes for endorsements. Tiger Woods received $100 Million for the use of his name, Rory McElroy received the same. College and professional sports teams are paid to wear uniforms with its 'Swoosh.'

"Advertising's job is to acquaint consumers with the product, boost the Prestige Quotient. You would give a diaper's Prestige Quotient zero, but don't underestimate the value of a name: Pampers' emotional Quotient may be 5.

"Perfume is different. Price alone adds to the Prestige Quotient. A scent at a higher price typically outsells that same scent at a bargain price.

"But make no mistake: All the advertising, endorsements, logos, catchy names, fancy packaging or impressive showrooms – think Lexus versus Toyota; same car, different logo, different showrooms – will fail to breathe life into an inferior or shoddy product.

"There, boiled down, is the secret: The driving force behind it all isn't Mad Men. It's market research. Researchers identify consumers' needs or wants; we get the easy job; we just write the words."

Chapter 49

Jaime pulled his car into the space next to Gerry's Jeep and climbed into her Porsche. It was coming onto six, the parking lot had almost emptied. Gerry took the top down and set off, meandering along tree-lined streets with well-appointed brick, wood and glass houses set far back behind lush green lawns. Rhododendrons, forsythia, jonquils, and tea roses were in bloom, the soft breeze was filled with delicious fragrances, Gerry nattered on about the vibrant economy of the Raleigh-Durham-Chapel Hill research triangle and Duke University's role anchoring the region.

"By the by," she continued, pointing out important buildings and churches, clearly enjoying the role of tour guide, "you might be interested in the derivation of the name Durham, an interesting bit of trivia. Celtic cities and towns, as a Professor of Literature you surely know –"

"Thanks for the promotion…"

"…correction noted," Gerry continued with a nod and a toss of her head indicating a particularly stately example of colonial architecture on the left bordered by a stand of red oaks, "often took names from the local geography. Hollywood, a town not far from Dublin in Ireland, originally called Holly Wood, probably derived from a nearby grove of oaks. In Celtic lore, groves of oaks were the dwelling place of holy men. Durham derived its name from 'dun,' which in Celtic is a hill fort, and from the old Norse 'holme,' an island. But some insist the name derived from the legend of the Dun Cow and the milkmaid who guided the monks carrying the body of St. Cuthbert to that site in tenth century. Dun Cow Lane is believed to be one of the first streets in Durham England. But some say that history, as later rewritten, is more valid than was observed by those who originally recorded it."

Jaime scrunched down behind the windshield, tightened his seat belt, and tried not to be obvious checking if the passenger side had an air bag when

Gerry stomped down on the accelerator as they left the local streets and entered the drive bisecting the University's lush grounds.

"Wimp," Gerry mouthed, catching Jaime out of the corner of her eye.

Jaime grinned. "I know an actual example of rewritten history. There is a town near where I grew up in New Jersey in which its history is pure fiction, the invention of a fraternity brother."

Gerry took her eyes from the road for a second, stealing a look, asking *what nonsense is coming*. The car swerved for an instant but quickly pulled back into lane. Jaime kept his eyes rigidly glued straight ahead, pretending not to notice.

Gerry wondered if she heard what she thought she heard, or if it was the rush of wind over the windshield, but Jaime's eyes remained fixed on the road. A glimmer of a grin creased his cheeks and pursed his lips.

"What?" she asked.

"What?" Jaime replied, as if clueless.

Gerry considered this. "C'mon," she demanded, accepting defeat.

"Oh," Jaime replied innocently, "rewriting history. You'll probably think I'm making this up. I didn't believe it myself... A fraternity brother of mine, Stan, a number of years older, told us this story late one night when the keg was spitting more oak shavings than beer.

"I don't remember Stan's last name. It was something like Corman or Corkman, but that's not important, for there was nothing unusual about Stan. In looks, you couldn't distinguish him from any other guy, except he had the bluest, guileless eyes you ever saw, which would not be odd, except that he had a face that seemed to be a combination of a beaver's and a gargoyle's, except his nose wasn't long and twisty, but heavy and hooked, and the beaver part came from thick lips and two amazing front teeth, but the oddest thing about his looks was that he didn't look like that at all. When you looked at him closely you saw that he looked like everyone else, but nevertheless, you had that impression. Anyway, as I said, you wouldn't be able to tell him from a million other guys except whoever made him got all the parts right, but attached them too loosely so that at times they'd all go their own way, though somehow Stan was able to get them to coordinate. Anyway, as I said, maybe because he looked like everyone else, he wanted to seem odd, so he would take odd positions on everyday things. He never ate vegetables, only meat, and potatoes, for one, but complained if a restaurant didn't serve vegetables. Anyway, as I said, he was not the kind of guy who would make up stories, though we knew he would exaggerate some, so when he told us this story, we didn't believe him.

"In 1989, a year when he was in high school, New Jersey was celebrating its centennial anniversary. Students throughout the state were required to write a term paper on their city or town's history. This was before the internet, when research wasn't googling Wikipedia, so it took more than a little work. A week or so, before the end of the term, a girl in his class, Peggy something, Miss Constitution, a kiss-up, stopped him in town loping along in the odd way he walked. 'What's your paper on?' she asked. 'Paper?' he looked at her blankly. 'Duh. On the history of Milltown that's due tomorrow.'

"She saw from his expression that he'd forgotten about it. 'You're gonna flunk!'" she said snarkily.

"Stan told us he raced home, dug out his IBM electric, the typewriter that had a round steel rotating ball with letters and numbers, inserted a sheet of paper, sat down, and then and there wrote the history of the town making it up as he went along, names, places, dates, events.

"A week later, the papers were returned. Miss Constitution, nose in the air, threw him a look. 'A.' His paper received a 'B.'

"The papers of all the students in the school were then collected and sent to the principal. A few days later, they came back. Stan's paper had been chosen best in the school; his grade was raised to 'A+.' Miss Constitution looked like she was sucking a lemon.

"But what happened next was the real story. The best paper from each school was sent to the Governor in Trenton. Stan's paper was chosen there as the best of the best.

"Stan was sure it would end badly, hoped the whole thing would die there, go away, but the next day, the school's librarian called him and asked for a copy of his paper. She said she had read his report and was amazed to learn all those things about the town she had never known. She wanted a copy for the town's archives.

"Knowing Stan's penchant for exaggeration, we listened to his story with the amusement we would listening to Mark Twain tell of his experiences in Roaring Camp. 'Hey! you pissy-assed skeptics!' he roared, seeing the disbelief in our eyes. 'It's all true. You don't believe it? Check the school's library. You'll find my paper there.'

"You know, damned if it wasn't! We drove down to the school a week later. The paper was there, in the archives, along with a copy of the award from the Governor."

Gerry swung her eyes over to Jaime disbelievingly. Her brow turned into wrinkles, her lips compressed. She snuffed in air through pinched nostrils and shook her head. All at once, the most beatific expression came over her face, as if she knew she had been had. "Hey," Jaime cried, "If you don't believe it, go to the school and look for yourself. I didn't believe it. But I swear. I saw it."

Gerry drove on, sneaking peeks at Jaime, looking for tell-tale signs that it was a hoax, but Jaime's face gave nothing away. She'd never check, he knew, enjoying her dilemma. She would never really know if he had seen it.

Chapter 50

As she turned into the circular drive around the front lawn leading to the front of the colonial style Chapel Hill Country Club, the sprawling golf greens stretching out behind it, she pulled the car over to the side of the drive and stopped. Her face became grave. "Jaime, there's something you need to know. After you called me, I called Leslie to tell her you were coming to dinner to meet her. She knows you're your father's son, but she doesn't know why your father left; he didn't want her to know, sure it would distress her. He told her he had some family matters to attend to, but she was terribly upset. I tried to quiet her, not knowing whether to tell her or not. I didn't know which would hurt her more, and your father made me promise. She was sure he never really cared for her. Every time I tried to talk to her about it, try to get her to open up to me, she shut down. I wanted you to know this. If she doesn't want to talk to you, if she shuts you off, understand it's not you she's angry with, it's your father. And it's me, too; she has as much as accused me, that it was something I did that made him leave."

The grin Jaime had held in came out but became a grimace. He knew she meant well, but she had no way to know what it confirmed to him. Everything his father touched, even when he was thinking of others...turned to shit. *Thinking of others.* From everything he'd remembered, from everything he'd witnessed since, the only thing his father ever thought of was himself. He'd let others heal the fallout. It was not going to be him.

As Gerry tossed the key to the valet and led Jaime into the appointed lobby of the clubhouse, he tried to fix his face to give away not even the slightest indication of the thoughts raging through him. Shafts of late afternoon sunlight, filtering through the sky-lit domed roof, supported by twin rows of tall ivory and brown veined marble columns, fell softly on multi-hued chairs and sofas nested around Venetian glass coffee tables that looked dwarfed under the high ceiling. Directly ahead, at the opposite end of the entry, a pair of glass doors guarded the opening to a stone balcony overlooking the first hole of the golf course. Two couples in pastel shorts, knit shirts, and visors caps, sipping tall, cool drinks, were standing comfortably about, watching a foursome getting set to tee off.

Gerry led Jaime directly to a recess at the left far end of the lobby where a small group of teenagers were laughing and chatting, using the arms and backs of the armchairs, as well as the cushions, as seats. In the group, with boys hanging on either side of her, was a twelve-year-old girl with Gerry's coloring, full lips, broad cheekbones, and hazel eyes. Labrador black hair hung halfway down her back tied with a red bungee elastic. She looked up as Gerry approached. Gerry reached to straighten a wisp of her hair that had slipped out of the ponytail and fallen over one eye and kissed her brow, Leslie rolled her eyes at her friends, as if, *please…*

Gerry smiled, grinned at her friends, reached for Jaime. "Jaime, this is my daughter, Leslie; Leslie, this is Jaime, Aaron's son. And these are Leslie's friends, Gail, Naomi, Thad, and Mark." A chorus of 'Hi's greeted her from all but Leslie, whose face became grim.

"Leslie," Gerry whispered in her hair, low enough, but not so low Jaime missed it, "Jaime came to bring something his father wanted you to have."

Leslie shook her off. Her friends looked on, not sure what was going on.

Jaime saw it, felt the tension. The girls had the appearance of leggy tadpoles, almost at the stage when they would burst out and metamorphose into the young women they would become. Gail and Naomi, like Leslie, skin bronzed in the sun, sprouted legs waiting for the rest of their bodies to catch up. They were all wearing Madras shorts, knit shirts embroidered with the letters CH over the left breast pocket and sandals. Thad, the taller of the boys, looked as if he had outgrown his clothes; his body had more angles than Pythagorean formulas. Mark, a few inches shorter, was muscular; what he was short of in height appeared to have made it into his biceps and shoulders. Had he, Jaime wondered, ever looked as gawky as either of them?

"Hey, guys," Gerry said, refusing to lose her upbeat self, "we don't want to rush off, but we have an early dinner reservation. Can Leslie catch up with you after?"

In the mystical wordless language that teens communicate with each other, Leslie made it evident to her friends that she was being dragged off to a fate worse than death by an evil person, leaving Jaime no less uncomfortable, as she intended.

The maitre d' in the dining room greeted Gerry and high-fived Leslie as, at a nod, an assistant appeared to lead them to a table under an umbrella on the slate lined patio. The table was set with frosty white napkins, gold-bordered bone china, and gleaming cutlery. In the center was a tiny spray of lavender in a miniature bubble glass holder. A black jacketed waiter in white ducks appeared with a pitcher of ice water, filled the glass tumblers, followed by another with menus who also took drink orders, Gerry's a Sam Adams, Leslie's a coke, Jaime, feeling the need for something stronger, vodka and a twist.

Jaime settled into his seat uncomfortably, wondering if he had been brought as a buffer, to diffuse the tension, and if there was a chance they could get through dinner without a conflagration, so he could leave and be on his way. There seemed little chance; the expression painted on Leslie's face was identical to the one he'd witnessed on the boat, Wendy's, surly anger for being forced into a situation not of her choosing, wishing for a way to escape as quickly as she could.

Gerry made small talk as the drinks were brought, which interested neither Jaime nor Leslie, both anxious to get this trial over with. It was clear to everyone that neither wanted to be here. Jaime tried to remember what he said to Wendy that helped, but it didn't seem to come. It was really Wendy's father, not he, who did it, asking her to go shoe shopping. But it was when he stopped trying to force the words they came to him.

Motioning Gerry aside with a slight movement of his head and a turn of his hand, he turned and slid his head a fraction nearer to Leslie. Leslie pretended not to notice, but he whispered low enough that only she could hear, *"I wish I were you."*

Leslie recoiled, startled. She stole a look at Jaime, her eyes saying, if she heard what she thought she heard, he must be from outer space. Jaime shook his head, whispered, "I do. *I wish I were you.*"

She turned now looking at him fully on, uncomprehendingly, a panoply of emotions racing through her face, her hazel eyes becoming watery.

"I do," Jaime repeated. "You were loved by my father."

It was as if the talk in the dining room became silenced, that all motion stopped, that only the two of them were there, by themselves. "Your father...your father loved...no..." she managed.

Jaime's head dropped. "He left a diary. I have a copy for you."

"He's...*dead?*"

"Yes."

"If he...loved me, why didn't he tell me why he left?"

"I don't know. Maybe he told you the only way he could. He went off because he didn't want you to grieve."

Leslie's eyes blurred with tears. She shook her head 'no.' "I'd want to be there. Were you with him when he died?"

Jaime shook his head. "No. The last time I ever saw him was when I was six. I never saw him again...alive. You knew him longer than I."

Leslie turned to her mother, tears streaming down her face. A waiter came over, pad in hand. Gerry motioned him away. "Did you know?" Leslie asked.

Gerry eyes filled. She nodded 'yes.'

"Why didn't you tell me?"

"He didn't want you to remember him that way. He wanted you to remember the way the two of you were together before he knew he was dying. I couldn't tell you. I was hurting too."

Jaime watched the two of them feeling the love they shared with his father, a love he never knew. Afraid he'd act a fool, he excused himself and headed for the washroom, leaving the two of them with each other at the table.

When he returned some minutes later, the mood had changed, the air that hung over them was sober, the tension was gone. Gerry looked up at him with mock severity. "Hey! I thought we came here to eat."

The waiter, standing by, looked at them, wondering why, what she said, had them all laughing.

Before he and Gerry left later in the evening to return to Durham, Jaime handed Leslie the envelope with the stock certificates his father left for her. Leslie whooped delightedly, kissing him. "It'll be for the flute I've wanted I've been saving up for forever."

Chapter 51

The drive from Durham to Omaha offered Jaime an opportunity to see some of the country he always planned to visit one day, like so many of the vague things he'd filed away and let gather dust in the storehouse he kept under lock and key in the recesses of his mind. He started in Ashville, the southern end of the scenic Blue Ridge Parkway after a three-hour drive from Durham, and followed the lush road framed by elms, and oaks and maples in full leaf, and low-lying shrubs in a painter's palette of colors, snaking along as it climbed from six hundred to six thousand feet above sea level, stopping to take in the stunning views from lookout points whenever the mists circling the tops of the mountains cleared. Rolling forests stretched as far as the eye could see in places, at others only as far as the next mountain. Down below, as if looking through the wrong end of a telescope, crystal clear rivers and slow winding streams curled through fertile fields and valleys, here and there a solitary house or hut. As he drove from one lookout to the next, he felt the pull of sadness, the wish that he could be making this drive with Susan, but it was a dream he knew could never be, for there was no way they could make a life together. It was better, be told himself, as he followed the winding road, often two-lanes, to rid his mind of those thoughts and focus on reality.

He and Gerry had stayed up late talking the night before over a couple of bottles of a wine with names he'd only read about and couldn't pronounce. He had been surprised that a woman who had to be so tough and level headed to have accomplished what she had, would have had a soft spot in her heart for his father, that she hadn't seen beneath the froth to the absence of substance. She saw the look that filled his eyes when she told him of the time they spend together, and the way it hit him when she told him of how his father had become the father Leslie never knew. "You love someone not despite their flaws or idiosyncrasies," she explained, trying to ease the sting, "but because of them." Your father was an amiable humbug. But in a way, so too am I. We knew each other for what we were and enjoyed and loved each other despite it, or maybe because of it.

"Is there such a thing as perfection?" she asked, decanting the last two drops from the bottle with the reddish brown cork and exotic label. "Or is what draws us the flaws and imperfections that endear that someone to us…and us to him, or her? How boring it would we be if we were all perfect, how difficult it would be to live with Michelangelo's David or Da Vinci's Mona. We seek gods and goddesses, but crave humans whose flaws and imperfections make them unique."

"And then," she added, narrowing her hazel eyes and half covering a wicked grin with her long fingers, "attempt to smooth away the edges."

It was coming on to two o'clock. He had rarely drank more than one, or at most two, glasses of wine in an evening and he had been feeling it. "Is it more likely," he'd asked, working at assembling thoughts that skipped and slid in and out of focus, "that there is a natural progression in the lovers we seek? In the diary my father left – I have a copy here for you – wait a second – let me find it –" he fumbled around for what seemed forever – until "ah, here is the passage: *Did you meet your soul mate? That always happens on the first day of school, right? We did make one determined attempt to restore the magic, but it was gone.*

"From the continual changing of partners everywhere, I suspect that the real reason for giving up on a relationship, more often than the reason given, is a longing to recapture that *first day of school magic*, but in time, I wonder if we don't come to realize that that *magic* is a siren's call, that there must be something more, genuine caring for the other one's happiness beyond one's own, and more, an appreciation of them as a person that transcends that *first day of school feeling.*

"But what do I know. I've never been in a committed relationship. Am I talking too much?" he tried to focus through the haze. Gerry's face had been fading in and out, the room was swimming. "What seems important to me now," he pushed on, telling himself not to, "– who knows – it may not seem important to me at some time in the future…" he stopped, sure there was an important point he was trying to make… discarded one, then another, finally decided on… "to use Henry Rollins' words… *Sometimes you feel like some kind of criminal, for wanting, knowing you are unable to offer in return all that that someone deserves because you know you've settled, afraid that the one you really want you can never have, that that's the closest you'll ever come to it, and you go along nagged by guilt, cheating someone who deserves better because you don't want to be alone.*"

He had tried to grab her eyes with his to see if she understood what he was trying to say, and when she looked up, he had the feeling that she could see into his soul, that it wasn't that it was so deep into the night, or the drink, and he felt naked, unmasked. He tore his eyes from hers, stared out beyond the leaded windowpanes into the darkness that seemed to have enveloped the world, with nothing there to see but the North Star. Sometime later, she showed him to the guest room. When he awoke, she was gone, but there was a note in her handwriting: "I hope you find whatever it is you are looking for."

Directionless, he had slept in, in no hurry to get on the road, finally heading off after a late start. Other than for a few places along the highway when, for no apparent reason, the traffic slowed to a crawl and, equally unexpectedly, flowed freely again, the drive was unremarkable, skirting the only city of any size, Greensboro. Three and a half hours later, he exited I-40W and pulled into Molly's, a truck stop along the local road heading into Ashville, wedging his sports cars between semis, pickups, clunkers, and vans, the sure sign of good food and hefty portions. There was a wait until a red plastic covered tall stool became available at the Formica counter between the tradesmen, workers, and truckers.

The guy on his right, in tan chinos and boots, with shoulders the size of an Olympic discus thrower, was mopping up what was left from a bowl of beef stew the size of Oklahoma with a chunk of freshly baked crusty bread the color of fresh cream, the dark complexioned dude on the other side, sporting a two-day growth of beard, hands scrubbed pink but showing mechanic's grease fingernails, was making inroads into a Caesar salad the size of the East River's Governor's Island as viewed from the top of the Empire State Building, washing it down with a diet Coke.

"Hey, Doreen," someone at the far end of the counter called. "How 'bout tonight?"

Without swinging her head around, the rangy, late twenties gal behind the counter tossed back, in a voice hoarse around the edges, juggling a Texas-sized bowl of hearty beef stew to one man with one hand and refilling his coffee mug with the other, "Sure. Give me your home phone number."

"My home phone?"

"Yeah," she agreed with a cute flip of her head, her dangling copper earrings swinging free of the pencil sticking out of her blonde highlighted chestnut hair, "so I can call your wife and ask permission."

"Hey, Doreen," another called, "I'm not married."

"Shouldn't wonder," she called back, grabbing a mile high tuna melt accompanied with potato salad and pickle and a stack of griddle cakes with strips of bacon from the shelf in the window to the kitchen.

"You," she asked, coming back to Jaime.

"Special and," she shouted to the kitchen Jaime's order, "fried chicken, mashed, gravy and biscuits!" turning back with a glow to chatter up a muscled hunk next to him in tan chino pants, shoulderless blue denim shirt.

He had his pick of 'Vacancy' signs along the road going into town, chose Day's Inn, $40 a night, nagged by shrinkage in his wallet. At the south-western end of the Blue Ridge Parkway he toured the mansion and gardens of the sprawling 19th-century Biltmore estate, the work of the architects Frederick Law Olmsted and Morris Hunt that may have been inspired by the formal gardens and rooms and hangings of the Palace of Versailles, and after dinner went on to visit the galleries in Ashville's downtown Art District.

A thirty-minute jog the next the morning before breakfast got the kinks out and helped ease his mind of the emptiness of traveling alone. Before leaving the motel, he called ahead, reserved a ticket that evening for Nashville's Grand Ole Opry and a room at the Nashville Marriot, a hotel converted from a train terminal from an earlier era, a time when passenger terminals were as majestic as Newport's mansions. That done, he set off to explore the neighboring small towns preserved from that earlier era, now lined with galleries and restaurants, general stores, museums, railroad memorabilia, launch sites for rafting and tubing down the Green River, train rides through the Great Smokey Mountains and hiking and camping.

After a lazy picnic lunch along the cascading river, little ones nearby giggling and laughing dodging the spray, wading near the edges, picking special stones for their parents, he set off for the five-hour drive to Nashville to see Larry Gatlin and The Gatlin Brothers singing *All the Gold in California, I've Done Enough Dyin' Today, Broken Lady* in the Grand Old Opry.

Coming upon the broad dome-shaped glassed-in Opry house façade just after sunset, its three circular chandeliers ablaze, each with fifteen cone-shaped frosted lights, was like trekking through a wilderness and coming upon Lincoln Center in a clearing, a far cry from the barn in which the Opry grew in 1925. That evening he sat with over four thousand, whistling, stomping, applauding, foot tapping along with people dancing in the aisles in dungarees, western shirts, tuxes, and gowns,

It was another three days, nine hundred miles, fourteen hours of mind-bending driving to the Omaha airport, with breaks to ride to the top of the Gate Way Arch in St. Louis, visit Legoland, and battle his way through a thirty-ounce t-bone steak at the Majestic in Kansas City.

Chapter 52

A glimmer of sun peeked through beneath a blanket of low-lying black clouds when he set off early the next morning on the last leg for Omaha whistling 'Everything's *Almost* Up to Date in Kansas City.' Chenny would be waiting at the Omaha airport three-and-a-half hours away. *Funny*, he thought, *how life turns 180°*. When he was a teenager biking up the Palisades, camping on an island in Lake George, the last things he, and the guys, wanted with them were girls. Now he wanted a woman…not just for the sex, but that, too.

An hour into the dreary hundred-and-sixty mile drive, drops began to splatter against the windshield. Within fifteen minutes, the dark clouds opened with a vengeance. His windshield wipers struggled to clear the sheets of water, the headlights offered minimal visibility, the tires lost traction planed at unexpected moments, traffic crawled, the three-and-a-half hour drive became a five-hour mind exhausting ordeal.

Radio stations faded in and out, red taillights blurred, headlights coming straight at him glared. Road signs rose through the gray mist and disappeared, mile after gray mile ticked the odometer, his eyelids grew heavy. The car lurched, the tires thumped, wakening him with a start. He yanked the wheel, pulled the car back too far, righted it, worried Chenny was waiting. He flexed his jaw, ground his teeth, worked the muscles in his mouth, rotated his shoulders to keep awake. Instead of noon, it would be two or later before he'd reach the airport.

Thoughts drifted in and out. He sampled one, then another, then another, settled at last on the last day he'd spent in Red Plains, dejected, without a plan, dogging his way along, coming upon Chenny sitting on the top step of the church. He began to reconstruct her as he saw her that afternoon, her burnished brow scrunched up grinning, pretending it was a coincidence she was sitting there, the sparkle in her liquid brown eyes, the curve of her high cheek bones, the set of her jaw when he teased her, the rhythm of the rise and fall of her breasts under the pale peach knit jersey, her matching shorts that reached only to the dimples in her knees, the curve of her calves, her long legs, the leather thongs round her ankles she tossed on the bank after shedding the rest of her clothes and climbed naked into the lake, and after making love on the shore under the hot, dry sun, he redressed her as he imagined her, as an Indian maiden in fringed buckskin, but when she was fully dressed, he was not sure that was really her, and he stripped those clothes from her piece by piece and redressed her as a Chinese princess in a multi-hued silk cheongsam that flowed down over her like a summer waterfall, falling down over her shoulders, the rise in her breasts, the planes and whorls of her stomach, the mounds of her slender hips, down, down, down, inch by inch, coming to rest on the beaded red slippers on her tiny feet.

And then he dressed her as a tiny ballerina twirling atop a music box, and when he came near and lifted her skirt to explore what lay beneath it, she turned and looked at him with sad, innocent, pleading eyes, but when he saw it wasn't Chenny but Susan, he shook his head and looked again and saw it was Chenny, and he scolded himself for allowing his thoughts to play tricks on him, for Susan was someone he could never have, it was Chenny who was waiting for him, and it upset him that the memory he had tried so to let go betrayed him. No. It wasn't his memory that betrayed him, he saw, it was that he lacked discipline, he had not tried hard enough.

But then his glance went to the digital display on the dashboard, and the angle of the hands reproached him, reminding him to hurry, that Chenny would be waiting, worrying at the reason for the delay, and thinking of her, he thought again of that afternoon at the lake.

When at last he arrived at the airport and searched for Chenny under the overhang at the arrivals area, he experienced an almost overpowering need of her. It was barely five weeks since he had been with her, but all at once he felt awkward. She looked at the unfamiliar car in surprise, made an awkward attempt to kiss him under the eyes of airport security amid the bustling comings and goings, but the kiss missed his lips and landed on his cheek, and when he stowed her valise in the trunk and she climbed onto the passenger's seat and clicked the seat belt, she busied her hands in her lap and made no further attempt to reach for him.

The need to touch her, hold her, gripped him, but her thoughts were unreadable in the charged air suspended between them. He was afraid to look too closely, afraid he'd see hurt and disappointment in her liquid eyes. It was too late. He should have drawn her into his arms at once, kissed her, and held her. But the moment had passed. But now, doing nothing was worse. He longed to reach for her hand, lace his fingers in hers, feel the warmth grow as their fingers determined to satisfy the need that could be satisfied only one way, but as he set the car in gear and headed off, the sheeting rain was an excuse to keep both hands on the steering wheel and his eyes straight ahead.

He took the exit leading to Route 29 north, the route that would take them to the first site they planned to visit, Mt. Rushmore, an eight-hour drive, too far now with this late start to make it today. Her nearness tugged at him, wouldn't let him be. The need to hold her, feel her in his arms, taste her breath was all but overpowering, and when a lay by appeared, he slowed, eased off the macadam and pulled in, sitting wordlessly in their little private world, enveloped in rain and mist, listening to the whisper of tires going by on the wet road off behind them, the almost silent purr of the motor, the swish of the wipers back and forth, the soft flow air from the air conditioner. Neither spoke, thoughts that were different and not different. They dared little glances, ducked back, surrendering again into their own private thoughts, until, as if of their own accord, their hands tested the tiny infinite space between them and, at once, their kissing had an urgency, a desperation to arrange each part of their body to each other's, pulling at the sodden clothes to reach what lay beneath.

"What is it?" Chenny whispered, pulling Jaime to her when he pried away from her. When he didn't answer, avoided her eyes, she pulled away her soaking panties, working her hand down between them to find him pleading, "Yes, please…please."

"No," he whispered, his mouth on hers, "no," trying to hold back, sucking the sweet moisture from her tongue.

Her eyes searched his, wordlessly asking '*why.*'

Jaime wedged back, bit down on his lips, afraid he would be unable to hold off. "Please," he whispered, "not here," trying to think himself down.

Chenny looked at him uncomprehendingly…

"Not here," he whispered hoarsely once more. "Where we can be naked, where I can explore every inch of you, where I can fall asleep inside you, where we can wake and do it again and again. Please," he pleaded, tugging at his clothes, smushing away the steam from the window with his fingers, turning the defroster on high to clear the sodden air. "We can be in Sioux City in less than fifty minutes," he pleaded, putting the car in gear, trying desperately to fix his mind on other things, Chenny, pressed tight to him, holding him, kissing him, his neck, his cheek, his nose, his ears as he put the car in gear.

"Again and again and again?" She pried her head from his neck to look at him straight on. "Hah!" she exploded with a hint of delicious mischief, leaving Jaime struggling to keep his thoughts on the road.

Chapter 53

They would have slept in at the motel, but decided to time the four-hundred fifty mile, six-hour drive from Sioux City to Mt. Rushmore to arrive no later than four in the afternoon so that they could watch the sun, as it slanted down, casting gold, orange and blue hues over the faces of the four Presidents. The temperature was a delicious fifty-eight, the landscape, freshly washed, sparkled, the morning sun lifted rainbows from the raindrops clinging to flowers and shrubs and hiding in clefts and fissures in the rocks alongside the road. Earlier, when they set out for a five-mile run before returning to shower and breakfast on chilled orange juice, fresh eggs, whole-grain toast, sweet rolls and coffee laced with heavy cream, the fresh, clean smell of warm water vapor was everywhere.

Chenny looked different when she climbed from the shower. He couldn't put his finger on it. Her cheeks weren't rouged but they were rosy, not from the sun, her hair was tied back with a yellow ribbon, away from her face, and her breasts looked fuller. A pair of Indian beaded moccasins were on her tiny feet – that bothered him some, wondering if they were a gift from Noah. But it was more than that. Her eyes were lowered shyly, avoiding his, as if embarrassed to look at him, as if what they had shared last night was more than intimacy. It was a turn on so powerful, so visceral, he had to restrain himself from reaching for her right there. He had never been able to get his head around the thought that women might have powerful sexual appetites, not the image he had of them as innocent, demure, timid…until, at last, awakened from Cinderella sleep by his careful, tender ministration, like the petals of a rose opens and unfolds in response to the patient warmth of the sun. Jamie prided himself on being logical and rational, yet it was one of the irrational beliefs he allowed himself.

"Doane Robinson," Chenny read, slipping on a pair of horn-rimmed glasses as Jaime set the car in drive, "who originally conceived of the idea for the monument in 1927 to promote tourism in the Black Hills of South Dakota, proposed it be carved in the Needles, a site in the Black Hills of eroded granite pillars…"

"Hey!" Jaime squealed, suppressing a grin, "Stop that."

"Just checking," Chenny replied, lowering her glasses to the bridge of nose, "to see if the granite pillar eroded. Shall I continue?"

Jaime glowed. Never had he remembered Chenny being so playful.

"I'd better not," she judged. "You're looking a little peaked. Where was I?"

"The eroded needles."

"Oh yes. Gutzon Borglum – pay attention, there'll be a quiz later – Gutzon Borglum, the sculptor who designed and oversaw the 14-year project (and died just ten months short of its completion in 1941), decided that the Needles were too thin to support the sixty-foot high carvings of George, Thomas, Abe, and Teddy…"

"George, Thomas, Abe, and Teddy?"

"Don't interrupt…and chose Mt. Rushmore instead, partly because it faced southeast and had the advantage of maximum exposure to the sun."

"Thank you, Ms. Wicked-Pedia." A shadow fell over Jaime's face but immediately lifted.

Chenny caught the change, puzzled at it, let it drop. "Not at all, sir," she quickly offered, "delighted to be your guide."

"I appreciated that last night."

"I wanted to make sure you didn't overlook places of interest."

They were stopped at a traffic light. "Places of interest," Jaime's eyes strayed to her breasts. "Your breasts seemed…excited…to see me."

Chenny blushed, her eyelashes, deep chestnut with touches of amber, rose as if about to soar revealing liquid brown eyes, but returned so quickly he might not have noticed if he hadn't been watching.

Chenny pulled away, studying him full on, as if trying to make sense of him but failed. "You're…"

"I'm…?"

Chenny shook her head, "All of the above. One minute you're happy, bubbly (if it's not too much of a stretch to use the word bubbly and you in the same sentence), and the next it's, like, the final day of judgment has come and you've been found wanting."

"Wow!" Jaime exhaled, wondering at Chenny thoughts. She was her own person, gave nothing away at times a million miles away, but he didn't ask, had never wanted to know. Their relationship had been the way he wanted it, uncomplicated, friendly; if she wanted more, she never said, he never asked.

She continued to observe him closely, keeping her thoughts to herself. A number of miles went by. Jaime kept his eyes straight ahead on the road, content to allow himself to believe she moved on.

"Jaime," she broke in when the silence extended for what seemed forever, "something came over you before when I was telling you about Mt. Rushmore and you said 'thank you Ms. Wicked-Pedia. What was it?"

Jaime scrunched up his mouth as if to rid it of a bad taste. "That limp 'Wicked-Pedia.'"

Chenny looked at him curiously. "That limp Wicked-Pedia?" They'd left the city and Jaime had ramped up the speed to more than eighty miles an hour in prospect of the long boring, barren drive, the kind he had become familiar with on long stretches with between cities and towns in Nebraska.

"It's hard to put into words," he admitted. "In a way, and this may seem – what's the word – dramatic – ridiculous – 'Wicked-Pedia' was…was just one more failure."

"Jaime. You've lost me."

"That pun…embarrassed me. It wasn't clever, it was limp. I know that sounds idiotic, making a big deal of something of no real importance, but in a way it was important – *to me*. I tried to come up with something clever, and came up with…*that*. It's stupid, I know, but to me it's why I've yet to set down more than a few pages of the book I always proposed to write, my failure to find the right words or phrases to express the thoughts I've tried to put on paper that meet the standards of real writers…you know what I'm trying to say.

"I've wanted to create something worthwhile, but I'd start, scratch out the words I wrote, start again, and after the sixth or seventh attempt, wonder if what I'd put down first wasn't best, or if it would be better to abandon it and try to find an idea I might be able to find words to say what I wanted to say."

Chenny pulled her head from Jaime and watched unseeingly as miles of inhospitable, hardscrabble road, as straight as if drawn by a two-hundred mile long ruler ran by. "Jaime," she struggled after some time, seeming to find it as difficult as Jaime to find words that fit, "trying for perfection sets yourself an impossible task. You wind up, inevitably, dissatisfied. If others don't like the work, you believe them justified; but if they find praise for it, you question whether they're competent to judge it. You write yourself into a box with no escape."

"So what's the solution, sendoff writing I'm dissatisfied with expecting it will be rejected?"

"Hey!" he added, "I got it." The corners of his hazel eyes narrowed into a mischievous smile puffing his cheeks and stretching the muscles in his jaw.

"I've always been exhorted to set the bar high. Now you're saying I set it too high."

Chenny shifted uncomfortably, unable to decide whether to take him seriously, or if he was having her on. "No!" she insisted, needing to make herself understood. "There are no perfect words. If every author was bottled up, unable to pen to paper, constipated, nothing would ever be written."

Jaime reached across and poked Chenny playfully. "You're saying I'm constipated? I will not stoop to offer the obvious reply."

"Jaime, it's the idea that is important, not the fear of failure. Tom Wolfe was rejected by eight publishers who send it back with the pat, 'We regret to inform you that...' before he found one willing to consider publishing his manuscript for the book that came to be entitled *Look Homeward Angel,* and even then, Wolfe had to agree to work with the editor to cut two-hundred pages from the eight-hundred-twenty-five pages."

"No. What I'm suggesting is that by not submitting anything, you don't risk rejection but accept failure. You know, I'm always amazed, living where I do so close to a Reservation, how much we have failed to learn from the Indians."

Jaime tore his eyes from the road slipping past at almost ninety miles per hour, arid, barren, stretching mile upon empty miles. This was not the woman he believed he knew, the blank slate, the tabula rasa, the woman who listened to him with encouragement without judgment. The face looking back at him was one he had never seen before, determined, fearless, not afraid to risk saying what was on her mind, someone who cared enough to the risk saying what he might not want to hear. The change did not match the easygoing manner he believed defined her. It was as if she was emerging from the kiln. He had always insisted he learned more from facing his faults than receiving praise for his merits, but now he found himself deciding if he liked a side of her he had never seen, and if, as he claimed, he really appreciated being laid bare.

"You've read of Tecumseh," she continued, "the chief of the Shawnee tribe whose father was killed in 1774 by white men who were violating a treaty by coming on Shawnee land. 'SLEEP NOT LONGER,' he entreated in a speech before a joint council of the Choctaw and Chickasaw nations. 'Will we let ourselves be destroyed without a struggle...you will soon be as fallen leaves and scattered clouds...driven away as leaves are driven before the wintry storms.' It was a wakeup call, warning the tribes not to surrender to their fate, but it was, as well, a message to any willing to surrender passively to their fate."

Jaime listened stunned, keeping his eyes straight ahead at the road without end, his insides twisting, the words grabbing and pulling at him, interrupting the pounding of his heart. For an instant, he wanted to respond in kind, but in the haze dancing over the macadam, an image of himself metamorphosed, not the image that looked back at him when he posed naked in front of a mirror, but the image of him Chenny must see, and he swallowed the words, wondering she would want to be with him as he really was.

Chapter 54

"You've gone native, I see," Jaime grinned, climbing out of the shower the next morning, fumbling naughtily with the terry towel sagging loosely around his middle. Chenny grinned, pirouetted, sending fringes of her beaded deerskin skirt swirling around her tanned thighs, offering a glimpse of black silk panties. She had cinched her waist-length chestnut ponytail with a beaded leather thong and an eagle feather.

The previous afternoon they had stood for over an hour, straining upward, etching into memory the sixty-foot tall faces of four Presidents that had been carved into the towering granite hills, a project it took skilled artisans fourteen years to complete, as awesome, in its way, as the Sistine Chapel created by Michelangelo in the Vatican. It was impossible to stand in the midst of the rugged majesty about them without a rush of blood, without the awareness of the greatness of the nation these men helped create out of an untamed wilderness, without being aware of the awed muted voices of fathers, mothers, and children, without thinking, this is my land, I was born here, I am part of the this, the greatest nation in the world, I am so lucky my ancestors made their way here, hearing once again the story of the founding of this nation, the roles these men and others like them played, men, women, children who dedicated gave their lives that this nation might survive, that these dead shall not have died in vain – that this nation, under God, shall not perish from the earth.

Tears blurring Jamie's eyes had run down his face unembarrassed. "I feel so lucky to have been born in this country," he whispered to Chenny.

Once the door to their room was closed behind them, she looked around and shook her head. "Has everything in America become homogenized?" she protested furiously. "Doesn't it eat into you, coming from where we were to…this. We are losing the diversity that made this country great, what our forefathers gave their lives for. I was expecting something…something rustic, hand-hewn logs, an Indian adobe, animal skin rugs, hand-loomed bedspreads, but it's another Hilton, a Marriot, a Days Inn. How long will it be before there is a McDonalds in Red Plains?"

"For a real treat, stroll down the Champs Élysées and see Americans who traveled to Paris eating hamburgers in McDonalds."

They should get on the road, Jaime knew, if they were going to reach Yellowstone National Park before sundown, a seven-and-a-half hour drive after a planned stop of an hour or so in Rapid City to visit another wonder on the itinerary, but he found himself wrestling with himself, diverted by the sight of the black silk panties and the stirring under his towel, surprised to discover what he had become capable of. Last night, the taste of Chenny's toothpaste, and another he never before remembered, set him off, and it was only a few hours earlier had they finally drifted off to sleep. As surprised as he was at his own endurance, he was amazed at Chenny's; he never seemed to need to ask. A story he once heard leaped to mind, that of the fellow who was promised he could rid himself of his shrewish wife in seven days by screwing her to death. The very next morning he set about it: morning noon and night, six times a day, he had her, in bed, over the sink in the kitchen, under the dining room table, against the living room TV, on the toilet seat, and again before sleep. In three day his cheeks were gaunt, his eyes twitched, he walked with a stoop, his voice rose to a higher register, but he kept at it with purpose. On the sixth night, as they fell off to sleep, he levered his head up painfully for one last look at the blush blossoming on his wife's face, musing, 'S-h-e-he-e-e…doe-s-n't…kn-kn-ow…i-t…b-b-but…o-n-e…more-ore…d-day…and…*she dies!.*'

"What," Chenny asked, aware he was far away.

"Nothing," he grinned, flushing, turning away to rearrange his clothes.

Chapter 55

Before stopping for breakfast, Jaime called to book a room for late arrival at the Old Faithful Inn. Built in 1903 of native timbers and stone, it was the most requested of the Park's nine lodges, according to the guidebook. "Late arrival?" the reservation clerk repeated. "*How* late?"

Jaime hesitated. He heard the clerk whisper to someone: "He wants late arrival!"

"How late," he chirped snarkily, "October?"

'A smart ass,' Jaime motioned to Chenny, flicking his nose.

"We've been completely booked since February. Would you like me to check availabilities at one of the other lodges in the Park?"

Jaime exhaled, leaving the receptionist on hold. "Damn!" he replied after a beat, winking to Chenny, "the Dean is gonna be pissed. I was supposed to scout the lodge and the services for a week-long seminar the University of San Francisco planned for next summer for the staff, fifty or sixty couples…"

"Fifty or sixty couples…?"

"Yeah. Well I guess we'll have to find somewhere else…"

"Hold on a sec," the fellow said, whispering to his partner. "Wait. I have a suite we were holding I can free up…I can make it available at the corporate rate for a standard. What name should I book it under?"

"What was that all about," Chenny said, puzzled. "What seminar?"

Jaime grinned. "I told him your name was Mary. Seems there was room at the inn after all."

The morning was crisp, the temperature rising slowly from the fifties during the night. In no hurry for another long, numbing drive, the two dawdled along the fifteen-minute drive to the Chapel in the Hills.

"It's like coming through a wilderness and coming upon a house Hans Christian Anderson built for Red Riding Hood's grandmother," Jaime marveled. The Chapel, covered with wood shingles, was an exact replica of the Borgund Stave Church in Norway built in the twelfth century, 'stave' from

234

the Norwegian word 'staver' for wood pole. Over one thousand existed in Norway in the Middle Ages, less than thirty remain today.

"If I were to tell the little ones of it in one of my classes during story-telling time," Chenny reveled, her fingers building images in the air, "I'd show them three pictures and tell them to close their eyes and decide which it looks like most, a fierce Japanese samurai warrior all dressed in medieval armor with his legs spread wide apart with his bulging arms planted squarely on his hips, a Christmas tree from the forest reaching up to the sky hung with wooden shingles, or a Japanese pagoda with roofs extending out in all directions with the ends curling up to catch the rain."

"That sounds like a lot more fun than trying to stuff Chaucer and Shakespeare down the throats of kids who just wanna have fun."

"At that age, they are so adorable. They want to do everything they can to please the teacher. And their minds, they're amazing, their imaginations are boundless. They sop up learning like…"

"Sponges?" Jaime offered.

"Hey! What a great word!" Chenny exclaimed, chucking him under the chin. "I can see why you're a professor of literature."

"Smartass. Find your own word in the future."

The road was boiling off mirages when they turned onto I-90 for the four-hundred-forty mile, seven-hour trip, allowing for a pit stop and a picnic along the way on an eighteen inch, freshly baked crusty baguette, 'rat' cheeses, Genoa salami, tomatoes on the vine, mustard and bottled water they picked up at a convenience store on the way out of Rapid City.

Along the way, radio stations offering an eclectic selection of talk radio and mountain music faded in and out. "Wow, this country is big," Chenny marveled as mile after mile flew by without a sign of civilization.

"Someday," Jaime observed, "it'll be faster to get to the moon, two-hundred-forty thousand miles from the earth, than going cross country."

"Only," Chenny groused, "if you don't have to go through security at the launch pad."

Chapter 56

"Talk about big," Jaime's eyes popped. "What a sight. Yellowstone is bigger than the states of Rhode Island and Delaware combined. And this lodge. It's monstrous."

They'd arrived at the Lodge shortly before seven just as a geyser shot up one-hundred-twenty-five feet into the air. "The Lodge looks like it was built by the Sorcerer's Apprentice."

Chenny's brow furrowed.

"Disney made a movie about it. The sorcerer goes away for the day, ordering his apprentice to sweep the room while he's gone. Instead, the apprentice attempts to set the broom sweeping using the sorcerer's incantation. The broom starts sweeping slowly, but soon sweeps faster and faster and wilder and wilder. Frantic, the apprentice tries to command it to stop but doesn't know the command and the broom continues faster and faster, wilder and wilder, until, at last, the sorcerer returns and stops it. The story is from a poem by Goethe that Paul Dukas, a French composer set to music."

Chenny grins, shakes her head. "Is there a point to this?"

"The lodge. Look at it. It looks like it was built by the sorcerer's apprentice who piled logs on logs, higher and higher, wider and wider, adding wing, then another and another, and by the time the sorcerer returned and commanded it to stop growing, the Lodge had grown to size of Massachusetts and the height of the John Hancock Tower."

The Lodge, over a hundred years old, constructed entirely of native logs stripped of bark, was cavernous. At its very center was a massive fireplace constructed of stones of various shapes and sizes dug from the nearby ground that rose to the apex of the six-story atrium, its base, like a tent large enough to shelter a tribe of Indians. Mammoth oak logs smoldering in the grate filled the room with their rich, biting aroma of burning wood.

As the two of them entered and headed for the check-in desk, a troop of ten-year-old girl scouts in green blouses and shorts, hiking boots and lanyards, led by a twenty-something den leader, was coming out of the dining room in pairs of two's and three's, chatting away excitedly about elk, deer and other animals that came out at sunset to graze in the meadows and drink at the streams, a hapless father was racing after a two-year-old, and in one corner, a family of five were sitting on suitcases impatiently waiting for transportation to take them to another lodge that had rooms.

Shit, Jaime mouthed, weary from the long drive, *I hope we're not going to be told we'll have to wait to get into our room, that there's been a screw up.*

"I don't want to sound negative," Chenny said when Jaime came returned from the desk, her eyes curling with mischief, in a way Jaime never before noticed, "but the accommodations you arranged with a view of the geyser doesn't include water-proof futons and an umbrella, does it?"

Jaime opened his mouth to reply, but nothing came out. This was a Chenny he had never seen before, uninhibited, free to say whatever popped into her head. It wasn't only in the words, or the way she said them, but the easy, relaxed way she had become with him. It was evident in her shoulders, no longer poised to back down, in the way she twitted him without restraint, a subtle sign that their relationship had climbed to a new level, that the balance between them had changed. It was unexpected. He found he was…amused…and delighted. If he wanted Chenny, he could no longer take her for granted.

He turned, bent to grab the handle of their wheeled valise, and with mock intensity commanded, "C'mon, woman, follow me."

"Aye aye," she grinned with a salute. "Let's recon that 'suite.'"

The Park was too big to explore in one day, even in seven. They rose early, set out as the sun, breaking over the mountains in the east, streaked through the trees and glades and bushes, the ground wet with dew, mist still clinging to the low-lying areas where a herd of elk grazed. They stopped to explore canyons, gaze at tinkling streams tumbling over rocks and fallen limbs, marvel at hot thermal springs, a shaggy bison with a calf at its teat, dozens of small animals, foxes, squirrels, rabbits, chipmunks, stopped for coffee and sweet rolls at the Blackwater Creek Ranch, returned to the Lodge at nine for breakfast, shower and change, set out again after lunch climbing mountain trails, fording streams, returned to have dinner in the lodge, disappointed to find neither buffalo, elk, bear or rabbit on the menu, nothing more exotic than corn-fed beef.

A grin stretched Chenny's cheeks from ear to ear at breakfast, her eyes fixed impishly on her tablet. The room was buzzing with excitement, hiking boots, backpacks, youngsters, parents, couples. "As Captain Sully said as his plane headed for the Hudson, 'do you want the good news first, or the bad news?'"

Jaime lifted his eyes from his plate, speared a strip of bacon, shook his head, the smile from last evening never having left his face.

"The good news is, it's a straight drive to San Francisco on Route 80 through Reno, where we're booked in at the Eldorado Hotel and have reservations for the ten o'clock show of Cirque le Noir, the 'Dark side of Cirque.' The bad news is, it's eleven hours to Reno. As they say in your native language, *Oy!*"

"*Oy!* If you have a secret wish to be Jewish, don't be afraid to 'come out.'"
"*Oy!*"

Jaime studied Chenny in the bubbling light slanting down from the lights high up in ceiling timbers, aware of qualities that had always been there that he hadn't, till now, been aware of. Her sparkling eyes followed his playfully. *Damn,* he thought, *there's more there than he'd realized.* Life with her would not be one he'd dreamed of, peaceful, comfortable. She would be worth fighting for. Susan was a dream, a dream that could never be. Chenny was real. When he thought of Chenny, he saw her in shades of white and gray, steady, predictable, comfortable.

But when he thought of Susan, he saw her in colors, exciting, unpredictable, thrilling.

Chapter 57

As the miles fell away, making little dent in the miles still to go, Jaime struggled with the ifs ands and buts. Cars whooshed past, the tires strummed relentlessly on the macadam. Answers led to questions ever more difficult to handle. Could Chenny really be the one? Was Susan no more than a fantasy? If she, Chenny, was the one, would she be willing to live somewhere else, make a life with him? Could Chenny survive living somewhere else, not only survive but would her qualities remain uncompromised, untainted in a metropolis where the tempo of life was fast, hectic, where temptations, diversions, enticements lay in wait. Would living elsewhere change her, make what makes her special be corrupted? Would she end up an empty husk in an alien world? Again and again the questions came without answers. There were no answers.

"Chenny," he began when he realized he was at an impasse, testing the words as they formed on his tongue, with no direction or idea where they were heading, "Tecumseh, the Indian chief you spoke of, his speech 'Sleep Not Longer' has gone round and round in my brain, 'Sleep not longer,' the words scolding me, telling me to wake up, stop making excuses, take charge of my life, begin the book I was going to write, finish projects I started I left half done, set myself a task, a plan, and tackle it, finish it, make productive use of my days. Can I ask you the same question: What is it you want to do with *your* life?"

Chenny exhaled, her insides crumbling. She pulled her head from the road and edged around to where she could look at Jaime, to see him as he was. He was, she knew, a man of many dispositions. On the surface, she saw how he tried to appear light-hearted, taking nothing seriously, make fun of life, but underneath she saw he was deeply troubled, saw the many concerns he wrestled with. His question, she sensed, revealed more about what was troubling him than what might be on her mind, that though he would deny that the question had deeper meaning, it did. She puzzled how to answer him, knew it hadn't been asked lightly, that if she were to answer playfully, the connection that was building between them would be lost. But she was also concerned that if she answered honestly, that she had no all-encompassing grand plan, it would not be what he hoped to hear. Yet how could she answer honestly otherwise. Not that she felt she was drifting. She had plans, but they were not the grand, encompassing kind she saw he harbored.

"Jaime," she ventured at last, taking a deep breath and letting it out, "that's such an easy question to ask – and such a difficult question to answer, I hardly know where to begin. I sense that you see your life still ahead of you, that you are not yet living it. I feel I'm already living my life, not waiting for some indefinite time in the future to begin living it. Wait," she said, sensing he was stirring, about to object. They were speeding along, passing semis and trailers, rarely was a vehicle driving less than ten miles above the posted speed limit. "Please. Let me finish.

"I have a loving family, my mother and sister and nephew and nieces, I have close friends, people around me where I live who come to each other's aid if needed, I don't know if there is a God, but the church is a cohesive family that brings us together, and I have a job teaching little ones that gives me great joy.

"Is this all I want in life? No. But I don't want to give any of it up. What I want, hope for, in addition, is to have children of my own, at least one, hopefully two – it's wonderful having a sister I shared secrets with, a best friend – and I'd like to be in a committed loving relationship and, in time, married. I guess if I would express it in its simplest sense, I want a life built around love."

Jaime tensed listening to Chenny describe the life she envisioned, finding it harder and harder to not make it obvious that it was making him uneasy, that the response he unexpectedly evoked went well beyond the usual meaningless banter they relied on to fill awkward silences, banter that revealed nothing more about either of them than whether they preferred white or red wine with dinner. For reasons he couldn't really make out, his insides were shaking. He had thought it was a game that they were playing, pretending that their interest in each other went no deeper than friendship, a game that had rules, keep it light, never dip below the surface, never reveal anything meaningful about their true selves. By breaking that unspoken pact, she had revealed more than he was comfortable discovering, not only about herself but about her thoughts of a future that might include him. The game they were playing had turned serious and he wasn't prepared for it. He had not dared breathe, but when it became more and more difficult to keep his face and body frozen, he tried to make evident, with a deep breath and a look of intense concentration, that he was not taking what she said lightly, as he would if they had stayed in the game, but that it was something that he needed to give deep thought to. And doing so, it surprised him to find that it was.

As Chenny's voice gave way to the shush shush shush of the tires tracking the seams in the road, Jaime felt it urgent to show Chenny how wrong it was to shut herself off from all the world had to offer, to show her that she was looking at only a tiny fragment of a much larger picture, to show her how frozen her thinking was, but each time he opened his mouth to say that, he shut it before it escaped his lips, locked up, unsure if the way of life she described might not be better than his, or if it not, if he might do an irreparable disservice to her – or to himself – by persuading her of it.

They switched drivers, mile after mile went by, the silence between them enveloping them like a shroud, sucking the air from the car, the banter, the upbeat mood that had sustained them, that had lightened the wearying drive, vanished. Jaime stared blindly straight ahead, settled in gloom, Chenny, infected by Jaime's despondency, sank into a morass of her own.

Mile after troubled mile went by. Chenny felt as if she had been punished for sharing her innermost thoughts, for letting her mask slip away, for allowing Jaime a glimpse into the real her, that she had shut him down, turned what had been an easy, fun trip, an opportunity to enjoy the brightness of each other's company, a feeling of two merging into one, into a tangled knot.

When the silence seemed to drone on forever, she wished there was a way she could undo everything she had said, pretend nothing had changed, tried to think of something, anything, that might lighten the mood, snap Jaime out of it, but the look on his face was so dark that she went back to staring straight ahead, fixing her mind on nothing but steering the car between the lines of the seemingly endless road. She felt as if she was sinking, inch by inch, slipping deeper and deeper into a bottomless oblivion, unable to see a way out of it until there seemed no option but to get off in Reno and fly back, let Jaime go on without her, when in the back if her mind she became aware that Jaime was saying something in a voice so low, so lacking in energy, it was almost swallowed up in the shush of the wind and the throbbing in her chest.

"…a number of years ago," she heard, trying to catch up with him, "my insides were screaming. I wanted to tell my fucking pig-headed boss, the head of the department, to take his fucking job and shove it. I was at an end. I had had it. There came a morning one day when I woke up, facing another dismal day ahead, determined to come in and chuck it when, like a flash, an epitome, something hit me…a blinding flash is the only way I can describe it. Instead of all the reasons I had to quit, all the injustices I'd swallowed keeping my mouth shut, all of a sudden I saw it all from the way he looked at it, from his perspective. In that blinding insight, I understood why he saw things the way

241

he did. I got under his skin. I didn't agree with him, I still believed him wrong, but I saw it the way he saw it. The anger that had me locked up, rigid, ready to quit, dissolved. I would not do things the way he did, but I saw that from his perspective, the way he was doing thing made sense.

"I had forgotten that. What you said brought it back. I had never imagined there might be a reason to live a life you described. I had never believed a life, a life so seemingly simple, could have real depth, a life that seemed on the surface to have nothing might have the entire universe. I can see now how it might be right for you, yet I'm not sure I can see it might be right for me. You opened a window, showed me something from a perspective I'd not been aware of. I need time to think about it, consider it, consider if there could be a compromise, or if one precludes the other."

As Chenny listened, the knot in her chest that had her ready to chuck it, seemed to untangle, dissolve, fall away onto the road behind them. It was a side to Jaime she'd not seen, been aware of. With all his 'sophistication,' she realized he was searching for answers too. She knew it would take some time for her to assimilate all of it, work it out. She saw something about herself, too; that like the person he described, she too had been locked into a way of life.

It wasn't over, she knew. He had shown he could appreciate what she wanted in life; he wanted more. If they were right for each other, could there be a path in between that could make them both happy?

The miles rolled on and on, mile after mile after wearying mile. Not until the end of the eleven-hour drive was in sight, when signs along the highway announced exits for Reno ahead, as the jumble of traffic poured onto the ramp to neon City with dreams of breaking the bank, did it occur to her to wonder what her answer would be if Jaime were to ask, now that she had said more than she intended, if she could ever think of living elsewhere.

Chapter 58

"So," Jaime asked as they pulled up to the Hotel Eldorado at seven in the evening under the glittering flashing neon canopy and pushed into the outrageously appointed lobby, slot-machine wheels spinning, yellow, red, turquoise, white lights flashing, bells ringing, as full of renewed zip as if he had just jumped out of bed instead of a wearying ten-hours on the road, "ready to hit the slots?"

"Ha!" Chenny grinned, infused with the charged air in the over the top circus, "the casino on the reservation took my wampum – along with my dream of retiring in Acapulco. What we have here *is the triumph of hope over experience.*"

"I thought it was Samuel Johnson who said that about his friend's second marriage?"

"No. He said it after visiting a casino on an Indian reservation. As a professor of literature, I'm surprised you didn't know that."

"WOW!" Chenny erupted later that evening as beaming performers, arm in arm, took their fifth bow to a tumultuous standing applause at the close of the performance.

"That was your fifth 'WOW!'" Jaime roared, on his feet along with Chenny and the clapping, shrieking riotous audience at the close of the sixty-minute, light/dark extravaganza, aerialists, mimes, dancers, costumes, music, techno, jugglers that burst seamlessly on and off the stage in dazzling arrays.

"What? I can't hear you over all this screaming!" Chenny screamed, following the euphoric mob into the casino bursting with hordes of players pouring over blackjack tables, poker tables, crap tables, roulette wheels, slots, slots and more slots, video poker, betting rooms, and still more slots, bells ringing, jackpot signs flashing '$$ WINNER $$,' pit bosses bossing, bunny clad cocktail waitresses waitressing, drinks on silver trays, $100-dollar bills disappearing into gaming tables maws, white, black, red, gold chips everywhere, tokens dropping into metal cups, clink, clink, clink, along one the side of the room a window, behind it another room, cigars and cigarettes puffing smoke, wrinkled, gray-haired women, eyeglasses as thick as Coke bottle bottoms, apple-cheeked, fair-haired boys with gelled hair, note takers, iPads, systems, croupiers raking, dealers stacking by touch, everywhere hope, one more shot.

"As the young bride said," Chenny grinned, "'Not tonight, dear, I'm tired,'" tugging Jaime's sleeve, pulling him away from the blackjack table. "Let's hit the midnight buffet and head up."

A blazing sun burst through the window blinding Jaime when he opened his eyes, wakened from a dream of a riotous party of drinking, boozing, and retching. Painfully levering his head up from his pillow, he squinted at the bedside clock, 8:15, shrugged, turned to look for Chenny. The bed next to him was empty. Shit, he muttered, shedding the covers. Stretching the kinks in his neck, he padded barefooted across the wood floor to the bathroom and tried the handle. "Chenny?" he called through the door, "you O.K?"

Chenny retched up something, spit, managed a weak, "Hold on a sec," spit again, flushed the toilet. "I think something I ate last night was bad. Maybe the crab." When she threw open the door, her cheeks were red, her eyes watering.

"You OK now?" Jaime worried. "You sure? I ate the same thing. I feel OK."

"Yeah," she nodded, struggling a smile. "I took something. I'll be OK. Go wash up and let's have breakfast. I'll make myself a cup of tea while you shower."

"So, what do you think?" Jaime asked as he finished a second toasted bagel with cream cheese and lox in the breakfast room adjoining the casino and washed it down with a second cup of coffee, his eyes fixed on the tableau in the casino, wide-eyed 'one-chip bettors,' jaded Noel Coward characters in silk, polka dot dressing gowns waving long, ebony cigarette holders, Bret Harte's unwashed, unshaven roaring camp desert rats in crusty khakis and scuffed leather boots, busloads of day-trippers, watery-eyed, blue-hairs in housecoats and flip-flops, the men in assorted fruit cocktail colors in slacks hiked up almost to the nipples, slick Rodeo Drive weekend jet setters in glove-leather loafers, pinch-waist Italian slacks, Parisian gowns, diamond chokers. "Should we stay a while and hit the slots or get on our way and hit the road to Frisco?"

"My vote is Frisco," Chenny allowed, stuffing a paper napkin into the pocket of her cut-offs, pushing her tea and white toast aside and rising from the cushy chair.

"I feel like a character from 'Blazing Saddles,'" Jaime offered, singing, "*I'm back on the highway again.* Let me ask you something. What did you think of the show last night?"

Chenny's brow wrinkled, puzzled. She turned her eyes from the road and looked at Jaime curiously. "I…" she began, then stopped. "Did I miss something?" She scanned his face, wondering if there was some sub-text she had missed, but his face gave nothing away. Instead of the crinkling in the corner of his eye she expected, a signal that some nonsense was coming, he seemed serious, more serious than she had expected. "Weren't five 'Wows!' enough?"

"Had you ever seen this, or portions of it, on television?"

"Yes. Some of it," Chenny turned her eyes back to the road, deciding she had over-read his question.

When several minutes passed and nothing more was forthcoming, she turned back to Jaime. She was beginning to know him. He seemed to be struggling with something. "Why did you ask that?"

Jaime took a breath, eyes fixed on the road straight ahead. His lips worked, in and out. He took another breath, and let it out. "How did being there…" he asked, searching for the words, "…watching it live, in person, compare to watching it on TV?"

Chenny searched his face, not sure where this was going, what he was looking for. She took in a deep breath, and let it out. "It was," she admitted, "like nothing I'd ever experienced before…I felt…wired…it…it was…electric…like I was there, up on the stage with them…like a light switch in me had been turned on, all the energy of the acts, of the audience…it was… Didn't you feel that? Didn't it affect you that way? I saw you bopping and tapping and levitating. You couldn't sit still."

A slow gleam rose in Jaime's eyes.

Chenny clunked back, searching Jaime's face more thoroughly, utterly puzzled. Her mouth opened, closed, opened again. She bit her lip.

"Don't you see it?" Jaime asked.

He pried his eyes from the road to meet Chenny's, but she lowered her eyes from his and looked away. Her voice was muted as if she didn't want to hear the answer. "Are you saying this is what you want in your life?"

Jaime wrestled about uncomfortably. "I'm not sure how to answer that. It isn't 'want.' 'Want' implies a decision. It's something I have no control over…like…like the force of gravity. I can describe how it affects me, but I have no more control over it than I have over gravity.

"It's…how can I explain it. It's not a choice. I have to be in the center, where things are happening, with the revelers in Times Square on New Year's Eve watching the ball drop, cheering, shouting, counting down from ten to zero along with everyone, feeling the energy, the exhilaration, being there in the middle of tens of thousands oohing and aahing, I have to be at the Battery on the Fourth of July watching the fireworks shooting up from barges in the East River, exploding overhead, glorying in the dazzling arrays, the spectacular colors, the dizzying lights, feeling the thrill of being an American – I've watched the broadcast from the Nation's Capital on TV, all the hoopla – it's not the same, no more than watching the Cirque d Soleil on TV – on Halloween I've stood in the middle of tens of thousands, shouting, clapping, jeering at the kooky paraders slithering down Sixth Avenue in way-out costumes, devils, fairies, queens, kings, jesters, crazy vignettes, exotic dancers – I've made it down to Chinatown under the colored lanterns during the Chinese New Year to watch the writhing snake prance down Mott Street…yes, I've gone to see operas broadcast from the Met in movie theaters – and yes, they're good – but they're nothing like the excitement, the thrill of seeing and hearing it at the Met in person, seeing the performance live, feeling the connection you don't feel in a movie theater – and music, yes I love hearing music on CDs – but there's nothing like going to a jazz club on 45th Street in Manhattan, being there stomping along with the all the others, or the connection you feel attending a concert under the stars at Tanglewood in Massachusetts or at Avery Fisher Hall or Symphony Hall in Philadelphia. It's the difference between making love au naturale, or wearing a raincoat and a rubber.

"How can I explain it? Why aren't physicists able to explain gravity other than it's the force that draws object to the center of a planet, or that it keeps the planets in orbit around the sun, or that it keeps satellites circling the earth instead of hurling into space or crashing down to earth?

"It's a force within me. I know it's there, I know what it does to me, but I can't explain it. Would I like to contain it, be able to turn it off if I could? It would be like feeling air leak out of me.

"You described what you want in your life. I admire it. It's like capturing the entire universe inside you in a lifetime – but wouldn't you want to feel what you felt last night as well, the exhilaration, the excitement, the energy – the spice that adds that little extra to a meal, to a day, to a life?"

Chenny sat silently, staring straight ahead, disturbed, her chest rising and falling unevenly, her muscles contracting involuntarily.

"I…" Jaime bit off the rest of what had been on his tongue to say. His stomach lurched. *Shit,* he thought, *what had he done?* He felt as if he had bit into something bitter, rancid, that he had destroyed something beautiful, something untainted, that he had opened a window that could never again be closed, that he was the devil offering an innocent a view of a life in exchange for her soul.

"Chenny," he began, deflated, empty, exhausted. "I… I feel… I feel awful. I… I apologize. I had no right to say any of that, make it seem that you have been missing something, that what you have isn't…isn't all that there could be, that the life you see, the way you describe it isn't… It's just that…that I…that I needed you to know what's…what's in me…what –"

"*Jaime.* What do you see me as? *What?* Do you think I am so…unworldly…so…insulated, so…naïve…that I haven't seen what else there is, that I've… I've shut my mind to anything else, that I…I haven't considered all that? Do you see me as timid, that I'm afraid, afraid to experience all the world offers? Maybe I am. Maybe I'm afraid to lose what I have rather than hunger for something I haven't – to hold onto what I feel sure of, comfortable with, instead of something I know not. Maybe. But I am…but I'm not ready to rule out the other, either."

Jaime sat, stunned, forcing deep breaths, feeling the starch seep out of his body. As Chenny spoke, said what she had, it came over him that it wasn't Chenny who was naïve, but he, that he had sounded like a puffed up savant, a fool, that he had failed to recognize that this woman sitting beside him had depth, that he'd allowed himself to believe that because the town she lived in was unsophisticated, she was as well. How much more did she see than he realized? He felt he had said too much, but not enough.

"Chenny, I feel like an idiot. I apologize. But there's something else I need to say. I… I don't know how to say this but… I can't lay…fallow, if that's the word. Say this is all I want in my life. I may never achieve much, but I have to try, even if the alternate to safety is failure."

"I know."

"You do? If I didn't, I'd feel like I was sleepwalking through life. I mean, it's like what you tell me you see in your classroom, the thrill youngsters have when they accomplish something new. I have to try. It's not that I want other's applause, though maybe it's that too, but I want to feel I've done something I haven't done before and then go on to try something more. It's not that it has to be earth-shaking, it's not that I shrink from tranquility, but I'd like to feel when I come to the end of my life I left the world a bit better, even in a small way, than when I entered it."

They drove on, both exhausted, as if they had returned from a five-mile run up a steep hill, enmeshed in their own thoughts, aware of the soft breathing beside them, aware of a feeling they couldn't define, that a level of intimacy had been reached that never before existed, only vaguely aware of the hum of the road, the occasional blast of a horn, the whoosh of semis rushing by in the opposite direction, of drivers playing mind games.

Chapter 59

As they approached the Bay Bridge, the City of San Francisco rose in front of them, the noon sun reflecting off the Trans America Tower spreading a halo in the fog hanging over the city. Chenny's toes tingled, imagining herself here, in the City she'd only read about, climbing Lombard Street, the 'crookedest street in the world,' sampling Dungeness crab on Fisherman's Wharf, gaping at jugglers in tatters keeping nine balls in the air, mimes dressed as iridescent jesters, black frock coated magicians in top hats and tails pulling coins behind children's ears, taking a walk up Grant Street in San Fran Fanny's China Town under Dragon's Gate, exotic smells, rosemary, ginger, sage, roast ducks hanging on hooks in restaurant windows, ebony and jade earrings and brooches in tiny shops with names like Look See, jogging with cyclists and skateboarders through Golden Gate Park past the arboretum, the Conservatory of flowers, stopping for tea and almond cookies in the Japanese Tea Garden, napping on a lawn under a Chinese red maple.

Is that what it would be, with Jaime? Or was it… She thought of that morning not so long ago with Moon Glow working her dark eyebrows into daggers, the way she did when she got worked up. *You're just gonna let him go, without telling him, without saying anything to him, so he doesn't know how you feel!*

Moonie! she'd objected, *We're just friends.*
Friends! I've known you too long.
And say what? I'm not going to throw myself at him – he's already going. If he wants me, he'll come back, or ask me to come with him. I'm not a charity case.

The trouble was, it was exciting. But…it was a big but. She wasn't sure of any of it, if it was the life for her, if Jaime was the one for her, any of it. Would she give up what she had, was comfortable with if he asked her to come with him? Give up her home? Give up her mother, her sister, her nieces, and nephews? Give up her job?

And what of… what of Noah, the life she could have with him? He was a good man, solid, dependable, settled. There'd be no surprises. He'd make a good husband, a good father, a good companion. And he wanted her. What did Jaime want?

Did he even want her? She and he wanted different things. He made it sound so…so exciting…the life he wanted to live, so different than any she'd ever imagined. But he's not even settled. His teaching job is a fill-in. He has no idea where he'll be ten months from now when the school year ends. Noah's real. Jaime is a fantasy, a dream, a fairy tale, a wanderer who stopped overnight in Red Plains, an innocent who would shrivel and dry up if he wasn't able to follow wherever his feet took him.

But it would be lovely, keeping house, hanging curtains, cooking dinner, sleeping in each other's arms, buying furniture, being a couple…until diapers had to be changed, bills had to be paid, until New Year's Eve was spent in front of a television set, until money set aside for opera tickets had to go to pay doctor bills, until the day Jaime looked at her and remembered dreams he once had.

No. Why am I so… It doesn't have to be that way. We could make it work. *She* could make it work. It would be she who made it work. Could he?

Why is she going on so. He hasn't asked her. Even if he had, it would be a long time before…and anything could happen in that much time. Unless…

Her thoughts went back to the book Jaime had given her, Willa Cather's '*O Pioneers,*' a tale of a young woman, Alexandra Bergson, who inherited the family farm in Nebraska, and her neighbor's son, her intended, Carl Lindstrom, how excited and wonderful it all seemed at first before years of crop failures drove most of the families, including Carl's, from the area, and how, after sixteen years of struggle, when she was finally able to save the farm, Carl returned and married her.

Sixteen years.

"Why so quiet?" They were coming off the Bay Bridge into the business district, Powell and Market Streets, passing cable cars on the carousal making the turn for the trip back up the hill. From the corner of his eye, he spotted Chenny's overly bright smile, the way her body was leaning into the turns, bracing for them rather than letting the bottom he cupped in his hands when they made love mold into the seat as it did into his hands, and her long tapered fingers absently fingering one of the jazz pieces she played for him.

249

Chenny, held her breath, snapped abruptly out of her reverie, came aware of trucks, pedestrians, cable cars, autos, shoppers carrying Nordstrom bags, turned and studied Jaime, completely at ease, dodging cars, trucks, and pedestrians that would have her sitting on the edge of her seat.

"Awe," she flipped back, feeling as if she'd been caught stealing a cookie from the earthenware rooster on the shelf in her mother's kitchen. "Even the air here is electrified. One minute I feel exactly what you described, the pull of gravity, the next I wonder if living here wouldn't be like, 'Live fast, die young and have a good-looking corpse.'"

"Isn't that a line from Goldilocks and The Three Bears?"

"No. You're thinking of The Treasure in Chenny's Mattress."

"Ah. I always get those two mixed up. The appointment with the realtor is at one-thirty. We should eat first. We may not be able to afford to eat afterward."

Chapter 60

Jaime found a small, one-bedroom furnished apartment in a high rise within walking distance of the university. Once the realtor left the keys, Chenny tore her eyes from the ant-sized pedestrians making their way along the street below, pulled from her oversized handbag a hand-loomed red, gray and ochre runner, spread it across the dinette table, smoothed out the wrinkles, positioned it carefully in the exact middle, crouched, and with knees high, stomped, circling the table, beating an imaginary tom-tom, chanting the Cherokee prayer blessing:

May the Warm Winds of Heaven blow softly upon your house.
May the Great Spirit bless all who enter there.
May your Moccasins make happy tracks in many snows,
And may the Rainbow always touch your shoulder.

Jaime snared her in mid circle, scooped her up, and planted kisses on her eyelids. "As the Great Father of my tribe says, 'May heaven fill your kiva with lotsa latkas.'"

Chenny levered her head from his, peered skeptically, and nuzzled his neck.

"Hey! No time for that. Tonight I cook. Let's shop for food."

"You're cooking? Add Tums, too."

The week sped by doing all the tourist things, the difficult decision, what to do first, what to save for last. Early in the week, they headed north, leaving behind the chilled, damp fog hanging over the city. Crossing the Golden Gate Bridge, they broke out into a bright, eighty-five degree sunny day in Marin County, craned to catch a fleeting glimpse of the art colony in Sausalito that clings to the side of the mountain at the edge of the bay, continued north on Route 101, taking the northeast turn off bringing them past broadly rolling grassy landscapes tenanted by wind farms, towering structures topped with lazily turning vanes harnessing the wind, little more than an hour later reaching the road north to the Napa vineyards sheltered on the west from storms that sweep in from the Pacific by a mountain ridge that allows the moisture laden clouds to gently release their rain, providing the benevolent growing condition that nourish row after row of grape canopies growing along both sides of the road in the vineyards of Robert Mondavi, Beringer, Domaine Chandon, and more than ninety others with names like Rolling Rock, Freemark Abbey, Ghost Block, Silver Oak new to them, all offering tours, sampling tables and stocked cellars,

Along the road they stopped at roadside stands choosing freshly picked tomatoes ripe from the vine bursting with juice, hard twisted salami streaked with white hoar, smelly 'rat' cheese, a 12" crusty baguette, and wine they purchased in the salesroom after touring the Moët et Chandon's winery, the first French-owned sparkling wine produced in the Valley.

Spreading a blanket in the shade under a canopy of trees well away from the stone building sheltering the stainless vats, rows of oak aging casks and bottles in which the sparkling wine began fermentation until ready to be bled and corked, contentedly full of the cheese, salami, baguette, tomatoes, and wine, they stretched out and idled away the afternoon.

"You know," Jaime offered lazily, laying weightlessly on his back, looking up into the canopy overhead, "it's hard to realize, when you look at this stunning vine-covered landscape, see the grapes hanging beneath the green leaves in clusters like chandeliers, marshmallow clouds gamboling off in the distance in the powder blue sky, observe the bees fertilizing the plants and feel the warm breeze tumbling across the vineyards, that all this is sitting on the St. Andreas Fault, the seven hundred-fifty mile ridge beneath which lay the Pacific and North American tectonic plates grinding and pummeling each other with the force of megaton atomic bombs waiting to erupt, as it did a little over one hundred years ago, in 1906, destroying over eighty percent of San Francisco, tumbling buildings, like matchsticks, pummeling an area extending four-hundred miles, killing three thousand people and injuring thousands more."

"Umm," Chenny acknowledged enigmatically.

Jaime twisted his head to look at her, wondering at the casual response. "Doesn't that… I don't know, I mean, doesn't that…say something to you…of the transitory world we inhabit, that aside from the deaths we humans visit on other humans, wars, guns, what have you, we have the arrogance to believe that we control our lives, our destiny."

He stared at Chenny, unable to understand her feline like countenance, the look he would expect her to confer on a precocious child who had, what he thought, was a startling understanding. Was this what she believed a higher power, or what?

Chenny was aware that he expected a response, but held her peace, enjoying his unease, allowing him to stew for a while. When she felt he had stewed long enough, she broke out into a huge smile.

"You're laughing at me, aren't you?" he grinned, playfully pinching her under the ribs, "as if at last I came to the understanding that there is a world out there that I know nothing about, that man supposes and God disposes."

Chenny leaned over and nuzzled him. "Not at all," she mumbled into his neck. "What we have beneath us here, the St. Andreas Fault, is small potatoes to what was beneath us in Yellowstone – which may be a lot more imminent. I hadn't wanted to say anything when you suggested we stop there – but you may not know – most people don't – that Nebraska is the site of what may be the biggest, bubbling cauldron of all."

Jaime looked at her skeptically. *"Nebraska?"*

"Had you ever heard of the town of Orchard, in eastern Nebraska?"

Jaime's face said he had no idea where this was going.

"I took my class there on a field trip two years ago," Chenny continued, enjoying his bewilderment. "Near the town of Orchard is what has come to be called Ashfall Fossil Beds State Park. At that spot, almost fifty years ago, a mass grave was found – the most extraordinary fossil bed ever discovered on this continent. In it were skeletons of umpteen animals – camels, rhinoceroses, turtles, zebra-like horses, and saber-toothed deer – that died almost twelve million years ago. They were found to have suffocated under a layer of volcanic ash as high as ten feet deep and a thousand-mile long…and you thought Nebraska is like in Paducah, that nothing ever happened here."

"I think all of the children had nightmares that night. Brian, a fearless little daredevil, told me dreamt of being eaten by dead animals, saber-toothed tigers and lions – and oh my. Jennie, a shy little cutie – you could drown in her brown eyes – dreamt that soap suds from the washing machine her mother washes her clothes in flowed over the side, crept across the floor and was about to climb up and suffocate her when her mother woke her wrapped in her covers, screaming in her sleep.

"Wait!" she insisted when Jaime seemed about to break in. "Just a darned minute, as the folks back home say. That ash was found to have erupted from a volcano in Idaho a thousand miles away six-hundred-thousand years ago. Imagine what it had been like. If suffocating under a ten-foot layer of ash wasn't horrendous enough, volcanic ash is abrasive. It cut into the animal's lungs when they gasped for air, and sliced open their guts – if somehow they were still able to eat or drink since all vegetation was blanketed by ash, and any water became a slurry of toxin."

Seeing the narrow-eyed skepticism that had stolen across Jaime's face, Chenny's serious expression dissolved into a broad, mischievous smile.

"Don't believe it, huh?" Chenny paused, enjoying Jaime's skepticism. "What would you say if I told you that you'd heard of it and probably weren't aware you had it?

"Aha! Where did the common household cleansers, Comet, Ajax, and others that your mother used, come from? Before that mass grave was discovered, for on to one-hundred years, that ash, that covered thousands of miles in Nebraska, was used in making those cleansers. And all of that ash, according to geologists, came from that one unimaginable hot spot, a huge bubbling cauldron of magma that erupted 600,000 years ago."

Chenny's dark eyes sparkled. "I didn't want to say anything before, but that hot spot is still there. It's called Yellowstone National Park. It isn't the site of an ancient supervolcano; it's the site of an active one. Geologists have worked out that the cycles of its eruptions appear to be every 600,000 years. The last one, 630,000 years ago, blotted out almost all human, animal life and vegetation for thousands of years. When the next may occur is unpredictable. The park has lots of small earthquakes – 1,260 last year, most too small to be felt. What they are sure of is that beneath the geysers in Yellowstone, waiting to erupt is a boiling cauldron of lava the size of Rhode Island. The park resembles a bubbling pot of tapioca pudding, rising and falling. In 1980, three square miles of the park was found to have risen three feet during the previous sixty years; the following year, the center retreated eight inches; the next year it began swelling again.

"I didn't want to say anything when you suggested we stop at the park, but what everyone believes is a huge tourist attraction, like the colorful dancing and leaping fountains in Las Vegas – we were walking on the mantle over boiling magma due to erupt.

Chapter 61

The highlight of the week for Chenny, an American history buff, was the show they were lucky to find seats for, 'Hamilton'; for Jaime, it was the all-Beethoven concert performed by the San Francisco Symphony that included Beethoven's Fifth Piano Concerto, the 'Emperor.'

"I don't remember who the conductor was the night I heard it performed in Avery Fisher Hall, but I'll never forget the pianist, Mischa Dichter. I sat mesmerized. I'd never heard it the way he played it: it sounded like water flowing over rocks into rushing waters below. How it came to be known as the 'Emperor,' no one is quite sure. Beethoven had wanted it dedicated to Napoleon.

"You really thrill to this, don't you?" Chenny beamed as they left the hall.

"I do. I can't explain it. It's like the music flows into my pores and turns a switch inside of me, and I feel as if I'm hooked up to an electric current, unable to sit still. I sometimes think of how wonderful it must be for conductors of the great orchestras of the world, James Levine of the Met, Zubin Mehta of the Israel Philharmonic, Leonard Bernstein when he was in Avery Fisher Hall, to be able to spend their lives in a cocoon of music. I remember, as an infant, pulling myself up in my crib, holding onto the railing, bouncing up and down with the music from the radio. I couldn't stay still."

"All music?"

Jaime grinned. "No," he denied, "mostly bel canto music (beautiful voices), operas, Puccini, Verdi, La Boheme, Traviata, classicist composers, Tchaikovsky, Mozart, Chopin, Haydn, but the aphonic, atonal stuff, Poulenc, Shostakovich, Mahler, *nein!*

"I have a funny true story. I had tickets for a violin concert in the 92nd Street Y in Manhattan one Saturday evening and asked a woman I'd never been out with if she'd like to come with me. The violinist was Shlomo Mintz. Shlomo Mintz. Sounded like an M-O-T, member of the great tribe – Itzak Pearlman, Isaac Stern, Pincas Zuckerman, Yascha Heifetz, Fritz Kreisler, Yehudi Menuhin. It turned out he was a fan of the atonal music I hate. Sitting there having to listen to that was like having a root canal. I couldn't get up and leave, even say anything, afraid she might be enjoying it.

"All of a sudden, sitting there, I started to laugh out loud. I couldn't help myself. She looked at me as if I'd lost it. I apologized later when we were leaving. What it was salvaged what had been a dreadful evening. Sitting there, it came to me that Shlomo Mintz preferred to perform in the evening. He was 'after-dinner' Mintz."

"You're weird."

"I know. But it got me through it."

They talked of almost everything that the week, except, as if by unspoken agreement, what would be when Chenny returned to Red Plains. Chenny could hear Moon Glow whispering in her ear – say something, don't let the opportunity pass. Speak up. Don't be like a silent squaw. But any time it seemed they might approach that subject, or how Jaime might fare in this new position, she sensed a brittleness coming over him, and she reverted to the breezy, light-hearted quips they used to steer the conversation from anything personal.

"There are two kinds of people," Chenny counseled the last afternoon before Jaime drove her to the airport for her flight to Omaha. They were on the Wharf, Chenny was holding her ice cream cone well away from Jaime who had finished his and was eying hers with a sorrowful hopeful expression. "There are ants, and there are grasshoppers. Ants eat slowly, savoring every slow lick, so they can enjoy their ice cream as long as possible. Grasshoppers, greedy little insects, gobble up their cones, then turn mournful, hungry eyes on the ant's hoping to get a lick of her's."

"Does it work?" Jaime grinned hopefully.

"Rarely."

Chapter 62

When Jaime returned from seeing Chenny off at the airport, the one-bedroom apartment that had felt welcoming, that wrapped the two of them in a homey, domestic warmth, seemed eerily cavernous and empty, the chrome-edged kitchen table, spindle-backed pine chairs, shag-covered living room sofa and faux-maple end table that seemed 'mod,' edgy, now seemed shabby, the single welcoming note, the hand-loomed red, gray, and ochre runner that Chenny had spread across the dinette table and carefully smoothed before her Indian ceremonial stomp around the table to her imaginary tom-tom…that and her lingering scent, bramble-berry soap.

More than once, as time for her to leave came near, he had dicked about, longing to say something meaningful, something of the future, something that might dispel the air of false gaiety hovering over them, something to ease the disappointment he saw deep in her eyes, but the words that swirled round and round inside his brain tangled before they reached his tongue, frozen in terror of commitment, the looming school year, the blank classroom faces – and, more than anything, the meeting he was scheduled to have the following morning with the Dean.

During the days and weeks since he secured this temporary teaching assignment in San Francisco, as he traveled around the country to deliver the bequests his father left, he explored ideas of how he might structure a course to energize students, persuade them that literature of previous eras had relevance to the fast-paced, intimidating lives they lived. How intimidating it must be, how different life today is from what it was when he was their age, how much faster paced. Today, change comes at the speed of light; the world's knowledge doubles every eighteen months. *Eighteen months*. Today's youth can hardly realize that much of what they take for granted did not exist when they were born – Netflix, video streaming, 3-D printing, touch screens, iPads, texting, selfie-sticks, Android Operating Systems that operate the billions of smartphones worldwide, robotic surgery, wireless electricity, hoverboards, GPS, tablets, self-driving cars, Facebook, YouTube – and those just a few of the most obvious, add to the list genetic engineering, DNA mapping, bionics, and so on.

Youths today, as in every era, have their own music, their own slang, their own culture, but today the choices are explosive – rock, progressive rock, emo, indie pop, rap, dubstep, deathcore, metal, metalcore, blackmetal, thrash metal, alternative electronic dance, jazz, hip hop, country, punk, grunge, pop-punk, bands with names like Radiohead, Joy Division, Placebo, Bright Eyes, Sigur Ros, Pixies, Gotye, Half Japanese, Mumford & Sons, The Vaccines – and the kids know the differences and have strong opinions on each. With so much to learn, so much to keep up with, it is easy to understand that the classics may seem irrelevant, easy to understand why their lyrics express their pain, their disillusion, their fears…yet beneath it all, what they don't say, may not want to admit, is their need for the security their families and society provide, the security that allows them to be armchair rebels.

He thought back to the dinner he had at the Algarve, the Portuguese restaurant in Newark, and what Darryl had said. 'When I tried to *sell*. I'd come up against resistance. People don't want to be sold; they don't want to be force-fed. Instead of *selling,* I discovered I could accomplish what I was after by going at it the other way round – by switching from an adversarial position, me against them, to enlisting them to become part of the team. I had an officer for basic training in the army in Ft. Dix whose job it was to teach under conditions, I would imagine, as resistant and abrasive as you find in the classroom. Imagine trying to wipe the bored look off the faces of a bunch of draftees or enlistees who were only there because it was the choice between basic training and jail.'

Instead of trying to force feed them, the lieutenant tried something new: he threw the ball to them. Hey guys, here are the problems. You have brains. How would you solve them? Seems unlikely, but he had them almost teaching him. It was like magic. He had the best training battalion in Dix. The ideas flooded in. Paint the day room? Not a problem. Hey guys. I'll get you the paints. How would you liven up this place? Same result. And strangest of all, poetry. How about he threw open to them, make up poems with the lessons in rhyme, paint them on signs and stick them in the ground around the training area? Poet Laureates they weren't, but they discovered poetry delivered a message.

On the way back from the airport, he had been buoyant, bubbling with ideas, brimming with confidence. He'd have the students eating out of the palms of his hands, lapping up the syllabus he set before them like a dish of sweet cream, eager to contribute, parade their favorite pieces before him, show him that the world had moved on, was no longer stuck in the rust bowl of the past, crippled with arthritic concepts, that it had opened a window and allowed

258

fresh air to seep in, sweeping away the musty suffocating works of dinosaurs, and then, when they accepted him, when they saw he was not there to stuff them full of dusty relics, they'd come to appreciate that grit expressed with a light hand rather than a sledge could be more telling, but now the what-ifs had set in again. He had been indulging a fantasy, sweeping away the sea with the flick of his fingers but it was now rushing back in again.

"Shit, stop you fucking wimp!" he screamed into the apartment's void. "Stop fucking putting it off, finding reasons why you can't!"

The walls bounced his words back into his ears. "Shut the fuck up!" he screamed at the walls. "Write. Put your fucking fingers on the keys and type, god damn it, or fall back into the fucking hole you've been in!"

A pounding on the wall answered, '*Shut the fuck up. Do you know what time it is?*'

Christ, he fumed, looking at his watch. 11:50. Shit. He stared at the blank screen. Write!

Chapter 63

Nine Months Later

The horizon had not yet begun to lighten in the east as Jaime, after a sleepless night, sat staring blindly out of the window of the Boeing 747 watching the lights of the San Francisco airport grow smaller and smaller in the distance, numb to all but the pull against his seat belt and the thrust of the powerful engines lifting the plane through the mist into the dark sky. The plane made a wide lazy circle over the Monterey Peninsula passing over Cannery Row, the waterfront street that once housed the string of sardine canneries immortalized by John Steinbeck, and turned east for Philadelphia. The apprehension that gripped him nine months ago when he first visited Philadelphia, gripped him anew, but now more powerfully.

He thought of how uptight he had been, setting out to meet the daughter of the woman for whom his father abandoned him, how Susan, no more than he, wanted to meet, the awkward moment when she, a doctor, a daughter of a well-to-do family, walked into the glassed-in two-story lobby of the Warwick Hotel overlooking Rittenhouse Square, how out of his depth he felt pretending to fit in, how he had risen when the hostess brought her to the table, uncertain whether to extend his hand, wondering if she saw his father in him, trying to keep his face from falling at the thought that this could hardly be the girl his father described in his diary, a young girl full of life, perky, bursting with fun. As a doctor, she would have a life he could only imagine, but everything about her was dull, faded. She had refused to make eye contact. Even her clothes were lifeless. All that was there was the depth of the blue in her eyes his father described and her clear complexion that needed no makeup to show it off. How he had dreaded meeting her – and less than a week later, dreaded even more agreeing that long-distance relationships didn't work.

He sold his soul. *For what?*

His thoughts went to the last words he had had with Susan that evening in the Italian section of San Francisco. They'd had dinner family style; he had been working up his nerve as they walked. Young boys in ragged shorts, tee shirts, and expensive sneakers were knocking a rubber puck about in the street with taped up hockey sticks, racing to the curb whenever a truck turned the corner.

"I don't want you to go," he had said to her at last, his gut aching, "but I need you to… I have to do this on my own. It has to be a clean break. For how long, I don't know. Maybe I won't make it, maybe I'll not do it all, but I have to see what I am capable of. If I don't, I'd not be any good to myself, nor any good to you, I'd always be looking over my shoulder, wondering what you would do, or what you would have me do, never sure if it's my decision, or not."

And he remembered the sinking feeling he had that morning waiting to meet the Dean, only a few years older than him, when he heard a coed giggle: "Yeah, it was a last minute thing. There was a dozen and a half registered for Van Bronson's class when the Professor had a heart attack. Dean Gearhard was stuck. He had to find a fill-in at the last minute or cancel the class. The only one he could come up available on short notice was some assistant prof who was out of work, couldn't keep a job in a tiny college in the boonies." He had felt ill, cold, sweaty, his breakfast coming up. He'd raced to the men's room. The students were stoked, ready for him. This one would go like the others.

He willed his legs to move. He'd been up half the night, writing and rewriting the lesson proposal he'd put together, the Dean's face was fixed, mocking. "Shakespeare. Hasn't that been done, and redone? Well," he'd continued looking at his watch with a dismissive wave, indicating the meeting was over, "I guess we'll see how it goes, won't we?"

He returned to his apartment calling up every curse with which the Irish embroidered the world's literature, adding a few of his own, wanting to scream it, tell someone. But the one he wanted to tell, the one he'd not tell it to, he couldn't.

But he had… she came… and he had sent her away.

The engraved envelope in his mail slot had her return address. The ground had fallen out from under him. He'd carried it upstairs unopened, set it down on the table on the runner Chenny had brought for him. There it lay, unopened… till three a.m. when sleepless, he could hold off no longer.

He had sold his soul. *For what?*

Chapter 64

Susan's mother shook her head, fixing Susan with the long-suffering look of St. Joan being led to the pyre. "I still don't see why you invited people you don't even know to the dedication," she insisted, lowering her cup of coffee and looking to Hermann for support. "It's embarrassing enough to have to explain why the room is being named for...*him*."

Hermann adopted the safe half-smile that assured his wife that he was in full agreement with whatever side of an issue she was in favor of at that moment, but the sharply inverted 'V' in her eyebrows made it evident to him that this was a situation that demanded more. Turning his heavy rubicund face on Susan, he coughed mightily shaking his head, setting his bowtie bobbing against his Adam's apple. Susan's mother accepted this as full agreement, and turned a righteous face on Susan.

From long practice, Susan ignored this and smiled aggravatingly. She had agreed to come to an early breakfast at Hermann's suggestion with the expectation that there was to be an inquisition accompanied by the threat of excommunication, but the difficulty her mother was having maintaining the modulated voice *Good Breeding* required made clear to her, as it did to Hermann, that this was a rather more important cause. "Mother," she offered, in an aggravatingly calm voice, "he was good enough to take into your bed less than two months after father died...and keep there for five years."

"Susan!" her mother exploded, flashing lightning. "I put up with an awful lot from you the year after Jonathan died to keep you from falling apart while you were grieving."

Susan's eyes threatened to tear up. "I know you did, Ma," she agreed, softening. "I'm sorry. But I've moved on, as you have, and I need to do what I think is right."

"Susan. You know all I ever had at heart was your welfare. You say you're over it, but I'm not sure. You know you've always been impulsive, like your father. You don't always think things through. You seem to come to your senses at times. At others, I see a far-away look in your eyes filled with uncertainty. Why are you dithering? You and Charles are perfect for each other. You're both on the same fast track. If the two of you choose, you can set up a joint practice. Charles is solid, dependable, someone you'll always be able to rely on...not someone who'd toss you aside, send you running when you've served your purpose. And his family can bring the right kind of people to you."

"Ma. That's water under the bridge. The other is over. Why are you bringing it up now?"

"Susan. How long have I known you? Do you think I don't know my own daughter? Is there any other reason why you arranged this dedication?"

"Ma! What now? There's no other reason. It's the right thing to do!"

"I hope so." Her mother rose from the table taking the dishes into the kitchen. "I've said enough."

At eleven a.m., Jaime's jumbo was just a speck in the sky above the Grand Canyon as the Delta flight from Atlanta with Gerry and Leslie, and the American Airlines plane from Raleigh-Durham with Leonora and Sydney, arrived in Philadelphia. Twenty minutes later, they were sitting with Susan under a blue umbrella next to the pool behind the Hampton Inn, eating nachos and sipping margaritas and cokes.

"It's good to put a face to a name," Susan said. "Jaime told me much about each of you, but it's really something to think we're all connected in a way."

"One degree of separation," Gerry agreed, "though I expect each of us has our own take on Aaron – or is it Arthur?

"Leslie was six when he came into our life, an amiable humbug, but Leslie adored him, and so did I. We all received a copy of his diary so there are no secrets between us. Aaron lived with us until a few months before he died, almost eight years. He had, you might say, his own sense of morality. He wanted to live the life he couldn't afford and didn't see any reason why others shouldn't make it possible if he couldn't, yet he refused help when he knew his end was near. Add to that his conception that he had been part of one big family and believed it important to bring us together."

Sydney's face darkened, about to disagree, but with a look from his mother, held his tongue. "*Amiable humbug?*" Leonora objected. "I have a hard time with that. Maybe each of us sees him differently, maybe he's a man of many sides, and maybe that's true of all of us. We're a different person to different people. I'd be more apt to describe him as an inept humbug, someone with big dreams who trips over his own feet. What's interesting is how, in some ways, Jaime is like him and in some ways exactly the opposite. His father was concerned largely for himself – I only spent one evening with Jaime, but they both had the ability to bring joy. Why else would we have allowed his father into our lives?"

"Joy is ephemeral," Gerry agreed, looking away, as if seeing herself at another time. "You can never make someone else feel a feeling you felt. When I was ten and a half, on my way home from school one day, I saw a book in a window. I wasn't even aware I loved my father until then, but I wanted him to have it. It cost every penny I'd ever saved from collecting deposit bottles, or running errands. I could buy a thousand books today and give them to my father, but buying that one book and giving it to my father gave me more joy than any I'd ever experienced before…or after…except having a daughter like Leslie."

"So," Leslie demanded, a grin peeking out, "how about buying me the book I wanted?"

"Lotsa luck!" Gerry shot back.

Susan had the sensation that rays of the sun had stolen out from behind the clouds spreading its warmth over her. It had seemed whimsical when the idea to bring them all together popped into her head, but she was happy she hadn't let her mother dissuade her. In a way, they shared a bit of history though in some ways they were so different.

Leonora arrived in white slacks, blue and white short-sleeved jersey and black sandals, her hair cut to chin length tucked behind her ears, Sydney in khaki shorts, black tee shirt with the U of Atlanta emblem 'Go Braves!' and black sneakers, his hair long and shaggy. Gerry and Leslie came dressed in cowgirl outfits, Leslie in pink and white striped shorts, a tee shirt with the picture of Mozart and white sandals, her hair in a ponytail tied with a leather thong. She had dickered, trying on one outfit after another, at last deciding on smart casual, knee length tan shorts, navy red and white striped scoop neck jersey, and navy boat shoes.

When they arrived, Susan was struck by something she'd never before been aware of, the difference money makes, how it changes lives. She got a sense of it from what she read in the diary, but seeing it in living color was something else again; the difference between Leonora and Gerry in their body language, in the way they held their heads, in the confidence they projected. Leonora, she imagined, had once walked down the street with her head high, but now it was an effort to pull it off, Gerry had probably always been cocky, but now her confidence was evident. She wondered what others saw in her.

Chapter 65

As the plane made its final descent into the Philadelphia International Airport just before three, Jaime wondered how he was going to get through it all, the dedication tomorrow afternoon, the dinner Sunday afternoon. Gathering his carry-on from the overhead rack, he followed down the aisle, made his way to the pickup area at the curb, and waited for the arrival of the Hampton Inns courtesy shuttle. Ten minutes later, at the Inn, plastic room key in hand, he headed directly for the elevator, hoping to avoid everyone when he heard a friendly voice.

"Chenny!" he exclaimed, letting out his breath. "You didn't tell me you would be here. Is that 'Wild Goose'?" Hugging Noah's chest, in a sling on was their newborn, 'Neka,' named for his father.

"Look," she glowed, hugging Jaime, lifting the blanket covering Neka's head and kissing a wisp of black curl on his tiny ruddy head.

Jaime smiled, delighted, swung around to Noah to give his hand an energetic shake. "You didn't tell me you were coming…even invited."

"Susan sent me an invitation. We folded our teepee and here we are."

Jaime cringed. When he had found the engraved envelope in his mail slot with Susan's return address, the ground fell out from under him, sure it was a wedding or engagement announcement.

"We were about to take a walk in the garden out back," Chenny offered, folding the blanket back over Neka's head. "Join us."

"Hey!" Jaime erupted. "Is that what I think it is?"

Chenny grinned, holding up her left hand. On her fourth finger, set in engraved silver, was a turquoise stone set in a cluster of small diamonds.

"Wow! It's beautiful. Congratulations. All kinds of good luck."

"It was Noah's grandmothers." She turned her hand admiring it, her nose crinkling. "It's an heirloom Noah told me. It's passed down generations, from squaw to squaw."

"Ugh!" Noah agreed. "Chenny's learning how to make woodchuck stew."

Chenny grinned the grin of a new bride.

"I want to dump my carry-on in my room, take a shower. You go ahead. I'll catch up with you later," he promised, heading back to the elevator feeling revived.

He was still smiling, delighted to see the two of them as he exited the elevator on the top floor and turned a corner towards his room at the end of the corridor. Instantly, he felt as if he had been sucker-punched; all the air in his lungs sucked out in a whoosh. Heading straight for him was Susan. He'd thought he'd prepared to see her again, but the cool he practiced fled. Flushed, he tried to offer an insouciant 'Hi' as he rehearsed, but he couldn't make it come out. Instead, he stood there with his mouth open, fussing with his carry-on, trying to make it seem as if it needed his full attention. He felt an idiot, an utter fool, aware of what she must be thinking. Not the slightest sign did he see that she had not been prepared to see him.

"I'm so happy you came," she said. "I wasn't sure you would."

All the pat words and phrases he had been able to find to say to the young girl on the boat, to Leslie, Gerry's daughter, and to the pupils in his class this past semester deserted him.

"I can't believe it was almost a year ago when I walked into the Warwick Hotel that morning to meet you," she said, as if this was an everyday conversation with someone she once knew, nothing special. "I almost didn't. Do you remember the balloon ride?"

"You were terrified," he managed.

"I was only pretending to be."

"I knew."

"You did not."

Jaime felt the tension that had gripped him begin to ooze out, replaced by a different kind of tension. He looked away, a smile leaking over his face, afraid if he looked at her, he'd make a complete fool of himself.

"What's funny?" she asked.

He shook his head. "If I told you that night what was running through my mind then, I was afraid you'd back out."

"What?"

"The words the rabbi reads from the Torah on Yom Kippur, *Who shall live and who shall die.*"

A door opened, and a middle-aged man, probably unaware he was rather disarrayed, stepped out, looked back over his shoulder awkwardly, and hastily headed for the elevator. Jaime had the almost overwhelming urge to add, 'and who shall procreate.'

"You're laughing at me."

Jaime shook his head. "I was thinking of that young couple in the balloon with us," he dissembled. "Do you remember their names?"

"Tom and Carrie?"

"Yeah. I guess I should dump my bag and take a shower before dinner," Jaime offered half-heartedly. Reaching for his carry-on, as Susan moved to go, awkwardly attempting to dodge each other, they collided, faces inches from each other's. Frozen, unable to pull away, staring at each other, the distance between them slowly grew smaller and smaller until their lips met, and then they were kissing, and Jaime was holding Susan, never to let her go.

"No," Susan uttered, tearing apart, her eyes wide with fright. "Don't. No. I can't do this. I'm... I'm seeing someone." Backing away, she fumbled around Jaime and hurried to the elevator.

Chapter 66

Numb from the sleepless night, the wearying plane ride and the wrenching encounter, Jaime fumbled the key-card into the slot, stumbled into the room, dumped his carryon on the canvas stand under the TV, kicked off his shoes and collapsed onto the bed near the limit of his reserves, losing the struggle to keep his eyelids from giving in to gravity, deciding to sleep until it was time to leave for the return on the red-eye flight Sunday evening.

He was certain he'd slept for twenty-four hours when he was awakened by the phone. His watch read 4:10. "Hey, cowboy," Gerry boomed, near to bursting his eardrum, "get your sorry butt down here. I didn't come up to this Yankee encampment to miss seeing your shining face close up. You got three minutes before I come up there, hog-tie you, and haul you down here."

Stumbling off the bed, Jaime doused ice-cold water on his face, ran his fingers straight back through his hair, struggled on his shoes, and headed downstairs and out into the back.

"Look at me, Pardner," she boomed, pirouetting and sending her buckskin skirt twirling around her tight hips, "I'm noshing a nacho."

Jaime shook his head. "You're incorrigible."

With a grin that could not be mistaken, she licked the salt from the rim of a glass of the margarita.

"I just had an image," he said, viewing her antics and taking a sweeping look over the party on the lawn, "of a Fourth of July lawn party in the Hamptons, blonde studs in white flannel trousers and striped shirts open to the puppick and willowy young things in silk and taffeta in deep conversation, swigging cocktails, characters in Gertrude Stein's off-off awful Broadway play, all engaged in animated conversations about recent parties they attended, the latest Broadway plays, who they ran into at lunch at the Four Seasons, who is having affairs with who, speaking (French intimate), it is all clear, and the characters were all speaking just two words, 'Saw Wood.'"

"You don't have much of an opinion of the rich dialog you've missed," Gerry replied, showing off her chaps. "That's a rather cynical take on your noathen brethren. What's got you in a twit? Ainchu got more urgent things to occupy you with?"

Jaime shrugged.

"If Leslie didn't like you so much, I'd take a switch to you. Aintchu learned nothing this year, young feller? Git over there and tell her."

Jaime felt the current of life flowing back in his veins. He liked Gerry. She acted tough, but she was the kind of person children and dogs loved. She had had a tough life. As a child, her father pursued 'other interests' away from the home, she had a mother she had to mother, but she asked no sympathy and bristled if any was offered, refused to accept that rules were not meant to be broken unless you were too much of a wimp to persist. She embarrassed Leslie, but Leslie's friends adored her. Once she made you her project, woe to him who defied her. But he learned this year that he was her equal. "Beggin' your pardon, ma'am, but I screwed up her life once all ready – or more likely twice. She's done found someone, from the looks of it. So let's drop it."

Gerry spread her legs in a wide stance and looked at him straight on. "God you're stubborn."

Jaime shrugged. "Tell me something important."

"Like what?"

"How'd Leslie's concert go?"

"Let her tell you herself."

Off to the side, near the pool, Leslie was auditioning the role of Lolita for Sydney's benefit. From his color, it appeared it wasn't a complete failure. "Leslie," Gerry called, "come say hello to this cowpoke here."

Leslie tossed Sydney a couldn't care less bird, ran over, threw her arms around Jaime, looked back over her shoulder, made a show of planting a kiss on Jaime's nose, gushing, without need for breath, "I brought my new flute. Susan said I could play it for you at dinner on Sunday. You're going to love it. Wait till you hear the sound. It's like Jean Pierre Rampal, Eugenie Zuckerman and Barthold Kujiken all rolled into one."

Brushing his lips over her hair, trying not to grin, Jaime fell back. "Changed your mind?"

"Changed my mind?" Leslie's chestnut eyebrows migrated together.

"Your mother told me that you squeaked like a rusty nail on a tin can at the graduation concert, the boys hooted, and you were so upset you insisted you were giving up the flute and becoming a missionary in Africa."

Gerry nodded energetically. "Leslie and I have already begun taking malaria pills."

"You are in for a treat." Leslie ignored them grinning, spreading her kiss-me lips to her ears. "I'm going to play *Entrance to the Gladiators,* the piece Kujiken played at this year's New York Flute Fair at Columbia University." With that, she flounced back to Sydney on her 4" black platforms, her pink chemise flapping, barely enough yardage to cover the essentials.

Jaime shook his head. "Were we ever like that? I don't remember. I have to pay my respects to Susan's mother and her stepfather. Have you met her yet?"

Gerry stroked her chin with a look.

"What does that mean?"

"A smile that could freeze ice cubes on the hottest day in August. I think Hermann was embarrassed."

"I'll be back. I may be in need of some TLC."

Chapter 67

Susan's mother was sitting with Hermann on the padded bench along the inner walls of the gazebo wearing a silk, knee-length, short-sleeved dress with a round neck in a mélange of spring greens, beige pumps, a strand of graduated pink pearls and matching ear studs. Her hair had honey brown highlights, curls on top, and fell softy to the nape of her neck. Hermann, sitting next to her, was equally as formal in tailored gray flannel slacks and a gray and white striped shirt open at the neck, His thick head of dark brown hair was edged with gray, his mustache wide and carefully trimmed.

Jaime fixed a smile on his face and made his way to the gazebo, taking the measure of the six-foot four-inch blue-eyed blonde Adonis in white flannel slacks and aqua cable-knit sweater hovering over Susan, who was oohing and aahing over Neka, while Noah stood by pretending to suffer the foolishness.

Aching from lack of sleep, he now regretted he had not changed from the clothes he wore on the plane, khaki slacks, red and white striped shirt and brown loafers, or that he had not done more than run his fingers through his tangled hair. "It's so nice to see you both again," he offered, uncertain whether to offer to shake hands with Marsha or just Hermann who sat enfolded in a mist of verbena and Brut after shave. Close up, he felt the way he had that day in the sixth grade when he was hauled in to see the principal in clothes that were torn and filthy from brawling during recess with Angelo Buccanzo.

The smile that Gerry described wasn't there. "Mrs. Goldbloom and Ms. Marino told me about your visits. They were quite…complimentary."

Was she trying to disarm him? He had found himself shaken in the past when he pre-judged someone before meeting them only to discover, too late regretfully, that he had been set up to dislike them before he had met them. He'd been guarded when Susan had brought him to brunch with her mother and found, then, that beneath the forbidding exterior, a warm welcome. Was he doing it again?

"They're very kind," he managed cautiously.

"Mrs. Goldbloom – Leonora – said that when you met her son, you became furious with him, that he was wasting his life, but he stopped hanging out and has enrolled in college. And Ms. Marino – Gerry – didn't know what you said to her daughter but – I saw her daughter go over and kiss you – and Sydney, Leonora's son, seemed happy to see you, as well. What was it you said to her?"

Jaime blushed, shifted around, embarrassed. "I said… I wished I was her."

Marsha's brow pinched, and her eyes seemed puzzled. "You wished you were a young girl?" She shook her head. "Is that why you sent Susan away?"

A deep shade of red swept over Jaime's face. "Oh my God. No! Not that at all. *No.* Leslie was acting out – she had everything and I had nothing." He shifted from foot to foot. "And what could I offer Susan… I couldn't… I couldn't let her… I…"

Marsha's face softened. "How did the year go at the university? You'll be staying on?"

There it was. Jaime smiled noncommittally. "I'm not sure."

"We wish you luck," she said, with a look at her wristwatch.

"Thank you again for inviting me," Jaime said, understanding the reunion was over.

As he backed away, Jaime had the sense that though she would prefer Charles for Susan, she would not be adverse to him, but was just as pleased he was on the west coast. But later, when he had more time to consider it, he wondered if it all wasn't misdirection, a magician's trick, that what he'd been led to believe didn't even come into the equation. Did it? His best friend always insisted he was gullible.

A light breeze had come up from the east stirring the leaves in the trees sending ripples over the water in the pool where youngsters, oblivious of the temperature, were playing with tubes at the shallow end under the watchful eyes of a mother while a father was stretched out on a chaise at the other end of the pool. One tow-headed little boy was hard at work, attempting to connect two tubes to form a raft to transport his red plastic dump truck, shooing away his sister who peeked out at him from behind her hand when he waggled his fingers at her.

"Susan has arranged a lovely tribute to your father, hasn't she?"

Wrenched from the reverie, Jaime found himself face to face with the fellow who had been with Susan. "I'm Charles," he beamed, extending his hand. "You must be Jaime, Aaron's son. Susan's her mother's daughter, isn't she?"

Jaime felt as if he had shrunk and climbed through the knothole in the fence, caught off guard, prepared to dislike Charles who, perversely, seemed a genuinely nice fellow. "Susan? Are we talking about the same person?"

"You don't think so? The elegant way she arranged all this. It's so like the receptions her mother gives."

Charles' eagerness was digging into Jaime's gut. He could imagine him on the fields of Eton, or some posh English public school, giving his adversary a hearty pat on the back, and a 'well done old chap.'

"She's quite a gal. She hasn't showed you my father's diary, has she?" Jaime asked with a guileless smile.

"Your father?" Charles shook his head. "Your father didn't care for Susan?"

"Care for her? On the contrary. He adored her. Said she was a little hellion."

"Susan? A hellion?"

Jaime smiled, as if it was an everyday thing. "I guess she hasn't shown you that side yet. Susan was a hero in high school. She organized a protest when her school refused to allow women to play football. They broke into the administration office and switched class assignments, scheduled boys to take sewing and home ec, girls to use the boys' lockers and showers. She spent half that fall on detention. She's quite a gal."

"Susan?" Charles asked, incredulous.

"Ask her," Jaime affirmed, with an ingenuous smile.

His bones aching from lack of sleep, bleary from carrying on a conversation with the white rabbit, Jaime backed away and headed for his room, planning to take a nap before meeting up with the others for dinner, but when he opened his eyes and looked at the time on his cell phone, it was eleven. His stomach complaining, having eaten only the excuse for lunch served on the plane, he pulled a pair of running shorts and jersey from his carryon, threw a sweater over his shoulders, and went down to the lobby in search of something to eat. The only place open was the cocktail lounge. Sitting at the bar, he ordered a burger and a beer, and when the burger came, carried both outside to pool, slid down on a lounge in the dark, finished both and lay there counting the stars.

"You get a reduced rate if you don't use your room?"

Jaime woke with a start, blinked the sleep out of his eyes, and struggled upright. "What are you doing here? Where's…"

"I couldn't sleep. Why didn't you tell me you came to Philadelphia last December?" she charged.

It was too dark to see the anger in her face but he heard the fury in her voice. "How do you know I came to Philadelphia?"

"Never mind. Answer the question."

"I… Would we be breaking one of the commandments on *Erev Shabbas* if you sat down while I answered?"

"Jaime!" she exploded, peering at him in the dim light spread by the lanterns along the path.

"I couldn't do that to you."

"You couldn't what?!"

"I… " Jaime hesitated, drawing quarts of air into his lungs. "I learned…you were seeing someone."

"What! I have to go."

"Do you still run in the morning?"

"Jaime!"

"Do you?"

Susan hesitated, *"Um,"* she admitted.

"Could I run with you?"

"Are you sure you are an English major?" she prodded, pissed.

"Could I?"

"I guess there's no law to prevent it."

"Six?"

"If you're late I'm not waiting."

Chapter 68

"From past experience, I didn't think you'd show up," Susan glowered, checking her watch. "What's this?" she scowled at the cardboard container Jaime was handing her.

"Cappuccino. Decaffeinated. Without sugar. The way you drink it."

Susan accepted the container as if it was wired with explosives. "The Inn's café is open?" she charged.

"I found a café open about a mile away."

Susan slunk back, unwilling to let go of her fury that easily. "Let's stretch."

They set off at a slow pace, Susan gradually ramping up the speed, both wary of bumping or even brushing against the other. Susan was in red spandex shirt and shorts, pink running shoes, her hair was in a ponytail tied with a red bungee cord. She had the Inn's white and gold-trimmed towel draped around her shoulders. Jaime was in the University's forest green, letters USF in printed in gold across his chest, the Inn's towel around his neck.

The first half-hour passed in silence, the morning's dew-swept air and the tranquility of the early Saturday hour stained only by a few dog walkers and early risers. Jet lagged and short of sleep, Jaime's breathing became increasingly heavy as he strove to keep up, refusing to fall behind. What had, at first, seemed all in fun became something more as Susan, aware of his distress, added still another burst of speed. Racing ahead, it was some time before she noticed Jaime wasn't behind her. Turning, jogging in place, she spotted him some hundred yards behind her, lying on the dew-covered grass, breathing painfully, massaging his calves and thighs. Jogging back, she asked sweetly, "Should I call the EMTs?"

Jaime attempt to smile fell short of success.

"My God you've aged," she charged. "Must be from late nights and the loose women you didn't push away."

Jaime looked away, miserable. "You're half right." The words were all but lost in the breaths he was drawing into his lungs.

"Half right!" Susan mocked. "I'll bet. Here," she said, kneeling down and massaging his calves, "let me."

"Can you get to your feet and work it out?" she asked, after working on both the calves and thighs.

"Could we sit for a few minutes?"

"Yeah. Wrap your towel around you so you don't cramp up so I won't have to hire a forklift to carry you back."

"Boy, I pity those little ones in your care."

"You bet your boots. It's a cruel world. It's better they find that out at a young age."

"Yeah. I remember. You're hard as nails."

They had been walking down the rutted road at Ringlehoff's B&B in Amish country, watching little ones feeding the goats. 'Doctoring isn't only about medicine and tests and surgery,' Susan had said. 'It's…it's hard to put into words, hard to even believe. I'd been out of residency only two years when a little three-and-a-half year old girl, Patty, was brought in by her mother. She didn't know what it was, the mother said anxiously – she wasn't that old herself, hardly out of her teens – but she said something was not right with her little girl. She was French Canadian, her native language was French, and she was having difficulty finding words to explain it. We took all the tests that seemed indicated, but they all came back negative. Nothing showed up. The hospital wanted to send her home, but her mother kept shaking her head. I sensed it too – something was wrong with the child. I can't describe how. If I said that I sensed that the child's *aura* was down, it would seem – mystical, or something – but that's what I sensed. I knew it was against hospital policy, but I refused to release her. That night, Patty went into convulsions – if she hadn't been in there, in the hospital, where we could treat her immediately, she could have died. She had a rare strain of meningitis we hadn't thought to test for.'

"Yeah," Susan agreed. "Like you. I see you melt when you see little ones. My mother told me what Leonora told her about you and Sydney, and I saw Leslie jump on you and kiss you."

"Anything I've ever done is trivial compared to saving children's lives."

By then, the sun had climbed above the horizon taking some of the chill out of the air, but their clothes, wet with perspiration and dew, stuck to them as they started back to the Inn. Along the way, a mother duck leading four ducklings across the road, the smallest, all legs and vestiges for wings, flopped along struggling to keep up.

"Hmmm," Susan commented with a meaningful look from the duckling to Jaime as the ducks waddled off into the shrubbery.

"Isn't this 'Be Kind to the Handicapped Week,'" Jaime asked.

Back at the Inn, on the way to their rooms to shower and change, they stopped for coffee and in the alcove off the lobby where continental breakfast was offered. "By the way," Susan said, carrying off a toasted bagel and cream cheese, "the dedication of the children's room is at two this afternoon in the hospital. Cars will be available at 1:30 to take everyone."

"Umm," Jaime nodded, biting a hunk out of a cinnamon Danish and washing it down with a swig of coffee.

"*Umm!* 'Umm' in Lakota means: (A) 'OK!' (B) 'So what!' (C) 'Me no speak with mouth full!'"

Jaime looked pensive as if to consider the options before heading off. He wiped the frosting off his mouth with the back of his hand answered, "(A) and (C)."

Chapter 69

Susan headed for her room pissed with herself. Seeing Jaime force a smile on his face when he lay on the grass in pain, as she had planned, hadn't given her the pleasure she had expected. Why had she acted this way? She had diminished herself, made herself smaller in her own eyes, had become the kind of person she disliked. She shook her head furiously. 'No, damn it!' she roared, charging out of the elevator, almost bowling over an elderly couple waiting at the landing, *'I'm entitled!'*

Almost since she was in rompers, Susan's mother had promised her that there was a lady hidden inside her that would appear magically one day. She had raced to her room that morning and looked carefully in the mirror, turning this way and that, studying herself, wondering where it was hiding. She still did, even to this day, though now it was to feel close to her mother, even when they had one of their many 'disagreements.' As hostess, she owed an obligation to her guests, but her obligation to herself was more important.

Twenty minutes later, showered and changed, she headed for Chenny, taking a path well away from Jaime who was stretched out on a chaise near the pool. Across the lawn, the white latticed cupola-ed gazebo was a storybook setting for her mother. Her mother's parents, her grandparents, had come over in steerage from Yugoslavia in their teens with little more than the clothes on their backs. With the help of an uncle who arrived earlier, they found a three-room apartment on the top floor of a lower east sidewalk up, and it was there that her mother, aunt, and two uncles were raised. There had never been enough money, often not enough food. Her grandfather, a big bellied bewhiskered fabulist who smelled of tobacco and garlic and told stories of heroic deeds he'd done when he was young, hiding from the soldiers under railroad cars, catching carp with his bare hands, supported the family peddling stationary, often gambling the little he earned playing pinochle with his cronies, slapping his cards down on the cardboard card table one by one with resounding snaps.

What always amazed Susan, in view of her mother's early life, was how she acquired her sense of style and taste. This morning she was dressed in a brilliant silk Balenciaga that cost more than her father earned in his lifetime, a dress a fashion writer with *Elle* might describe as *what to wear to afternoon 'affairs.'* Her pukka sahib was in colonial white, flannel slacks, Van Heusen shirt, with a crimson bow tie under his neck larger than Neka's diaper. 'Ah,' she could imagine her mother saying, 'but we lost Indiah.'

What is it that binds parents and children, Susan wondered? She and her mother had different tastes and never really understood each other, but her mother always had her interests at heart, doing what she believed was best for her.

Catching up with Chenny, she arranged her face. "How do these meatballs compare with roast woodchuck canapés at pow-wows?"

Chenny caught something in Susan's voice but wondered if she was imagining it. She didn't know Susan that well, hardly at all. "Not as flavorful," she answered, puzzled. "But I don't have to pick the hairs out of my teeth."

Susan smiled and turned to look at Neka sleeping in the sling on Noah's chest. "Your son has the longest dark hair of any infant I've ever seen. He's what now, two months old?" she babbled. "Does he talk yet?"

"Yes," Chenny nodded beaming. "*Goo goo...* but Noah's teaching him *Ugh.*"

"You must be thrilled," she went on... "and your dress. It's lovely. Did you make it?"

The dress had a tiny waist, turquoise beads at the bodice and hem, and flared out over her hips and calves when she turned on her matching beaded leather moccasins.

"Noah told me he shot the deer, skinned it, his mother chewed the skin to soften it, and his father, who'd been a tailor in London in Savile Row, sewed and beaded it."

"Ugh," Noah's eyes sparkled, as if wanting to eat Chenny up. "I bought it at Wal-Mart."

Susan produced the laugh expected. "Have you and Noah set a date?"

Chenny paused before answering. Why the questions? Something in Susan's voice puzzled her. She sometimes wondered if people believed that those living where living was slow were slow. Susan seemed as brittle as icing on a cake at a PTA bake sale that even a gentle tap would be enough to shatter.

"We're planning on making it during the Harvest Moon Ceremony in November. Noah and I hope you'll come."

"I'd love to," Susan gushed. "Did Noah get down on his knee? Where did he propose? What did he say?"

279

Chenny looked at him fondly, remembering the evening. "He was so cute. We were in Sally's Tea Shoppe with our friends drinking firewater – ugh – but I wasn't allowed to because I was pregnant. I was slurping up a banana slurpee and almost choked. At the bottom of the glass was this ring. He panicked, carried me out to his truck and drove off, like he was at the Indy 500…to the vet…*to the vet!*"

Noah blushed. "The vet was the closest. I was afraid to use the Heimlich maneuver. Now she's stuck. She can never give the ring back."

"Was Jaime there?"

Chenny shook her head. "No. He was in San Francisco."

"San Francisco? You drove there with him, didn't you?"

Chenny took a breath and let it out. There is was. The penny dropped. This is what it all about, what Susan had been leading up to. She wasn't crazy. This is what she sensed. It was clear now why she and Noah had been invited though they didn't know Jaime's father, never lived with him. Susan was hurting. Why was it so difficult for people to ask what they really wanted to ask? It might have been her, she realized, imagining what Susan was feeling.

"Jaime didn't tell you?" she asked, the tension that she sensed starting to dissolve.

Susan shook her head.

"I thought you knew," Chenny said kindly. "My mother's breast cancer metastasized… triple negative…*you know…I*…he made an excuse, but that's why he stopped off on his way to San Francisco…"

"Oh my God," Susan mouthed. "I didn't know. What's her prognosis?"

Chenny shook her head. "You knew Jaime flew to Philadelphia in December, didn't you?"

Susan shook her head. "Not until this morning."

"He didn't tell you about the class?"

Susan hunched her shoulders, shook her head.

"It took a bit, but the students got interested and ran with it. They put on plays at the end of the term, formed themselves into groups, chose a theme – romance, murder, jealousy, revenge – and showed examples from the time of Shakespeare to the present in literature, music, plays, poetry…even hip hop and graphic novels. For the end term performance, they constructed period sets, added music, and costumes. Soon, the whole school was buzzing, students signed up for class for the coming semester…he flew out to tell you…"

Susan rocked from foot to foot. She shook her head, stunned.

"I told him to. I insisted. But he discovered you were seeing someone and… Don't tell him I told you. He asked me not to say anything. If you'd like you can find more about it on the internet in a thread from the University of San Francisco."

Chapter 70

"Hey!" Charles called, catching up with Susan. "You look like you received unhappy news.

Susan shook her head, trying to sort all of it out, not knowing why she should be angry, not even with whom, or for what reason.

"Did Chenny say something that upset you?"

Susan dragged her eyes from the ground, saw the caring, the concern in his face, the caverns that hollowed his cheeks, the fine blonde hairs around the corners of his eyes she kissed, saw how he was there for her, knew he'd always be, becoming still angrier.

"Charles. I need some time to myself. It's nothing to do with us…" She tore her eyes from him, looked back down to the ground. She heard the children shrieking and playing in the pool, refused to look, knew Jaime would be there. "Do you like children, Charles?"

Charles flicked back, confused. "Do I like children?" he asked. "Do you mean would I like us to have some one day? We never talked about them. Does that mean that you…"

"No, Charles. No! Not that. It was just a question. I'm sorry, Charles. I need some time. I think it's the time of the month. I'm going up to my room. The dedication is at two. I'll see you in the lobby at 1:30."

Flashbulbs popped, reporters and crews from NBC and CBS TV news sprang into action when they got out of the limos at the hospital greeted by heads of the city's social departments, charitable organizations, hospital staffers, residents, and doctors. Susan tried to remain focused, not let the tumultuous greeting, the reporters and news teams, all the excitement, and the glow in her mother's eyes, undo her, but only with supreme willpower did she keep her knees from giving way. Hardly was she through the front doors when normally reserved Dr. Hemplewhite, the tall, slim, distinguished, sixty-three-year-old director of the hospital, in white coat and midnight navy trousers, swept Susan into his arms, hugged her and whispered 'well done,' all but undoing her. Sweeping his chestnut hair in a wave back over his right brow with a flip of his hand, turning his familiar thousand-watt smile to the cameras, he shook hands with her mother and Hermann, greeted Charles, and led them all to elevators waiting to whisk them up to the children's ward.

As they exited the elevator, the staff of the central nursing station rose as a group and applauded as Dr. Hemplewhite led them down the freshly painted colorful walls, stopping in front of a red satin ribbon stretched across a pair of doors. Signaling for quiet, he introduced the man standing next to him, a three-hundred-pound former right tackle of the Philadelphia Eagles, with shoulders the size of bread boxes and thighs like tree trunks, enough to intimidate many opposing linesmen, Mayor Tim Mahoney.

Wearing an exquisitely tailored, double-breasted suit in a rich deep shade of chocolate, a shirt the color of sweet cream and an amber tie in a tone between the two, the mayor accepted the accolades with an endearing why all the fuss smile, and began, "I am proud to be here today at the opening of another first in this City's services to the community, an example of what private initiative and the city government can accomplish working hand in hand. I…" As he got underway, Jaime wanted to shush the anchor on the news desk of the TV station who whispered, 'Since only half of those in attendance here are registered Philadelphia voters, maybe he'll cut his speech 50%.' Her cameraman's suggested it was unlikely, but Jaime and the others hung on every word and applauded enthusiastically.

"Thanks so much," Dr. Hemplewhite applauded when he wrapped up, "for showing us once again what a team player who puts his weight behind it can accomplish…in the metaphorical sense.

"This morning, at breakfast, my youngest daughter, on her twenty-first birthday said, 'You know, Dad, I'm not so young anymore.' I couldn't help remembering thinking that it was just six years ago when Dr. Susan Abramowitz, then only a few years older than my daughter is today, joined our staff, could a woman this young not only have what it takes to face what a doctor on the staff of the children's hospital has to face day in day out, but also the heart to work with children facing illness that can tear the heart out even calloused doctors. I needed to have no doubts. Not only has she become one of the leading members of our staff, but she has shown compassion we all admire.

"When Susan proposed ten months ago that if we would dedicate a room to bring joy to the children whose bodies we treat, she would endow it with a bequest she had received, we agreed on the condition that she, in addition to her other heavy responsibilities, organize and oversee the work. And so she has, pouring as much energy and dedication into this project as she has to all her other responsibilities. Today, we are proud to unveil the product of that effort.

"Dr. Abramowitz. If you will."

Susan's eyes filled as she accepted a pair of red scissors from Dr. Hemplewhite. The audience laughed encouragingly as she looked at the scissors seemingly uncertain how they worked. She took a moment to compose herself, looked up at Dr. Hemplewhite, looked back at everyone standing there, chewed her cheek, turned, carefully inserted the ribbon into the blades of the scissors, cut the ribbon, and as the two halves of the red ribbon slid to the floor, she turned again to everyone. "Thank you Dr. Hemplewhite. Before we open the door, as my grandmother used to say when she sat down with neighbors for the afternoon to chat, I'd first like to say one word."

When the laughter died off, she began. "There are a number of people who helped make this room a reality, among them my mother, Marsha, who worked tirelessly to recruit volunteers who have agreed to come to entertain and teach the children, Dr. Hemplewhite, without whose support and encouragement this could not have been accomplished, and many of the medical and managerial staff of the hospital. This was a joint effort and I have been proud to have been a part of it."

Standing to the left of Susan, Hermann offered his handkerchief to her mother to staunch the tears beginning to flow down her face. Charles glowed. Susan stopped, choked up, unable to go on for a moment. Jaime took a breath. In the white silk dress that fell just below her knees with its sweetheart neckline and capped sleeves, accented with an over the shoulder flowered aqua shawl, matching high-heeled shoes, turquoise beads and turquoise and gold earrings, she looked like how he imagined the goddess Diana must have looked.

Wiping her eyes, Susan turned back to the others. "I also want to add that credit also goes to an anonymous donor whose contribution enabled us to install fitness and physical therapy equipment for the children.

"And now…" Susan hesitated, looking about as if she'd forgotten what was to come next. Seeing Dr. Hemplewhite motioning, she paused.

"I thought you would like to know. For reasons of security, our comptroller chased down the source of that anonymous contribution. He found it was the advance on a book to be published this summer, 'The Bequests' that was funneled through MacMillan & Co., a west coast publishing house, by the author, 'J F,' who prefers to remain anonymous."

Susan smiled uncertainly, and with a decision, threw open the doors and motioned everyone to follow her in.

The room proved to be slightly rectangular, some thirty-feet long and twenty-five feet wide. It was painted with wide diagonal stripes in primary colors, alternating red, yellow, green and blue, there was a scalloped fringe above, like that found on a merry-go-round, and high on one wall, a discreet bronze plaque:

Aaron Frommer Room
Gift of Dr. Susan Abramowitz.

Sturdy laminate tables and chairs in the colors of the rainbow stood in each quadrant of the room, four-year-old sized in one, progressively larger in the others. Shelves along the walls were stocked with toys, games, crayons, and paints appropriate to that age and cubby holes for children's belongings, there were two flat-screen TVs, work-out mats, weights, treadmills, recumbent bicycles, pull-down and pull-up machines in the fitness area.

A glass fronted upright refrigerator held containers of water and juices, there was an erasable bulletin board on the wall to list volunteers who staffed the room hour by hour which would be open from 8:00 a.m. to 10 p.m., as well as an hourly calendar on which to list patients' schedules.

Jaime walked around in silence, oblivious of the excited chatter, trying to focus on the furnishings and equipment, blotting out the image of Charles never far from Susan and her parent's side. If he had any doubts before, he had none now: the close affection Susan shared with her mother was clear. He made the right decision: he'd always be an outsider.

Chapter 71

Jaime turned down the opportunity to visit the Liberty Bell and the Naval Yard with the others and returned to the Inn, beating himself for being an idiot, with no one to blame but himself. Chenny and Noah invited him to have dinner with them but he made an excuse, fit company for no one, holed up, had a sandwich in his room, changed his ticket to an earlier flight after the noon luncheon, and packed his bag ready to leave.

Aching, he fell into a troubled sleep, set the alarm. He'd say goodbye to Susan – if he could before she went running – avoid everyone else until lunch, leave immediately after. Minutes before five, before the alarm went off, he switched off the alarm, climbed out of bed, washed, pulled on clean running clothes, and headed to the lobby to wait.

"Susan!" he exclaimed, stunned, getting out of the elevator. She was standing in the lobby just to the side of the entrance. "What are you doing here at a quarter after five?"

"I owed you a cappuccino," she insisted, handing him a cardboard container.

"You owe me…? How long have you been here? This is…*cold*."

"Never mind!" she hurled back, furious. "Why aren't you asleep? What are you doing here at this hour?"

"I'm…" Jaime declared, "I'm…*going to run*."

"At a quarter after five?" she taunted.

"And you? You got up before five…*to run?* Or is it you wanted to be sure to catch me for another chance to humiliate me?"

"Is that why you're here so early?" Susan demanded. "You wanted to be sure to catch me so you could be humiliated again?"

Jaime stood, looking down at her, glaring. Susan glared right back up at him, determined, making it a contest of wills. When minutes went by, neither giving way, a hint of amusement crept over Susan's face, and all at once, both were unable to keep from laughing uproariously.

As suddenly as Susan gave way to laughter, the laughter gave way to fury. *"Don't laugh,"* she demanded. "There is nothing to laugh about! I'm furious with you. Who do you think you are? A character in a novel, throwing yourself on the guillotine to show your feelings…*it is a far far better thing I do…*

"Why didn't you tell me this? And this!" she demanded, rising on her toes to face him full-on, pulling two computer printouts from her pocket, slapping them on the table next to her smoothing the creases.

San Francisco Chronicle: December 27th, 2016
From Shakespeare to Hip Hop
University of San Francisco Students Drama
Production a Smash Hit

Members of this year's English Literature Class, with the guidance of Assistant Professor Jaime Frommer, staged a performance this December tracing how love, jealousy, villainy and comedy developed over the centuries in literature, poetry, theater, music and art, from the time of Shakespeare to the present, with costumes, scenes and musical period instruments themed to each era. Love themes dated from the 14th century, French 'Courtly Love' from Juan Ruiz, Arch Priest of Hita,' 'The Book of Good Love,' *El Libro de Buen Amor;* 15th century, Romeo and Juliet; 16th century, Unrequited Love, a poem in a book by Chaucer by Elizabeth Dacue, a Catholic, written to Sir Anthony Cooke, a protestant: 'The goodbye I tried to speak but could not utter with my tongue by my eyes I delivered back to yours'; 17th century, 'The Lunatik Love,' English Street Song,' or 'The Courtship of Kate and Will'; 18th century, 'The Sorrows of Young Werther' by John Wolfgang von Goethe ; 19th century, 'Great Expectations' by Charles Dickens: 'It is a far, far better thing I do'; 20th century, Phantom of the Opera by Gaston Leroux: 'It is a corpse that adores you and will never, never leave you'; 21st century, 'Drunk in Love,' by Beyonce & Jay Z: 'We be all night, love, love.'

San Francisco Chronicle: March 15th, 2017
Asst. Professor Jaime Frommer Addresses Chicago Academic Conference

"And what lame idiot with the initials 'J.F.,' may I ask," inches from his face, "is the author who made the 'anonymous' donation!"

"He wasn't lame until you ran me into the ground yesterday," Jaime tossed right back.

"This is no laughing matter," Susan exploded, struggling not to laugh.

"Susan, what do you want of me? You're in a relationship. Didn't Charles propose last night?"

"He did. You owe me."

"He did. I owe you?"

"You waltzed into in my life when I was hurting…and waltzed out again, leaving me hurting worse."

"Then…you aren't…"

Susan shook her head limply.

"Then…"

"Then…?"

"You're free to…to run with me this morning…*and every morning?"*

"Jaime! You idiot," Susan exploded, wrapping her arms around him in a boa constrictor hold and kissing him.

"Susan," Jaime worried, his face inches from hers, "I can't do this."

"What???" Susan glared, holding him, refusing to let him go.

"I don't have a ring."

"No ring! Not so fast, buster, you're not getting off that easy. "C'mon," she demanded, refusing to release her grip, pulling him behind her.

"What? Where are we going?"

"Never mind. Just get in the car."

"Uncle Jack!" she screamed over Bluetooth, "it's me, Susan. Susan! Your niece!"

"Susan! Do you know what time it is? It's Sunday morning."

"I need your help."

"My help? At this hour?"

"Could you come down to the store? There's an officer here that wants to arrest us."

Jaime shook his head, mouthing, *you little storyteller.*

"Why are you at the store at this hour of the morning?"

"I just got engaged and I need a ring."

"You what? At this hour?"

"He got away twice. I'm not going to give him a chance to find another reason why he's not good enough for me…which he's not…and he has an airline ticket out of here. So please hurry."

"Susan, you did some crazy things when you were growing up, but this is the craziest."

"So, will you come?"

"Oy. I'm in my pajamas."

"Please."

"Oy. Are you meshugenah? Is this the fellow you went ballooning with who left and you went to San Francisco to get and he sent you away?"

"He tried to get away again, but I'm not going to let him this time."

"Oy. Let me put my pants on. Tell the officer I'll be right down."

"Hurry. He's threatening to arrest us for loitering with an attempt to burgle."

Chapter 72

"Oy. So this is the metziah? For this you dragged me from bed at six o'clock on a Sunday?"

Susan beamed, planting a kiss on his whiskers. "Yup! This is Jaime. Jaime, my uncle Jack."

A silly grin creased Jaime's face as he shook hands.

"I'm not even washed or shaved yet. Look at me. Your aunt Min told me when you were young you'd grow out of it, then when you became a doctor she said, 'now, you'll see, she'll become dignified,' but still, I'm looking, it hasn't happened. Maybe this fellow can... *he's an M-O-T?*... Susan shook her head *'um hm'*... OK, come look at rings...so where are you gonna live...in San Francisco...you're gonna commute?"

"If I have to."

"You will?" Jaime roused, stunned.

"If I have to."

"Nope. You won't," Jaime grinned.

"I won't? How are we...?" Susan blinked, puzzled, unable to tear her eyes off a sapphire and diamond ring on blue velvet tray sparkling under a bright halogen light in the window. "You want me to move to Hippy City?"

"And give up the Wannamaker organ? *Never*. How 'bout I move here?"

"Become my consort?"

"Absolutely. We'd help each other. You'd tell me how to run my classes and I'd go into the operating room with you, point and say, 'Cut here.'"

"*Your classes?* What classes?"

"How about if I accept an offer from the U of P?

Susan's eyes went wide. "The U of P? The University of...?"

"After my talk at the conference. I was offered..."

"What? You'd live here?"

"Yup. Hey, stop that."

"Susan! Save that for after the wedding," her uncle scolded."

"I told you to hurry," Susan insisted.

Susan's uncle unlocked the door, shuffled into the store, shut off the burglar alarm, spun a dial on a vault in a wall, opened a safe, reached in and pulled out a tray. "Look. See if you like one of these," he glowed, kvelling over Susan. "Maybe," he said, pulling out his cell phone, "we should take a picture to show your aunt."

In the mirror behind the counter, Jaime caught a glimpse of Susan's uncle hovering over them, the halogen light reflecting off the ruddy scalp sparsely covered by uncombed pepper and salt hair.

"Here," he said, selecting a square cut emerald ring in his liver-spotted hands, "what do you think of this?"

"Does it come with a lifetime guarantee?" Susan asked.

"Rings I can supply. Lifetime guarantees are up to you. Tell me *maidele*, what did your mother say when you told her?"

A sheepish look spread over Susan's face. "I prepared her last night."

"What!" Jaime cried. "You little vixen. You put me through all that! I already changed my plane ticket to leave immediately after the luncheon, and you…"

"You deserved it, sending me away in San Francisco, and then fixing it so I'd let on I'd even commute."

"So, how did your mother take it?"

"The restaurant was noisy, but all of a sudden I had this out of body feeling that it quieted down and everything was happening in slow motion. The waiters returned to remove the salad plates and bring the main course, I'd ordered poached wild Alaskan salmon with Hollandaise sauce, buttered tiny new potatoes and steaming asparagus, and then, as conversation started to swell again, Charles tapped his fork on his wine glass, the room went lethal, and everyone in the restaurant turned to look at us, forks in the air.

"Mother let out a breath, bosom heaving and falling. Her eyes swung from Charles to me, 'Oh, honey,' she sighed, 'this is so…'

"My breathing became shallow. Mother was beaming. I looked at the exquisite ring nesting in a white satin lining in the blue felt-covered box. Charles was on his knees, looking at me anxiously.

"I was afraid this might happen. I began to cry. 'I can't,' I sobbed, 'I've loved only two men in my life.'"

Jaime took a breath, grasped Susan's hand and squeezed it. She looked up at him.

"Mother shook her head, the smile on Charles' face froze. 'Susan!' Mother insisted, 'You're excited. You're not thinking clearly!'

"'I'm sorry,' I told her. 'Charles is a wonderful person, but…*you loved dad, didn't you?'*

291

"'What's that got to do with it?' she bristled.

"'You loved him, *didn't you?'* I insisted.

"'Loved him?' She reached for Hermann's hand, laced her fingers in his. 'God knows I did. I couldn't see straight once I met him. He drove me crazy. But I did. I loved him.'

"'Well, I'm your daughter,' I told her.

"'There are different kinds of love,' she insisted.

"'I know,' I told her. Tears were falling down my face. 'I want the kind that you had.'"

Jaime looked at Susan as if he wanted to eat her up. "I loved you," he said to Susan, "from the moment I met you when you walked into the breakfast room of the Warwick Hotel looking as forlorn as a waif. I wanted to take you into my arms that minute… I was afraid you'd think I was demented."

Chapter 73

Everyone was already seated when Susan entered the private dining room at the Inn where luncheon was to be held. "Wow!" Gerry exploded with her distinctive brand of un-restraint, spotting the sparkling diamond and emerald ring on the third finger of Susan's left hand. "Where's your fiancé?!"

"Right here," Susan beamed, pulling the grinning hunk behind her.

"*Jaime?*" Gerry detonated, jumping up and rushing to examine the ring, offer good wishes and congratulations, followed by everyone else.

Cell phones popped out snapping pictures.

"Susan!" her mother cried, hugging and kissing her, smushing her face with tears and insisting on hugging Jaime, *"You'll let me make your wedding?"*

The room exploded with laughter.

The 'Presidential Room' was hung with heavy satin brocade drapes the color of sweet cream, a floral arrangement with chrysanthemums, roses, and birds of paradise in a cut crystal vase in the center of the long table, sweetened the air, crystal goblets of ice water at each place setting dripped moisture, bone china plates rimmed in gold sparkled under the twinkling lights from pairs of antique wall sconces around the room, silverware gleamed beside damask napkins in a matching cream. Waiters retired, Hermann rose, lifted his wine glass, everyone joined his toast to the engaged couple as wrapped together, Jaime's lips formed words only she could hear, vowing he'd always be there for her.

"Hey Buster," Susan grinned mischievously, "hold that till later. I'd like to welcome all of you – and for those from the south – you all, to the first meeting of the E F O A F, *the Extended Family of Aaron Frommer,* known to some of you as Allan Fisher. In *As You Like It,* Shakespeare said 'All the world's a stage, and in his lifetime man plays many parts.' Aaron must have been the man he had in mind. But for whatever he may have been in his life time, in death he touched our lives, blessed them in a way that made them better."

Before the luncheon ended, Leslie entertained by performing Julius Fučík's *Entrance to the Gladiators* on the Burkart Handmade Flute she had bought with his father's bequest, and Sydney, with more than a bit of prodding, allowed that he expected, with what he earns at summer and part-time jobs, the bequest would enable him to complete a four-year bachelor of science degree at the University of Atlanta. As the celebration ended, with handshakes, hugs and good wishes all around, Leslie and Sydney were still bantering good-naturedly over which of them received the best gift from Jaime's father.

***

Epilogue

As the plane to Omaha lifted off at four that afternoon, Chenny cuddled Neka in her arms and snuggled up against Noah. Noah looked down at her and the new little person in his life. "It was a nice thing of Susan to do, to plan that tribute to Jaime's father, wasn't it?"

"Hmmmmmmm," Chenny offered, drowsing off.

"Wasn't it?" Noah prodded, running his lips over the crown of her head.

"If Susan ever decides to give up medicine," Chenny murmured, "she could become the greatest illusionist the world has ever known."

Noah's brow creased. He'd become used to trying to decipher Chenny's enigmatic observations, but this one had him stumped. He bent over to ask her to explain, but she was already asleep.

***

Later that night, wrapped in Jaime's arms, feeling the steady beat of his heart and listening to his breathing, Susan thought of Leslie and Sydney's bantering about which of them received the best gift from his father.

She smiled.